MW00755363

SOLERI

SOLERI

MICHAEL JOHNSTON

TOR

A TOM DOHERTY ASSOCIATES BOOK

NEW YORK

This is a work of fiction. All of the characters, organizations, and events portrayed in this novel are either products of the author's imagination or are used fictitiously.

SOLERI

Copyright © 2017 by Michael Johnston

All rights reserved.

Map by Michael Johnston

A Tor Book
Published by Tom Doherty Associates
175 Fifth Avenue
New York, NY 10010

www.tor-forge.com

Tor® is a registered trademark of Macmillan Publishing Group, LLC.

The Library of Congress Cataloging-in-Publication Data is available upon request.

ISBN 978-0-7653-8648-9 (hardcover)
ISBN 978-0-7653-8649-6 (e-book)

Our books may be purchased in bulk for promotional, educational, or business use. Please contact your local bookseller or the Macmillan Corporate and Premium Sales Department at 1-800-221-7945, extension 5442, or by e-mail at MacmillanSpecialMarkets@macmillan.com.

First Edition: June 2017

Printed in the United States of America

0 9 8 7 6 5 4 3 2 1

For Mel

RIFKA

KINGDOM OF
RACHIS

KINGDOM OF
FEREN

THE
SOLERI
EMPIRE

THE FEREN RIFT VALLEY

CATAL

THE SHAMBLES

THE
DROMUS

KINGDOM OF
HARKANA

SOLUS

HARWEN

KINGDOM OF
SOLA

BLACKROCK

THE WYRRE

GATE OF
CORONEL

DESOUK

THE
CRESSEL
SEA

SCARGILL

SOLERI

⋛ THE BLACK SAND ⋚

They used to be fishermen, but that night hunger made them thieves. Under a moonless sky the men set out from the island in small wooden skiffs, sailing across the ink-black sea toward the distant kingdom. They were crowded in the long thin boats, crammed shoulder to shoulder, some turned sideways or doubled over to shield themselves against the waves. Gusty wind and angry water forced a few ships to turn back, while others were lost to the surf, and those who journeyed onward kept their eyes focused on the horizon, searching for the dim silhouette of the Dromus. The skiff rolled and the boy caught sight of the desert barrier. The great wall was hewn from cinder-gray rock and reflected no light, its jagged ridge biting at the low-hanging stars like a blacker piece of night.

A cresting wave propelled the boy's craft to shore. He clutched his oilskin sack and held it tight against his chest. The skiff tipped as they neared the black sand, and everyone went overboard. He was first in the water, overwhelmed by the dark, the rushing swells, the screams of men. In all his ten and five years, he had never left the southern islands. Now here he was, scrambling for footing on a foreign beach, staring at the desert wall.

As he marched up the black-sand beach, he wondered if he had made a terrible mistake, if he should turn back. Others were whispering, afraid to go on ahead.

As if in reply, the eldest among them urged them forward—reminding them that for the last several months all they had to eat were the bones of last season's salt-dried fish and those were all gone. There was no going back now. There was nothing to go back *to*. The men turned once more to face the Dromus, that ash-stone monolith, onyx black, impenetrable, they said, impossible to breach—this wall that kept Sola rich, protected, and apart from the lower kingdoms. In the distance, as the sun rose and its light spread from the barrier's rim, they saw the first glint of what they had come for—the riches promised beyond the wall—gold.

All the gold of the Soleri. The words rang in their heads, the proverb they had heard as children at their fathers' knees, words from their deepest memories: "Before time was the Soleri, and after time the Soleri will be." The ruling family had been in power longer than even the calendars that stretched back 2,942 years—first in stone, then clay, then parchment. Those records told a history of conquest and domination by a family descended from gods, a family older than anything in the known world, ruling with nearly absolute authority for three millennia. There was no world without the Soleri—they were the center of everything, the end and the beginning—and so it was to the center of the empire, to the Dromus and all that lay beyond, that the men from Scargill, dressed in sea-soaked rags and driven by desperation, now turned.

They pressed on, passing into the wall's growing shadow with a mixture of dread and determination. They had crossed the burnt-sand beach and were within striking distance, but now they were vulnerable to attack from above, from the dead-shot archers of the Soleri Army. They scanned the wall for signs of its inhabitants, upward and down, following the ragged contour of the Dromus until it disappeared into the horizon. Nothing.

The line of the wall thinned out along its broad curve, and they moved more quickly now as the ground became more certain underneath their feet, the wide plain of the desert opening up around the ash-stone barrier. There it was. The Gate of Coronel, the southern gate of the Dromus, three days' march from the city of the Soleri. The boy could see the two panels of the gateway, each one the size of a great raft turned on end. But what was this? The doors stood open.

A trap, some said. But others disagreed, said it was just a bit of luck, that the guards must be napping in the first light of dawn. They should take this chance, they murmured, while they still could. The boy remembered that the Feast of Devouring approached. Perhaps the guards had gone off to prepare for the high holiday.

The open doors stood before them.

The elders made the decision: the fishermen of Scargill would charge the gate as planned.

They crossed the Dromus and entered the gate. Steeled themselves for spears, for swords, for fire, for the emperor's soldiers, warriors of exceptional skill and ferocity who were bred to conquer and slay. Who were said to be able to kill with a breath, with a look.

They were ready for anything, but nothing rose to meet them. No fire. No arrows. No soldiers. The Dromus was empty. Unguarded.

There was no one there.

No soldier stood guard, and even the gold they had seen from a distance was nothing more than the sun's first rays reflecting off the temple's tattered dome. No army and no riches here. No food or fresh water either—the storehouses and water barrels stood empty.

The fishermen from Scargill, their limbs thin, bones poking out at the joints, who had come if not for gold then simply for food for their children, could not go home, not yet.

Past the temple, past the fields of spears and upturned earth, the men pushed onward till the air turned foul. Here at last were the mighty soldiers of the Soleri. But the fighting men were not arranged in serried ranks, nor were they spread out in a mighty phalanx of spears and helms. The soldiers lay lifeless, stacked in mounds, left to rot in the sun and the wind, left for the crows' next meal.

The men from Scargill, woolly bearded elders and smooth-chinned boys stopped their advance. There was nowhere else to go, nothing left to see. The boy flung his oilskin over his shoulder, scratched his cheek, and spat.

Around them, the Dromus stretched to infinity—its black line holding the last traces of night.

Everything else was just sand.

THE DYING RAY

1

Will I see the sky today?

Ren Hark-Wadi sat in darkness, awaiting the sunrise.

As the first finger of dawn came sliding down the steep wall of the lightwell, it changed the color of the stones in his cell from black to brown to a faint, muddy yellow. Ren stood from his wooden pallet, took a scrap of polished iron from beneath his blanket, and slid the metal through a narrow slot in the window. It caught the light, filling the small chamber with streaks of blue-gray illumination. Ren let the faint rays wash over his face, hoping they might warm his skin, but the light was too dim.

Perhaps the upper rings can see a bit more of the sky? He didn't know.

He leaned closer to the window, pressed his head to the slot, and peered upward. If he held himself just-so, sometimes he could see a wedge of sky—a blue sliver no larger than a nut. In his free moments, when he was certain no one watched, he would stare at that blue dot till his neck cramped, hoping to catch sight of a bird or an errant cloud, some sign that the world outside existed, that the breeze blew and the clouds drifted, but his neck was too stiff to find the sky that morning. He saw only rows of narrow windows, one above the next, five rings of arched windows, one for each level of the Priory, trailing far underground where the outside world never intruded—where the outside world, and all the people in it, were nothing but rumor.

Maybe tomorrow. Maybe then I'll be able to steal a glimpse of the world beyond these walls.

Dousing himself with a bucket of foul gray water, his morning shower, Ren sputtered, rinsing the sleep from his eyes, as well as yesterday's dirt from his cheeks and his long hair, which was always flopping into his face. The water poured across the floor and out to a stone scupper, where it disappeared. He suspected that it was simply used again the next day, the

same water with more grit in it. The men who ran the Priory were nothing if not stingy with the necessities of life.

Pain makes the man. The priors said it every day. The Soleri taught their
people that pain built character. *Pain makes the man.* It was their mantra,
but Ren didn't think it was a particularly good one. If pain truly made
the man, then he had been made a man many times over. *I don't think
pain makes a man. I think we become men in spite of it.* He had seen pain drive
boys mad. He had seen it drive them to cruelty. He had never seen it make
them into anything Ren thought a man should be, but what did he know?
All Ren knew were boys. And all the boys he knew were ransoms.

In the distance a trumpet blared, high and tinny and full of self-
importance. The Feast of the Devouring had begun; in five days the sun
would blacken for a brief span, the daylight turning as weak and shadowy as twilight, the people hushed and awed at the yearly spectacle of
the sun god's blessings.

*Mithra-Sol dims his light to acknowledge our emperor and the whole of the
empire watches as if it were some great miracle.* Ren didn't care if the sun
dimmed for a brief span. He'd never even seen the sun, not even a sliver.
The fact that the sky blackened each year didn't seem particularly special.
He was well accustomed to darkness.

Ren Hark-Wadi, the youngest child and only son of Arko, king
of Harkana, had not seen the world beyond his prison walls since the
emperor's soldiers had delivered him to the underground city of the Priory ten years earlier. Only three years old at the time, Ren could not
recall the moment he had been taken from his family, could not remember
his father's face, or his mother's, or his sisters'. He knew his sisters' names,
Merit and Kepi, his teachers had told him that much, but he could not
remember what they looked like. He wondered if they remembered him.
If they would recognize him now. If anyone cared that he still existed.

Am I a name without a face? An empty chair at the table each night?

Surely they would know him if they saw him, even if he was now nearly
as tall as a man. His hair, once honey-colored, so different from the other
boys', was dull and mousy now from years of living underground,
though it had attracted a lot of attention when he was younger. Ren
had sharp cheekbones and a narrow, angular face marked by fox-colored
eyes and a mouth that sometimes seemed set in a permanent frown. He
was tall for his age, but surely there was something left in him of the boy
he had been. Surely his father and his sisters would see it, if no one else
could. He spent his nights trying to recall his childhood, searching his

memories for a glimpse of their faces: his sisters, his father and mother. *Did they love me? Were we a family once?* Did they eat meals and tell stories and were the children held at night until they fell asleep? He longed for memories, but had none. Even a dream would have been acceptable, but he had never dreamed of them either. The idea was too foreign, too distant to conceive. He recalled only these rooms, the boys, the priors, and the bitter nights he had spent in this cell.

A prior tapped his door. "Out of your room, Hark-Wadi." Already the boys were gathering for morning meal. *Time to go, time to eat, time for lessons.*

Ren removed a stone from the wall. Behind the rock, a blade occupied a stony niche. Ren palmed the knife, tugged a linen tunic over his head. He needed to hurry. Their rations arrived once daily and were seldom sufficient: thin soup with bits of tough dried meat or stringy vegetables; sometimes a paste of dried dates or figs and thin, unleavened wafers; sometimes nothing but hard bread with oil to dip it in. It had been a long time—a very long time—since they'd had enough to fill their bellies. That was how the men ran the Priory. "Pain makes the man," a prior shouted as he walked past the boys' cells, banging on all the doors, waking them up.

Ren stumbled into the corridor and caught sight of his young friend Tye Sirra of the Wyrre. An older boy, Kollen Pisk, was talking to Tye, going on about the Devouring. Ren slipped behind Kollen and shoved him playfully in the back. "Priors are calling for you." It was a lie, but Ren wanted to get rid of the older boy, and a call from the priors was the surest way to do that. "Probably best be on your way," said Ren, slapping the tall boy again.

"Later then," Kollen said. He knocked Ren on the shoulder, but his eyes did not leave Tye, his gaze lingering up and down, as if taking measure. Then he laughed and disappeared down the corridor.

Ren waited until they were alone. "Do you think he knows?"

"I'm not sure—he might," said Tye.

"Then we need to be more careful. You should grow your hair longer," Ren said. "And maybe a different tunic?"

"My hair won't grow any faster—or longer," said Tye. "And this old tunic is the mangiest I could find. I already stink like a rat, do I have to look like one as well?"

Ren shrugged. "It's better than being discovered. No one looks twice at a rat and they certainly don't want to stand by one." He pinched his nose.

"It's no joke. Sooner or later someone is going to figure it all out and then—" Tye glanced around to make certain no one was listening.

"We can't give up so easily," said Ren. "We've fooled them for years."

"Years, yes, but I was younger then and didn't have much of anything to hide," said Tye, brushing a bit of dirt from what had become a slight swelling in her upper chest. Tye was a girl. Only her friends Ren and Adin Fahran, the heir of Feren, knew the truth. Her father had swapped his daughter for his son when the Protector came to fetch the boy from their home in the Wyrre three years ago. Now twelve, Tye was tall and thin, and for the most part lacked the curves that would come with womanhood. She had the light hair and eyes of the southern tribes, a slender nose, and a sprinkling of freckles on her cheeks. She was growing more beautiful every day, and took great pains to hide it. She could still pass for a boy, though each day she looked a little less like one.

"What are you doing in this part of the Priory?" Ren asked. Tye's chamber was on a different floor.

"Looking for you."

"Aren't you sweet—" he teased.

"Shut up, I'm here for a reason," she said.

"What reason?" Ren asked, seeing her face turn anxious.

"Just follow me." Tye darted down the corridor and Ren followed. *What was so urgent that she would risk missing morning meal?* The answer came soon enough when they saw Adin.

"My father's dead," Adin said, squinting in the gloom to look for his friends. He stood in the door to his cell, a yellowed parchment clutched in one hand, his skin dusky in the lamplight. Adin was a few years older than Ren, tall and lanky, his hair messy, his chin stubbled, shoulders hunched like a boy afraid of his own height.

"It's over," Adin said. "I'm leaving." The Priory boys were unable to return home until their fathers died or were killed.

For a moment Ren just stared at his friend. This was the moment they lived for every day. Freedom. Home. But Adin looked far from joyous. "What's wrong?" asked Ren.

"There was a note, from my uncle, Gallach. All is not what it seems. There was a revolt a year ago. A merchant named Dagrun Finner declared himself king of the Ferens and took the throne. He kept my father hostage, then sent him to the gallows for treason. Now the emperor has recognized Finner as king and since my father is dead and I am no longer the first son of Feren, I'll be set free. My line is ended."

Heavy footsteps echoed outside, the priors were coming. Their yellow robes emerged from the dark of the corridor. The Prior Master, Oren Thrako, walked at the head of the group. He was stout and strong, the skin over his bald head stretched smooth and bulging like an overdeveloped muscle. He gripped Adin by the neck.

"Time to go, boy," Oren said.

"Give us a moment," Ren protested

The parchment shook in Adin's hand. His eyes darted between the Prior Master and Ren. "The new king will surely kill me once he learns I have gained my freedom. They're sending me home to my death."

"Save your worries for someone who cares. Time to meet the Ray," Oren said.

Ren put himself between Adin and the Prior Master. "Just a moment," he begged.

"Go back to your cell," Oren said.

No. He would likely never see his friend again. But before Ren could speak, Oren slammed him against the wall. His fingers wrapped around Ren's neck, slowly tightening. Ren gagged, his face turning red, fingers twitching. Then something made the Prior Master let go. Tye had taken hold of Oren's tunic and was frantically tugging at it. The loose threads of the tunic caught Oren's bronze necklace. She gave the cloth another tug and the necklace bit into his neck, drawing blood.

Oren forgot about Ren. He lashed out at Tye, slamming her with his fist and knocking her to her knees. "Stupid boy," he said, gesturing for one of the priors to hand him his cudgel, meaning to beat her, right there in front of them.

No, no, not Tye, this is my fault. Ren swiftly drew his blade and pressed the iron against Oren's back.

The Prior Master turned slowly around, his eyes settling on the little knife. "What are you going to do with that?" he scoffed. "Skewer a mouse? You'd be better off threatening me with a thimble," he said. "Throw it down or I'll carve you with it myself."

More priors hurried down the corridor. Seeing the knife, three of them immediately surrounded Ren. A fourth took Adin and led him away. His friend resisted the prior's pull. "When you get out, find me, you sons of bitches!"

"Go, you idiot!" Ren backed toward the wall, the knife feeling heavy in his palm as he faced the priors and an enraged Oren Thrako. *At least he's forgotten about Tye.* "May you share the sun's fate—and all that!" he called to Adin. "We'll find you sure enough, I promise. If we ever get out of here," he muttered to himself.

Adin twisted to look back at his friends, and seeing them in obvious jeopardy, struggled to return to help. He struck the prior who was leading him down the hall, knocking him on the jaw and hurrying back down the corridor. But two more priors arrived, blocking his path. They faced Adin with a snarl and each one took one of his arms.

"I mean it—come to Feren," Adin yelled before he was pulled back into the shadows.

Before Ren could reply, Oren took him by the fabric of his tunic. "You should have dropped the bloody knife," he said. "I'll take a finger in payment, or maybe two." He held Ren by the neck while the remaining priors scrambled to take hold of the blade. It took two of them to restrain Ren while the other pried the knife from his hand, peeling back his fingers one by one. The knife clattered to the floor.

Oren took a step back, removing himself from the melee, straightening his tunic, and fixing his necklace. His hand came away red with blood from the ugly cut on his neck. "You'll go to the wells for this, Tye," the Prior Master raged. He held up his red fist. "We'll let the sun judge you for your sins."

"No," Ren said. "I'll do it, I'll stand beneath the sun. I drew the blade. Let me take his place." He knew the Prior Master would not pass up an opportunity to punish him, so he offered himself in Tye's place.

Oren glanced from Ren to Tye and back again, weighing the matter. Then he grunted his acceptance, as Ren knew he would. "Good enough, Hark-Wadi." He smiled grimly, as if this was what he had wanted all along. "In place of a finger, I will send you to the sun. You will stand and face the Sun's Justice," said Oren.

Ren had seen a boy survive the Sun's Justice, had seen the ransom's charred and flaking skin, his blind eyes and cracked lips, his neck and shoulders dotted with yellow and white pustules that ruptured when the boy bent his arm or flexed his neck. Now it was he who would stand and wither in an oven-sized shaft while the sun's heat turned the stones around him into searing coals. If he survived the ordeal, he was innocent. If he died, he was guilty and would be sent back to his kingdom in a casket, and the empire would demand a new ransom.

Already the priors were grabbing him by the hood of his tunic, taking him to the roof. "Go," he told Tye, who had tears in her eyes. "Forget about me." *At least she is safe.* It was comfort enough to know he had kept her from the worst of it. And Adin was free. His friend had escaped the Priory. Ren had spent the better part of his brief life dreaming of the day when the three of them would be free. It was all he wanted for himself and his friends. He tried to take some solace in Adin's freedom, but his thoughts were a jumbled mess. Soon he would face the Sun's Justice.

Strong hands lifted him by the armpits while he kicked and strained. His foot met the face of a gray-haired prior. He kicked again, but a younger and stronger man took hold of his ankle and wrenched the joint into a painful half-turn as they dragged him down the corridor.

They enjoy this, he thought, *they like watching us squirm.*

Ren saw an arch above him, which meant they were on the stairs. He had struggled for years to see the sun, to catch a glimpse of the sky, and now it was here, bright and blistering.

A door banged open and everything went white. Warm air buffeted his face. Ren squeezed his eyes closed, but sunlight pierced his eyelids, filling his vision with a red-veined panorama.

"Open your eyes, boy. We're on the roof," said one of the priors.

"No," he murmured, "I don't want to see the sun." In truth, he had wanted to see it his whole life, but now that the moment had come he wasn't ready. No matter. Ren did as told and saw a pair of crooked teeth smiling at him. The prior turned his head and spat into a lightwell. The spittle hung in the air, falling and falling, then disappearing into the darkness.

"That's where you're going—into the well, to bake like bread, to cook like a goose," he chortled. "Pain makes the man. Pain makes the man," the prior hummed the words.

Two and ten shafts dotted the roof of the Priory—long, narrow cuts dug into the flat stone, wells that fed light into the underground chambers of the Priory of Tolemy, the house for the emperor's ransoms.

"Here you go," said the crook-toothed man as he fed a rope under Ren's arms and tied a knot behind his back. "Careful not to touch the stones, you don't want to burn yourself," he japed.

Ren closed his eyes, the sun was too bright—he wasn't ready. The rope tightened around his chest. He felt a tug as the prior led him forward. His eyes clamped shut. He wished he could shut his ears too. The city was loud, almost suffocating. Dogs barked and hawkers cried.

"No, I—"

The prior's foot hit his back and Ren fell, tumbling into the darkness. The rope caught beneath his arms, the knot tightening like a hangman's noose. He grabbed the cord and tried to steady himself as his feet hung, kicking in the air.

"Help," he said.

A grunt echoed from above as the priors struggled with the rope. Ren was dropped again, but more slowly this time. When he kicked, his foot hit stone. *A ledge.* He put one foot down, then the other, until he stood on a small foothold within the lightwell.

"Is this it? Is this where I'll stand?" he asked, but no one answered.

The shaft felt like nothing more than a narrow pipe, one that was slowly tightening around him. He wanted broth on his lips and amber in his belly. There was an angry pulsing in his head that only a meal could fix, but he would not eat this morning. There was no knowing when the next meal would arrive, or if he would eat at all.

I wish I were back in my cell. He had not appreciated how much he had until it too was taken away.

The priors pulled up the rope and soon they were gone.

It had all happened so quickly that he had not yet had time to consider what was in store for him.

He was alone on the ledge. The light shaft provided no shade, nowhere to shit or piss. He could jump, he could end his life, plunge to his death. But even then the fall might not kill him. If he was only maimed, the priors would surely nurse him back to health just so they could abuse him once more.

The sun was rising, and the rocks were already growing hot. Soon the stone would be too hot to touch, the air too smoldering to breathe, and the sun and his justice would be upon him.

Ren wanted to be back in the dark, loamy comfort of his cell. *I want to eat bread and drink amber and see my friends.* A ransom had no other desires, no other privileges. Standing alone beneath the vast sky, trapped inside a veritable oven, the absence of those comforts struck him as a blow mightier than any the priors could strike.

He pressed his shoulders to the stone. The rock was warm.

I'm ready.

A ray fell across his face, and after ten years in darkness, Ren raised his head, opened his eyes, and finally saw the sun.

2

"Dear friends," Merit Hark-Wadi said, projecting her voice across the stadium so that each person in the arena could hear her words, "people of Harkana, honored guests from Feren, on this last day of the feast, I wish each of you a good death." The crowd applauded as she sat back down on her father's chair. Adjusting her finely pleated dress, it occurred to her that she did not truly wish each of them a good death. After all, it was the bloody deaths that made the crowds cheer loudest.

"May you honor Sola with your presence, and Harkana with your blood," she said as she waved to each of the combatants, her eyes lingering on a tall and powerfully built Feren warrior in silver armor. Merit settled back into her chair. The first daughter of Harkana was a woman of regal bearing and a cool, calculating gaze. She was a decade past coming into her womanhood but still a grand beauty at six and twenty, with long black hair that fell in thick ebony waves down her back, bronze skin, and full pink lips. Dressed in a dyed-blue linen so new it sweated color on her elbows and ankles, giving her elegant limbs a shadowy, bruised look, she raised one silver-bangled arm and waited—for the sounds of the crowd to die down, for a silence that she deemed sufficiently respectful of her place and position.

"Take arms and let the contest begin," Merit said.

The warriors saluted with a dip of their swords, first toward the visitors from the neighboring kingdom of Feren as a measure of respect, then the Harkans. Only a handful of them would survive the ring, and even fewer would be afforded a good death. But it was early in the games' last day, and the combatants were still fresh, still convinced of their own strength and skill.

The contests were an annual tradition and had been around for years, for centuries as far as Merit knew. The Soleri calendar held three hundred and sixty-five days—twelve months of thirty days each, which left five remaining days unaccounted for. During these five days, the people of the empire observed the high festival, the Devouring of the Sun. These five days existed outside of normal time—no work was done, no animal was slaughtered, no field was plowed. Five days out of time—a period of rest, five days to drink and play as the people of the empire waited for the sun to turn black.

Every year the feasting paused on the fifth day and exactly at noon the moon eclipsed the sun and the sky turned dark. The Devouring. Throughout the kingdoms, the people of the empire gathered together as Mithra-Sol dimmed his light in acknowledgment of the emperor. In the blackthorn forests of Feren they buried torches in the red earth. In the Wyrre, the beggars banged iron pots and smashed clay vessels to ward off the devourer. In Rachis, the mountain lords lit blazing pyres that turned the coal-black sky orange. But in Harkana, where hatred of the empire ran strongest, the people observed the festival in a more personal manner. The Harkans could not work or sow, but they could play and so they played at war. If they must commemorate their own defeat, if they must toast in honor of the emperor, the Harkans would do so with blood.

Merit shaded her changeable blue-green eyes as she surveyed the field. Below her, the sound of iron striking wood shot through the arena. A Feren warrior cried out in pain as he fell to the arena's dusty floor. Merit looked away with a grimace. Though it was her duty to order men to commit acts of violence, she didn't much like watching it. She could stomach brutality as long as she didn't have to look at it.

To Merit's right, the queen's seat was empty, as it had been for nearly a decade. Her father, the king, was absent. Her brother, Ren, the heir, was locked in the Priory of Tolemy, so it was left to Merit to represent the royal family and to sit on the king's chair as the combatants clashed swords, a duty that by rights was her father's, but Arko Hark-Wadi, king of Harkana, refused to display patronage to the empire. The king was hunting in the north as he did each year during the Devouring.

A thought occurred to Merit. Did the boys in Tolemy's house observe the festival? Did they stand and watch the sun dim? Did Ren know that his people spent the day battling one another with spears and swords to remind the kingdom of its once-brave history? Her own father, the king, had never served in the Priory. His father had fought a war to keep his son safe at home. She wondered if that was why Arko always left Harwen for the Devouring. *Is he too proud to salute the bravery of others?*

"The Soleri emissary will take it as a sign of disrespect, Father," she had told Arko, watching him ride out with his hunters. "Any slight will be noticed."

But her father had dismissed her with a wave of his hand. "Fear not, Merit, I'll raise a cup when the sky darkens and I'll offer the emperor's spies a drink if any are watching." Then he had left, not even looking back at the place and the people he was abandoning. He did not even acknowledge the burden he had left her to bear. The queen's duties came naturally to the king's first daughter, but the king's obligations were another matter. As much as she tried to fill his place, she was not his heir, and as much as she cajoled and flattered their allies, it was clear that no man save Arko could command their respect, and the king showed little interest in his duty. She longed for permanence, for recognition, for a power that was hers alone. Since her father would not grant her what she desired, she had decided she would take it for herself. She would find her own path to power and if that meant getting a little dirt on her hands, well, that wouldn't bother her a bit.

Merit stood up once more, as her duty required, raising her hand to the crowd. "To arms," Merit said as the second of the matches, the contest of kings, began. This next bout pitted highborn warriors from competing kingdoms against one another in a melee. In practice, the servants and soldiers of wellborn families often fought in the contest, but the rules of the game did allow for the participation of the highborn and even the king's family. Such participation was rare but not unheard-of in the contests, and so on a day such as this one, a day when the wellborn citizens of both kingdoms stepped into the ring, the games held an added tension, a thrill that was palpable. Noble blood meant the possibility of noble death.

Finally something worth watching, she thought.

On the field, a fierce battle raged between the Harkans and their Feren adversaries. Her eye tracked the Feren warrior in silver who had caught her attention earlier. The swiftest and most nimble of the Harkan warriors, a slim figure in a royal set of black leathers, with the horns of Harkana emblazoned upon them in silver, one Merit knew well from many previous celebrations, one the crowd knew as well, advanced on the Feren in the silver, but was driven backward by a pack of Ferens. There were five of them against just the one Harkan, and the Ferens were taller and their swords were longer and heavier. The Harkan had every disadvantage, but the warrior in black was undaunted. The Ferens, with their heavy armor and heavy weapons, moved slowly, giving the Harkan time to lift a short sword from the sand, where someone had dropped it. With two blades, the Harkan held back the five Ferens, parrying blows with one arm while attacking with the other.

The crowd roared its approval, and even Merit clapped.

Moving with confidence, the warrior in black executed a deft maneuver, throwing the short sword like a dagger and striking one of the Ferens in the leg, bringing him to the ground while the Harkan slashed at another, knocking the sword from the man's hand and taking a finger with it.

The remaining Ferens pressed their advantage. Two attacked from the front while the third came at the Harkan from behind, moving with exceptional speed, thrusting his sword at an exposed patch of the Harkan's armor. The blade drew blood, and the warrior in black retreated to the edge of the field.

Merit edged closer to the lip of the platform. She hated when the fighting dragged on like this. The air smelled like blood and sinew and her stomach churned.

On the field below, the Ferens pressed the lone Harkan. Injured but still defiant, the warrior in black blocked a fierce blow from above while from the side a gauntleted fist pummeled the Harkan's cheek. A second blow sent the Harkan stumbling. The Ferens pushed in for the kill.

Damn it all, Merit thought, *this will ruin the games.* Merit wondered if she should call an end to the match. It was within her right to end the contests, to declare a winner without further bloodshed. She raised a finger and the crowd's gaze swung from the field to the platform where Merit stood. The people waited. A word would end the melee, but no sound issued from her lips—as there was no longer a need for her to act.

What's he doing?

The highborn Feren in the silver armor had advanced across the ring and was attacking his own countrymen, clobbering one soldier with the pommel of his sword, sending the man crashing to the sand while taking the second man by the collar and tossing him outside the ring, ending his part in the contests. The last of the three Feren warriors, unwilling to raise his blade against the noble warrior in silver, dropped his weapon. The crowed roared as he scurried from the ring.

Clever man, thought Merit. *He wants her all to himself.*

Two combatants remained, one from each kingdom, the tall and powerful Feren in silver, the small and stealthy Harkan in black. Her head swung from one to the other, watching closely. These next few moments would be the critical ones, the moves that would decide the match.

The Harkan advanced, feet shuffling in the dirt, stirring gray clouds, sword gleaming in the light.

The crowd went silent.

The Harkan lunged with frightful speed, then faltered midstrike.

The crowd gasped.

Merit bit her lip.

Searching for an explanation for the Harkan's failure, Merit noticed blood seeping from the black armor. Taking advantage of his opponent's injury, the tall Feren struck at the wounded Harkan, disarming his opponent, putting his blade to the Harkan's neck, ready for the kill.

"Halt!" ordered Merit. She swallowed an uneasy breath. "Show yourself!" she ordered the Harkan.

On the field, the Harkan angrily tore off her helm, revealing the face of a girl of ten and six years with close-cropped hair and brown eyes.

Harkana's last warrior in the field was Kepi Hark-Wadi, second daughter of Arko, king of Harkana. Merit's younger sister. *I told her to stay out of the games.* Merit had urged Kepi to sit alongside her on the platform, but her sister had little interest in Merit's advice—little interest in anyone's counsel save for her own.

The tall Feren took off his helm. His dark, wet hair was plastered to his head, his strong jaw lined with dark stubble. He was Dagrun Finner, the young king of the Ferens.

Below Merit, the crowd surged with anger at Kepi's defeat.

Merit held her breath, waiting for Kepi to yield so that the match would be over, but her younger sister gave no sign, no indication that she would relent. *Right,* thought Merit. *She isn't going to make this easy for me.*

The two combatants stood, unmoving, the Feren blade held at her sister's throat, the crowd whispering, as soldiers from both sides began gathering at the edge of the field, ready for war. All eyes turned to Merit. But she remained impassive, unwilling to release her sister from her fate. Instead she caressed the folds of her blue dress as she watched Kepi shudder beneath the blade, watched her squirm while the crowd held its breath. *Let Kepi worry.*

When the moment had stretched for a sufficient time, Dagrun, the king of the Ferens, tired of holding his sword, let his blade nip her sister's throat, drawing a sliver of blood.

Forcing Merit's hand. Save her sister or send her to her death.

She had little choice.

Merit slashed the air with her hand, surrendering the match to Dagrun. *You won't taste death today, Kepi.*

After all, Merit had plans for her little sister.

3

"I should have gutted Dagrun while he held the blade to my throat," said Kepi Hark-Wadi, the king's second daughter, as she threw her black leather armor across the room so that it expelled a trail of blood onto the floor. It left a star-shaped stain on the dusty brown sandstone, a mark she knew her father would see, no matter how much she would scrub it later. "I'm fine!" she barked, waving off the consolatory murmurs of her waiting women, the worried clucking of the physician who wanted to see to the bruise on her cheek and the cuts on her neck and chest that were still dripping blood from her fight in the arena. "Leave!" she told the physician.

Kepi didn't care about cuts and bruises. She seldom shied away from pain; in fact, if the words of her physician were to be believed, pain was the thing she sought most in life. Pain helped her forget. Whenever there was even the smallest chance of remembering her past, she would pick up a blade and pick a fight instead. Hitting things made the memories go away, and on occasion, taking a good hit did the trick as well.

She had taken more than a few hits in the arena that day, but her humiliation hurt more than the slash of any blade.

Merit should have let the king of the Ferens kill her; surely death was better than this. So close. She had come so close to defeating Dagrun. She could see it in her mind's eye—if she had taken one more step to the right, if she had used her size and speed to react just a moment faster, she could have ducked his arm and come up behind him, caught him around the neck and pressed her blade against *his* throat, made him submit to her while around him rang the cheers of her countrymen. A Harkan victor in Harkana's games. A victory against the people who had wronged her. She touched the cut on her throat and her finger came away wet with blood.

"My, my, look at all these cuts," murmured the girl who was washing her.

"You're black and blue," said another. "You look like you been stompin' grapes—like you're covered in wine stains."

"I've had worse," Kepi said as she untied the last of her leathers. Around her, the girls fussed and fretted, cleaning the dirt and the blood from her neck and chest, bringing her fresh water and a clean gown, something suitable for the gathering in the King's Hall.

"That's what I'm going to wear?" Kepi looked at the flimsy linen dress and laughed without mirth. At ten and six years, slender as a teenage boy, with her wide shoulders and high forehead, Kepi was not as conventional a beauty as Merit. Her hair was a mossy brown and cut at the nape, short as a boy's, and she had her father's black eyes and thin nose. But Kepi cared little for her looks. In truth she had her own brand of charm, a beguilingly crooked smile, a brightness in her eyes, but as she was often standing next to her sister at public events, many found her plain.

"You'll make a poor sight in the King's Hall, in your fine gown and golden bangles, and that bruise blackening half your face," said the girl who was helping her with her dress.

"You forgot about the cut on my arm," Kepi said with a wan smile. The slash on her forearm was festering, turning purple, a sorry sight *indeed* for the people of Harkana, not to mention their guests from Feren.

"I rather like the way I look," Kepi said as she glanced at the patchwork of red and blue that covered her skin. The girls all shook their heads as they adjusted her gown, tugging it up across her slight breasts and flat stomach, correcting the pleats. The fabric was thin and she wore nothing beneath but her contempt, ill at ease at having to stand in the King's Hall during the Devouring with a man whose people she so despised. Whose idea had it been to invite them to Harwen? Especially Dagrun, that brute and no-name. *How can Merit tolerate the man?* She had heard the rumors about her sister and the new king of the Ferens and hoped they were not true. The mere thought of the Ferens—liars, slavers—made her stomach roil.

Kepi's history with Feren was something she tried daily, without success, to forget—how as a child the emperor had promised her in marriage to a warlord of the blackthorn forests. How she had nearly died at the hands of her new husband and his kin. Imprisoned, starved. Abused. Her year in Feren was easily the worst of her young life.

Kepi tried to push the thought from her mind as her cuts burned and her bruises throbbed. On any other day the pain would have distracted her, but not today, not with the Ferens so close. On a day like this, she could not forget what had happened to her at their hands.

The betrothal itself was not unusual. Since the War of the Four and the penances that came from losing to the Soleri, every year legions of commoners from the lower kingdoms were sent to Sola to serve as slaves, while the ruling families sacrificed their children. Sons were sent to the Priory of Tolemy, while daughters were matched in marriage by the emperor himself. Like slaves, the children of the lords and kings of the lower kingdoms had no choice: they had to submit to the emperor's will, for the good of the empire, for the sake of their country, for peace.

And submit they did. Three years ago, Kepi had traveled with her father and sister and a small coterie of lords and ladies and soldiers, crossing the Rift valley on a rickety wooden bridge and making their way into the strange, dark land where green plants and trees grew wild, monstrous blackthorns so tall their tops were hidden in the low clouds, keeping the land in a cool gray shade, in a perpetual twilight that made everything seem hushed and secret. Even the noisy Harkans had been silenced and spoke only in whispers when they entered the forest kingdom, where there was no horizon, where the trees themselves seemed to lean in to listen.

It had all seemed so exotic—the land, the lushness and greenness of it, so different from the deserts of Harkana. So empty. Met only by the calls of the black-winged kestrels wheeling high overhead, the Harkans traveled two days without seeing another soul, not a village, not a city. Kepi started to think the Ferens were a dream, not a people as much as a myth.

No. She didn't want to recall her tortured little wedding, the night of drunkenness that followed, and the way her husband's body had looked when she found him dead the next morning, lying on his face in a pool of his own spit. She tried not to think about it. She always tried not to think about it, but was seldom successful. She'd spent a year in a Feren prison, accused of the drunkard's murder, before her father had arrived with a legion of Harkan soldiers and demanded her release. When the prison guards balked at the Harkans' demands, Arko's men had cut down the Ferens, hacking their way into the prison. It was Arko himself who broke through the great wooden door of her cell, shattering her chains and carrying her to his horse.

When she crossed the Rift valley, passing from the Feren kingdom into Harkana, she had spit upon the earth, vowing never to return. When she arrived in Harwen, Arko declared Kepi's commitment to the Feren kingdom fulfilled. She had married Roghan Frith as the emperor had commanded and Roghan Frith was dead. Kepi was free.

The Ferens felt differently, of course. They believed that Kepi was a widow of the Gray Wood and one of them now. She was owed to them. When Dagrun took the throne, the new king of the Ferens had quickly petitioned her father with offers of marriage to his various warlords. The fact that Kepi had been accused of murdering her first husband was not a deterrent. The Ferens would claim her, Dagrun had threatened, by the emperor's decree.

Arko swore to his daughter that he would never allow it. And in the meantime, Dagrun had proven to be nothing but a saber-rattler. So far he had not gone to war over her, even if the threat of another Feren marriage was ever in the air.

I should have beaten Dagrun today. She was no longer ten and three, but sixteen, and the most nimble soldier her Harkan trainer had ever seen. *I wanted to bring him to his knees.* She was disgusted with her failure to do so. Since the wedding, she had dreamed of nothing but her freedom. She wanted to make her own way in the world, to be free of the empire's influence, free of Feren marriage proposals. She wanted to determine her own path in life.

A knock rattled the door. A messenger. From Merit, no doubt, who was wondering what was taking Kepi so long and had sent a boy to fetch her younger sister to the gathering in the King's Hall.

"A moment," her servant called. Kepi was not yet ready.

"A long moment," Kepi muttered, still not certain if she wanted to go through with the gathering.

"What are we going to do about the bruises?" asked the girl who had dressed her. The others all shook their heads; they were clearly at a loss. "Isn't there some way to hide them? Chalk powder? Ochre?" The girls fiddled and murmured until Kepi lost patience with their fussing. She pushed them all aside, glanced at her reflection in the polished silver, and laughed.

"I think I look splendid," Kepi said. She would not conceal her wounds. If she must make an appearance, if she must face Dagrun, let her meet him not with the face of a king's daughter, but that of a warrior fresh off the field—bruised but defiant.

4

Ren's stomach tightened as the first drop of honey landed on his forehead. He caught a second splash on his nose and cheek and licked what he could. *Is this my morning meal?* Had they come to feed him? The honey ran over his shoulders and down his stained tunic. The heavy syrup clung to the loose, homespun fibers. He brushed at the honey, catching it on his palm, licking it up greedily.

A day had passed since Adin had left the Priory, since Oren Thrako had sentenced Ren, the Harkan king's son, to the Sun's Justice. His skin was red, his forehead burnt, his lips cracked. He had seen the sun as it wound its way across the sky; he had stood in darkness and watched the daylight approach. *I've seen the sun, but it's nothing like what I imagined.* In his cell the sun was nothing but a vague, barely perceptible glow, something to be hoarded and conserved, like water or food. But in the light-well, that same sun was a tyrant, a fiery demon that spun through the sky, burning his skin and eyes.

"More," Ren cried, the honey clinging to his lips. "More," he said again, but no one answered.

A fly buzzed. Ren swatted at the creature but missed.

"Is that it?" he asked, but no one replied.

The buzzing came again. Tiny legs tickled his skin. The thick, syrupy honey had trapped a fly on his brow. Ren smashed his fist against his forehead and the buzzing stopped. He rubbed his hand on the hot stone, smearing fly guts over the rock. *I miss the gray water, my morning bath.*

He licked honey from his lips.

Not much of a meal. In truth, it had only made him hungrier.

The buzzing resumed. A gnat tickled his eyelashes, a black fly bit his nose, another crawled across his chest. "Do you think I'm a corpse? I'm not dead," he said, swatting at the flies, "not yet." His head ached, as did his stomach and the muscles in his arms and legs.

Pain makes the man. He hummed the priors' favorite mantra, hoping it meant something. *I'll be quite a man if I survive this.*

He smashed another fly, the wings sticking to his palm.

This was not a meal, he realized. The honey was not enough to fill his belly, nor was it meant for him to eat. *The priors are feeding the flies.* The honey's scent had drawn the black-winged creatures to him. They swarmed his head, landed on his ears and nose, on the nape of his neck, and the ridge of his forehead. "Get off me," he said as he brushed aside the honey with his sleeve, but he could not scour the sweet scent from his face. The flies nipped at his eyelids and ear lobes, they slithered across his back beneath his shirt.

How long is this going to last? Ren nearly fell from his perch as he flapped his hands in the air, scattering the flies, but only for a moment. "Do I taste good?" he asked.

Ren wanted to kneel, to make himself as little as possible, but the ledge was too small. There was nowhere to go, nowhere to hide. He could cry out. No. His voice would ring through the shaft, then the sound would echo through the Priory. Every ransom and prior would know that he was broken. It was too early for that, too soon to submit. Ren bit his lip and punched the air.

Get me out of here. The words thundered in his head.

The sky turned white, the sun seared his neck and shoulders, his forehead, and the tops of his feet. In Solus, the twelve hours of the day were divided evenly between sunrise and sunset. In the summer, when the time between these was longer, the hours were longer as well. A *summer hour* was a long hour. *In this well, every hour is a summer hour. Every moment feels like years.*

Ren was no stranger to isolation, to boredom. In the confines of his cell he had learned to pass the long hours. He had built towers in his head, constructing the spires one stone at a time. He had made up stories, tales that sounded funny spoken aloud but in his head provided marvelous entertainment every night. Some evenings Tye would sneak over, and they would pore over old scrolls she had stolen from the archive. *At least I spared her this torture.*

As evenfall approached and shadow filled the well, he tried to recall one of his stories, but his head hurt too much to think. He tried to create a tower, but the pain in his legs made it difficult to focus. Only thoughts of Tye, safe in her cell, gave him comfort as he shifted uneasily, as the stiffness spread through his joints, the pain rising through his legs and midsection.

What have I done to deserve this?

Sandals slapped on the stones above, a voice rang in the shaft. "Alive?"

Ren grunted.

The sandals slapped again, fading away as the prior left him.

"I'm alive," he said, thinking the prior had missed his reply. *I'm here and I'm hungry. Feed me or kill me, but please don't ignore me.*

The tapping of footsteps returned and this time a shadow passed over the shaft. A prior upended a wooden bucket, spilling its contents into the well.

"Eat, gutter rat," the prior said as objects hard and soft clattered against the stone, striking Ren's head, falling on his lips, his shoulders.

"Eat this?" he asked. The sickly sweet smell of rotting meat and wilted vegetables made him wince, but he was hungry, terribly hungry. He caught a half-eaten date and took a bite from it without hesitation. It was likely a leftover, a discard from the priors' table. The ransoms ate everything given to them.

"Wait, boy. Don't fill your belly yet," said the prior. "I have more."

No doubt, thought Ren as the prior cast a second bucket over the lip of the well and more rotten fruit fell around him. Ren caught a sweet-smelling fig. He devoured it without thought or hesitation, and quickly regretted it. There had been maggots wriggling through the sweet flesh of the fig. His stomach heaved, he coughed and spit it out.

"Give me something decent to eat," he said as he shook the filth from his tunic.

There was no reply.

"Say something—you can't ignore me," Ren said, but the only reply was the soft thud of a door slamming shut.

The day passed, the sun vanished, and the sky turned black. Flies swarmed in and out of the lightwell, coalescing into black clouds. He ate what he could scrape from the shaft wall, watching as half-chewed olives hardened on the warm stone. Ren was prying a seed from between his teeth when he heard footsteps once more. The tap-tapping of sandals on stone echoed from the roof above.

"Alive?" a voice called.

Ren snorted, shifting his weight in the darkness.

A hand reached over the rim of the lightwell, fingers glowing orange and red, shadows mixing with the light. The prior laid a stubby candle on a protruding stone, then added a second, and a third.

"Why?" Ren asked.

"For company," said the prior with a mean chuckle.

The candle spread golden rays across the shaft. *This is no gift.* The light might keep the rats at bay, but the flickering glow would bring moths and black beetles. *Leave me alone. Let me rest. Let me die in peace.*

"You can keep your candles," he said as he transferred his weight. He raised his right leg, shaking out the cramp, massaging the muscles as he swatted at moths. His fingers swept something acrid into his nose. *What's this?* The odor was rich and loamy. The scent stung his eyes. A trail of smoke crept up from the darkness below, weaving its way toward the night sky as slowly and carefully as a thief stalking the darkness.

Pipe smoke. And the smell was familiar. Oren Thrako often walked the Priory, pipe in hand, smoke trailing behind him. Ren followed the line of smoke down to the midpoint of the shaft. *There you are.* A faint glow emanated from an opening in the wall. The light brightened, grew warm and orange. He saw a pipe winking red in the darkness, a yellow sleeve and five stubby fingers.

"Alive?" the question reverberated in the darkness. The smoke swirled, its white tail curling through the air, the familiar scent filling Ren's throat. The Prior Master stood at the opening, provoking Ren. *Alive?* He asked. *Still fighting? Why resist? Why not jump?*

It would be easy to jump. One step, then another—then the end. No more pain, no more flies, no more rats. No more tap-tapping of sandals on the stones. No more rotting remains. No.

He waited as the smoke drifted through the air, rats scurrying at the edges of his vision, head spinning, and almost without trying, without thinking, he began to hum a few bars. It was the "Eld Song," a Harkan song he remembered from childhood, one of his few memories of home. He sang quietly, then more loudly, his voice cracking at the lilting melody, the dramatic highs and lows. The song distracted him from the moths, from the rats that scurried in the shadows. He sang his tune as Oren's pipe smoke rose through the shaft.

His voice cracked again, his throat was too dry to sing, and he did not know all of the words, but he continued singing anyway. He was a miserable vocalist. The priors had told him as much. No matter how much he tried, he could never carry a tune. He just couldn't find the notes. But in the shaft, lips dry and throat aching, the song came out beautifully. The song made his throat burn, but he kept up the tune. He sang it without ever pausing or straying from the melody.

In the gap between notes, Oren coughed, clearing his throat.

Ren guessed Oren had come to hear him sob, not sing. *Do you want me to beg, to cry for mercy or my morning meal?* He had considered begging, crying like a child on his first night in the Priory. But no amount of pleading would better his situation—ten years in the Priory had taught him as much. If he wept, the boys would only mock him. So he sang as best he could and for as long he could manage.

The glow from Oren's pipe faded; the smoke drifted toward the stars.

"Sorry to disappoint you," Ren said, but Oren was already gone.

The black sky faded to purple.

The great clock wound its way through the sky. Each day the sun felt brighter, its heat more intense. His skin blistered and peeled off of his shoulders and neck. The days passed and Ren's body withered. He wished the sun would make up its mind. *Damn me or set me free,* he thought. *Have your justice and be done with me.*

Sandals tapped on the stones again.

"Alive?" the prior called.

Ren refused to acknowledge the question.

"Alive?"

Ren leaned against the hot stone, his head hanging down as if he were unconscious. The prior's shadow crossed the shaft. "Alive?" he called again, louder. Ren heard mockery in the prior's voice. *What are you waiting for, Hark-Wadi? Jump, boy. Jump so you can be free of the shaft. Jump so we can tell your family you were a suicide. Do it now and we can be done with you, and you with our questions.*

Ren shook off the imagined voice. He heard the prior ask the question once more, heard sandals drumming on the smooth stones, but he didn't move. He refused to acknowledge the prior's question.

"Is the boy alive?" A rock fell and struck his head. Curses echoed from above. More tapping. More talking. Ren did not move, he couldn't move. He hadn't slept in days, his thoughts were chaotic, his limbs ached, his skin burned. He was out of breath, out of everything—he had only his defiance: a primal urge to resist the priors. He held on to that urge, his head hanging low, unwilling to acknowledge their questions. *If I must die, let it happen now, while I still have my wits, while I can resist.*

Voices boomed from the rooftop, panic coloring the conversation.

Do they think I'm dead? If so, why do I hear fear in their voices?

The bickering continued, closer now, the voices nearly at the rim.

"If you've killed him it's your ass," said a voice that could only belong to Oren Thrako, then more softly, "and mine too. The Ray is not a for-giving man."

Ren wanted to laugh, but his throat was too dry, his lips too cracked. He coughed, his chest heaving, his body shuttering.

"He's alive," Oren exhaled in relief before the anger returned. "Fuck-ing runt's alive. Get him up. It's time to meet the Ray."

⇒5⇐

Following the morning's tournament, after Merit Hark-Wadi, the first daughter of Harkana, had bestowed laurels on the champions, after Shenn, her husband, had read out the names of the victors and the vanquished, Merit retired to her bedchamber. Her waiting women greeted her there and removed her blue linen dress, stripped the gold from her hair, and brushed out her long black locks. They rubbed moringa oil and lime into her skin, drew green malachite around her eyes, and painted her lips with ochre and her arms with carob. Merit sat still as long as she could, then waved them off with a jingle of her bangled wrist. "Please," she said, "I just want to lie down for a moment. I want to rest before the gathering. It's so hot today, and the games were so bloody. I ask not to be disturbed."

"What if the king asks for you?" asked Ahti, her servant.

"My *father* is away and I ask not to be disturbed. By anyone."

Ahti bowed, a gleam in her eye. Merit was sure she and Samia knew her secret, but it did not matter, her ladies were loyal to her alone, she had seen to it. Besides, no one would believe the word of a servant over the king's daughter.

When they were gone, Merit placed a green-stemmed flower on the stones outside her chamber door, then returned to her stool and waited. The flower's rosemary scent clung to her fingers as she rubbed them across her arm.

There was a time when she'd had more suitors than she could count. Even when she was a stripling, she'd had boys twice her age shadowing her through the corridors, leaving blue-tipped lotuses at her door or poppies on her bed. Despite her age and marriage, little had changed.

Merit waited, tracing a circle on the floor with her foot. Her servants had scrubbed the stone that day, the girls had worked the weathered rock with brushes made from palm twine—polishing the stone until its amber color shone. Her visitor would notice such things—just as he would notice the way the malachite made her changeable eyes glow green.

When he came at last, he did not knock. Instead he opened the door with a bang, catching Merit in his long limbs. She embraced him and stepped back, looking behind her as the door banged shut. "You saw the bud?"

He held up the white flower and nodded, "Good thing too, it would be a shame if I kicked down someone else's door."

"Careful," she said.

"Here?" Dagrun laughed.

"Yes, here. Everywhere in Harkana. You know we cannot be seen together. Not yet."

His hand cupped her cheek, his eyes bore into hers, and he smiled when he saw the green malachite on her eyelids, just as she knew he would. She had worn the green powder when they first met, and she had worn it again each time after.

He had proposed to her more than once, asking her to throw off the marriage the emperor had arranged.

Merit was impressed by his bravery, even if she understood it to be a foolish, impulsive move. Dagrun was a commoner who now wore a king's crown on his head and sought validation in the only way possible, through blood and name, and only the Soleri rivaled the Hark-Wadi dynasty in history and prestige. She understood his desire, but if she succumbed to his wishes war would rage through the empire. Tolemy was merciless, no doubt the army of the Protector would march into Harkana for her head. She always turned him down. But his endless proposals inspired her to devise a way for both of them to get what they desired.

The king of the Ferens rubbed his bearded stubble against her forehead. She worked her fingers through his clean, wet hair and buried her face in his neck. He still smelled faintly of horse and dust, a gorgeous, living smell. Like victory. His victory.

"You did well today, rescuing her," she said. "It would not have been much of a celebration if the king's daughter were hacked to bits."

Dagrun shrugged, "It was you who did the rescuing. I was the one holding the blade to her neck, if you recall."

"You knew I'd spare her. But I doubt she would do the same for you. If Kepi had had her way, she would have taken your head."

"Perhaps," he allowed. "She's good with a blade, marvelous actually."

Merit waved away the comment. "I knew you'd win the day, and you did."

"Not quite yet," he said, stealing a long kiss. His hand wrapped her back, unfastening the dress. Merit stepped back. She could not let him have her this way—not yet. It thrilled her, the way he desired her. She could sense his desire, almost like despair—he was hers, she could do with him as she wished.

Dagrun pulled her to him. His breathing was slow and even. "How much longer must I wait?"

"Not long," she said, running her finger across the skin of his stomach. "Everyone's waiting in the King's Hall. When we gather for the Devouring you can make your proposal at last."

"And then I'll have you?" he asked. "A queen for a king? Two kingdoms joined—a way out of this mess?"

Merit raised her eyes to him. "We'll both have what we desire." She had at last found a way to achieve the power and influence she desired.

He frowned. Pensive, which was unlike him.

"Come, they are waiting for us in the King's Hall," she said, tipping her head to the side, letting her blue-green eyes go wide as a girl's, though Merit was no child. "You know we must do this now, while my father is absent."

"Are you certain we should go through with this?"

"Yes, darling. With all my heart," she said with a sweet smile. "I want you to marry my sister."

⇒6⇐

"It's nearly noontime—I am ready," said Sarra Amunet, the Mother Priestess, as her servants fitted the last of the golden stalls onto her fingers. She wore a collar of carnelian on her neck, gold on her fingers and toes, and a flowing robe of white linen. Nearing her fourth decade, tall and slender, her hair a rare shade of red, her skin so pale she seemed suffused with an unearthly light, Sarra bore the blood of the southern islands. It was said the men of the south came from a place beyond the Cressel Sea, where the air was cool and the land was rich and green, full of flowery meadows and gentle wooded vales. Women in the capital whispered that the sun had never touched her skin, it was so fair and strange, though Sarra knew for a fact that was not true. There had been a time when she had been very much at the mercy of the sun.

"Mother, shall we away?" said Ott, her scribe. He was barely older than a boy, and had an underdeveloped arm, which he concealed beneath his robe. The absent limb gave Ott a strange, asymmetrical appearance.

She nodded. "I said I was ready. Open the doors."

The Devouring approached. Soon she would stand on the Shroud Wall of the Soleri and receive Mithra's blessing. As the great doors of the Temple of Mithra opened, the light washed over her face, the roar of the pilgrims swept the temple, and Sarra strode out into the temple's columned hall.

She walked directly into the blood-soaked body of a priest.

"What's this?" she gasped. *As if I didn't have enough to worry over today.*

"Mother what's wrong?" asked Ott, right behind her.

Sarra struggled to keep her composure as she studied the lifeless body. She knelt and put a hand on his chest. The skin was warm, but the heart was still. Blood caked the priest's white robe. *This just happened.* She searched the columned hall, but saw no one. She was alone. The crowds, held back from the high steps of the temple by her priests, could not yet see the body. *Only I was meant to see this,* she thought. Someone had set the body here, at her door, hidden among the columns for her to find.

Saad.

"So this is how Amen Saad welcomes me to Solus," Sarra said as she stood. This was her first visit to the city of the Soleri since Amen Saad had taken the Protector's sword and control of the empire's armies. She came here, to the Ata'Sol, the priesthood's home in the vast capital of Solus, once a year to observe the Devouring. Her true home was in Desouk, the city of scholars and priests.

"Are you certain?" Ott asked, his shaved head glowing in the light.

She glanced once more at the columned hall, at the steps beyond and the crowds that waited in the distance. "Back into the temple."

"And the body?"

"Pull it inside before the damned pilgrims see it," she said as she retreated into the temple. Ott followed, dragging the corpse, mumbling to himself. As the doors sealed behind them, she checked the sun's angle. Noontime approached; the moon would soon devour the sun. *I should be on the wall, but there is a dead man in my temple.*

"What now?" Ott asked. There was blood on his hands and her priests were staring at him, gathering around Sarra. Their anxious whispers made it difficult to think.

"I need a moment," Sarra said, gesturing for her priests to retreat into the sanctuary. *I need more than a moment, but I fear that's all I have.* She must respond to this aggression, but at the same time she could not ignore her sacred duty. The Mother Priestess must stand on the wall. *I need to be in two places at once.*

Ott tapped a finger on his chest, "The sun will not wait, Mother. Corpse or no corpse, we should away."

She knew as much, but she could not go on as if nothing had happened, not today, not with a bloody corpse on the floor of her temple, and not after what she had discovered that morning in the depths of the Ata'Sol.

"The Mother will stand on the wall at the appointed time," Sarra announced. She had a contingency, a way to address her duties without actually being present. "You there," she said, pointing to one of the servant boys, "bring parchment and ink."

When the boy returned with what she had requested, Sarra scribbled on the parchment and handed it back to him. "Fetch Garia Asni. Give her this note. The girl has reddish hair, like mine. Look for her in the scribes' chambers."

The boy vanished down a dark stair, descending into the labyrinth of corridors beneath the temple.

"You're sending Garia to stand on the wall?" Ott asked, guessing at her intentions.

Sarra nodded. "The pilgrims will not notice the difference. The girl knows the words and the customs as well as I do—I trained her myself. The wall is high, and the crowds are distant. Only we will know that a surrogate stands in my place."

"Let us hope," said Ott. "For three millennia the Mother has stood on the wall and observed the Devouring. It would be a shame if you were the first to break that tradition."

"It would be a more terrible shame if something were to happen to me." The wall was not a safe place for the Mother Priestess today, and for a moment she thought about Garia, whom she was sending there.

Ott tapped his fingers as he paced. "Everyone in Solus is in peril, especially us." He exchanged a meaningful glance with Sarra.

"Yes, that is clear. And we will still need a way to exit the temple unnoticed. Perhaps Garia should slip out the postern?"

"The stable entrance—why?" Ott asked.

"Because that's what Saad would expect. A dead priest left on our temple steps. The Mother is worried for her safety, so she left through the postern door."

"And where will the real Mother go?"

"Out the front."

Ott raised an eyebrow, but Sarra paid him no notice. She was not yet ready to share the plan she had only just conceived.

"You there," she called to her priestly servants, "hand over your robes." The servants exchanged glances, confused at first, but when she glared at them, they doffed their sand-gray caftans. She stripped off her collar and the golden stalls her servants had just fitted to her fingers and toes. She took the gray robe and drew it over her white one. She motioned for Ott to do the same, watching as he wiped the blood from his hands. Her priests wrapped the dead man in linen.

"If we conceal ourselves," Sarra said, "we can walk out the front door like a couple of servants fetching date wine for their masters."

Ott was tapping his fingers again, screwing his face into odd contortions, his withered arm looking ghostly beneath his robe. Throughout the empire, boys such as Ott were often cast out into the streets, or left to die in the desert, but the priesthood gave shelter to the weak, the unwanted, and the abandoned. Sarra had, many years ago, benefited from the priesthood's charity. Ott had done the same, as had many others.

"If concealment is the goal," said Ott, "perhaps we should add a third to our party." It was well known that Sarra always traveled with Ott at her side. The two were inseparable.

Sarra nodded her agreement. "You there," she said, motioning to one of her acolytes, the boys who operated the golden doors of the temple. "What's your name?"

"Khai Femin."

"He has only recently arrived from the Wyrre," said Ott.

"He'll do."

"For what, may I ask, Mother?" said Khai as he drew closer to her, his eyes wide, his skin pale in the lamplight.

"For what I tell you to do. Take a gray robe and come with us," she said.

"Where, Mother?" he asked, but Sarra gave no answer. She was thinking about her next move, how to counter Saad's aggression and use the discovery she'd made in the depths of the Ata'Sol earlier that day, trying to decide which was the greater threat.

Sarra raised a hand, indicating the doors. "Open one, slowly now," she said, the roar of the crowd filtering in through the narrow opening. "Just wide enough for us to exit." This was how the servants of the house came and went from the temple. Sarra bowed her head and drew her cowl down across her face. She slipped between the doors, her priests following close behind.

"So many people," Khai said as he stepped out into the streets teeming with pilgrims. Sarra walked around the boy, Ott at her side, scissoring through the crowds of Solus as she made her way past the temple steps, motioning for Khai to follow behind. Sarra had forgotten that Khai was a peasant from the Wyrre, and in the southern islands ten men made a crowd.

In the streets below, ten thousand thronged the plaza. In the whole of Solus, ten times ten thousand crowded the backstreets and courtyards of the capital, sleeping in dry fountains, on smoldering rooftops, and in winding alleys. Tattered cloaks and barefoot children packed every temple and yard from the Cenotaph to the Statuary Garden of Amen Hen and the Golden Hall. The pilgrims were everywhere, all of them gathered for the Devouring, to watch as the sun dimmed to acknowledge Mithra's continued support of the empire and its emperor.

Sarra caught sight of bronze helms glinting in the distance. Soldiers hidden in the shadows kept watch on her temple. No doubt these were the men who left the body at her door. *Murderers,* she thought.

The Protector is nothing more than a common thug. Amen Saad had ascended to the position of Protector and commander of the armies after his father, Raden, was found dead of poison only two weeks prior. Sarra was almost certain the son had murdered his father to attain the position. Raden had murdered *his* predecessor and half the army's generals when he had taken the Protector's sword. It seemed only appropriate that his son would do the same.

But Saad is not content with the Protector's sword. He wants my mantle as well.

Seeing the soldiers, she pinched her cloak beneath her chin, cinching the fabric and hiding her red locks.

"Khai, hurry," Sarra said to the hesitant boy, hoping their exit from the temple was unobserved by Saad's men. "The streets will only grow more crowded as the Devouring approaches." Ott offered the boy his good hand.

"Mother," Khai asked, "where are we going?"

"I . . . I . . . was wondering the same thing," Ott stuttered as he waded through the ever-thickening crowds. The boy was acting coy.

"Ott, you know where we're going," she said.

Indeed, Ott looked to the great circus and beyond, his eyes fixing upon the tip of a black and spindly tower. "There," he said, shaking loose Khai's grip so he could point.

"That's the Protector's Tower," said Khai.

Sarra gritted her teeth. "I think I know a way to end this conflict before it truly begins."

"Are you talking about our little revelation?" Ott asked. He was referring to the discovery they'd made earlier that morning. She would need to stand with Saad for the Devouring if she wanted to use what they had learned against him.

"We have no choice. Saad put a corpse in our temple."

"He is under great stress, and not all of it is of his own making," said Ott. He was referring to the recent insurrection. A captain in the army had led a revolt against his general. Two weeks prior, the rebel, Haren Barca, had murdered half of the soldiers in the Outer Guard before stealing away to the southern islands. The Gate of Coronel, the southern gate of the Dromus, stood open to the sea, and raiders from the Wyrre were pouring through the doors. It was Saad's duty to pursue the rebel and retake the gates, but he had not yet gone after Barca.

"This is about Saad's ambitions," she said. "That is why he has not left Solus, why he is here in the capital playing politics instead of defending the empire. He means to take as much power as he can, moving quickly, before too many complaints can be raised."

"You think he's bullying you, trying to get you to step down?" Ott asked.

"He wants me out of the way."

"So he can attain the Ray's seat?"

"What else?" she asked. The First Ray of the Sun was the most powerful *man* in the empire—as the emperor was *not* a man, after all, but a god. The First Ray was the eyes and ears of the emperor, the only one permitted to pass through the Shroud Wall and stand in the presence of the Soleri. The First Ray of the Sun, Suten Anu, was ailing, and rumors of his impending death or long-standing illness were everywhere. If he named no successor, she was next in line for his seat. Sarra herself had long coveted the post and had campaigned to Suten to make certain he named her as his heir, but he had refused her recent requests for an audience. Suten would not speak to her regarding succession. So she was left to wonder at what would happen next. Sarra and Saad, the Mother and

Father, sought the same seat of power, and neither knew who would get it. The title of First Ray was the highest post any mortal could attain. She coveted it above all other things, but the high seat remained always outside of her reach.

The street angled sharply upward, leading them to a wide set of steps. The old city, the Waset, sat thirty steps below the street level of the outer rings. The city of Solus had literally risen around its most ancient temples, growing in height and circumference over the millennia. Pilgrims camped among these ruins, pitching tents beside the Mundus of Ceres, sleeping between the tall statues of the garden of Amen Hen. Hawkers sold trinkets: carved viewing devices for the eclipse, tiny sundials, and weathered charms. A blind man, cursing ominously, predicted doom. Pilgrims chanted while a white-robed priest guided their prayers. He held aloft a copy of *The Book of the Last Day of the Year*, the tome the Mother Priestess read as the sky turned black. Sarra hoped Garia was well on her way to the Shroud Wall. She pulled her cloak tightly to keep her red hair hidden as she passed the priests.

Step after step carried her up and out of the Waset, Khai close at her side, Ott a few steps behind, the old statues and crumbling temples disappearing behind her as she crested the great stair. Beyond the last step, the calcium-white towers of the White-Wall district rose on all sides. Sarra stepped into the shadow-spotted street. She checked the sun's angle and hurried onward, past the bronze gates of the city's highborn families. House gods decorated each entry. Gifts of fresh persimmon wilted in the morning sun.

Up ahead, a call shot through the crowd as a soldier clad in the yellow mantle of the city guard caught a woman's tunic with the tip of his spear, carving a gash in her shoulder. She screamed and the soldier panicked, and as he spun away the butt of his spear struck a mop-haired boy on the head. The pilgrims pressed in, their arms raised, complaining angrily as they gathered around the yellow cloak.

Sarra felt their anger. If she trusted her discovery, the entire city would soon be filled with rage, but that time had not yet come, Mithra had not yet given the pilgrims cause to rebel. The sun had not yet reached its zenith, but the shadows were shortening, the midday drawing closer.

"Mother," Ott said.

"I know," she said. Sarra needed to arrive at the Protector's Tower in advance of the Devouring.

Farther ahead, the crowd parted as white-robed priests walked by carrying a mighty bier supporting a statue of Mithra-Sol. All eyes were fixed on the golden statue. Mithra's likeness carried good fortune—all who saw it were blessed by the sun god's grace.

Khai craned his neck, watching the statue wade through the crowd. *Perhaps he is a true believer.* It had been years since Sarra had any faith of her own.

A priest stumbled and the bier tipped, as did the statue. Horror darkened the faces of all who witnessed it. The golden statue tilted, but was soon righted before it fell from the platform. Pilgrims gasped, some sunk to their knees. Mithra was saved, a miracle. True believers all. Sarra shook her head. *I wonder what will happen to their faith when the Devouring comes.*

Everyone was moving in the same direction now, toward the Shroud Wall, pressing shoulder to shoulder, pushing against Sarra and her priests who were the only ones headed away from the wall. Buff-colored stones gave way to black, sand-covered earth. Ash-colored monoliths rose from the sand. A winding track loomed in the distance, a great cylinder wrapped in pillars. Flags whipped in the air and the smell of horse wafted in the breeze. A slender turret poked above the circus.

"The Protector's Tower," Khai whispered, looking fearful.

As they made their way around the circus, the tower's ebony façade was revealed floor by floor, until they reached the field where the turret stood. The carbon-black edifice, the citadel of the Father Protector, was older and stranger than any structure in sight, with a jagged, spindly appearance—like a tooth bent out of place. An arch framed the entry. The names of the vanquished, the conquered tribes and kingdoms of the empire, were carved into its stone. The names were so numerous they covered the entire surface, the words so small they could hardly be read.

Perhaps the name of my fallen priest should be added to the arch. Maybe they'll add mine after today, thought Sarra.

Almost noontime.

The moon approached the sun.

The crowds raised their heads to the heavens in supplication as Sarra and her priests passed under the black arch, their eyes raised to the sky, their hearts drumming beneath their robes.

7

In the King's Hall, the vaunted throne room of Harwen—a torchlit space made of dark, rough-cut stones that echoed with the voices of the old kings of Harkana, and the cries of a thousand generations of Harkan warriors who had come before—the king of the Ferens, Dagrun Finner, made his proposal to Kepi, second daughter of Arko, king of Harkana and son of Koren. Dagrun had filled the hall with dozens of broad-shouldered slaves, the strongest and best of his lot. He himself was dressed in a fine gray-green tunic, a bright jewel around his neck, his cheeks freshly shaven—the portrait of respect as he took Kepi's hand in his tenderly and pressed it to his heart. The courtiers of Harwen were hushed, watching this ceremony play out during the last day of the Harkan games, as the sun neared its zenith and the Devouring approached. "A lady of virtue and wisdom," he intoned, "a lady of beauty and grace and fire, birthed in the Year of the Kite."

Kepi withdrew her hand with a frown. The bruise on her cheek was still throbbing; the cut on her neck was still fresh. *The man nearly took my life, now he's showering me with compliments?*

"A woman who nearly bested me in today's games," he continued, "one I consider my match and my equal. A lady of cunning and strength, a lady I will be blessed to call my queen."

Queen? You should have cut my throat. She wished again that he'd killed her in the arena, or better yet that she had taken his head. Standing before him like this was worse than defeat, worse than any surrender she could imagine.

"Kepi of Harkana," he continued, "widow of a Feren lord, a man of knowledge and humility—Roghan Frith, the Lord of Redmud, long may he be remembered. My lady, you clearly learned your strength as his bride."

Clearly. Kepi could hardly believe that the wretched fool who had beaten her repeatedly on their wedding night was the same man Dagrun was trying to describe. Her fists turned white and her eyes narrowed.

Where's my blade? Kepi hated when she did not have a sword at her side.

"And though Roghan was taken from you too soon, you remain a credit to him and to the people of Harkana as an honorable widow."

Kepi scoffed. *How long must I endure this?*

She had expected Dagrun to bring her a husband, a minor warlord to replace Roghan, and she was momentarily shocked to realize the great king was proposing marriage himself. Just when she though herself free, the Ferens had come to her with yet another proposal. Why was he doing this? Was he baiting her? Was he actively trying to start a war with Harkana over her? The possibility had occurred to her more than once. Or perhaps the rumors were true and Dagrun was looking for a way to gain control over Harkana by courting both of Arko's daughters, Kepi in public and Merit in private. One of them, at least, he would find unwilling. *He spared me in the ring, but it will take more than an act of mock gallantry to earn my hand.* She wanted her freedom, not another husband.

Kepi touched the bruise on her cheek, which had turned a ruddy purple in the time since she had left the ring. She liked the way it stung.

Not far from Kepi, Merit sat in their father's place on the Horned Throne, beneath her father's banner, her face cool. Blank. One would have thought Merit was watching a game of Coin rather than a marriage proposal. Kepi stared at her older sister and Merit met her gaze for a long moment. Shenn, Merit's husband, was conspicuously absent, and Merit's eyes darted to the empty chair where he would have been seated. Then she lifted her chin, surveying the room with eyes narrowed, her lips opened slightly to reveal her teeth. Was that triumph in the set of her sister's jaw, in the flush on her cheek? *If you think I'll bend to your will,* Kepi thought, *think again.*

Merit had never been much of a sister. She was the one who had to be responsible for all of them when her mother left. *I had no childhood,* Merit had said to Arko once, in Kepi's hearing. *You were only too glad to rely on me when you needed me. Yet because you refuse to name me regent in your place, you keep me from having any real authority. The people think I am your favorite, the beauty, the one who rules in your stead. But in truth I am neither monarch nor regent. I am nothing in Harkana.*

Yet it was precisely Arko's love for her that kept her from what she wanted. Merit misunderstood their father's actions. For Arko, power was an unyielding sun—if you lingered beneath its glow, it was certain to burn you. He wanted to keep his eldest daughter safe from its burden. Merit believed she was denied, slighted by her father's indifference. She had never understood Arko. Nor did she understand Kepi either, that her little sister wanted naught from Merit but kindness. *She doesn't know me.*

Kepi wished again that she had finished this in the arena.

Another Feren wedding felt like a fate worse than any death by arms, worse than growing old and wretched.

"This is for you," Dagrun said as he took a cloth-wrapped object from his slaves and faced Kepi. He drew back the smooth wool to reveal a stout blackthorn timber. He set the iron-gray mass on the floor, where it landed with a dull thump. "This was cut from my birth tree." Every Feren had a birth tree. The commoners carved brush handles and wood combs from theirs. The king used his to supply furnishings for his queen's chamber. She knew the Feren traditions—Roghan's envoy had promised them that his lord would build Kepi a set of chambers fit for a lady when they were negotiating her marriage dowry in Harkana. Roghan had made many promises, but kept none of them. She expected no better from Dagrun. Standing before him, Kepi felt lower than the lowest servant, more helpless than a Feren slave. *But I am no servant.*

The sudden quiet in the throne room made her realize Dagrun had finally stopped talking. The king of the Ferens unsheathed his sword and drew it across his palm.

"Kepina Hark-Wadi, I, Dagrun Finner, king of the Ferens and lord of the Gray Wood, beg for your hand in marriage." He held up his bloody palm. The blood oath was a Feren custom, she knew, and it meant that he had pledged himself to her and that his honor was bound to this pledge. If she refused, it would mean war. *He gives me no choice, I must accept.*

All eyes were on Kepi, her hands folded, her gown draped over her slim frame. Risk war or damn herself to a second Feren wedding—she had to make a decision. Everywhere Kepi saw apprehension on the faces of the crowd. The Harkans gripped their spears; the Ferens clustered around Dagrun. Everyone waited for her to speak. The room was utterly quiet. No one dared cough or whisper for fear of missing what Kepi would say.

She gathered her nerve. "I thank you for the honor of your proposal." Her voice began to falter, but she steadied it. She would not give him the satisfaction. Kepi took a step toward Dagrun. Her soldiers edged closer to Kepi, and Dagrun's men gathered about him. She took her open palm and pressed it to his bloody one.

"I accept."

There was clapping in the chamber, a sigh of relief, the crowd exhaling. Merit relaxed on the throne and the Harkan soldiers slackened their hold on their spears as Dagrun's men shook off their scowls. Everyone seemed relieved, except for Kepi who had not yet finished.

"I accept your proposal," she repeated. "Yet I regret that I am still in mourning for my dear dead husband. Every day I see his face before me and weep for his loss. No other man will ever supplant his place in my heart, at least not for a time. It would not be fair to you, my brother-king, to accept your love when my heart still belongs to another," she lied.

Dagrun's eyes flicked in Merit's direction, but Merit's face revealed nothing, no surprise, no dismay, though Kepi knew she was burning within.

"Though I do accept your offer of marriage, as per tradition, I must wait until more time has passed. I must mourn for seven years, as is Feren custom," she said, her eyes downcast. The old laws of Feren allowed a widow to mourn for seven years before she wedded a new husband. Kepi had accepted his proposal, yet denied it.

Dagrun's eyes grew dark. Dangerous, the way Roghan's had as he watched her on their wedding night. *Such a tiny thing. Like a little girl, still.* That was what he had said to her before he pushed her facedown onto the table. Kepi resisted the urge to step back. *Hold your ground.*

Dagrun took a step forward. The sword was still in his hand. He raised the blade, wiped the blood from the edge, and sheathed it. The hilt gave a loud ring when he jabbed it against the scabbard. "I will leave you to your grief."

"I grieve for Roghan every day," Kepi said, smiling faintly. Roghan had been a miserable husband, but his name sounded sweet on her tongue when she spoke it just then. She may not have bested Dagrun in the arena, but she had no doubt taken the upper hand in the throne room.

Go, Kepi thought, watching Dagrun leave. *Go and don't come back.* But when she gazed up at her sister on the Horned Throne, Merit's eyes flashed angrily at her and Kepi knew she had only delayed the inevitable.

8

A low moan drifted down the spiral stairwell of the Protector's Tower as Sarra Amunet, the Mother Priestess, cocked her head at the sound. "Come, follow me. Those cries are meant to intimidate lesser men," she said as she climbed up the steps, Ott and Khai following close behind her. In truth, Sarra had felt a stab of intimidation when she heard the first cry, but she didn't want her priests to know she was afraid.

The spiral treads of the tower were deep, rounded at the edge and steeply angled, designed so that a chariot could drive from the base of the tower to its summit without stopping. *Or perhaps the long, twisting steps were designed to delay a guest's arrival?* Even a horse-drawn chariot would be forced to move slowly over the uneven ramps. Amen Saad, the Father Protector, must have been aware of this, as he had left the doors open at the top of the tower. Sobs rang from the doorway, followed by the crack of a whip. The cries increased in frequency as they neared the top. Khai covered his ears while Sarra fixed her gaze on the tower's slitlike windows. She was watching the crowds, looking for the sun, making certain she would not arrive too late. She was weary from the long walk through the city, and the climb only made her more tired. *There must be thousands of steps in this tower. It's a wonder anyone visits the Protector.* If her life did not depend upon what happened next, she swore she might have turned around and given up.

From somewhere above, there was a sharp word, and the sobbing ceased.

Good, I'm tired of listening to it, she thought.

Outside, a horn blasted. The raucous cheers of the crowd filled the stairs: the sound of the people awaiting the eclipse, the end of the year. Awaiting Mithra's blessing on all of them—man, woman, child, on the crops and the rain, on the emperor himself, to whom the sun would bow. *If I were them, I wouldn't hold my breath.*

At the top of the stairs Sarra stepped through the gates without announcing herself, but her arrival had been anticipated: Amen Saad sat facing the door, a hand on a knee, his face screwed into a challenging glare. There was a partridge on a bronze plate before him, while behind him, in a separate chamber, a prisoner hung from manacles. The captive man wore no clothing and his chest was colorful with whip marks and bruises. A man dressed in the black robes of a torturer drew long cuts across the prisoner's chest. Sarra hardened her gaze; she would show no discomfort. The room was full of the prisoner's muffled cries, and Saad merely continued to eat his midday meal, ripping the wing from the bird with delight. The Protector waved his hand and the torturer ceased his interrogation.

At last, some quiet, thought Sarra as she laid eyes on the new Protector for the first time. Grease covered his fingers and he chewed with his mouth half-open, a sliver of onion wedged between his teeth. *This boy thinks himself worthy of the Ray's seat?* Sarra chafed at the notion.

"Welcome to the citadel," said Saad, gesturing with his knife. He was stout, roughly bearded, and shiny with perspiration. Not yet twenty, Saad retained the temperament of a boy, wrathful and impatient. He wore the pristine armor of his father, the former Protector. Not yet tailored to fit him, the plackart hung crooked on his chest, and it ground against the rest of his armor whenever he moved.

It was said that no man would dare strike the Protector, but Saad did not look like a boy who had never felt the sting of a blade. A bold scar split his face in half, stretching from forehead to cheek. The cut, carved into the young man's face when he was only a boy, was rumored to be nothing less than the work of his father. *Pain makes the man,* thought Sarra. *No wonder Saad killed him.*

Sarra removed her gray cloak to reveal the white robe of the Mother Priestess. "I was hoping to surprise you, but your soldiers spied me on the temple steps—did they not?" She guessed his men had watched her at the temple, followed her through the city, then rushed ahead to warn him of her arrival. The soldiers who murdered her priest had followed her here.

"My men are everywhere." Saad did little to conceal his grin. "You, on the other hand . . . isn't there somewhere you should be? On the wall, awaiting the Devouring?" Saad asked, eating as he spoke. "To partake in the blessings of our precious god? It is through your hand that the blessing of the sun is passed on to the emperor, is it not? Or do you not wish to bless the empire this year?" he asked, amused. Sarra wondered if he would ask her about the dead priest.

"Mithra blesses the empire," said Sarra, deciding that it would only make her look weak if she mentioned the dead man at the outset. "I am merely the conduit."

Saad chortled between breaths. "So Mithra-Sol has commanded you to make a mockery of the Devouring?" he laughed again, a rattle somewhere deep in his belly. He was a skeptic, she guessed. The pilgrims had faith, but the educated—the viziers and generals, the scholars and scribes—no longer believed in Mithra's light. They observed the rituals, but put no faith in their meaning. *I must make a believer out of Saad, even if I myself have ceased to believe.* Her victory would depend on it. The knowledge she had attained would only serve her if the Protector held some shred of faith.

"Do not worry, Saad. The Mother Priestess stands upon the wall," she said, motioning for him to join her at the parapet. In truth, she did not know if her surrogate had yet reached the wall, but she would find out the truth soon enough. She covered her red locks with her cowl. Together they walked to the balcony and stared across the city, to the Shroud Wall. The noise from the cheering crowd was nearly intolerable. Her head throbbed, but she was relieved to see that Garia had reached her spot, a small balcony about halfway up the wall. Her priestess was dressed in full regalia, her arms raised to the sky.

Saad nodded at the sight of the white-robed priest. "What caused you to breach custom by letting a common priest do your work? Why are *you* here?"

"Be patient."

"I am patient when I know what I am waiting for—care to enlighten me?" The scar on Saad's face swelled when he spoke, and his cheeks reddened. How old was Saad when his father drew the blade across his skin—ten years? Was it even possible to intimidate a man raised by the cruel fist of Raden Saad? She would find out soon enough. When the sun reached its height, she would reveal what she knew.

Down below, among the people, drums beat loudly, their rhythm accelerating as the time of the eclipse approached. The noise jarred her nerves, making the room seem too bright, too hot. The boy, Khai, was shaking, uncertain of what to do. Ott was rocking back and forth.

"What's wrong with him?" A soldier snapped, drawing his sword and moving toward Ott.

Sarra faced Saad and spoke again in the voice she used with the common people, the one dripping with belief, with power. "Tell your man to lower his blade." The guard at Ott's side hesitated. "Mithra Himself spoke to me," she continued. "I'm here to share His wisdom, to reveal to you what He revealed to me." She needed to prepare Saad for what would come next. She needed to make him believe.

"I'm not interested in your fairy stories, sheepherder, save your lies for your flock."

Her voice softened once more into her real one. "It's not a story, Saad. Mithra's power is as real as the iron in your soldier's grip." She met his eyes, probing their depths. She'd had little time to prepare for this encounter. For the most part, she was making things up as she went, but she checked his face now and then, trying to ascertain whether he believed her. "I heard a voice. A whisper in the night. Mithra-Sol called to me in the darkness. I heard your name, Saad. Mithra-Sol spoke the name of the Protector. *Go to Saad,* He said. *Go to Saad so that he may understand.*" Her knees were trembling beneath her robe, but he could not see that. "Now watch and know that I am the wife of Mithra-Sol. His earthly ambassador. I am not your enemy, Saad. We are two rays cast from one sun. Come."

She could see the hesitation in his eyes, the uncertainty. A part of him—a small, superstitious part—was wondering if maybe she were telling the truth, or so she hoped. Less than an hour ago, outside her temple, he had sent his soldiers to kill her priest. A warning. He wanted her to step down, to get out of his way. He wanted the Ray's seat, but she wasn't going to let him have it. The position was hers, as far as she was concerned, and she would fight him for it. She would fight him with the only weapons she had: knowledge and faith.

Saad stood and went with her to the parapet and gazed down upon the crowds of Solus once again. The drums stopped. The crowds pressed around the statues in the clearing. Her acolyte on the wall below held up *The Book of the Last Day of the Year.* The sun was at its high point, throwing the full weight of its heat upon the people of the empire.

The city held its breath.

"Watch. Mithra Himself warned me what would happen next," said Sarra, knowing full well what was about to happen.

"What are you rattling on about?" Saad asked with a sniff.

Sarra pointed to the sky. "Something is about to happen that has not occurred in a very long time. When I spoke to Mithra, He promised me a sign. He wants you to understand His will. There is too much strife in the empire, too much death, too much suffering. The people will believe *He* has abandoned them, but you will know otherwise. Mithra-Sol demands *peace* between priest and protector, that whoever harms the Mother Priestess and her flock will himself come to harm. Watch and you will know that what I say is true."

He cast her a doubting look, but she shook her head.

Watch.

9

So this is the First Ray of the Sun.

A man in a golden mask approached Ren. The disguise was carved with the likeness of Tolemy, but the face beneath was not the emperor's. It was Suten Anu, the First Ray of the Sun, the one who was permitted to pass through the Shroud Wall and enter the sacred domain of the Soleri. Ren trembled a bit, but not from fear. His legs were still weak from the time he had spent in the lightwell. After Oren had called down to Ren, the priors had pulled him from the well, had bathed and fed him. They had tended to his burnt skin with ointments and fatty creams, scrubbing him from ass to ears. With dull scissors, the men had cut his hair and tried to make him look presentable, but there were black guts crammed beneath his fingernails and at every turn he feared he might collapse.

If they make me take another step I swear I'll fall to my knees. He'd spent five days in a lightwell. It was the longest any ransom had stood and faced the Sun's Justice. *Surely the sun found me innocent?* He had survived, after all. Though no one here seemed to care the least bit about what he had endured. *I stood in that piss-soaked well for five days. The least they can do is to tell me I'm guiltless.* For his part, Ren wanted desperately to forget about his time beneath the sun, but the burns on his shoulders and neck would remind him of his pain for weeks to come. The sun outside was already making his sunburnt skin itch.

The Ray was nearly upon him, his mask glowing like the sun itself. Oren stood at Ren's side.

It was nearly noontime. The time of the Devouring had come. Suten had duties to perform. *So why has he taken time out of his day to meet me?* Ren wondered. *Why aren't I standing in the lightwell or rotting at the bottom of it?*

"Bring the boy forward," Suten said, his golden mask shifting as he spoke. "We must hurry."

With a push, Oren sent Ren stumbling into the street.

"Come closer," Suten said. "Do not be shy, my boy."

"I'm not shy," Ren said. "I only want to know why I'm here."

"You are here to observe the Devouring. Come," said the man in the mask. "Let us bear witness."

The Ray urged him forward with a nudge from his staff. Ren refused. *Why must I witness the Devouring?* He'd never heard of the Ray inviting a ransom to do such a thing. A ransom only met the First Ray of the Sun when he was released from the Priory. If Suten was about to set him free, why not bid him farewell and send him on his way?

"Do as he commands." Oren shoved Ren forward, interrupting his thoughts, threatening him with an ugly grimace and a shake of his scabbard.

"I'm going as fast as my feet can march," said Ren. Not wanting to anger the man, he held up both hands, signaling his compliance. He was too weak to resist, to weak to even walk, but he forced himself to do it anyway.

So this is Solus, he thought. *The city of light.* He had lived most of his life in Solus without ever having seen the city. Now he was outside of the Priory, so he turned slowly in a circle, taking in the sights for the first time: The temples stacked upon temples. The ruins stacked upon ruins—every surface etched in gold and worn by the ages.

Suten turned his golden mask to Ren and beckoned. "Do you know why the Soleri wore masks?" Suten asked. The light reflecting off his disguise was almost blinding.

"To gaze upon the Soleri is to gaze upon the sun itself, and no man can survive that light," Ren said, repeating what the priors had taught him.

"Yes, centuries ago, before they sealed themselves behind the Shroud Wall, the Soleri walked the streets of Solus in their masks of gold. These golden visages shielded the people from the light of the Soleri, from their fire. I wear this mask to remind us of our past each year as we celebrate the Devouring," Suten said. "Do you understand the solemn rite, boy?"

Ren shrugged. He understood it, but had never actually witnessed the eclipse.

"You'll learn all you need to know today," Suten said as he led them through the crowded streets, guards at his side. "These are the great temples of Horu and Sen," Suten said as they walked. "And this is the house of Re, first of the emperors," he pointed to a structure so ancient it lay half-buried in the stones and sand. Its rooftop was packed with men in golden caftans, its edges guarded by soldiers.

"In the distance, you might catch sight of the Protector's Tower, the high Citadel of Solus," said Suten.

Ren looked, but he didn't see the tower, and the Prior Master nudged him forward before he could steal another glance.

Everywhere they went, the streets were overflowing, the houses and temples empty. Everyone was gathering in the streets for the culmination of the Devouring, for the eclipse.

"This is the Golden Hall," Suten announced as they approached a grand structure with four massive domes. The curved stone walls of the domes—the height of fifteen or twenty grown men—towered above their heads, and the great circle of the sun, carved into the gleaming golden doors, reflected the light of the real sun into their eyes. *It's like looking into the eyes of Mithra Himself.*

"I suppose the view must be impressive," Suten said. "But it has been many years since I've felt impressed by much of anything."

Ren didn't know whether he should be impressed. Everything in Solus was new to him—everything except the sun. He'd seen enough of that. The strong sun reminded Ren of his time in the lightwell, and its heat made his red and peeling skin throb. He stumbled and Oren struck him with his elbow, sending him faltering. Ren growled at the man and reached instinctively for the knife he did not have.

"Come this way," said Suten, shaking his masked head at Oren as he led them to a door and unlocked it with a small click, revealing a dark passage.

"Where are we going?" Ren asked.

"To the lip of the fourth dome. Come," Suten said.

The walls inside were patterned with gold and electrum, the doors edged with silver and carved with curling runes. They climbed a long flight of stairs, ducking their heads, circling the very rim of one of the four great domes of the Golden Hall. Suten led them out onto a balcony and back into the light. On the wall behind them, there was a great circle of bronze with white and gold marks spaced evenly around its perimeter.

Drums mixed with the roar of the crowd below, hundreds of thousands gathered in the plaza, more people than Ren had seen in his lifetime.

Below, in a city square festooned with yellow banners, a ring of gold knitted in the center of each one, the people cheered the appearance of the Ray. Dressed in the colors of every kingdom—the somber black of Harkana, the silvery green of Feren, the vivid indigo of Rachis, the azure of the Wyrre, the buttery yellow of Solus—they sang songs to Mithra-Sol and the emperor, awaiting the moment when the sun would dim and their god would rain His blessings down upon them once more. As He had since time immemorial.

"Each year," Suten said, "I stand here to witness the Devouring. Since before you were born. Since your father was your age."

The sun had nearly reached its highest point in the midday sky. "Do not look directly at it," Suten warned. "It will blind you, but you don't need me to tell you that." The reflection of the light off the colossal city wall *was* nearly blinding. Everyone shaded their eyes, and Ren did the same. He'd spent his childhood yearning for sunlight, but the Sun's Justice had cured him of that desire.

A hush fell over the crowd below, the people looking through the cracks between their fingers. Some used clever viewing devices. The songs died down; the crowd held its breath.

The moment had arrived.

"Look now," Suten said. The Ray turned his back to the crowd, meeting the gaze of a white-robed woman who stood on the wall. They both glanced to the Protector's ebony tower, where two figures stood at the rail, then upward to the spot where the emperor observed the Devouring from behind a veil—unseen, secret.

The crowd fell silent.

Time ticked past. The sun shone brightly. A crow cawed, the shadows drifted, but the light in the square was as strong as before. A murmur started in the crowd, an undercurrent, hushed at first, disbelieving, then more urgent, a rising voice, a hum of concern, then mounting fear, cresting, a wave that built and built until the people below were pushing at one another, shouting, fear turning to terror in their voices as the noise rose to the balcony where the First Ray of the Sun waited, standing still, his face masked in gold, expressionless.

The sun did not bow to the emperor, did not dim.

No Devouring. No eclipse.

The masses roared their fear and disapproval.

Suten turned away from the crowd, his golden mask still shining like the sun above.

"How did you know?" Ren asked, awed. It was clear that Suten had known what would happen. The Ray was the only one who wasn't cowed by the sun's failure to darken. Even the soldiers were staring up at the sun, waiting for it to dim.

"How did you know?" Ren asked again.

"Patience," said Suten. "There is a way to predict the yearly eclipse, an instrument that simulates the motions of the earth and the moon.

I knew the sun would fail to bow this year, and so I prepared for it. Follow me."

The noise from the now rioting crowd faded behind them as the Ray led Ren along a tight corridor, Oren and the soldiers still close behind. Through a priest's chamber and down a narrow stairway they went, passing a row of soldiers spiky with weapons, before walking through a pair of heavy iron gates. This second journey was much longer than the first, and soon Suten dismissed the guards, all except Oren Thrako and one of his priors.

They stopped in a circular room with a heavy door on the far wall.

"What is this?" Ren glanced from Suten to the Prior Master, realization dawning on his face. "You are setting me free—aren't you?"

"Well, of course. You *are* outside the Priory," Suten said. "A ransom doesn't leave Tolemy's house unless it's time for him to replace his father."

"My father is dead then." It was not a question. Ren swallowed twice, his insides knotted with fear.

"Not quite yet," Suten said. "Oren will guide you through the Hollows, it's the only way to avoid the rioters. At the gates to the underground you will find an escort assembled by the city guard, who will take you safely to Harwen." Suten placed a silver ring with an eld skull ornament on Ren's finger. He told Ren that the ring had belonged to Arko and would prove that Ren was the heir of Harkana. Arko had placed the ring in an imperial soldier's hand ten years prior. Oren offered a cloak and Suten handed him a pair of scrolls. "Give this to Arko for me."

"To Arko?" Ren asked. Suten's words made no sense. "My father isn't dead?" If Arko was alive, why had Suten set him free? And why had Suten called him to witness the Devouring?

As if in answer to his question, Suten offered a final message: "Tell your king that at long last, the emperor demands his tribute. The sun has failed to bow and the people will require a sacrifice. We return his heir, but Arko Hark-Wadi, the king of Harkana, is owed to the emperor."

10

When the sun refused to darken, when the light would not bow to the emperor and bring blessings to the populace, Sarra stood in the Protector's Tower and watched Amen Saad gawk at the sky. He was not a believer, neither priest nor pilgrim, but he was afraid. The Mother Priestess saw it in his eyes. He had not once thought to question the Devouring. The sky turned black once a year just as the tides rose and fell and the harvests came and went—these were the rhythms of the world. But now those rhythms had faltered. For Saad, for the people of Solus, the sun was out of alignment, its axis drifting, unhinged. The world was out of balance and the empire was to blame.

Or so the people think. Sarra knew better of course. She had known the sky would not darken. In the bowels of the Ata'Sol, there stood a curious device that predicted the exact hour of the annual eclipse. That morning, the mechanism had predicted this exact event—that there would be no eclipse. There was a second device in the Empyreal Domain, but the Ray had made no announcement and no one else knew the truth of the day, so she had chosen to act on what she'd learned.

Even now there was worry on the Protector's face, worry in his tightly clutched fists as he leaned over the low wall, watching as the crowds overturned carts and ripped banners, smashing urns and overturning braziers. Thousands of angry men, women, and children lifted oil lamps and cast them onto carts and rooftops, tearing spears away from soldiers, and stealing oil from shops. Fire rippled through the crowded city. Smoke drifted from rooftop to rooftop, spreading like their rage. "Attend to the rioters," Saad ordered.

Soldiers bolted from the tower, beating a path through the crowds, calling to the city guard, hurrying toward the distant courtyard where the false Mother stood on the Shroud Wall, where the emperor stood behind his veiled window. The shadow of Tolemy, the god-emperor of the Soleri, retreated from the screen, but the white-robed girl, Sarra's surrogate, continued her vigil, *The Book of the Last Day of the Year* held before her in trembling hands by an acolyte. The priestess read the prayer, the solemn vigil, the words that were spoken each year at the Devouring. *That was my duty,* thought Sarra.

Now the rioters crowded at the base of that Shroud Wall, pushing aside a cadre of well-armed soldiers, men holding shields as wide as their shoulders and spears twice their height. The rioters scaled the narrow stair, climbing to the place where Sarra's proxy stood, hands raised, reading from the book. The mob engulfed the narrow walk, their bodies sweeping over the balcony like waves tumbling over rocks, washing away the soldiers, drowning the white robes of her priestess.

Sarra gripped the rail.

On the wall, the girl who wore Sarra's robe ceased her praying. The boy who held *The Book of the Last Day of the Year* faltered, and the ancient manuscript, the tome from which the words had been read for millennia, fell from his hands. Fumbling for the book, the boy lost his balance and plummeted from the balcony. For a moment, Sarra thought Garia would follow the boy. The white-robed priestess teetered at the balcony's edge, the rioters surrounding her.

One tugged at her robe. She whirled, trying to free herself, moving desperately to avoid the pilgrim's hold, to find shelter, an exit—a way to escape the encircling rioters, but there was none. There was no escape. She had sent Garia to stand among the crowds while she was safe in the Protector's Tower, sheltered from the riots, from everyone except Saad himself.

The rioters took Garia.

The men who had once been pilgrims stripped her bare, naked in front of the city.

Sarra turned to Saad. Her eyes flashed with victory, her calm face a contrast to the churning violence and shouts from the crowd. "The wall was not safe for the Mother Priestess," she said, nodding slightly, tilting her head toward the crowds and indicating the place where the rioters had finished their work, where the body of the girl who was once Garia Asni lay like an urn dropped upon the stones, broken and scattered. In truth, Sarra had not been certain what would happen to the priestess who stood upon the wall, but she'd guessed it would not be good.

"The second death," muttered Saad.

Sarra bowed her head. The girl was not simply dead. The crowd had given her the second death, the end from which there was no afterlife. A dismembered corpse, a body torn apart, could never enter the next life.

A terrible fate, one Sarra had deftly avoided.

"Dreadful," she said, her eyes fixing on the body. She did not want Saad to miss the significance of what had transpired. "There is your sign, Saad. The sun did not bow. Never before, never in three millennia, has the sun failed to dim. Can you not see what is happening on the streets? Mithra gives shelter to those who do His bidding. He did not want the true Mother to stand on the wall. He wanted her safe. He always wants her safe," said Sarra. It was a lie, but that didn't matter. She had predicted the impossible. She had known the sun would not darken and she was using that knowledge against him. "Mithra protects the Mother," she continued, not wanting to stop, not wanting him to doubt her for a moment. "Can you say the same for yourself? Do you think he would spare your life? Did He come to you in the night, Saad?" She shook her head. "Or does He speak only to me? Can you not see the sign—do you not hear Mithra as He roars His disapproval?" The sound of the crowd was indeed defeating, and it was growing louder.

Saad scowled. He ran his teeth across his lip, turning the skin white. "I hear the people," he said. He was studying the crowd, but his eyes kept darting to the wall, to the bloodstained body of Garia Asni. He was shaken—she had him.

Saad rubbed his scruffy chin. At last he said, "We will hang every last one of them."

"You *cannot* hang every pilgrim in Solus—you'd run out of rope before you got started. Don't you understand, Saad? You cannot fight the faithful," Sarra said, meaning to make him think that she and her god had caused all of this, that the power of the faithful was greater than any army, more fearsome than any sword. In truth, there was hunger in the empire, a drought, a grain shortage, and a revolt at the Gate of Coronel. Everywhere there was unrest and it had boiled over into a seething riot. The failed eclipse was the spark that set the kindling ablaze, nothing more, but Sarra needed to make it appear as if her god had spoken.

"Feel their anger," she said, "their rage." She tightened her fingers and made a fist. Now she would make her final argument, she would hit him with his own aggression. "This is the beast you prod when you kill a priest on my doorstep," Sarra cried. "From now on there shall be no more animosity between the army and the priesthood. Mithra-Sol commands this. Tell your soldiers to stand down."

"What soldiers?" he asked.

She stood up straight, making herself taller than Saad. She raised her

voice. "The soldiers at my temple. The men who followed me here. The ones who are no doubt preparing to assault my priests and take my seat."

"Your seat?" he asked, trying to deny what he had done. Saad was wavering now; he was stuck somewhere between fear and anger. *You're just a pup,* she thought, *a rabid one, but a whelp nonetheless. You can be cowed.*

She stared him down and refused to look away. Both of them coveted the Ray's seat, but only one of them could have it.

After a long moment Saad shook his head. "Fear not, Mother. I'll leave your temple and your priests in peace for now as I need my men to defend the city." He pulled back from the rail and called to his men, told them to bring maps and to gather the captains of the city guard. He motioned to go, but she took him by the hand so he could not walk away.

"This is about far more than my temple and my priests. This is about respect, Saad. Did you think I would hurry home to Desouk when I saw a bit of blood on my floor?" she asked. Sarra needed him to know that he was wrong about her, that he had underestimated the Mother. "Do you think I am powerless, a woman who would cower at the sight of a sword? Iron is not the only weapon in the empire." She glanced one last time at the spot where Garia had been standing until the crowd assaulted her. "It's not hard to find yourself alone with the crowds teeming all around you."

He pulled away from her grip, drew his ceremonial sword, and held it to her chest. The blade was bronze and the edge was blunted, but he could still skewer her if he struck with enough force. "Are you threatening the Father?" Saad asked.

"I think we are past the point of arguing about threats."

"I make no threats, Mother. If I want someone dead, the deed is done," he said, the sword held to her chest. The two were not alone, soldiers watched, as did her priests. Saad held the blade for the space of a breath. Perhaps he was taunting her, maybe he was deciding if he'd let her live.

But in the end, he turned and walked to where his soldiers had gathered around a table. *He's backing down.* Saad slammed the sword into the table. He knew he had acted rashly when he struck down her priest, that he had made an error.

She made her way toward the stairs, motioning for her priests to follow. Her work was finished. It was time to go and she was almost out the door when Saad stopped her with a word. "Mother," he said, his voice growing louder. "I will let you go. I have no more time for you," said Saad. "But you should know this: My father told me never to trust a pries

I do not know what foreknowledge you posses. I cannot guess at its source, nor do I care to try, but take note of my words. Leave Solus and do not return until your duty demands it. I am no pilgrim. I will leave you in peace, but if you cross me there will be no tower for you to shelter within, no robe to protect you."

Sarra bristled at the naked threat to her person. She was the Mother Priestess and she commanded the faithful. "There is no need for such discourtesy. I had always planned on leaving for Desouk this afternoon. May you share the sun's fate," she said, giving Saad the traditional farewell.

Sarra left the chamber at a measured pace, followed by Ott and Khai. She had done what she had come to do. She had put the boy in his place. He was still a threat, he'd try again to claim her mantle and put himself one step closer to the Ray's, but at least she had brought herself a reprieve. *He's clumsy,* she thought. The boy had revealed his intentions. *Clumsy, but dangerous.* She would need to be careful with Amen Saad.

When they were clear of Saad's chamber and well outside of his hearing, Khai whispered to Sarra. "Mother," he asked, descending the stair, "the crowds saw your body torn from the wall. They think you are dead."

"Do not fear," said Sarra. "When we reach Desouk and we are safe in the city of priests, I will announce my escape from the crowds: how Mithra's hand led me through the angry hordes, how a kind peasant helped me to a cart, and a blind woman hid me from the crowds till the carriage was outside the city walls. The body they saw was not mine." Sarra would have little trouble claiming she had survived the day. Already she had conjured up the false story her priests would spread throughout the kingdoms.

"I see, but how will *we* escape?"

"I have a carriage in the stables of the Ata'Sol," Sarra said, slowing her descent to allow Ott to catch up to them. *If we make it to the stables.* She hadn't had much time to prepare their flight from the city.

At the base of the Protector's Tower, soldiers guarded the gates. A captain of the Alehkar, the Protector's sworn men, addressed Sarra, "Lord Saad commands us to provide escort, to keep you safe, Mother."

Sarra did not want an escort; she had donned her gray robe and planned once more to hide among the pilgrims, to blend into the crowd. She feared the soldiers would draw undue attention or, worse, turn their swords against her and her priests, but she had no way to stop the men.

"Go," she said. "Lead the way if you must."

The Alehkar, shields strapped to their arms, spears tilted at the mob, plunged into the crowded streets. Around them, smoke hung in the air, pierced by shouts from all directions. Fear colored the faces of everyone—the Alehkar, the city guard, the pilgrims as they clashed in the alleys and arcades, in the wide plazas and columned halls. *I've escaped Saad, but now I must survive the people.*

"Mother, the way is not safe," said Khai.

"Would you rather we stayed in the tower?" she asked. "Nowhere is safe in Solus today."

It was true. Everywhere, pilgrims scuttled through the streets, some looting, others simply trying to escape but not knowing where to go. Sarra shouldered through the crowd, shadowing the soldiers, holding her priests close, keeping her eyes on the ground, trying not to trip.

Up ahead, the great circus was ablaze and the soldiers had to reverse course to avoid the smoke. They stumbled upon the stairs of the Waset. The stones were slick with oil and wine, the air thick with smoke. She held her robe to her mouth as she elbowed down the steps, Ott at her side, the boy tripping behind them.

"Mother, we should go," said Khai.

"Where?" she asked. There was nowhere else to go.

The steps were abruptly blocked. Sarra crashed into the soldiers' backs. The Alehkar had come up against a wall of angry protesters and were fighting their way through the crowd. Pilgrim after pilgrim fell to the stones, cut down by the soldiers' spears, skewered like cattle, their bodies lying in heaps. All around her, angry faces pressed in, pressed closer, shoulders jostling her from all sides. The crowd surged; it swarmed so closely around them that the Alehkar could not wield their spears.

"We should away," said Sarra as she seized Ott's robe and drew him close, tumbling backward and nearly falling over Khai. It was time to abandon their escort. She had only to detach herself from the Alehkar, to disappear into crowd before—

The gray homespun cloth fell from Khai's shoulders, revealing the boy's priestly attire: a flawless white robe, bright and glistening.

"Help!" he called to the soldiers, to Sarra, as the crowds descended upon the boy, snatching at his hood, grabbing at his hair and his face. "Mother!" His gaze caught hers; his eyes begged Sarra to save him.

"Guards! Attend to the boy," she shouted, but it was too late. The crowd had Khai—they had her soldiers too. The rioters gathered around Sarra. Hands pawed at her robe, tearing the fabric. In a moment she would be uncovered, but she held her ground, crying out to the captain of the Alehkar, ordering him to protect the boy. Her caftan tore, but it was not the crowd that pulled at her robe, it was Ott. He was dragging her away.

"The temple, it's not far," Ott cried out, his words barely audible against the clamor of the crowd. Sarra resisted. She called to the soldiers; she shoved at the rioting pilgrims. She stayed until the last of the Alehkar were swallowed up into the crowd, until she could no longer see Khai. She would not turn away, so Ott dragged her away, mumbling to himself as he led her down the steps, toward the Ata'Sol.

Ott stopped just shy of the temple yard.

"Gods, what now?" Sarra asked.

"The way is blocked," he shouted above the din of the crowd. Indeed, the space outside the temple of Mithra seethed with soldiers and rioters. It crawled with pilgrims wielding clubs and broken pottery, soldiers hurling spears and arrows.

Sarra motioned toward a narrow back street the rioters had not yet discovered.

"We'll use the stable entry, around the side." Sarra led them along a wall, down the narrow street, and into a yard, the cries of the boy still ringing in her ears, the image of Garia's torn robe and bare skin flashing in her head.

Up ahead, a wide archway sheltered a golden door. It opened as she approached, and the priests inside motioned for her to enter. Sarra glanced once more at the crowd of rioters. She thought she saw Khai or some bit of his robe, but the flash of white was nothing more than the sun glinting off a soldier's spear. The city was a cyclone of smoke and arrows and fluttering robes. *He's gone. Dead like the priest on my temple steps.*

Nervously, a priest ushered Sarra through the entry. Ott followed, the doors sealing behind them, the roar of the crowd fading.

The carriage was not far.

They hurried through passages deep beneath the ground, not pausing, not even lingering to catch their breath. Passing through the great wooden doors, they came upon the stables where a carriage waited, the horses watered and ready. Sarra thanked the groom as she slid into the coach, the door slamming shut as Ott sat across from her.

A moment later, a whip cracked, and then they were bolting, fleeing Solus until the burning city was an effigy in the distance.

⇒ 11 ⇐

The sun did not bow. The people will require a sacrifice. Ren recalled Suten
Anu's words as Oren Thrako grabbed his tunic and shoved him forward,
dragging him out into the light and chaos of the streets of Solus, where
the people were rioting and clashing with men in bronze-studded armor.
The shouts of the angry pilgrims assaulted him once more. The sky, once
limitless, was obscured by smoke, by the whizzing of arrows, by the desperate shouts for help. Ren waded through the crowd, navigating the bodies and the motion in the marketplace as quickly as possible, time to go
now, hurry. Oren was leading him out of the capital. He was nearly free,
but he thought only of Suten's words.

The emperor demands his tribute. His father was the sacrifice, and Ren
was the messenger sent to collect him. He had the urge to crumple the
scrolls Suten Anu had given to him, but he knew it would be pointless.
Message or no message, the Protector would send his soldiers to retrieve
the king. There was no stopping this; Ren would have his kingdom and
the Soleri would have their sacrifice.

Ren followed the Prior Master through the Waset's tightly spaced
temples and around overturned carriages and dying bodies. His limbs
were still weak, his skin burnt from the days he had spent on the Priory
roof, but he hurried as best he could. Sounds echoed like thunder around
the square as up on the walls, members of the Protector's Army lobbed
clay jars filled with black powder at the people down below, or shot arrows tipped with burning tar at thieves looting from the marketplace. A
group of laughing soldiers had backed a few girls into a corner, their intentions clear. Ren started to falter, turning toward the screaming children.
To do—what? To save one or two and run away?

"Quit staring." Thrako pushed him forward. "You'll have plenty to
gawk at where we're going."

"Where's that?" Ren asked.

Oren pointed to an iron gate directly ahead. He pushed Ren toward
it and they descended four flights in the dark before coming to a great
metal door.

"These are the Hollows." Oren thrust open the gate and they emerged in an even darker space. The sound of the door clanging behind them, shutting out the sounds of death and bloodshed from the streets above, was like the shutting of a tomb. It echoed in the darkness, giving a sense of great emptiness and space, and as his eyes adjusted Ren began to see the shapes of staircases and landings.

Solus had been built over the site of a great system of caves, natural passages carved by ancient waterways. The Hollows was an underground city of the same immensity and complexity as the world aboveground, a mirror image of the city of light.

So much darkness here. Ren almost felt at home. The spaces were low and wide and the floor was uneven. It was impossible to grasp where they were, what function the cavern held.

"What's this?" said Ren as they came to a sort of bazaar, with towers of crates, and tent walls.

"The Night Market," said the young prior, but he gave no further explanation. None was needed. The market was packed with goods Ren guessed were illicit: slaves and strange urns, vessels made from the hollowed out bodies of animals, stitched together with sinew and packed with exotic herbs and bubbling liquids. As they made their way through the stalls, Ren noticed a man in a drab linen cloak dashing behind a stack of crates at the sight of them while a second man ducked through a warren of tents. Ren lost track of them in the lamplight. *Who are they?* He stopped, glancing quickly around, the hair on the back of his neck prickling in anticipation.

Before he could warn the others, a shield glinted in the torchlight. A dagger flashed in the dark. Oren whirled, his cloak enveloping the long knife. The Prior Master twisted the blade from his attacker's grip; his foe stumbled backward, disappearing into the darkness.

"A thief," said the young prior who had come with them.

"No," Oren replied. "He fought like a soldier." He sneered at Ren. "Looks like someone wants the heir of Harkana dead."

"Who?" he asked. *Someone wants me dead? Who in the world even cares that I'm alive?*

The Prior Master pulled at the neckline of Ren's tunic until Ren was choking.

Ren hoped Oren would trip, lose his sword. More than anything, he wanted Thrako's blade. If he had a sword he could defend himself and take vengeance on the man who had sent him to meet the Sun's Justice. But the Prior Master's hold was unwavering, and Ren had no weapon.

Thrako's words haunted him as well. Someone wanted Ren dead.

"This way," Thrako said. "Into the gooseneck." He pushed Ren toward another narrow passage, their movements made more urgent by the unexpected attack. The corridor was long, narrow, and winding. *It really does feel like a goose's neck*, Ren thought as they ran, beating their soles through the corridor, Ren ahead and Thrako behind, followed by the young prior, each one glancing over his shoulder, searching for the gray cloaks of the men who had attacked them earlier. Ren's head brushed the ceiling; his shoulder scraped the rough wall. The passage split and he dove right, but found the way was too tight to walk, and he was trapped. Thrako grasped his hand and led him backward, dragging him out of the crevice and pushing him the other way.

"Go, boy!" He urged Ren forward with the tip of his blade while footsteps echoed in the distance. "If they come upon us in the tunnel," Thrako told the prior, "you will block their path to allow for our escape." The young man grunted a hesitant reply.

"Faster," said Oren. "Move." The light ahead grew brighter until they came to the end of the narrow passage, to a gate of black iron bars. Outside the gate the cavern opened up into a wide chamber filled with men, their faces black as kohl, only the whites of their eyes visible in the dark.

"Who are these people?" Ren asked. The stink was rich and made them gag. Ren saw a legless man dragging rags from the pile; a blind man tripping through the dust.

"They are the untouchables," the young prior said.

"The thralls who keep the shit flowing. Out of our way!" said Thrako as he shoved the sightless man aside. He raised his sword, motioning toward the distant gate. He no longer needed to push Ren forward. If someone wanted him dead, that was all the motivation Ren needed to quicken his pace. *I've waited my whole life to find my freedom.* It hardly seemed fair that someone was trying to take it from him before he'd even had a chance to taste it.

Ren in front, they pushed through kohl-stained shoulders toward a second gooseneck, even smaller than the first, lit by oil lamp and covered in greasy soot. This corridor led to another cavern, where men huddled in crowds, jostling them. One man tried to steal a dagger from Thrako; another tugged at Ren's cloak, looking for a purse he did not have. He held the scrolls tightly as hands clawed at the rolled parchment.

"Where are we?" Ren murmured. He felt lost. The hot stink of sweat filled his nose and the light was so dim he could not tell a gray cloak from a black one, a beggar from a murderer. They stumbled over trash and bones. *This must be some kind of sewer.* They passed through the tunnel and out into a tall chamber, fetid water cascading around them as they dashed toward the next gate. He looked for a moment to turn on Thrako, to seize his weapon, but the Prior Master kept his blade on Ren's back, his hand gripped tightly on his tunic.

"Try me and I'll gut you like a pig," Oren said. The man must have seen the anger in Ren's eye, the desperation.

"There's the next passage," said the young prior, pointing to a passageway that was so narrow they had to turn sideways to make the journey, and Ren felt his chest tighten, fear climbing up his throat. If they were attacked here, combat would be nearly impossible. The tight space made his heartbeat audible, his breath loud. A gray-cloaked form huddled against the passage wall. Thrako struck without hesitation, forcing his sword into the spindly silhouette. He pushed the body forward until they came into the light, where Ren saw that it was no soldier. The body belonged to a bone-thin beggar, a man too weak to move or cry out. Thrako pulled back his blade and the man sunk to the ground. *A life ended for no reason.*

On the other end of the gooseneck passage, beyond the lamp that sat high above the archway, the cave was completely black. They stumbled into walls, stepping on things in the dark, living things that moved.

"There are people here," said Ren. "I can feel them, but I can't see them." Knobby elbows and lumpy ribs pushed against Ren as he made his way forward. The young prior held up his torch, but the cramped space, even when lit, was too cluttered by bodies, posts, and other obstructions to allow them to see much. "Move aside! Move!" Oren called, and the mob parted, but only slightly.

Ren spied a handful of tall, gray-cloaked men at the edge of the crowd. "There!" he cried as he tugged at the young prior's robes, pointing toward the men, but they were gone when the prior turned, and the next gate was upon them.

A cool draft wafted through from the other side, but it was dark there, the lamps burned out. The hair on his arms danced painfully.

"Can you see anything?" Thrako asked.

The prior wiggled his torch and it came back alive, he thrust it at Ren. "Here," he said. "You look."

Ren would not move.

Thrako scoffed. "Put your eyes on that gate, boy," he said, pointing with the tip of his sword. "Or I'll cut them out and do it myself."

Ren knew it was a false threat, that the Prior Master wouldn't hurt him, he feared Suten too much, but nevertheless he leaned forward, pressing his face against the bars. Dimly he saw a guard dead on the ground, an arrow through his gut.

"We should go back. It's not safe here."

"I didn't ask you if it was safe. I asked what you could see," Thrako said.

Frustrated, Ren threw the torch through the gate so it fell on the ground, illuminating the narrow passage, the body, and a pool of blood spreading across the stone floor. "There," he said. "Now we can all take a good long look."

Thrako grabbed him by his tunic and smashed him against the bars so hard the room went white. "Do that again," he said, "and the kingdom of Harkana will be short one heir."

Footsteps beat in the distance; Ren looked beyond Thrako and his man to see gray-cloaks trembling in the dark. The men who pursued him were not part of the city guard nor were they imperial soldiers—they wore long cloaks and heavy robes, gray and brown homespun like crofters or shepherds. No armor, though their weapons were heavy, well made, and well honed like soldiers' weapons. Their skin was dark, tanned almost, as if they were not from the underground city but someplace above. Not slaves, then, but likely soldiers as Thrako had guessed. But whose soldiers? Who wanted him dead? Thrako let Ren go and opened the gate with his key, pushing him through the gooseneck and following close behind.

"Who are they?" Ren asked, picking up the torch he had thrown into the passage.

Thrako did not reply, he was too busy cursing. "Hold them off!" he ordered the young prior. He moved to lock the gate behind them, but the men were already pushing at the bars, shoving them open. Armed men were approaching from the front as well, from the dim passageway, like wraiths in the darkness. Behind him Ren heard blades collide. A cry, and the young prior fell in the entrance to the passage. The torch slipped from Ren's grip, the fire died, and the corridor went black. Ren had no weapon, no torch, and nowhere to run.

A cloaked man approached, his form like a shadow, a black outline accented by the swift movements of a curving dagger. His attackers had chosen their weapons carefully, the short blade would be easier to wield than a long sword in the tight space of the gooseneck. Ren scrambled for the extinguished torch, lifted it from the ground, swung it at his attacker, but missed—dust filled the air. The gray-cloak struck the torch, missing the flesh of Ren's arm by a narrow width. The man swung again, his blade slashing at Ren's cheek, drawing a slender stream of blood.

Angry and desperate, Ren swung again, sweat pouring down his forehead, stinging his eyes. Thrako defended their rear. His back pressed Ren's, inadvertently pushing Ren toward his attacker's blade. Trapped between what felt like two foes, Ren roared as he swung again, hitting only the corridor wall. His attacker's blade slashed Ren once across the shoulder, the cut stinging wildly. It was too dark to see his attacker's movements, to parry or dodge; he sensed only the whistling of a blade, the rippling of a cloak. Thrako knocked into him once more and Ren stumbled, tilting his torch like a cripple extending his cane. The torch's iron shaft made contact, its smoldering tip swallowed into the darkness of his attacker's cloak. Thrako forced Ren toward his attacker, they fell, iron pierced flesh, and Ren's attacker cried out. The corridor brightened, a distant light appearing behind the man.

Ren stood, his chest heavy, his breath like fire. In the slim passage, there was not space enough to run past the fallen man, so Ren trampled him and Thrako followed, the air loud with the cries of the dying man.

Blood pounded in his ears. *I'm alive. Still alive.* Ren had likely killed a man, though not by choice. *It was an accident. If Thrako hadn't pushed me, if I hadn't fallen into the gray-cloak, he'd have killed me instead.* Ren crashed into the gate at the far side of the passage.

The Prior Master shoved him aside, knocking him hard against the stone as he opened the lock, flinging up the large wood bolt and tossing it at him. When the door was open he pushed Ren through, grabbed the bolt from him, and barred the gate once more from the outside. Their attackers beat their shields against the gate, but the barrier held. Through the bars, Ren caught glimpses of their faces: stern jaws, long black hair, and skin the color of old leather. *Who are they? Who's trying to kill me?*

Gasping for breath, shaking with adrenaline and fear, Ren found himself standing at the base of a winding staircase. Faintly, dusty light came down from above.

"Go." Thrako pushed Ren forward as the soldiers hacked at the gate behind them, trying to break it down.

They followed the narrow stairway through thick rock, passing a gate manned by the city guard, their familiar yellow uniforms a relief after the strangeness of the Hollows. Thrako spoke briefly to their captain, low words Ren could not hear, but the older man indicated the path behind him, alerting the guards to the men pursuing them.

Past the gate, beyond the gooseneck and stair, Thrako led Ren toward a buttery-yellow light.

The sun. I'm nearly free.

Outside, the streets were alive with people, men and women rushing away from the city center, people frantically gathering their children inside to keep them away from the Protector's Army. Thrako opened the gate and motioned for Ren to pass. Staggering into the street, Ren heard the click of a latch, the spinning of gears. He turned to face the gate through which he had passed. Thrako did not follow.

Ren realized it was his last chance to strike at the Prior Master. He lunged and his arm shot between the black iron bars and caught hold of the Prior Master's belt, pulling so that Thrako stumbled forward and slammed against the iron gates, his face wrenched into a fearful scowl. The cut on the Prior Master's neck opened, a drop of blood inching down his chest. Stripped of his guards, Oren Thrako appeared diminished, afraid, but no less sinister. He snapped the gate closed with almost unnatural speed, and tore his cloak away from Ren's grip.

Ren cried out, rattling the heavy bars, but it was over.

With a bang, cold iron stood between him and the Prior Master, who was already backing away from the closed gate. "Goodbye, heir of Harkana," Thrako said, but his voice was faint, half drowned out by the howls of the rioting pilgrims. "Suten's men will take you home. See that you live long enough to get there." With those words, Oren Thrako faded back into the darkness of the Hollows.

Ren stumbled backward from the gate, nearly colliding with his imperial escort, the men who would take him to Harwen. They were looking him up and down when a throng of rioters poured out of a nearby alley, swarming the courtyard outside the gate. Suten's men drew swords and hurried to push back the crowd. In the chaos that followed, they lost track of Ren.

Now, while they aren't looking. I should fly. Better not to trust anyone, he thought as he staggered backward, fleeing from the soldiers and losing himself in the unruly mob.

12

Merit bustled through the stony corridors of the Hornring, pushing past waiting women and soldiers alike, slipping around the girls who gathered at the archways, eyes fixed on the bright-blue sky, waiting for the sun to darken. Some stood agape; others were squinting, shading their eyes at odd angles as they searched for the shadow that in any other year would slowly devour the sun. But there was no shadow. The time of the eclipse had come and gone and the sun had not bowed to Tolemy. For the first time that she knew of, the sun had stayed its hand. Mithra-Sol had chosen to rebel. *Perhaps the sun is Harkan,* she thought with grim merriment.

"A curse," a servant girl whispered as Merit passed. The girl was standing at an archway that faced the Ruined Wall, and the soldier at her side was shaking his head. "No, it's just the bloody sun, it don't curse people, and it don't bless them either. It just burns things. If you keep staring at it, it'll burn you too." He chortled, trying to catch the girl's eye, but she would not turn away from the sky.

The gossip was everywhere.

"It's an ill omen," said a waiting woman.

"This is about Barca," said another, referring to the Soleri traitor.

"No," said a page, "this is about the grain, the amaranth. The sun is angry—that's why I've got nothing to eat but spoiled amber and old bread."

Merit passed them all, trying not to listen to their chatter. She did not care about the sun. She cared only about Dagrun, but he had left the Hornring, returning to his camp just outside Harwen's walls. She had sent messengers, asking for him to remain in Harkana, but there had not yet been sufficient time for him to reply. She needed to set things right with Dagrun, but she didn't know how to do that, not yet. *Maybe the sun has cursed me,* she thought, but quickly put the notion aside. Curses were for children and servant folk. No, the sun didn't care if Merit lived or died, or if she whiled away her days in solitude.

Merit hadn't truly known how much she desired the king of the Ferens until he walked out of her father's hall. She hadn't expected the quiet pang of grief that struck her when he left. *I didn't know how much I needed him.* How could she have known? It was all so complicated. Dag-run desired her as she did him, but he wanted more than just her soft skin and her eyes drawn with malachite. He needed her name and the prestige that came with royal blood, but she could never give him that, not as long as Tolemy sat on the throne.

She'd crafted a plan to fulfill all their wishes—an unconventional way, perhaps, but one that was within the emperor's laws. Kepi was owed to the Ferens, and if she married Dagrun, his children would carry the royal blood he needed, and their marriage would guarantee a powerful alliance between their kingdoms. And this way, it would be Kepi's sons with Dagrun who would be sent to the Priory, not Merit's.

Because in secret, Merit would have a man who loved her, a man she had chosen for herself and not one who had been assigned to her by the emperor. One day, their two kingdoms would stand together and defy the empire. Only then could they live openly together as husband and wife.

But since Kepi had refused Dagrun, there was no alliance with the Ferens. There was no Dagrun in her bed. There was only Shenn, her husband, who had not even bothered to stand at her side for the gathering. *Now I'm forced to seek you out, Shenn, so I don't look like a bloody idiot at the feast.*

Pushing past the servant boys who were still gawking at the sky, past the soldiers who guarded the king's family, she pressed deeper into the Hornring until she came upon her husband's chambers. She threw open the door, and there was Shenn, sitting on a low stool, a young man kneeling between his legs, pleasuring Shenn's manhood.

"I'm sorry. I didn't know you were busy," she said as the door shut behind her.

At the sight of Merit, the young man jerked bolt upright. He was naked and his flaccid cock bobbed up and down like a fish on a line as he searched for his robe.

"It's in the corner." She nodded toward a sand-gray robe, draped haphazardly over a half-played game of Coin. The young man nodded his thanks as he took the robe and slipped it over his head. Shenn fussed with the laces on his breeches, but the young man just stood there, uncertain of what to do next, confused, a bit embarrassed.

"Go," she indicated the door. "Out. Don't worry, it's nothing I haven't seen before." And indeed it wasn't. This was not the first the time she had found Shenn in the company of someone else, and she doubted it would be the last.

"Go on," Shenn said. He too looked embarrassed, but not as much as the boy.

Merit waited until the door shut behind the young man, her eyes exchanging a knowing look with Shenn.

"I thought I'd find you here," she said.

"I'm sorry. I didn't mean for you to see that," he said as he donned his ceremonial tunic of dyed black linen.

"No doubt, but still . . . I wish you were a bit more discreet," said Merit as she watched him dress. "You have duties to attend to—you are my husband, Shenn. I expect you to stand by my side, and I don't enjoy looking like a fool."

Shenn was a friend, a co-conspirator, everything except for a husband, really. They made a handsome couple in public, Merit with her mother's blue-green eyes, her father's dusky skin, Shenn tall and strong-jawed and deeply bronzed. That the great beauty of Harkana was married to a man who was immune to her good looks proved that Tolemy, the bastard who had arranged her marriage, was not without a sense of humor.

"You were absent in the King's Hall."

"I know I should have been there, Merit, but you know how I dislike ceremony."

"You are worse than my father, but at least you are not hunting in the north. Perhaps in the future you can see fit to wait until the evening to seek out the company of others. It's what the rest of us do."

"Right," he said. Shenn fixed his hair in a circle of polished silver, moving his strong jaw from side to side. *He could have made a decent husband, if only it were in his nature to love me.*

"The Devouring has come and gone," she said, continuing her rebuke.

"I was detained, by a messenger."

"That one?" Her eyes flicked toward the door, in the direction of the man who had just left.

He shrugged. "Your waiting women told me about the sun and what Kepi said in the King's Hall. I know Dagrun left the Hornring." Shenn made his way across the room. He gave her a brief but comforting embrace. It felt good to feel the warmth of another pressed against her body. She'd loved him when they were first married. Even when she discovered he could not return her love, as her dearest friend and ally, she loved him still. But an endless parade of lovers had made her the butt of every joke from Harwen to the Cressel. Beyond, even.

Merit longed for something of her own. Someone of her own. "Dagrun's not gone," she said, "not yet. I can still make this right. But for now we have duties to attend to. The Devouring is not yet finished." Each year, when the games were over, Harkana observed a feast as part of the five lost days. The sun had not dimmed, but the ceremonies continued nonetheless—there was nothing else to do. The tables were set, the bread was warm and the amber cool. Merit saw no sense in canceling the whole affair.

"Shall we?" she asked, ready to take her husband's arm. She motioned to go, but something caught her eye. The young man had left a white linen scarf on the chair, the kind worn by the acolytes of the Desouk tribe.

"That man, who was he?" she asked. Merit recalled his dark skin and shoulder-length black hair. "He wasn't Harkan."

"No," said Shenn. "I'd almost forgotten to tell you. He was a messenger. The Mother Priestess sent a scroll."

Merit gave no reply.

"The Mother Priestess, she's asking about our repository."

Shenn passed the scroll to Merit, who nodded as she read through the correspondence, keeping her face calm, even if the very mention of the Mother Priestess made her twitch. Shenn was watching her carefully. He never quite understood why Merit did not take better advantage of such a powerful affiliation, why his wife shunned any contact with the priests of Desouk. He had badgered her to reconsider her stance on the issue, but Merit was firm: she would have nothing to do with Sarra Amunet.

She tossed aside the scroll, "Anything else?"

Shenn shook his head.

Merit walked to the door, her thoughts returning to Dagrun. *I'll try once more,* she thought. *I can't go one like this, not with a husband who mocks me, and a kingdom with an absent king.*

"*Merit.*" Shenn's voice held an edge. "What should I do about the Mother Priestess's request?"

"Give her what she wants. If the priests are after a few old scrolls, let them have them. Send your boys, have the scrolls ridden to Desouk."

Shenn shot Merit a questioning look. He was not accustomed to hearing her acquiesce to the Mother Priestess's demands, but Merit was feeling generous that day, her usual stubbornness weakened by her sister's disappointing cleverness, her father's absence, her husband's dalliance.

"You heard me," she said, her tone wry. "Give her what she wants. For once, I'd hate to disappoint my mother."

13

"Order three cakes for my supper," Kepi Hark-Wadi, the king's younger daughter, told her waiting woman. The two were standing at the door to Kepi's chamber in the Hornring. "One black bread, one barley, and a star of fast bread."

As her lady scurried toward the kitchen, Kepi took a heavy black cloak—a woolen mantle reserved for funerals—and threw it over her shoulders, meaning to ride as fast and as far from Dagrun and Merit as her horse's hooves could take her. She had not attended the banquet that followed the Devouring but instead had stayed alone in her chamber, listening to the guards chatter about the failed eclipse. Kepi hadn't given the sun much thought; like any Harkan, she had little patience for Soleri superstitions. But now she was hungry, not only for food but also company. So she fetched her mount from the stables and made for the nearby city of Blackrock, riding along a path she had taken many times, a trail that allowed her to avoid the guards who stood on the Hornring's wall, and the sentries at Harwen's gate.

I need to be free of this place. For a moment she thought she might not return at all. If the empire would not grant her the freedom she desired, Kepi would take it for herself. She would flee and never return. *As if that were even a possibility,* she thought.

Kepi rode through a postern door, past the low hills and scattered dwellings, riding out across the lonely road that straddled the basin of Amen, the great plain that stood between the Dromus and the hilly highlands of Harkana. It was not Harkana's safest road, but she had always been careful—she had never encountered any kind of trouble that her horse's hooves could not outrun, and she concealed a pair of curving blades beneath her saddle.

Ash, her gray-haired rouncy, carried her mistress quickly across the desert hills toward Blackrock. The steady thump of the saddle made the cut on her neck burn and the bruise on her cheek throb. Kepi was aware that once again she was trying to forget, to escape, though she knew she could do neither. She missed her absent father. *Was it a month now?* The king had never been gone for so long. *I wish he would return.* She needed allies, she needed the king at home and not off hunting as he usually did during the five lost days. She had so little family left. Her father was away, her brother and her mother too. Kepi had not seen either in a decade. The king of Harkana had his flaws; he could not abide the Soleri holiday, so he left Harwen each year at this time. But he always returned. *Isn't that what matters?* she thought. *Isn't that the one thing a parent must do? Stay. Yes, that was it*, she thought. Sarra had left them all behind when she fled to Desouk, and Kepi had never forgiven her for that. If her mother had a reason for leaving, Kepi didn't know it. She didn't want to know it. *I've fled the Hornring, but I know I'll go back. I'll face Merit and Dagrun.* She would not flee from her problems as she guessed her mother had done.

Not long after the low sun had turned the desert's gray sand into a shadowy mass of purple, Kepi caught sight of the *badgir*-spiked silhouette of Blackrock's wall. She rode toward the black stone pylon with her cloak bunched around her shoulders, her hood pulled down. She rode past the city gate, past the statue of Ulfer, past the stables and barracks that housed the garrison's men and horses. Up ahead stood the lime-washed walls of the Elba—an amber house whose only advertisement was its chalk-white walls and the loud sounds of drinking and cursing that echoed through the open archway. Kepi slipped from her mount and tethered her horse. A boy rushed from the archway; she flipped him a copper turn and asked him to make certain Ash was watered and fed.

Inside, she strode past the crowded front toward the alcoves that ran along the back walls. There in the far corner she saw a boy sitting at a table with three cakes of bread. One black, one brown, one shaped like a star.

"You got my message," she said, taking the seat across from him.

Seth caught her eye and grinned. "How could I miss it?" He laughed. "No one ever orders black bread. I think the kitchen girls are starting to suspect something."

She beamed as she tugged back the hood of her cloak. Seth tracked every order that came through the kitchens. If Kepi asked for anything—a glass of amber, salted quail, or a cake of bread—Seth was the first to see her order. *Courgettes and olives* was an invitation for Seth to visit her chamber; *tagins in pots* meant to meet at the market; *lamb with tagins* meant the stables. *Cakes of emmer* meant Assur. *Black bread* signified Blackrock. *Fast bread* told Seth to come quickly, that same day, when he had finished his work. *Barley bread,* in this case, told Seth to meet her at the Elba.

"This is the third time this month you've ordered black bread and everyone *hates* black bread," said Seth.

"So do I. I don't like barley bread either."

Seth shook his head. "Barley bread was all I ever ate growing up."

"So you hate it too?"

"Can't say I do, it's like hating amber—what's the use in hating something you can't live without?"

"I assure you a person can live without barley bread—it's as hard as rock," Kepi said as she lifted the cake and broke it in two.

A girl arrived with a cup of amber. Kepi took the clay vessel before the girl could place it on the table. She drank and nearly emptied the cup. "Did you know that my brother was born on the last day of the year?" she asked, putting down her cup.

"Today?"

"Ten and three years ago, but I doubt he knows it. They say the ransoms don't celebrate such things," she motioned for another drink.

"I don't know much about the ransoms," Seth said, taking a sip of amber. "Do you remember your brother at all?"

"Not really. I was only six when he left. I think Merit remembers him, but she won't admit it. I tried asking her about him once, but she said she couldn't recall much, nothing worth sharing."

"I've got eight brothers, but I can't imagine having one taken when we were young."

"I would like to see his face. They say the ransoms have gray hair and white skin. They are boys, but they look like ghosts, like withered old men who have never seen the sun." She shook her head. "That sounds silly—doesn't it? There are so many stories, but no one really knows the truth." Kepi took another drink. "Tell me something happy, Seth." Even if she had seen him only the day before, it felt as though months had passed since they last spoke.

"Not till you tell me what *he* said. I heard Dagrun proposed, that's what the cooks are all saying. You replied with some long speech that no one understood, but in the end you turned him down. The bakers all said there'd be war, that Dagrun would come for you for certain."

"I know." Kepi lowered her voice. "Dagrun will return. He won't rest until I've married him or one of his lords. The damn Ferens have too much pride, they think they own me," she said, shaking her head. "Even my own sister seems bent on arranging the marriage. The two were practically grinning until I told him I was still in mourning for my old husband." Kepi sighed. "You should have seen it, Seth, the Feren slaves, packed shoulder to shoulder, an entire army of them, barely clothed—it was a strange sight, ugly and cruel."

Seth scratched lines in the table, digging the pointed end of a knife into the soft part of the wood. The candle on the table tipped forward, dripping wax. "You don't have to marry him—or anyone else," he said, righting the candle.

"It looks like I have no choice—if not Dagrun then some other Feren. I'm only stalling."

He shook his head. "There has to be another way."

She stuck her finger in the melted wax, liking the sharp pain from its heat. They had had this conversation before, and there was nothing she could say to him that he wanted to hear.

"So that's it then? We just accept it?" Seth's eyes were red, he wanted to help, but there was nothing he could do. "Maybe one day we could . . ." His sentence trailed off to nothing.

"Yes, one day," she echoed faintly. It seemed too cruel to raise his hopes. Try as she might, she could see no way out of the marriage Dagrun had proposed. She knew she was only stalling. Arko was stalling—but what good did it do? The emperor decided on her fate, and her fate was tied to Feren. The empire would threaten war if she did not do as she was told. And when it came down to it, she would not resist, she would not put her life above the lives of her people. Arko had given up Ren, his heir. Arko had seen his father revolt against the empire. In the Children's War, Koren had fought to keep his son, Arko, out of the Priory. He succeeded but her father suffered nonetheless. Arko lived with blood on his hands—he dreamed each night of the fathers and sons who had died to keep him out of the Priory. They haunted his every moment. She did not want to live as her father had, burdened with guilt. She wanted her freedom, but she saw no way to attain it.

Seth reached out his hand, but she drew back hers. "Let's get out of here tonight. Your grandfather resisted the empire's edicts and he's practically a hero. In the north they sing songs about Koren."

"Thousands of Harkans died to keep one child out of a cell—Koren was brave, but foolish. I think sometimes my father would be happier if he *had* gone to the Priory—he'd be free of his guilt then. He wouldn't spend half his time in the Shambles drinking and hunting. My father did the right thing when he sent my brother to the emperor—no one admires him or tells stories about his decision, but he made the right choice, the hard choice."

"You're not your father," Seth said.

"No. But I am his daughter."

Seth did not reply. The room felt big and empty, hollow for a moment. The two sat in silence: Seth's eyes downcast and Kepi studying his features. The three cakes he had brought from the kitchen caught her attention. A fourth cake, one so slim she had not noticed it, sat beneath the black bread. "What's this?" she asked, breaking the silence.

"That? Nothing—just a little something extra," he said, looking as if he wanted to hide.

She knocked the upper cakes aside. Below sat a curious square of white, flat bread. "What is it?"

"It's nothing really."

Kepi picked up the crumbling square. Her eyes widened. "You're from Barsip, aren't you?"

He dipped his head in acknowledgment. The northern tribes—the villages that populated the hilly lands north of Harwen, near the Shambles and the Feren Rift valley, where the land was rocky and crops were hard to grow—made a special cake, a cake reserved for weddings.

"It's a Barsip cake," she said.

Seth frowned. "I wasn't going to propose or anything. Don't worry, I won't make you turn down two men in one day. I just thought it would be nice. It's a special cake, the most special we have, and so I baked one for you."

Though they were part of Harkana, the northern tribes practiced customs unique to their lands, customs not shared in Harwen. Kepi had never tasted a Barsip cake, but she had heard of it and heard it was quite good. Seth took the flaky bread, snapped it into halves, and offered one to Kepi. She took a bite. The cake was hard, almost brittle, and when it broke, the crack revealed a hundred finely rolled layers, one piled on the next. It tasted sweet on her tongue. She wondered if he was lying, if he *had* meant to propose, and she had cut him short with her comment. She hoped he had not. She wanted things to remain as they were, there was no use taking the arrangement any further.

Seth reached across the table and held her hand. He gave her another piece of bread.

Kepi drained the last of the amber from her cup. The cool liquid made the downy hair on her arms prickle and her cheeks feel numb. The cut on her neck no longer ached and her bruises had ceased their throbbing. She dropped her cup and the clay chipped. Lamplight flickered in the alcove. The crowd thinned. Her head was already spinning, the drink flowing through her veins as she motioned for the girl to bring more amber. She locked eyes with Seth. *I should end this, I should set him free, but I can't. Not yet.*

She didn't want things to change, not with the boy from Barsip, the boy who knew nothing of the ways of kings and courts. She wanted to stay here and pretend they were just another boy and girl in the back of the Elba, sharing what was supposed to be a wedding cake.

⇉14⇇

"Halt! Stop where you are, boy," the soldier said, his armor gleaming in the sunlight. Carefully etched symbols depicting a raven and an eye decorated the chest plate. The marks, Ren knew, were wards—blessings from the gods to protect the man from harm. This soldier belonged to the Alehkar, the Protector's sworn men. He stood before an arched opening in the Dromus, brandishing a spear. The soldier guarded the eastern gates of Sola. Ren would be free once he passed through the arch.

"I'm bound for Harkana," he told the Alehkar and held up the scrolls. The long walk from the gates of the Hollows to the great wall that marked the edge of Sola had left him exhausted, but he tried not to look it.

"Come closer," the man said, motioning for the scrolls. He noticed Ren's sunburnt skin and his eyes narrowed. Behind him there were more soldiers, spearmen at the gate and archers on the walk.

"Alone?" the man asked.

Ren nodded. *Of course I'm alone. I've just been chased though the Hollows and half of Solus. I don't trust anyone in this this kingdom.*

Ren turned over the rolled parchment and the soldier bent to study the seal. Swirling grooves of hardened yellow wax clung to the leathery sheet. The paraffin was as hard as rock and had already chipped in one spot, but the detail was still legible. The soldier chewed some awful-smelling thing in his yellowy teeth, taking his time as he studied the wax.

A feeling of dread shivered through Ren's body. *If they turn me back, I'll have no way to reach Harkana.* He studied the soldiers on the wall. There were too many to fight and he had no weapon.

"You're the dingiest messenger I've seen in weeks," the Alehkar said, spitting as he talked, wrinkling his lip as he looked Ren up and down. "Well, what're you waiting for, boy? Move on—Suten doesn't like his messages to be delayed." He lowered his spear and motioned for Ren to pass through the gate.

"Can I have a bit of—"

"On your way, boy, I've got no time for your questions," the soldier said.

Ren had only wanted to ask the man if he could spare a bit of bread or a sip of amber; he'd had neither since he left the Priory. *He thinks I'm below his courtesy, a lowly messenger not deserving of his time.* The soldier had already turned his attention to a group of pilgrims.

No matter, thought Ren. Past the gate, he found a narrow ditch filled with muddy water that belonged to the men's horses. It was dark and smelly, but Ren dunked his head into the muddy trough and drank all he could. He swallowed, sipped again, grinning. He drank his fill before a soldier noticed and he had to run away again.

He ran for a long time before stopping to look one last time at the wall, the great barrier that marked the edge of the kingdom of Sola.

He was outside the Dromus now. He was about to think himself free when he caught sight of riders in gray cloaks. This time, the men followed at a careful distance behind him, talking softly and greeting the carriage drivers and pilgrims who passed them.

What do you want? Ren thought as he faced his pursuers. *You came for me in the underground city, why not come for me now?* He lingered for a moment, then turned back to the trail. The great basin of Amen stood in front of him. To the east, across the basin, lay Harkana. The road that stretched between them, the Plague Road, would take him home, as the dry, beaten path was the only road connecting the two kingdoms. Perhaps that was why the gray-cloaks kept their distance. If Harkana lay at one end of the trail and Sola at the other and everything in between was desert, Ren was as good as trapped. There was nowhere else to go, no other path to take. *They'll kill me in my sleep. They'll come when the road is not crowded, when no one will notice another dead desert rat.*

The gray-cloaked men kept their distance, ignoring Ren for the time being, but never disappearing from his sight. *Just as well. Two against one isn't terribly good odds. It's better to run, better to stay alive.* He had forsaken Suten's guards to take his chances on his own and he vowed not to regret it.

He hoped to reach Harkana before nightfall, but he was uncertain of the distance. He had seen maps, and had studied the history and geography of the empire, but it was one thing to look at illustrations of roads and another thing to walk upon them. *I'm a stranger here.* He studied the wide expanse of the desert. *I'm a stranger everywhere except that awful cell in the Priory.*

The sun was beginning to sink in the sky when, on the horizon, he spotted the first mud-brick buildings and black stones of a distant town, and rising above every house was a *badgir,* the angular wind scoops that cooled every Harkan home. They were smaller than he had imagined. Less grand. The city's defensive walls were cracked and crumbling—sticks and logs poked from the muddy surfaces and black handprints dotted the sun-caked turrets. *It looks like a wasp's nest,* he thought, having once seen the insect's muddy tubes from the window of his cell. While the white walls of Solus had a solid, stately appearance, radiating strength and longevity, these walls were more suited to a beggar's hovel. *This is only a border town,* he had to remind himself. *This is not yet Harwen.*

As he made his way toward the city, Ren spied the gray-cloaks. Fearing they would come at him before he reached the gates, he abandoned his slow march toward the city walls and dashed through the gate and into a yard. He looked for Harkan soldiers, for anyone who might help him, but the town was quiet, locked down for the night. The streets and buildings were dirty, the open sewers in the middle of the road choked with garbage, filled with human and animal waste, and the stench was immense. Graffiti covered the walls of the buildings, spelling out crude warnings and curses worse than the ones he and his fellow ransoms had scrawled in the Priory.

Ren slipped down a back alley and tried to look like one of the townspeople. For a moment, he regretted returning home without the Soleri entourage that would mark him as the king's son, returned.

Down narrow streets and dark alleys he went, trying to keep the wall at his back so that he would not walk in circles, but the wall disappeared behind crumbling buildings, and before long Ren was lost.

He came upon a clearing, where a fountain splashed underneath a horned statue. Water! So much of it! The sound of it—the wet splash, the sound of water running—left him half-crazed, and stumbling forward nearly on his knees he cupped his hands below the cool stream, gathered as much as he could, and drank deeply. He splashed it on his face, letting it run over his chest and down his back.

Then pain—a man was slapping him hard on the ear.

Ren fell backward into the dust.

"The water belongs to the god," his attacker barked.

Ren gazed up at the fountain. A word came to him from someplace deeper than memory—Vatuk, the horned god of ancient Harkana. The statue did not depict the first king, Ulfer Wat, wearing his ram's horns as he had assumed, but one of the ancient gods, from the time before the Soleri.

The fountain was not a fountain at all, but an altar. As Ren stood and peered into its depths, he saw it had no pool, no bottom: the water fell without splashing, disappearing into endless dark depths below the city.

Ren had drunk from the god's offering. *I know nothing of my people. How will I ever rule here?*

"Forgive me," he said, making his best, most sincere apologies. "I am new here, and thirsty. I am afraid I saw nothing but my own relief." *And I had lost my wits at the sight of that water.*

A curious grin grew across the stranger's face when he heard Ren's imperial accent. Ren tensed. Out of one kind of trouble and into another.

"I must go," Ren said, but the man who struck him was already shaking his head, his lips curling into a dreadful grin.

"I've found the boy!" he cried out, and Ren saw that there were others, hidden in the shadows. They emerged with swords drawn, and with dismay Ren noticed that the men wore the gray homespun of herdsmen and crofters—the same cloaks worn by the men who had pursued him through the Hollows. His assassins. He cursed himself for his lack of foresight. They had found him.

I'm a damn fool, he thought as he bolted, heading down a narrow street, through a crowded market where women haggled over rough linen and hard bread. He rushed down an alley and into an intersection; the gray-cloaks close behind, Ren stumbling. The alley ended in an intersection. He looked right and left, but there was nowhere to flee—the men approached from both directions. Ren took one step back, then a second, nearly tripping over a hunk of wood. He lifted the heavy timber. It was no weapon, but Ren didn't care. *I'd rather fight—I'm tired of running.* He was tired of cowering, tired of scurrying and hiding. If he bolted once more, they would only catch him, he saw that now. There were too many men, approaching from too many directions. He retreated to the edge of a courtyard, his hands gripping the wood. The club made him recall the blade he kept hidden in his cell. It reminded him that he was not defenseless.

"Well, what are you waiting for?" he asked, but the gray-cloaks did not respond, nor did they approach. Instead, all but one backed away, hiding their weapons and disappearing into the crowd. The remaining gray-cloak drew a short sword from beneath his cloak. Raising the weapon, he threw himself at Ren, sword flailing, anger on his face. *Finally, a decent fight,* thought Ren. He swung, as did the gray-cloak, but the blows never landed. An arrow pierced the gray-cloak's shoulder, arresting his advance, dropping him to his knees where a spearman struck the deathblow.

Ren let go of the hunk of wood and turned to see who had done this.

Harkan soldiers packed the courtyard.

The men surrounded him, their faces awed and respectful, the eyes of the nearest man focused upon the ring Ren wore on his third finger.

He had forgotten about the silver band. The ring that Suten had returned to him glittered in the lamplight. It was Arko's ring, and his father's before that. The ring worn by the Harkan heir.

Their captain, a stout, hardy man with a dark beard wearing a full suit of black leather armor, his hands gauntleted, moved closer to inspect it.

Ren cringed but to his surprise the man bowed deeply. "My lord," the captain said. "We've been waiting for you."

≥15≤

Crow-hopping his horse between a broken chariot's shattered wheels, cutting around the trunkless legs of a half-buried statue, Arko Hark-Wadi, king of Harkana, pursued a pack of horned deer to the edge of the Shambles, Harkana's sacred hunting ground.

Breathing fast but even, Arko turned his mount with his knees, leaving his hands free to nock an arrow in his longbow and take aim. He had chosen the largest buck of the herd, a ten-point beauty the size of two strong men. For weeks he had pursued this particular deer, the oldest and craftiest of the lot, losing it time and again as it disappeared into the heaps of brush, the broken trees and ancient cities of stone ground to dust by the wind.

Nearly three and fifty years, his dark hair flecked with silver, Arko was strong-featured, with an angular nose and a cleft chin covered with a week's worth of stubble he never bothered to shave. A white stone hung from his neck, a charm that he always wore. His golden-brown eyes took in everything in one great sweep—the desert, the plain, the herd—and found it lacking. Himself, most of all. Thick and strong-limbed, shoulders as broad as his horse's withers, he was a formidable hunter and a formidable man, but his people called him the Bartered King, and more often than not he felt he deserved their contempt and to be called such a name.

The desert plains were baking under the midmorning sun. Spiky patches of needle grass rose like enemy traps amid the scattered stones. To the east were distant gray hunchbacked mountains, while to the west the verdant green line of the riverbank cut a lone lifeline through the arid landscape. He sighted along the arrow for the sweet point just behind the deer's pumping forelegs, but as soon as he let fly, he knew it was too soon. The buck jumped around a jutting piece of rock and the bolt sailed free, skittering across the field littered with the bleached skeletons of old ballistas, rusting arrowheads shot long ago. The herd bounded away, unscathed.

Arko cursed his luck, the deer, the desert. His mind wasn't on the hunt, not anymore. Not in this place.

He gulped amber from an oilskin. His love of hunting was exceeded only by his love of drink. He emptied the oilskin and drew forth a second, wondering if it was time to leave the Shambles, guessing he had stayed too long. The five lost days had come and gone, and the sun had not dimmed. *Time to go home,* he thought, *but not before I fell this deer.* He kicked his horse again and started off after the herd, ignoring the Harkan soldiers waiting at the edge of the field, shading their eyes warily.

The deer fled into a rocky outcropping some distance away, the buck leading, sniffing the air, nostrils flaring. Arko rode to the far side and waited for the herd to emerge from behind the rocks. He stilled his heart, his breath. Soon those magnificent antlers would come into view, and he would loose another arrow.

The stillness did little to allow him to forget where he stood, what had happened here.

This place had a name that stuck to him like a shadow, like a reproach.

The Blood-Dyed Reg. It was on this field that his father stood against the empire, it was on this sunbaked patch of desert that so many of his father's men fell to ensure one boy's safety. His. They had died to prevent Arko from doing what every Harkan heir had done for two centuries— serve in the Priory until their fathers died. Five times a thousand men had died in the Children's War, had died for Arko when he was still a child. A war to keep him home with his mother and father, a gift of which he had never felt worthy, or able to repay. The war, the men who died for his freedom, shadowed his every thought. He wished only to be free of the burden of that guilt.

At last the buck took a tentative step from behind the rocks out onto the sandy field, lifting its head, its haunches still hidden by the stone. Arko had grown patient in his age, no longer the impetuous youth he once was, and weeks of chasing this particular buck had taught him the value of that patience. Too many times he had lost his chance at victory to reck- lessness, a too-quick movement here, a bad choice of cover there. Not this time. *I plan on drawing blood before I take my leave.*

He drew his arrow with his full weight. Breathed in. Waited.

When the buck took his next step, exposing that sweet spot behind its front haunches, Arko released the string, sending the bolt flying straight and true. It passed through the buck's foreleg and out the other side, frothy pink blood bubbling up from beneath. A perfect shot. The deer tried to take off, but Arko was on it in a heartbeat, jumping off his horse, drawing his knife, and slitting the animal's throat, ending its pain along with its cunning.

His black leather armor covered in blood, Arko felt a great emptiness at his core. This small success only served to remind him of the many failures he had suffered, was still suffering. The memory of his father's strength—the strength of his love, the strength of his courage, had done the opposite to his son. It always made him feel a lesser man. Koren, after all, had lived to survive the Priory. For all his life Arko wished he could say the same.

Ten years ago Arko had delivered his only son, Ren, to the Priory. He had no choice, he told his wife. He was not Koren, he was not his father, and he did not aim to be. Sarra had complained bitterly, she'd told him to fight, told him to stand up for his family, but Arko possessed nei- ther the funds nor the fighters to wage war against the emperor, and even if he had, the people of Harkana still had painful memories of the last campaign, an entire generation of young men lost. He felt it when he walked among the people, their accusing eyes, their resentment. How many had lost a father, a grandfather, to keep him out of the Priory?

But money and manpower were only excuses. Arko knew that if his father had been no match for the imperial forces, no one was. *Your father did not send you, yet you will send your own son,* Sarra had said, holding their baby in her arms. *My son will never go to the Priory. You are a coward.* And coward he still believed he was, even if he knew he had done the right thing, that one man's life, even a king's life, should never be worth more than any other one.

Now Ren was ten and three, and his emissaries in the capital had heard rumors that the boy had been released from the Priory hidden inside the great city of Solus that Arko himself had never seen. A boy returning from the Priory before his father's death was unheard-of; it had never happened before, and why it had occurred, and what Ren would do when he returned, was anyone's guess. For all Arko knew, his son was coming to kill him and take the throne. *I wouldn't blame him if he did.*

He was within earshot of the camp when he saw riders approaching fast from the south. Two were soldiers on horseback, carrying a third, smaller figure before them in the saddle. Arko drew his dagger. Even on Harkan land, he had learned to be cautious: the emperor and his agents were nothing if not unpredictable.

The riders drew close enough that he recognized their Harkan uniforms—black leather emblazoned with silver horns. The third was a stranger. A young boy. When they came close enough the soldiers dismounted, one of them helped the boy slide from the horse's back and come unsteadily to his feet. "Sir," they said, and bowed, their chins touching their chests. "We found him."

The stranger with his father's face.

He was the right age, though nothing about the boy seemed Harkan. He was too slender, scrawny even, with an expression of suspicion and arrogance that made Arko feel a stab of contempt. His tunic too was thin, impractical for horseback and hunting, made not of the heavy weaves worn by Harkan tradesmen nor even the leather of Harkan soldiers but a flimsy silken texture. The clothes were plenty dirty, though, and it seemed they'd been recently torn. Spots of blood stained the front of the gray cloth, and his skin was red.

"So, this is my son," Arko said, studying the boy, who was almost as tall as he.

"We found him in the border towns looking for a drink. He's lucky we arrived first."

Lucky indeed. Arko had sent out his soldiers as soon as he had heard reports of Ren's imminent return. He gave the boy another look.

His son.

The one he had given up.

So this is my heir. The boy who will lead Harkana. He hadn't seen Ren since he was a child, fair and unsteady and sweetly charming, still a baby in many ways. He had clung to Arko that morning when they sent him to Solus, and he had been forced to pry his son's arms from his neck. He recalled how the boy had held out his arms and called, "Mama! Papa!" as the imperial soldiers had taken him away. How Merit, then fifteen years old, had glared at Arko as if he had sent the boy to die—as if he were a failure as a father and a king. She looked at him that way still, sometimes.

This boy was nothing like the child he remembered, with none of his son's easy smiles and sunny looks. Darker now, sullen with fear, the boy in front of him was doing his best to pretend to be brave. If Arko had raised him, he would have taught the boy to mask his feelings. The stronger the emotion, Arko would have said, the stronger the need to hide it, or risk giving your enemy too much power over you. But he had not raised this boy. He had not had a chance to teach him anything yet. *He has no father,* thought Arko. *No one has ever cared for this boy.*

"Why are you here?" His voice was louder than he meant it to be, more brusque than he had intended. He took a heavy step forward. "Who sent you?"

Ren did not reply. He did not move, did not flinch. Arko saw the ring upon his finger.

"Do you remember your family at all? Do you remember your mother, or your sisters? Your home?"

Foolish questions. The boy had been only three years old. He had spent most of his life locked up belowground. God knows what had happened to him there. He had heard the same stories about the Priory that everyone had—the beatings and abuse. Pain makes the man—that was the rule of the Priory. But only the ransoms knew what it meant and even Koren never spoke of his time in the emperor's house. He said the hardships he'd suffered there had taught him a bit of humility, nothing more.

The king's shoulders slouched when he looked at his son. *If only I could have been a father to you, if I had raised you.*

"You remember nothing of your kingdom?" he asked again, but his questions seemed to embarrass his son, so Arko let it go. The boy carried a pair of scrolls in his hand. "Is that for me?" the king asked.

"Yes, sir," Ren spoke at last. The boy looked down at the scroll as if he had forgotten what he carried. It was sealed with the insignia of the Ray of the Sun, the emperor's mouthpiece.

"Suten gave this to you?" Arko took it from him and broke the yellow seal carefully, with more respect than he felt. Inside was the parchment that Arko signed ten years ago when he agreed to send Ren to the Priory. The signature was faded, and the blood and wax he had sealed it with had dried and flaked away, but this was the paper that had shamed him for almost a decade, that had led to the end of his marriage, such as it was. He resisted the urge to crumple it.

I should not have signed this parchment.

The second scroll was not as weathered as the first; it bore a newer seal with a slightly different design. This seal showed only a ring with a star shape at its center. He cracked the wax, studied the brief text, suppressing a bit of rage as he read.

When he finished, Arko looked up at the boy and asked, "What about me? Do you remember anything at all about your father?"

The boy shook his head.

"No. I suppose you wouldn't. I suppose there isn't much you'd care to remember, about any of us . . ." Arko dropped the scroll into the dust and picked up the reins of his horse. "It appears the emperor has made a trade. He has returned my heir so I must take your place, but not in the Priory. The emperor demands an audience with me." He nodded at his son, his boy. Years had been stolen from them, and years would be stolen from them still.

The king addressed his men. "Take the buck, I must leave immediately."

≋16≋

Harwen's silhouette jutted from the horizon like a sheaf of barley, tall and jagged. Through the day's first light, Ren saw a line of *badgir* protruding from the wall, trying to catch any small breeze. *The badgir. The flags of Harwen.* The wind scoops rose and fell, swaying beneath the spires of the Hornring, Harwen's fortress. High and spindly and punctuated by stakes, the towers were older and stranger than he had imagined back in the Priory.

I'm home at last, but this wasn't the homecoming I imagined.

Ren and his father, Arko, had ridden almost without stop from the Shambles. The men were tired, the horses spent. Arko raised a black gauntlet and the procession halted. The horses bent their heads and searched for grass, shook their tails and whinnied. A lone goat bleated from some distant corral. There was a hollow loneliness to the air. Ren had returned to the city of his birth, but this place was not his home, not yet. In Solus they called the lower kingdoms the barbarian lands, and for a guilty moment, he thought they might be right. Still, he could not tear his eyes from the man. *This is my father, my blood at last.*

The king was on foot now. People were streaming out from the city gates and down the Plague Road, the last of the crowds leaving Harwen after the games the Harkans staged each year to coincide with the Devouring, the king explained. Soldiers in bloodstained coats of black, boiled leather called after young girls, servants held highborn men up on litters, white-robed priests smelling of oil shuffled by, while dregs—beggars and outcasts he could smell before they approached—shifted between the carts, their faces caked with dust and dirt wiped clean at the mouth from too much drink. They emerged in a long, tired stream from the heart of the city, eyeing the soldiers and Ren himself, bowing respectfully to the king. Some stole glances or sideward stares, but no one lingered.

Ren ignored the crowd. His father had been called to an audience with Tolemy. *To gaze upon the Soleri was to gaze upon the sun, and no man could survive that light.* Once the king stepped before Tolemy, Ren would not see his father again. Only the Ray could pass through the Shroud Wall of the Soleri and live. Like it or not, he had brought his father's death with him. This was the sacrifice the people required. *They want my father, but I want him too. Have I no right?*

In the distance, soldiers in ornamental bronze armor, the Alehkar, gathered at the gates of Harwen. A few mounted their steeds and made for the king's caravan. This would have been Ren's entourage back to Harkana and now it was his father's back to Solus.

"Walk with me," his father said. "We haven't long. The Alehkar will soon take me to Solus."

Ren nodded but was paralyzed, too overwhelmed to move. *For years I've dreamed of this moment.* For a decade he had filled his head with questions. Would the king have the same slender nose, the same crooked teeth as his own? Would his father know his face? He peered into the king's eyes and searched for himself, for something he could recognize or latch onto. *This is my father?* He saw nothing—no recognizable similarity. The king had a face like one of the city's soldiers, hard and expressionless.

What had he expected? Affection? Approval?

Yes, that's what I want. I want my father to see the man I've become and approve.

Ren waited, searching for some hint of acceptance. But it was clear Arko did not have time for that. Instead the king rested his hand on the pommel of his sword. "I want you to listen carefully, my son. I won't be here"—his voice caught—"what I mean is, I have only a little time to teach you what I know about Harkana. About being a king."

"Father, I—" The words did not come. "Must we start with formalities?" he asked. Ren had no interest. He wanted a father. He wanted to be part of a family. Even if he had to cram an entire childhood into a single moment, he would take that moment.

One memory would be enough.

So let it be a good memory, he thought. Ren wanted the king to speak to him about something other than politics. *Tell me about hunting and skinning oryx. Tell me how to get drunk on amber—not how you rule.* He'd had enough of that in the Priory.

"Ren," Arko's voice was strong, a king's voice. "My own father, Koren Hark-Wadi, did not send me to the Priory. I spent my childhood in Harwen. Do you know this, do you know our history?"

"They taught us lessons, histories of the lower kingdoms."

"Lies."

"Perhaps. But I heard it was true that you were never ransomed to the emperor."

His father heaved a bitter sigh, his breath raspy. As he walked along-side Ren's horse, an awkwardness grew between them. Ren knew he should dismount, but he did not act. It seemed more natural to keep his father at a distance. He was a stranger. His scent, his manners, his crudely burnt skin, it all seemed odd, foreign, *barbarian.* Once more, Ren felt guilty for thinking such a thing, but it was clear that life in the Priory had made him into a boy from Sola, with imperial airs.

The sound of hooves beating on the sand interrupted his thoughts. The Alehkar approached, a yellow banner waving atop a pole. The approach-ing soldiers rose and fell as they climbed the low hills. His father caught him watching them. "You want revenge, I suppose. That's what I'd want. I'd want to take revenge on the men that jailed me, the priors that stood at my door and barred the gates each night."

Ren nodded. Maybe he didn't want to learn about skinning oryx, or Harkan amber.

"We are not so different, boy." His father's face turned an angry color of red. Perhaps pain and resentment were what the two had in common, the only bond that existed between the newly reunited father and son. *Pain makes the man,* he thought bitterly.

"Take me with you back to Solus. I want to punish them, the priors, the Ray, all of them," Ren said, finding his voice.

"As do I," the king said. "But you can't go back with me. You are needed here. That's why they returned you to me. As soon as I'm gone you'll take the Elden Hunt, and when you've claimed your horns, you'll come back to Harwen and take the Horned Throne and the blessings of the kingdom. That's the way it has to be. That's the way it's always been."

Not for you, he almost said.

"We should be grateful to have this time together." His father guided Ren's horse. "It's more than most kings and sons are granted."

Ren knew that his father was right; most kings never even met their heirs, except when they were just babes. He wanted to feel something—anger, hatred, love—for the old man next to him, but Arko Hark-Wadi did not yet feel like a father to him, and Harkana, a strange and alien land, did not yet feel like home. They shared the pain of Ren's imprison-ment, but little else.

The imperial riders approached, their shields clanking against their ar-mor. A shout rang out over the desert hills. His father shrank, and then his face lost its stern mask, softening into something sadder. "Ren, when

I gave you up, I had no choice. If my father could not triumph against the empire, how could I?" he asked.

Ren blinked. "I . . . I don't blame you." It was not quite the truth, but the words felt good to say. He had blamed his father for abandoning him. If Koren had resisted the empire, why had Arko not done the same? Why hadn't he fought for his son? *Isn't that what a father and a king ought to do?*

His father exhaled. "We should be grateful you arrived safely in Harkana. The same cannot be said for Adin, Barrin's son."

"What do you mean? What happened to Adin? Did he not return to Feren?"

"No. No one knows what happened to that boy," his father said. "I sent soldiers to find him. A tribute can be a powerful ally or a valuable prisoner. My men had no luck, though. I heard Dagrun's men found him."

Ren felt as if a hammer blow had struck him. Distant memories flashed in his thoughts: the jests he'd shared with Adin, the days spent learning their lessons. He recalled how his friend had once swiped a bit of bread from the prior's table, and how Adin had shared it with him. Ren had only two friends in the world, and now one was gone. From Ren's earliest memory, he had dreamed of their mutual freedom. It was all he wanted, but that dream would not come to pass. "He's dead then?" Ren asked.

"In prison, more likely."

Ren exhaled.

"A king's blood has worth," Arko continued. "Such a person could be made to serve one's interest."

His father's frankness surprised Ren, but his words rang true. Arko had once traded Ren to keep the peace. The empire treated the kings of the lower kingdoms as a currency. Arko was an unpaid debt, a coin Suten had come to collect.

As the Alehkar approached, as the men dismounted, his father pointed to Harwen's wall. One section lay blackened and crumbled like a rotted limb. "Look," he said, "while we still have time. The Ruined Wall. It's a kind of Harkan monument, burned into the battlements two hundred years ago during the War of the Four, the first revolt, when Nirus Wadi's army at last fell to the Protector's men. When the Harkans rebuilt, they created a new wall around the old. They wanted the scar to remain."

"Why?"

"It's a place where the Harkans find strength by remembering the harm the emperor has done to them." When Arko turned to him, Ren glimpsed the naked grief in his father's eyes. "You are not alone, you know. The

entire kingdom, the entire empire, suffers the ransoms together. Some more than others, of course, but we all suffer nevertheless."

Arko, at last, put his arm around him. His grip was awkward and stiff, almost perfunctory at first, but as he drew Ren close, the tension fell from his limbs and Ren could feel the warmth of his skin, the dull thud of his beating heart. He had never imagined the power an embrace could have, the way it might soften, in an instant, his resolve. This was his kingdom; his family was here. He belonged to Harwen. He had trekked across the dry, sandy basin, his skin was burnt and he had nearly starved to death trying to reach this place, but it was all justified now. He was home. *If only my father did not have to leave.*

The Alehkar approached, swords drawn, faces looking grim. Ren broke the king's embrace. He reached instinctively for the shank he always kept with him, until he remembered the Prior Master had taken it away. A soldier advanced, his arm outstretched and he gripped the king's shoulder. Abruptly, his father's hand moved to his sword and he drew. Silver streaked through the air, metal scraped metal, and blood splattered on the sand. In a heartbeat his father had turned, drawn his blade, and nearly severed the offending soldier's arm from his shoulder.

"You boys should know better than to lay hands on a king," his father said. "Keep away and I will not fight you." The men nodded sullenly and Arko sheathed his sword, not even bothering to wipe the blood from the blade. Deep lines faded from the soldiers' faces. Some lowered their weapons, others kept their swords raised. Though the imperial soldiers were superior in number, none were eager to engage the king. "Give me a moment," his father said. "A moment with the boy and a moment in the Hornring with my daughters. Give me that and I will go in peace."

Their captain stood in front of the others, his armor dense with ornament. He tipped his helm. "Keep that blade in its sheath and you'll have your moment." Behind him, the Alehkar attended to the wounded man, whose cries echoed in the cool morning air as the soldiers tried in vain to stanch the bleeding.

Arko turned to his son, blood on his hands, the imperial soldiers surrounding his convoy, more men approaching in the distance. The Ray had sent an entire legion of Alehkar to retrieve his father. There was no way they could resist. These would be their final moments together—the first and the last coming all at once. "Don't return to Harwen," Arko told Ren, "not yet. Travel to the Shambles and find the old hunting grounds. Complete the hunt and prove yourself worthy, as all Harkan kings have done. My soldiers—your soldiers—will escort you there. Find the eld, make your sword, and then you can take your throne."

"I don't know how." It was not one of the lessons he had been taught at the Priory.

"You'll learn. Remember the wall, the scar. It's been sitting there, without repair, for two hundred years. The wall tells us to be patient, to build our strength, to never forget. This is what it means to be Harkan. Show the kingdom your strength, return to the Hornring not as a ransom from the emperor's Priory but as their Horned King. Be my father's son in the way that I could not be."

He drew a dagger from his side and handed it to Ren. The blade had ridges on one side. "Take this, you'll need it to claim the horns." He pressed the iron into Ren's palm, the blade still warm from his father's touch. "The knife was Koren's and now it is yours." Arko drew his wine-skin, took a long sip, and swallowed. "Now I must bid your sisters farewell. Goodbye, son. Leave Harwen. Go! I would rather you were not present when I am forced to give myself up for dead."

⇒17⇐

"My father is dead," Merit whispered as the last imperial soldier departed, as her father, the king, left Harwen. His eldest daughter remained alone at the city's Ruined Wall, staring at the slips of parchment naming the dead, the tiny yellow rolls tucked into the wall's cracks. Behind her, soldiers darted through the courtyard, running with their shields, pulling swords from the racks and spears from the walls. There were so many of them they covered the wall walk with their black leather, blotting out the sun.

Fear had seized her people. The king was gone, a legion of imperial soldiers had collected the king of Harkana. Only Merit stood, ever calm in the confusion, ever aware of who was watching. She ran her hand across the blackened stone of the Ruined Wall, feeling a loose piece between her fingers. She picked it up and crushed it, opening her hand to reveal ash. *The emperor has taken my father and given me his servant in return. He's put a king on the throne I've kept warm all these years*

A moment earlier, Arko, tired, weary-eyed and half-drunk, had stood shouting in front of the Ruined Wall, issuing his last commands. He had told Merit that Ren had returned from the Priory. Tolemy had sent him home. When Merit asked where was the heir, Arko explained that he had sent the boy on the Elden Hunt to prove his rightful claim to the Harkan throne. "When he returns with the eld horns, he will take Ulfer's chair in the King's Hall and sit beneath our family's banner," her father had said to her. "Until then, you are Queen Regent in his stead."

Merit had nearly choked at these words. She would rule, but only until Ren returned, triumphant, and carrying the eld's horns on his shoulders. Once he came back with his prize, Tolemy's lap dog would sit on the Horned Throne. Couldn't her father at least have given the family a moment together to meet the boy? After ten years, were they not due a short reunion, a moment to assure one another that this was indeed the small boy who once crashed through the courtyards knocking over planters? The one who spent his days wrestling dogs and drawing horses in the sand? No. He had sent the boy on the honored hunt without even the slightest hesitation.

A soldier approached, then a second, urging her to leave the courtyard. "Let us take you to safety," they said. The men wanted her back in the Hornring, but Merit would not cower or hide.

"No," she said. "It is important for the people, the waiting women and the cooks, to see me, to see their sovereign standing tall and unafraid." With a wave of her hand, she dismissed them. She brushed the ash from her palm. It had a salty sting that made her fist clench. The Ruined Wall was a place she and her father cherished equally. She had many times seen him standing at the crumbling fortifications, thinking of Ren, of his lost wife, of the sacrifices her grandfather had asked of the kingdom.

When they stood together at the Ruined Wall, Arko would allow her to comfort him. It was the one place where they could speak without arguing—the one place where she felt like his daughter. If only they could agree on the wall's meaning. They shared a reverence for the ruin, but not an understanding of its importance. When Arko stood at the wall, he saw a call to arms, a wound that would fester until the Harkans had burned down every wall in Solus.

Merit saw something different.

She saw failure. The wall's broken remnants stood there because her ancestors failed, and Koren had failed, and Arko too. Each Harkan king had failed to stand against the line of Tolemy. Each one thought the sword was their only weapon. Merit knew the Harkan Army alone would never triumph against the empire. The Harkans needed help, allies from every kingdom, if they hoped to erase this scar from their history.

At least Koren had attempted to wield the sword; Arko never even unsheathed his.

Merit breathed a slow breath as she smeared the last remnants of the ashes across her blue dress, kneading its charcoal dust into the finely woven gown.

In spite of the old resentments, the arguments they'd had over her mother, over the kingdom and its tending, she would miss her father. She missed him already and would miss him each time she came to the wall or glanced at its broken stones.

A hand touched her shoulder. It was Shenn, soldiers at his side.

"What did Arko say? Where's he gone?"

"To Solus. Summoned by Tolemy. My father is to meet the emperor. He will walk through the Shroud Wall and gaze upon Tolemy's face."

"He is gone then," Shenn gasped. "What of Harkana?" he asked as he directed the soldiers, pointing them to unlatched gates and gaping doorways.

"As we feared, my brother has returned from the Priory. He rode with my father, but did not enter the city." They had heard whispers of the boy's release and had prepared as best they could. "My father left me in charge of his kingdom for now," she said.

"Why?" Shenn motioned to the remaining soldiers, telling them to stay back.

"Arko sent Ren on the hallowed hunt. Once he has his horns, he will take the throne."

"A boy-king fresh from Solus to lead Harkana?"

"In his panic, my father gave Ren the throne without allowing time for us to meet our new liege," she said, her voice hardening with bitterness.

"So, a ransom will rule Harkan. It's been decades since one has sat on the Horned Throne. It won't go well. He's too young, and too inexperienced. He's not Harkan, not truly. The Harkan lords will not kneel to Tolemy's lackey."

Merit knew as much. "We will have open revolt—it happened in Feren and it will happen here," she said, her eyes filling with tears of worry. If the boy could not hold the kingdom together, what would become of them? *Will some lowly Harkan lord try to pry the kingdom from our family?*

"I won't let it happen," said Merit.

"Agreed. Arko was always too rash. He should have named you as regent for a longer term—at least until the boy had lived in Harkana for a number of years. The child needs time to curry favor among the lords, and to learn the ways of the kingdom." Shenn was right, of course, but her father did not think in such terms. A king was an absolute ruler, that's what her father would say. A king was subject to the emperor and no one else. But Arko lived in a world that no longer existed. He respected rules that were no longer applicable. The power of the Harkan throne was tenuous; every bit of power in the empire was tenuous. The Priory had weakened the old lines, humiliating the royal sons of the lower kingdoms, fomenting insurgencies and agitation among the common folk.

"Where is your sister?" Shenn asked.

"Where do you think?"

Shenn nodded. They both knew Kepi was in Blackrock or Badr, hiding with the boy she believed she had kept secret. But Kepi's waiting women answered to Merit, and they knew her habits, what the black cloak meant.

Merit walked to the edge of the courtyard and gazed through Harwen's arch, the gate leading to the Plague Road. The last imperial soldiers were only now disappearing over the hills outside Harwen, the same hills that housed Dagrun's encampment. The Feren contingent remained close by at her request.

She shivered, but not from the cold. She was Queen Regent now and she did not intend to lose her post. "My brother has suffered enough," she said, drawing Shenn close to her. "I won't allow the boy to make a fool of himself when he returns. And I won't allow my sister to put off her duty to the empire. We must move quickly. I'll retrieve my father's seal, and you must leave the Hornring."

Shenn did not argue and he did not ask questions. After so many years together, he knew what she wanted him to do.

18

"The king was met by soldiers in bronze armor at the city gate," her waiting woman said. Kepi had only just arrived at her chamber in the Hornring when the woman came knocking at her door, pounding until Kepi had come to answer.

"The Protector's men took my father?" Kepi asked.

"Yes. While you were away, they took the king to Solus."

"Solus?" Kepi spoke before she could fully grasp her servant's words. *Solus. My father has gone to Solus.* "Why?"

"To meet our lord and emperor." The girl told her what had happened.

"Merit is Queen. My brother is free . . ." Kepi shook her head. "And my father is to meet Tolemy himself?"

The girl nodded, her eyes downcast. Everyone in the empire knew what Arko's visit meant.

"Dammit. When did the king depart?" Kepi asked.

"He left just after midday." It was now late in the afternoon.

"They took the Plague Road?"

"Yes—but mistress, your sister seeks your presence—"

Kepi pushed past the girl and her protests. *My father is headed for his death and I was not here to say goodbye. I'll be damned if I'm going to wait around for Merit.* She hurried toward the Hornring's stables. She had become exceptionally good at slipping unseen from the Hornring. This time, however, her secrecy had worked against her. She had spent two days and two nights in Blackrock and no one had known how to find her. *Mithra's ass,* she thought. *My brother is free, but I was not here to greet him.* Now she must wait until he completed the dangerous hunt before she could embrace him. *At least I'll get to meet Ren.*

Her father was another matter. The emperor had summoned the king. *To gaze upon the Soleri was to gaze upon the sun itself, and no man could survive that light.*

Her heart pounding, Kepi strode through the stable's wooden doors, hastening past soldiers and messengers alike. Ash stood near the stable's entry, her saddle still strapped to the horse's midsection. The horse was not yet fed or fully watered, but perhaps her father was still close to Harwen, and the ride would be short. Ash was not the stable master's fastest mount, but she was nimble and reliable and would not balk at a second ride that day.

Kepi tugged the reins and bolted through the open doors, retracing the path she had taken earlier that day. Outside, the streets were empty, the Hornring silent. The city was locked down, doors shut, gates barred. *Why? Her father was gone, but why lock down the city?*

A spear answered her silent question, an obsidian point blocking her path. "The queen regent commands you to remain in Harwen."

"As far as I can tell my father is still alive, and hence still king of Harkana, and as his daughter I answer to him alone," she said. "Until my brother sits on the throne, my sister holds no more power than I—now, let me pass."

The man hesitated. He looked to his fellow guardsmen. While the men exchanged hushed words, Kepi broke past the gate, brushing aside their spears with an outstretched arm. *I must find my father.*

She rode past another company of city guardsmen who called to her, but she refused to slow her horse. Even if her sister was regent and she had given orders for Kepi to stay within the city walls, the guards would not dare harm the king's daughter.

Ash pounded the sandy earth, bolting through the outer fortifications, past the Ruined Wall, over the Blackwood Bridge and out of Harwen. She rode over the low plains, her eyes bent on the horizon, searching for the Plague Road's first marker. White plaster glinted in the distance. The road was not far. The Protector's retinue was no doubt large and well armed; such a force could not move as hastily as a single rider. She had heard imperial soldiers rested often and seldom rode swiftly. The men conserved their strength for conflict. She hoped the soldiers would take their time. If she rode quickly, if she drove her mount to exhaustion, perhaps she could catch her father before he reached the Dromus. She wanted to see him before he disappeared behind the walls of Sola. She could not even recall the last words they spoke to each other. *Let me look at him one last time,* Kepi begged. But there was more than simple sentiment in her prayer. She was riding to win a promise from the king, an order that would release Kepi from her vow.

Merit would not dare work against a king's decree.

She passed the first marker, crested a low hill, but saw only stray carts and goat herders. She cursed. In the distance, light shimmered on the second marker. She had hoped to sight imperial soldiers when she arrived at the top of the hill, but she saw only sandy knolls, broken trees, and distant travelers. *I should have taken a fresh mount.* If her ride continued past the low hills and into the desert, she would need to water Ash, and she would lose precious time and might not catch the soldiers before they reached Sola.

I can't lose him. I won't let him disappear—not like mother.

Ten years ago, Sarra had slipped out in the night, leaving Harwen and fleeing to Desouk. Sarra Hark-Wadi, the woman who would become Sarra Amunet, the Mother Priestess, had never even bothered to say goodbye to her children. She had simply disappeared. Now Arko had disappeared too—the Protector's men had stolen him while Kepi was away. *I cannot allow both of my parents to leave without bidding me farewell.* She'd been cheated once, but she would not allow it to happen a second time. More than anything, she wanted to see his face one last time.

The clop of iron shoes thundered in the distance. Horses approached from behind, from the direction of Harwen. Kepi hit her steed with a hard but steady kick. Ash responded, beating out ever-quicker paces, her strides lengthening with each gallop. Kepi pressed her feet into the stirrups and lifted her torso to avoid the pounding of the saddle. She flew, her horse's hooves stirring dust and sand, wind at her face, hair whipping at her brow. Her bruises ached, but she ignored the pain. She kept her eyes on the trail, leaping over rocks, dodging ruts in the road as the clop of the approaching soldiers reached a crescendo.

Ash was at her limit and the riders were nearly upon her.

A soldier in black leather approached, motioning for her to halt. His mount was a destrier, a powerful horse, and likely well fed and well rested. A second rider advanced on her right flank. *I cannot outrun these horses, but can I fight?* Her saddle concealed a pair of curving blades. If pressed, she would draw her knives.

The Harkan soldiers drew closer. The road ahead was clear. She could stop, order the men to turn back, to leave her, she could fight them if needed, but she had no wish to spill Harkan blood. Yet each moment that passed, her father was closer to the Sola. She beat her mount, but she could not outrun the soldiers. The rider at her right blocked her path. He came at her so quickly he spooked her horse. Ash reared, hurling Kepi forward, knocking her head against the horse's mane.

"Let me be!" she cried. Kepi spurred her horse and tugged one rein, trying to turn her mount, but she could not swing a circle narrow enough to avoid the destrier.

"Halt!" said the soldier blocking her path.

Relief washed over her when she saw him clearly. In the failing light she had not recognized their silver-crested leather, their black shields. These were not, as she had feared, Merit's hired soldiers. These were her father's sworn men, the kingsguard, the black shields of Harkana.

"Where is my father? Why have you abandoned him?"

"He travels the Plague Road with a legion of Alehkar. He bid us to come find you."

"How far away is he?" she asked.

The soldier shaded his eyes and searched the desert hills, his gaze lingering on a cloud of dust at the horizon. "One hour's ride, maybe less."

"We're wasting time on words," Kepi gripped the reins. "We should ride."

The man waved to his comrade. "Off your horse, the king's daughter needs a fresh mount." He motioned for Kepi to dismount just as they heard the pounding of more hooves, more soldiers riding up the Plague Road.

"Your men?" she asked.

"No." The captain shook his head and squinted at the horses, a worried look on his face.

Who, then? Kepi studied the horizon. The men wore the jade-green rings and the gray cloaks of the Wadi clan. Merit's hired soldiers at last. Among them she saw Sevin, her sister's captain. The approaching riders, five in all, bearing long spears, sent dust into the air as they encircled Kepi and the kingsguard.

"Back to the Hornring with you," cried Sevin as his horse ground its hooves into road. "Queen regent's orders," he said, his jade rings jingling, his soldiers fingering their weapons. Sevin had drawn his sword, though neither Kepi nor the kingsguard had drawn theirs.

"Queen regent, Sevin? Is that what she is calling herself?" Kepi said, watching his blade bob up and down. "My father has barely stepped from the Hornring and my sister is calling herself queen already? Tell me, is she seated on Ulfer's chair?"

Sevin grimaced, his fingers tensing on the grip of his sword, the deep lines on his dark face furrowing. "Damned if I care." He motioned for his men to draw blades. "We're just doing what we're told, child." He leveled his sword, the point resting no farther than a finger's width from Ash's nose. "It's not in my nature to strike a lady, so do as you're told. There's no need for violence," he said, his blade saying otherwise.

Kepi's eyes flicked to the Plague Road. She saw black shapes dotting the horizon. Her father's caravan was not too far. She could still catch up to him.

"Please," she asked. *I have to see my father, just this once, before he vanishes.*

"There's no use in begging," said Sevin. "I've got my orders and it'll be my head if I don't follow through." The others shrugged. There was no sympathy here, just men doing as they were told.

"Sevin, don't," she said, but the Wadi man did not lower his blade. He drew a scroll from his satchel. The black letters smudged as he unrolled the sheet—the markings were fresh, the ink damp.

"What's this?" she asked.

Kepi did not want to read it, but he shoved the parchment in her face anyway. A few short words filled the top half of the sheet, a waxen seal dotted the bottom. The message was clear: the king of Harkana had released Kepi from her seven years of mourning and ordered her to wed, without delay, Dagrun Finner, the king of the Ferens and Lord of the Gray Wood.

It was sealed with Arko's mark, an eld skull with a swirl of horns at its base.

"Dammit," she cried. "This is not my father's decree. Look at the seal." She knew the mark was not made by Arko's signet ring but with the large stamp her father kept in his chamber, and she knew exactly who made it. "This is my sister's doing," she said, her voice raised. "Arko did not even enter the Hornring." This was not her father's orders but her sister's, using the king's seal. Arko had slaughtered more Ferens than she could count when he pulled her from Roghan's prison and he would do so again if needed. But that no longer mattered. What mattered was that it was a king's decree with the king's stamp. She could no longer protest, she could no longer put off Dagrun's proposal. Without Arko, without the king to protect her through law and threat of violence, she must comply and she must do it immediately. She had only the kingsguard and the blades she concealed beneath her saddle.

"My father—your king," she tried again. "He's left for Solus. This is a forgery."

Sevin bared his teeth, his sword trembling in his hand. "I only do what I'm told, my lady. I've been plenty patient, but now you're starting to try my nerves. Drop the blade and we'll all ride back to the Hornring. We can have a swig of amber and a nice ride."

Kepi was finished with talking. She crumpled the letter, but the Wadi man tore it from her grip before she could wreck the scroll. Not hesitating, she drew the knife she concealed beneath her saddle.

"You can have a swig of whatever you like, but I'm going to find my father," she said, her blade glistening in the moonlight, black and wicked. She reached for the second knife, but Sevin was faster. He pinned the saddle flap closed with the point of his sword. "How dare you, Sevin." She glared at him, spit on her lip, fire in her eyes. Anger clouded her vision.

"You have no right to detain me—you are my subjects—I am the second born of the king," she said. Her father would have their heads.

But my father is gone. Kepi knew it and Merit's soldiers knew it as well.

"Draw swords," she said to the kingsguard, but the men were already drawing their blades. They were two against five and they held their swords uneasily. Their eyes darted, uncertain of how to proceed.

"Remember your oaths," Kepi chided her father's men. *Sevin's bluffing,* she thought, *his men will not harm me.* Kepi tightened her grip on the black knife. She was still smarting from her defeat in the ring, still eager to prove her worth with a sword. So she hurled the curving blade at Sevin's throat, making him cower as he fumbled to block her attack. She missed his neck, but the blade tore a swath of leather from his armor. He dropped his sword, giving Kepi a moment to draw the other knife. The iron was heavy, the blade felt good in her grip.

"Clear a path," she told the black shields. Perhaps she could escape while the kingsguard delayed Merit's soldiers. Iron rang in the cool desert air as the swords of her father's men met the spears of the Wadi soldiers. There were shouts from both sides. A man in black leather, one of the kingsguard, tumbled from his horse. He struggled to stand, but the Wadi men drove their spears into his black leather before he could right himself. The second kingsguard struck the nearest Wadi spearman, knocking him from his mount. He swung his sword in a wide arc, driving back his attackers, but he was outnumbered three to one and the Wadi men held spears, not swords—they could strike from a distance. They drove their points into his armor. A wet thump rang across the desert hills as the last man fell to the sand.

In the span of a few heartbeats it was done.

Kepi was alone.

She kicked her mount and tried to ride off, but the Wadi men made a ring with their horses, sealing her in.

"Move or I'll cut you down," she cried, but the men would not move. "Fight me," she said, but they would not strike her.

Instead, one drove his blade into Ash's withers. The horse issued a strangled whinny. Kepi—who had ridden Ash since she was a child, who had loved her horse as a friend—screamed as the gray-haired rouncy fell to her knees. She tumbled with her horse to the sand.

The Wadi men, with their jade-beaded hair, brushed the dust from their cloaks and dismounted. Kepi lay on her back, knife in hand. She feigned injury and clutched at her thigh while she searched for the man who had struck Ash. When he came close, when he bent to look down at her, she drove her blade into the place where the neck met the body— into the place he had struck Ash. Her knife entered at the collarbone and exited just below the neck. She held it for a heartbeat before withdrawing the blade. Much like the horse, the Wadi man fell to his knees, alive, pained, crying as her horse now cried. The two of them made a terrible sound.

"Ash was my horse, and a better servant than any of you," Kepi said as she stood. She took notice of all the men, their armor and their weapons. She composed her stance, bending her knees and readying herself for the fight, the blade feeling light in her hand. For a moment she was back in the ring, driven by the awful crying of her horse, she was ready to fight again. She motioned to strike, but a loud pounding interrupted her attack, the clop of horses coming up the road. More of Merit's soldiers, perhaps ten in all, crowded the Plague Road. The odds had turned against her.

With a loud crack, a carriage followed the soldiers over the hill. The coach was ironwood, gray, and gleaming like stone. The curling mark of the Feren kingdom decorated its outer panels.

So they were taking her to Gray Wood already.

There were too many of them to fight. Gritting her teeth, Kepi took her blade and sunk the point into Ash's skull, ending her horse's pain.

At least one of us ought not to suffer, she thought as she withdrew the blade and surrendered it to her captors.

⇒ 19 ⇐

Arko Hark-Wadi stood before a massive stone arch, inlaid with a circle of gold, and flanked by rows of imperial soldiers. He was here at last, in the golden city of light. The eternal city of the Soleri. The buildings, the walls, even the crowds were larger than what he had imagined. Rank upon rank of soldiers stood in lines beneath the stone archway, their bronze mail burnished and blinding. Angry commoners called out his name, tossed rocks, and spit on his cloak, but he gave no indication that he noticed. Nor did he give a moment's thought to the stone-carved faces that stared from every building, their eyes vengeful and condemning. Only the great steles caught his eye. They covered the faces of every building, their tall carvings depicting victories both recent and remote. *This city has forgotten more history than I can recall. It has witnessed the lives of more men, great and small, than I could ever hold in my head.* That his own father had dared defy an empire with such great a history was almost unfathomable.

He had been ordered to leave his soldiers behind when they reached the outer circle of Solus. Dismiss your men, the Alehkar commanded, or leave them to slaughter, as foreign armies were forbidden to enter the city. Arko had clasped the forearm of his captain, Asher Hacal, and bid him go back to Harkana and to serve his eldest daughter, the new queen regent, and if fate looked kindly on his house, the soon-to-be boy king, his son, Ren.

"I'll wait outside the walls, sir . . . until it's over," he said as the last of Arko's men departed.

When they were gone, Arko Hark-Wadi was alone among strangers. He became nothing but a civilian, with no rank or title, not even a Bartered King, nothing but a subject of the emperor, one of many. He was surprised at how easy it had been to shed the past and the last of his responsibilities. He would meet his end not as a king but as a man—flawed, human, and ready.

As he passed beneath the stone archway he saw in the distance the Shadow Gate, the door that led through the Shroud Wall and into the Empyreal Domain. He thought of his older sisters, Eilina and Atourin, both married to Rachin lords. He had not seen either in years but he wished them well and hoped they would find a better death than him. He thought of Barden, his younger brother, who, having died at the age of four, was also spared from the Priory. He thought of his children, of Ren and his daughters. He had bid his farewell to Merit, but not to his youngest daughter, who had been out riding. He had sent two of the kingsguard to find her, but they had not returned. It bothered him deeply that he had not said his goodbye to Kepi. He hoped it would be his last regret. He touched the white stone at his neck, felt the grooves of the six letters inscribed on its back, and pictured the woman he once loved. *Is there another path I could have taken in this life? Is this how it was always fated to end?* He contemplated his death in much the same way as he had contemplated his life—with a potent melancholy, a pensive shrug.

Now he stood before the Shadow Gate and the passage that led through the Shroud Wall. When he passed through the gate, he would leave this world. He would never see anyone from his life again. Never see his son become king, never hold his grandchildren in his hands. *This might as well be the moment of my death.*

Legend had it that the Shadow Gate cast the last shadow a man would ever see. Past the gate, within the Empyreal Domain, all things were touched by Mithra-Sol and made of light. A smirk crossed his face. He doubted the legend's veracity, but it was a good story nonetheless. Arko guessed he would see a few more shadows before the day ended.

The crowd surged closer as his escort approached the gate, but Arko focused only on the path ahead, one slow footstep at a time. These few moments, looking at the red sun rising over the edge of the horizon, would be his last, yet his heart was curious instead of fearful. Soon he would be privy to the hidden mysteries at the center of the empire, and he would stand face-to-face with Tolemy himself, the god who sat at the heart of the circle of power that governed Arko's life and the life of everyone in the empire. He was looking forward to showing the emperor that Arko Hark-Wadi was no weakling, no fool, before he died. No one who entered the Empyreal Domain ever came out. All those who looked into the eyes of the god-emperor burned from within and perished within moments of gazing upon the emperor's face. It was more than his own father had done, or his father's father—to look into the eyes of a living god. Arko was looking forward to experiencing the divine before his death.

They passed beneath the Shadow Gate, moved beyond the archway, down a corridor that terminated in a single door carved with an array of radiating lines. The ceremonial captain ordered the main body of the force to remain, and then taking only five Alehkar, he opened the door and stepped inside.

Arko followed them down a passage, deep into the maze of corridors, and quickly lost track of direction, of a sense of place. Only the light of a single oil lamp illuminated those dusty corridors, and he kept his eye on it like he had the sun in the world above. The only sound was the shuffle of footsteps across stone, the only view the back of the ceremonial captain's dark, sweaty head. *There is no world other than this one,* Arko thought. *There is no place beyond this place. When I pass through the Shroud Wall, I leave this world.* Arko would submit to his fate here, today, and be satisfied that he had done his duty and submitted his tribute, the way his father did before him, and his son after him. *At last I am no better, nor worse, than they. No longer the Bartered King, but fulfilled in my allegiance.*

The passage opened up into a larger space, a surprisingly airy chamber where the stone walls and ceilings were carved in monumental relief. Arko had heard of this place. The Hall of Histories. He read the titles, but the events were often unfamiliar to him, at least until he saw an image of the second revolt, the Children's War, etched in figures twice the height of a man. Rougher than the rest, more hastily done and plain, without the richness of gold and riot of color that adorned the older pieces, this carving illustrated the moment his father, Koren, had surrendered to Raden Saad, the former Protector and father of Amen Saad. This was the moment when Koren had agreed to end the war, if, in exchange, Raden would not collect his son. He would spare Arko from the Priory. This was the moment his father had bought him his freedom. A reprieve that had lasted until today, until the emperor had at last called Arko and summoned him to Solus.

At the end of the passage the heavy wooden doors swung open, and the captain gestured for Arko to proceed alone. As Arko stared into the dark abyss beyond the door, it occurred to him that the captain might be the last man from the world above to whom he would ever speak. "What happens to me after I enter this room? Are the stories true?"

"I don't know," the captain said as he withdrew.

Arko Hark-Wadi stepped through the darkened doorway, and they sealed the doors behind him.

He had heard there was only light beyond the Shadow Gate, but all he saw was darkness. He stood alone, in the black, for a moment or two before he saw a dim light approaching: oil lamps. The light grew and multiplied, splitting into two, three, four separate flames. Women filled the room, imperial handmaidens who served the royal family from birth, or so the stories went. The women lit the lamps, greeting Arko with a nod of their shaved heads—pale, silent, captive creatures, like blind mice living far underground. Female eunuchs, Arko had heard, as children they had been sacrificed by their families into imperial service. He grimaced at the sight of their mutilated fingers, the fingertips had been removed so they could not hold a weapon or a writing utensil, their tongues cut out at nine, ten years old, their breasts and feet bound tight. They walked with the shuffling movements of newborn dogs, their feet rendered useless so they couldn't run away. He had heard their breasts were cut off as well and their genitals partially sewed shut so they could not be a temptation to any man, nor bear any children. Their sexlessness made him recoil, their gentle movements and silence masking the horror of what had been taken from them, what they had become.

The women surrounded him and began to help him undress. He was still wearing the bloodstained tunic from the hunt, during his last morning in the Shambles, before Ren had returned. They removed everything but the white stone that hung from his neck. Arko would not allow them to touch the necklace. They took him by the shoulders and led him to a basin, where they bathed him completely, from his dark, shaggy hair to his hands and feet, and dressed him in a long white robe, similar to theirs. A sacrificial robe. *So this is what I will die in.*

The women pointed the way, down a dim space that Arko had not seen. What else could their eyes see that his could not? One of them took him by the hand and led him through the dark, like a dead man being taken into the underworld. The space was not narrow but great, cool and open and echoing with the sound of their footsteps, a far more disorienting feeling than being in a tight space. Without the eunuch to guide him, he would not know which way to turn.

In the distance a dim light grew—brighter, and then brighter, the hall now flickered with oil lamps high above, illuminating a hall of statues, each as tall as a desert palm, with toes as big as Arko's head. He saw the statue of Re, the first emperor of the Old Kingdom, his effigy a smoothly abstracted figure, the features rounded and bulbous, like a figure billowing out of smoke. His children and their descendants ruled for three centuries. The Soleri were a family, five boys and five girls, always interbred. After Re came the rule of Nejeb, fourteen emperors in all, their round features—puffy cheeks, round eyes—fading into the black sandstone. Djet and Horan followed, fifteen in one line, twenty in the next. The statue of Khaba was the first to be carved in the buttery stone of Solus, its form still glistening, its features more realistic, more familiar than the older carvings. Polished stones sat within eye sockets, the pearls followed Arko as he passed. The emperors of the Middle and the New Kingdoms followed the emperors of the old. Sekhem Den was the last. There were no statues after his line. Nothing to mark the reign of the Tolemys—the hidden emperors, the gods that lived and died behind the wall. Looking back at the long hall of finely chiseled figures, Arko could not help but feel a stab of envy. *Ulfer's statue back home is made of carved olive wood.* The statue of Harkana's first king was old and cracked, the face chipped in spots and stained with water. *One day, the termites will chew through Ulfer's face, but all of this will still be here.*

Beyond the statue of Den stood a final pair of doors located at the apse end of the gallery, and behind the doors, just underneath the sill and at the cracks, was a gleam of pure yellow light. Even this far belowground he recognized it not as the dim flicker of torches or oil lamps but the steady white light of the sun. The light of the god-emperor. The emperor himself lay beyond those doors. This was where Arko would face his fate at last, to serve his tribute, to face the divine.

Arko was alone. No soldiers accompanied him now, no women.

To meet the emperor is to forfeit one's life. No man, save the Ray, may see the face of the god-emperor and live.

He forced the great doors open and entered.

≋20≋

Kepi didn't have to look out the window to know where her carriage was headed. Since the moment they set out from Harkana she had felt the Feren border creeping toward her like some kind of sickness. She only slid the shutter open when the convoy stopped. Outside, green forest grew tall against gray mountains, and the smell of blackthorn drifted like smoke through the window. *It smells like Roghan.* Kepi thought it stunk like the cage she had slept in for a year.

Sandals sloshed in the mud, the sound drawing closer. The clank of the lock coming undone rang through the carriage wall. Someone had unlocked the door.

"Who's there?" she asked, but there was no reply. She pressed her face to the window to try to see what was happening, but the door flung open instead.

"Expecting someone else?" said Dagrun, sitting so close she could feel the warmth from his body. Kepi pressed herself to the wall, her breath quickening. She had never been alone with the king of the Ferens and did not trust him, especially since she had made the first portion of her trip from Harwen to Rifka in almost complete isolation. For days, as they rode toward the Rift valley, she ate with the soldiers and slept on the hard bench of her carriage like nothing so much as a prisoner.

But now her soon-to-be-husband had come to sit with her. His very presence in such close quarters made her fingers shake, her eyes itch. But she noticed that he seemed nervous as well, as he looked her up and down, possibly uncertain himself. His teeth were white, whiter than any Harkan's, perhaps the rumors of his wealth were true. His eyes were big and dark and never blinked. They radiated a strength she found at once intimidating and disquietingly appealing.

"We are nearly there." He broke the quiet.

Kepi pressed her lips shut. She knew as much.

"Can I get you anything? You must be hungry after so much time on the road. Some amber, or bread?"

"A fast horse." She put her hand on the window. "I can ride, there is no need to lock me in this carriage."

He shook his head as if she did not grasp her situation. "You'll soon be the queen of the Ferens and the roads between our kingdoms are unsafe. I've lost three riders to stray arrows so far. The outlanders are following your caravan. They're everywhere in the border region between our kingdoms. Mount a horse and you might also catch an arrow. Their bolts are as thick as your thumb and one arrow can fell a man twice your size."

"I can fight."

"Yes," he said, glancing at the cut his sword left on her neck, the bruise on her shoulder. "You have skill, but there is no pointing in testing it against the outlanders."

Kepi put a hand on her shoulder. "It was a lucky blow."

He grunted. "In a fight, it doesn't matter if you win with luck or with skill. Dead is dead. I'm not going to risk your life." He took her wrist in his hand. "I am protecting you—nothing more." His touch made her recoil. Seeing her displeasure, he withdrew his hand. "I am not the man you think, Kepi. To the empire, Feren is a mystery, a puzzle, and I exploit those fictions. I play the rebel, or the blackthorn thief, when it suits me. But you will find I am not the man those stories tell."

"Maybe so," she said, flattening her shoulders against the carriage wall. "I want my waiting women."

"They are here."

"And my clothes." When she'd asked for a fresh set of clothes, Dagrun's soldiers had offered her a brightly colored gown of the king's choosing. She'd put it on, but the dress made her feel awkward and ladylike.

"My soldiers have your wardrobe. Anything else?"

"My freedom," she said, and from beneath her she slid out the knife she had concealed all the way from Harwen, one of the curved blades she kept stashed beneath her saddle. It was nearly as long as her forearm, double-edged and sharp.

"Right now," she said as she pressed the knife to the soft spot under Dagrun's jaw.

But quicker than she anticipated, he took her wrist, crushing the skin against the bone. "You mistake my intentions. Kill me"—he pushed the blade deeper into to his skin, daring her to do it—"and my men will cut you down. I am trying to protect you, but you're acting like a child. I don't expect gratitude, but I could do without your threats."

A loud knock on the carriage made them both start, and Kepi's hand jumped, and the blade slid farther into his skin. Dagrun put his hand to the wound and came away with a smear of bright blood.

Outside there was the sound of shouts and running, and the *thunk, thunk* of projectiles striking the carriage. "Arrows?" she asked.

Dagrun flung open the carriage door. War cries thundered outside. Spears whistling through the air, the sound of horses.

"You'll be safe here," he said as he locked her inside.

I'd be safer if you lent me a sword and some armor, she thought as she peeked through a crack in the shutter. Outside, a band of pale-skinned warriors covered in white ash from head to toe threw themselves at Feren and Harkan both, cutting throats and making guttural cries of pain and pleasure. Like ghosts running through the twilight, their banshee noises raised the hair on the back of her neck.

The San warriors, outlanders from the High Desert, answered to tribal warlords and fought with a terrifying brutality. Her father had twice driven their tribes from Harkana. She had stood with Arko on the field years before and watched as the Harkan Army routed them, sending them screaming back to their lands. Kepi had no wish to meet them here, trapped as she was inside the carriage like a dog in its cage.

The door opened again and Kepi brandished her blade, but instead of Dagrun or a ghostly outlander, she saw Seth in front of her, his face covered with dust and streaked with sweat. He must have accompanied her waiting women; he must have told the Ferens he was her servant. *Clever Seth.*

She nearly fell on him in relief.

"We should hurry," he said as he handed her a Feren sword and told her the San were overrunning the Ferens, that it was only a matter of time.

"Run to the stones," he panted. He meant the monumental rock circle, a well-known place where the stone trunks of the nearby Cragwood parted and a ring of standing stones kept watch for the sunrise. "They're just across the rope bridge. I'll join you there." He embraced her quickly, ran a hand down her hair.

"How?" she asked, but there was no time for explanations.

"Kepi," he said, his eyes holding hers for an extra moment—two, three, "be safe."

Kepi took off across the bridge, though behind her she could hear the hollow footsteps and wordless battle cries of the San following. She turned to look for Seth. He was drawing his blade, the cries of the San shattering the air. They were on him. She watched a man smeared in thick tar and hoary ash run his blade across Seth's belly, drawing a bright spurt of blood. "Help!" he cried. "Someone help!"

Kepi raised her sword and ran toward Seth, but a pack of outlanders blocked her path. With a stolen sword they hacked at the bridge supports, forcing her to retreat to the far side of the rope bridge before it collapsed into the rift, rattling as made its way down the rocky cliff.

With the bridge gone, all she could do was watch as the outlanders, hundreds of them, hurtled their ash-white bodies through the camp, overrunning the Ferens. She lost track of Seth and Dagrun—the haze of battle obscuring everything.

She was cut off from the Ferens and the fight but not safe from the outlanders. Three had crossed the bridge before it fell and they eyed her greedily, their mouths slashes of red in their ash-white faces, their teeth small and brown. One grinned wildly, his tongue rippling across his sharpened teeth. They would bludgeon her and dine on her entrails or tie her to a tree and use her as they pleased.

She ran.

⇥21⇤

Prepared to face the divine, to look into the face of god and perish, to burn or fall to the floor with a stroke that would end his life—Arko Hark-Wadi entered the Empyreal Domain, his breath heavy in his chest. In spite of all his preparations, in spite of how ready he thought he was, it was another thing entirely to walk into the room under his own power and present himself to die. He found himself strangely aware of every muscle, every fiber of nerve, every bit of blood and bone that belonged to him. He felt his heartbeat throbbing in his ribs. He felt the coolness of the floor under his feet, the scratch of his new ceremonial garments, the wet hair curling along his neck, the pain in his muscles from the long journey. He felt how good it was to be alive, and a momentary twinge of regret that it would soon be over. *All men die. Only most don't know the day or the hour. At least I will face the sun before I go.* He could not decide if that knowledge made him grateful, or bitter. Either way, he pressed forward, deep into the heart of the empire.

Ready to face the divine and meet his death.

But death did not come.

Instead, there was nothing.

No one.

A single beam of sunlight pierced the gloom from somewhere far overhead, falling off-center, momentarily blinding him, throwing the rest of the hall into darkness. The room was filled with silence, along with the musty scent of old dust, mildew, stale air deep underground, the coppery tang of rust or blood. There was the sound of his breath and his heartbeat in his ears but nothing more.

Arko had the sudden, distinct realization that he was completely alone. *Where is the emperor? Where is the eternal light of the Soleri?*

Arko listened, but nothing stirred. No one spoke, no one moved or breathed. Not a dog barked or a flame crackled. No sound of beating drums, or the rustle of a scroll, nor the pad of bare feet on stone.

Nothing. It was completely silent, the silence a blanket that smothered him.

A loud and overwhelming quiet.

His eyes adjusting to the dim light, ready for anything now, Arko stumbled upon a scene of a calamity. The golden throne of the emperor, twice the height of a man and covered with intricate carvings, lay crushed by the weight of a fallen beam from the ceiling above. Bits of gold glittered on its surface, showing where it had once been richly overlaid. Had thieves been here? Marauders? The rioters—could they have reached the palace, and if so, where were they now?

Around the throne, the walls were littered with black scars that looked like the remnants of fire perhaps, or the ghastly remains of long-dried blood. Arrowheads and half-rotten spear shafts lay in piles along with broken stone blocks from the ceiling above, an overturned cup, a bit of bright-blue cloth clinging to an ax head—the remains of a battle. But the room was two, three fingers deep in dust and sand, soft and brown and undisturbed by footprints or tracks of any kind. No one had been in this room for generations. Whatever had happened in the emperor's chamber must have occurred long ago.

"Gods," he sighed, "what happened here? Where is everyone? Where is the emperor?"

From the shadows, a voice answered him. "This is all there is, all that is left," it said. "What you are looking at is the great secret at the heart of the empire."

Arko shaded his eyes and squinted through the gloom. At the periphery of the chamber, he could see the outlines of a man take form, as if from the dust itself—an old man, from the look of him, white-haired and rangy, dressed simply in a robe. But in the middle of his forehead a great yellow jewel gleamed in the single beam of light.

"Who are you?" Arko asked, even though he had an inkling.

"You know who I am, Arko Hark-Wadi. I am Suten Anu. I am—or I have been—the First Ray of the Sun, right hand of Tolemy Five, the living god among men. Or I *would* have been, if such a person had ever existed."

Arko nearly choked. "You're speaking treason. Or you're mad, one or the other. What have you done with the emperor?" he asked, though the answer hung on his lips.

The old man gave a mirthless laugh and set an overturned chair upright. He sat down on it and sighed with gratitude. "There have been many days when I wished I were mad, when I wished I could believe as everyone else does. Madness seems to be our national occupation in Sola. Sanity, on the other hand, is a tremendous weight. It's a relief even to tell you this much: there is no emperor. There hasn't been, not for centuries. Den was the last." He took another deep breath and blew it out again. "You can imagine how long I've waited to say those words. Since my father said them to me, really."

Arko considered the chamber, wondering if this were all some terrible joke, a diversion meant to entertain before he went to see the emperor. But no one was there—only stones, and dust, and decay.

"No one knows what happened or why the Soleri vanished," Suten said. "There are no records or witnesses. There is only this shattered throne room. A scene of destruction preserved for each Ray to witness. We don't know who destroyed the chamber, or how the destruction was achieved. There are no bodies, and no bones. We have only the testimony of the first Ray, Ined Anu. He was the Father Protector of the Dromus during the War of the Four, the first great revolt, when the lower kingdoms banded together and rebelled against us.

"Two hundred years ago, when Ined's armies routed the Harkan rebels and liberated Solus at the end of the war, when the Empyreal Domain was liberated, they waited for the Soleri to return. A month passed, then another, but there was no sign of the emperor. Ined waited, but it was soon apparent that the emperor's family was not returning, and since Ined did not know where the Soleri had gone, he could not seek them. No one knew where they hid except the Soleri themselves, and their servants, and none of them ever returned. The gods had abandoned him. But Ined Anu knew the empire needed stability after decades of war, that we needed our gods back, and so he reinstated the rule of Mithra's children. He sealed the Shroud Wall, closed off the Empyreal Domain, and established the Ray of the Sun as a conduit to the Soleri and named himself to the post. We do not know who destroyed this chamber, perhaps it was the Harkans—it may have been burnt when the rebels arrived in Solus, but what evidence we have is conflicting and lost to time. My predecessors searched for answers, I searched for answers, but found none. Whatever secrets the Soleri had, they took with them. They are gone."

He pushed himself up and beckoned Arko to follow him out of the throne room. "I'll show you what is left."

Through the centuries of dust they went, crossing through a set of double doors into a long set of rooms where lavish feasts must have once taken place, where ladies would have paraded in their richest clothing. The rooms were still full of tables where no one sat, hung with alabaster lamps that gave off no light. As he made his way, Arko stumbled over a broken sword, an upturned bowl. They passed an ancient well with its rope rotted, its handle rusted, a distant repository where scrolls rotted on aging racks.

They took a passage up a set of blackened treacherous stairs, leading to a long gallery that must have once been richly lined with carved wood. Now the panels lay on the floor in pieces, eaten by termites, by rats. They passed through bedrooms where the beds had turned to dust, the heavy woolen tapestries still hanging to warm spaces where no one slept, no one dreamed, no one made love. No sound except their own footsteps, their own breathing. The old man chortling to himself as if it were all a great joke. Perhaps it was.

But the realization hit him with the force of truth: the old man was not lying.

There was nothing here. No center to the empire. No authority. No emperor. There hadn't been an emperor in centuries.

It was a lie, all of it. The emperor, the royal family, the empire itself . . . A lie.

It seemed like hours had passed before they saw daylight, but there it was up ahead—a bright ball of sunlight streaming in through an open door. The two men shaded their eyes and stepped out of the inner sanctum, back into the world above, and shut the door behind them.

Outside the inner palace, in the Empyreal Domain, there was no evidence of the emperor's absence. The stony yards were swept clean, the trees trimmed, the flowers pruned. A gleaming temple sat hard upon the inner wall, and near it a warren of workers' homes, and guardhouses. Everything was well kept and in order. Suten explained that the Empyreal Domain was populated entirely by men and women of the Kiltet—a service cult, one that had existed for centuries. Suten's acolytes culled servants from the villages of Sola. It was an honor and privilege to be chosen for the role, to live behind the Shroud Wall, within the domain of the god-emperors. Like the women who had bathed Arko, the citizens of the domain were all deaf, dumb, and mute. Their tongues were cut out and they were taught neither to read or write.

The cult considered its sacrifice a divine offering, but Suten admitted outwardly that it was nothing short of barbarism. Another necessary evil, he called it. The Kiltet maintained the gardens and trails, the high walls and temple exteriors. Stable boys mucked the stalls while gardeners trimmed the hedges and gathered grain and leeks, endive and onions.

"Dear gods," Arko murmured. "They don't know, do they?" The sun was high in the sky. The air was quiet, the Shroud Wall blocking out the noise and chaos of the rest of the city.

"Perhaps they suspect," Suten said, "but whom could they tell? No one can leave the domain."

"But there must have been thieves or spies—men who scaled the wall?"

"Of course no wall is impenetrable. Over the centuries, many have tried to enter the domain, most failed, but a few have succeeded. When they crossed the boundary, they saw nothing but date palms and rye grass. One spent the night hidden among the goats before the Kiltet found them. None have found the emperor's true domain. It is buried beneath us and the inner chambers are forbidden to the cult."

"But they do not wait on anyone, so they must suspect something?"

"The men and women of the Kiltet believe that only ethereal servants, creatures that can bear the light of the Mithra-Sol, serve the Soleri. When your life is predicated on a series of lies, one more mistruth is easy enough to accept. I've lived the better part of my life propping up one lie or another."

"So no one knows the truth." It was a statement more than a question.

"No one. Only the Ray of the Sun is allowed to pass in and out of the Empyreal Domain. My longtime adviser—Khalden Wat, the servant of the Ray—cannot enter the domain, but he will assist and serve you as best he can."

Arko was confused. "Serve me?" he asked. A dim, nagging feeling at the back of his head told him there was something more happening here, something monumental—something that would be far more important to him personally than the revelation about the emperor.

"Why yes, isn't it clear, Arko Hark-Wadi? You are to be the new Ray of the Sun. Only the Ray of the Sun can survive the divine light. Once the people discover you have survived the audience with the emperor, they will acknowledge you as his holy conduit."

"This is folly," Arko said. "You mock me. I am no Ray. My father could have been Ray, but not me. Kill me or send me back to Harwen, but leave off this nonsense now, before you make a mess of everything." Arko shook his head. He had been expecting to meet the emperor, to gaze into the face of a god and perish. Instead he would live, and Suten expected him to serve the empire as the next Ray of the Sun. It was impossible. He was Harkan. He was the enemy.

Suten's hand on Arko's forearm was dry and cold, too cold for the warm day, but soothing. "Perhaps this will make you understand," he said, and Suten led Arko to a chamber deep beneath the earth. He left Arko at the door and moved to the center of the room, picking up a burning torch and throwing it into a round iron receptacle. A dim light filled the chamber, a circular space with a domed roof and curling symbols carved into the walls. Two spheres hung from the dome, one large and one small. Suten stoked the brazier, the flames brightened, and the spheres rotated about the center of the room. One represented the Earth, the other its moon. The fire was the sun, Suten explained. As the spheres spun about the dome, the moon continued to pass between the sun and the Earth, but with each revolution the moon went slightly out of sync with the planet. Finally, it missed the yearly alignment that caused the sky to darken. "The failed eclipse," Suten said, stoking the brazier as the spheres continued their silent revolutions.

As Arko watched it fail he sensed some deeper meaning. The machine was telling him something, but he didn't know what it was. "What is this?" he asked, tugging at his beard as the spheres came to rest, the flames darkened, and the room went quiet.

"That's a question I've pondered for a great many years." Suten stoked the brazier. "This instrument was crafted by the Soleri and imbued with their wisdom and light. It signals the yearly eclipse, but that is not its true purpose—it was designed to predict the coming of a single event, one it has now revealed. And that is why I have brought you here to be the new Ray."

"But those people, your citizens, think I am some sort of sacrifice to soothe their anger. When I become Ray their anger will only double. So why place a Harkan on your throne?"

"The Devouring."

"What about it?"

"Ever wonder what the name meant?" asked Suten.

"The Harkans—"

"Do not properly honor the Devouring," finished Suten. "Yes, I know. I've heard of your games. The Devouring is a tradition that stretches back to a time before the empire, and even before the Soleri." Suten drew in a long breath, his wrinkled features hidden in the darkness. He stoked the brazier, but the flames were gone, only embers remained, and their light was fading.

"On the last day of the year, the moon devours the sun, but this is not the true Devouring. The very *first* Devouring was not just a dimming of the sun but a devouring of the land and the cities upon it. The stories of this first Devouring are etched in the burnt ruins of the Shambles and the worn temples of the Waset, in the fractured caverns of the Hollows and the crumbling fortresses of the Stone Reefs. In these places, there are walls that lay crumpled like parchment or shattered like glass. There are whole cities reduced to ash, leaving only desert.

"Have you ever wondered why so much of Solus is built beneath the earth, why the Soleri chose to hide half of their great capital beneath the sand? Why the throne of the sun god's children lies buried beneath the desert stones? And why the Soleri erected the Dromus, and the Shroud Wall? *What were they hiding from? What did the gods fear?*"

Arko did not know, he was out of answers, out of breath too. *A first Devouring.* What did that mean? And what creature could devour the very landscape?

"What *do* they fear?" he echoed.

Suten shook his head—he didn't have all of the answers, but it was clear the old man had been frightened enough to invite his enemy to stand with him as a friend. "The last Devouring is upon us. The moon and the stars are misaligned. The amaranth, the sun god's sacred plant, is in scarcity. The people rioted, they set fire to the city of the Soleri and tore a priestess of Mithra from the wall; more will follow unless we have a leader who can hold this empire together by force of will alone . . ."

"And you expect me to be such a leader," said Arko. If the Soleri could not abide it and created their entire empire in preparation against a hidden, shadowy enemy, what could one Harkan accomplish against such a foe?

Arko stared at Suten, speechless. He had expected death; he had not expected this. "I suppose you don't know me very well if you believe me to be the kind of leader you require."

"In that you are incorrect. I know you well. They call you the Bartered King, but in truth you are the last true king. Save for the interloper who now sits on Feren's throne, you are the only king untouched by the Priory. If I ally your kingdom with Sola, we need no longer prepare for another Harkan-led revolt. Only the outlanders will possess a force large enough to challenge us, but you have proven deft at subduing them.

"Two decades ago, when Raden Saad and the armies of the Protector failed to hold back the San, it was you who sent their hordes scurrying back into the High Desert. You twice defeated their riders, while ours were forced to retreat. It was Raden's defeat that led to the expansion of the outlanders in the first place. And if Amen Saad's father could not hold back the hordes, surely the son cannot do any better. The house of Saad is unfit to rule, as is the Mother Priestess, who would only use the post to advance the interests of her cult. I've spent a great deal of time contemplating the matter. In a way, I've pondered this choice for your entire life." The old man paused, his eyes were fixed on some inner distance, some memory. "I saw you once before, you know. Long ago, when you were only a child, during the second rebellion—the Children's War. You must not have been older than four, sitting atop a horse at the head of your father's soldiers as he rode out to meet Raden Saad on the battlefield."

My father. The Children's War. The second revolt. Suten was talking about the day Arko's father stood against the empire and secured his freedom. On that day, after the battle, Raden Saad, the former Protector, had agreed with a handshake that Arko Hark-Wadi would still be owed to the emperor, but the empire would not collect him, not that day or any day after. Not until today.

"You were there?" Arko guessed the Ray was at least ten and twenty years when Koren met Raden in battle. "I never knew."

"No one did. I rode along in disguise, as one of Raden's guard. I wanted to see firsthand the man who would destroy the empire." Again, the old man's eyes went out of focus, as if they were probing some unseen depth, a place seen only in memory. "Your father was a strong man. I admired him for his courage, for his conviction in denying your entry into the Priory. He nearly destroyed his kingdom to protect his family." Suten stood up straighter, stretching as if his limbs hurt him. "My own father did little to protect his. My only brothers were murdered as my father quibbled over power. Your father rode out with every man in Harkana to protect you. My father despised Koren for that act, but I feared him, feared what Koren would do. In turn I feared and punished you and your family. I sent your son to the Priory as soon as possible. I married the Harkan beauty to a man who would not appreciate her, a lord with no power or prestige. I wed your younger girl to that miserable little lordling in Feren. I thought it would ruin your alliance with the Ferens, and it did."

"We have no need for an alliance with Feren," Arko said.

"Some feel otherwise, our generals are among them. They fear the lower kingdoms." Suten gave Arko an admiring glance, "Lately, I have come to see my fear as nothing more than jealousy. Your father loved you enough to wreck his kingdom for you, how could I not envy such a man?" Suten stood up straight and looked him in the eye. "We are all children of the Priory. Where others have succumbed, your line has tried to do what is right, in spite of everything I have done. You carry the blood of Koren Hark-Wadi—you have more strength than you guess. Stop mourning your setbacks in the old wars and use that strength. Think on this: Sola was not always an empire and its leaders were not always conquerors. The rulers of the Middle Kingdom were wise and compassionate men. You could restore the values they once instilled in our people. The empire is a tool; it can be used for good as well as evil. The men you despise, the ones who subjugated your kingdom, are mostly dead. I am one of the last and I choose to begin anew. You are that beginning." Suten glanced one last time at the great throne room. "I am done here."

"Where will you go?"

Suten smiled, his gaze distant. "To my vineyard in the Denna hills. It is quite lovely this time of year. I hear this year's harvest is excellent."

"And if I say no? If I refuse the position?" Arko had no interest in fulfilling this man's designs, Devouring or not. Suten Anu had engineered the marriage of his youngest daughter to Roghan Frith and given his eldest to a man who could not love her, and when Ren was three years old, he had demanded Arko deliver him to the Priory. Some did not surrender their boys until they had reached a decade in age at least.

Arko had more than once pictured his hand on Suten's throat. He had dreamed of taking back the Amber Throne of the Soleri. He could start now, he could take Suten's life, expose the emperor's absence—a good enough start to a revolt. He took an aggressive step toward the Ray.

Suten retreated but did not wince, and Arko guessed he was not the first king to menace the Ray. "You will not refuse. I offer you the Soleri Empire. Only a fool would refuse such an offer and you are no fool."

Arko's head was spinning. The world had no center anymore, and he— he would be First Ray of the Sun. By all rights, he was the emperor. Free to arrange the world as he saw fit. Was he really capable of such a thing? To decide who lived, who died, who received power and who had it taken away? Was this really where his life had brought him? He saw that it would be foolish to deny Suten's request. No hatred he held for the man could overcome the appeal of what Suten offered. Arko Hark-Wadi would be the First Ray of the Sun.

But what of Suten?

Arko studied the aging Ray. A vineyard in the Denna hills was it? A peaceful retirement after a life spent in service to the empire?

Suten held out his hand and offered Arko the glowing citrine, the stone that had once rested on his own forehead. "Take this," he said. Suten picked up Arko's hand and placed the jewel in his palm.

It was heavier than he guessed. He tightened his fingers around the stone, his thoughts revisiting the grief Suten had thrust upon his family—Ren's gaunt face, Merit's bitterness, Kepi's tattered dress.

There would be no vineyard and no peaceful retirement. Not for a man such as this.

Arko Hark-Wadi swung and in a single blow took the life of Suten Anu, First Ray of the Sun.

In death, Suten looked like any other man, old, withered, and afraid.

Arko pressed the jewel to his forehead. "A life for a life," he said to the empty throne room. "You are correct, I do carry the blood of Koren Hark-Wadi. And my father was not a forgiving man."

And thus would begin Arko Hark-Wadi's stewardship of the empire, wrought in blood and light, marked by the cries of a dying man.

THE WAKING RITE

≡ 22 ≡

Sarra Amunet wore black on her first day in Desouk.

The sun had not bowed to the emperor. The crowds in the city of the Soleri had torn her surrogate from the wall. Mithra had shown his displeasure. As the Mother Priestess of the cult Sarra felt it necessary to acknowledge these indignities, so she went to the temple of Mithra at Desouk and told the Dawn Crier to leave the temple. Today the Mother Priestess would perform the duty of her lowest acolyte. As the morning light raked the temple columns, she sang to the statue of the sun god an ancient hymn, "The Song of Changes," a sweet and simple tune about the sowing and growing of the amaranth. She didn't much like singing or the recitation of prayers, she preferred her scrollwork, but she sang the song anyway. She needed her priests to believe that she had been saved by Mithra's hand, so she walked the prayer circle, tracing a careful ring in the temple's center.

Priests gathered to watch, some simply congregating as they did each day to honor the god, others whispering about her miraculous flight from Solus. The false story of her escape from the crowds was already spreading through the empire. The chatter was all around her, but she pretended she could not hear it.

As was custom for the Dawn Crier, she fasted throughout the day, pausing only to catch her breath or to take a draught of water. The fasting and the singing made the day drag on, and she let her exhaustion show on her face. Today she must look penitent, contrite. She must appear humbled, and grateful. The people must believe that Mithra himself had ferried her through the riots on the last day of the year. *They mustn't know that Saad put his sword to my breast, that my cloak was ripped and the crowds nearly tore me limb from limb.*

As the darkness crept across the open-air temple, her thoughts drifted. She pictured her childhood home in Asar, the rocky little keep where her family weathered the wet season. She thought about the family she left behind in Harkana. She remembered Arko, bitterly, and her daughters more fondly. *I'd like to see their faces again.* She had sworn she would never return to Harkana, but perhaps the girls would one day come to her.

As the sky darkened and the air grew cold, she heard the cries of the young boy, Khai Femin, echo in her thoughts. The image of Garia's severed limbs flashed at the edges of her vision. Sarra wondered if she had acted wrongly, if she should not have sent Garia to stand on the wall. Was there another way—something else she could have done? No. She needed to put Amen Saad in his place, to halt his aggression. By her own estimation, she had been only partially successful in subduing the young Protector. The matter of succession was still unsettled. Saad remained a threat.

Sarra realized she had stopped singing. The cold air made her skin prickle.

The sky was black, and only one or two priests lingered at the temple, shuffling their feet as they hummed the song.

She drew her robe about her and left the temple, bowing slightly as she stepped outside of the prayer circle.

Sarra wore white on her second day in Desouk. She attended to her duties in the temple, ordaining acolytes, and celebrating the start of the new year, the first days of Soli, the first month of the Soleri calendar.

On her third day, when the formal duties of the Mother Priestess were complete, Sarra journeyed high into the Denna hills, to a place where the ancient amaranth fields sheltered in green vales beneath walls of sheer rock. Months ago, the Mother Priestess had uncovered a narrow opening that had once been a doorway, but had centuries ago been covered by an avalanche. Her priests had done their best to remove the obstructions, clearing a narrow passage that led to a set of underground chambers. A young priest who had only just arrived in Desouk, Nollin Odine, waited by the entrance to the excavation, sitting atop a pile of stones, studying a scroll. He was a scribe of the Hierophantic Order, the interpreters of sacred symbols. At a very young age he'd made a name for himself deciphering texts written in hieratic script. She'd heard the boy spent all of his time studying scrolls. Her priests said he ate with a scroll in one hand, and slept often with another beneath his head. Ott had joked that the boy had been glimpsed on the privy, a parchment in his lap, tearing off corners to wipe himself as he read. She hoped his ample knowledge would be of some assistance.

"Come," Sarra beckoned warmly. "Follow me, Nollin."

"It's Noll. If that's okay?"

"Noll." She ushered him toward the narrow shaft, lifting the edges of her robe so the hem wouldn't drag as she slid between the stones. She was eager to show him the mountain chamber, to hear his thoughts on the curious inscriptions that had puzzled their most talented scribes. In their effort to decode the markings, her priests had requested scrolls and clay tablets from across the empire, including Harkana, and her daughter Merit had been kind enough to allow her request. But they had made little progress in their work.

A few steps in, the passage swelled, the walls opening into a vast rotunda hewn from amber stones.

"Where are we?" Noll asked.

Sarra took an oil lamp from the wall and raised it to the distant ceiling. At the dome's apex, rusted iron bars half sheltered an oculus. "This is a storehouse," Sarra said.

"For the amaranth?"

"Yes, an old one. We are standing at the base of a grain depository. The priests dropped seeds through the oculus." Sarra pointed to the opening above. "The grain was stored here and emptied through there." She motioned toward the floor, then the passage through which they had entered.

"It is a sacred place," he said, rubbing his eyes.

"Yes, the storehouse once sheltered our sacred crop."

The amaranth. Not even a plant, but a gift from the gods themselves. When mixed and ground, the leaves of the amaranth formed a thick paste that made the dry soil of Solus fertile—so vital that the priesthood of Desouk, in whose domain the oases existed, had long ago woven the sowing and harvest of the amaranth into their religion. Only a priest or priestess could touch the seed and tender the plant.

"A year ago, you sent a large number of translations to the repository, translations of imperial scrolls dating to the reign of Den, during the War of the Four. One of those documents, a lengthy chronicle of grain shipments, contained this storehouse's location."

"Those scrolls were centuries old."

"Two centuries. Sekhem Den, last in his line, erected the storehouses. His builders left their marks."

"Yes, I've studied Den, but I don't see the connection. What interest do we have in old storehouses?" Noll asked.

Sarra laid the lamp on the chamber's grain-speckled floor. The room darkened. She cupped her hands against the stone, scraping sand and pebbles into her palms. She raised her hands to show the young priest what she held. Amber kernels lay among the dust and sand. "See these seeds?" she said. "What if I told you these seeds, and ones like them—the seeds hidden away in the empire's vast storehouses—are the last fertile amaranth seeds in the empire?"

Noll shook his head. "I don't understand. I saw a field of amaranth on my walk this morning."

Sarra's eyes darted around the empty chamber; even in the safety of Desouk she was careful where she spoke. "You have served only as a hierophant—am I right?"

Noll nodded. "I've only just arrived from the southern islands."

"Your order is not privy to the information I am about to share with you. Only the highest circle of the priesthood knows this." Sarra lowered her voice. "The gods have rescinded the gift of the amaranth, or at least my predecessor, Pouri Amunet, thought so. There is a drought, but the lack of rain is not the source of our seed shortage. The amaranth is in short supply because the amaranth seeds are infertile and have been for two hundred years. The seeds of the newly planted amaranth do not bud or grow. We sow seeds from the empire's old storehouses, reserves that are nearly emptied. The field that you saw outside was the last of the supply."

"Impossible," Noll whispered. "How?" he shook his head. "There would be records, ways to trace such things. You've kept this hidden?"

Sarra tilted her head to one side. "Is it really that hard to believe? That the priesthood could keep secret the truth behind its sacred crop—the one only we can tender, whose very nature has been protected by the priesthood for three millennia?"

Noll did not argue with her. The scribe was quiet, then he asked, "There will be no more amaranth?"

Sarra pressed her lips together. "When the seeds are gone, the amaranth will be gone. Our stores of seeds were once vast, but they are nearly depleted. The gift of Mithra, the amaranth, cultivated by the priesthood and sold to the people of Solus, will be no more, and the desert will be uninhabitable. Right now the forests of Feren sustain much of the empire, but there is not enough food in the Gray Wood to feed all of us."

"The priesthood has been keeping this a secret? Why?" Noll asked.

"My predecessors felt it best to conceal the amaranth's infertility. A drought is an easy thing to understand. The empire will not blame the priesthood for a drought. But tell the people that our sacred crop, a plant tended only by the priesthood, is infertile? We will surely be blamed."

"I understand, but why are you telling me this?" asked Noll. "I study symbols. There is nothing I can do."

"I hope you're wrong." She led Noll through a corridor, down a ramp, and into a room no wider than Sarra's outstretched arms. The lamplight revealed faint indentations on the walls and ceiling. "Can you read the marks?" Sarra asked.

"A few—most of them, actually."

"Good. My priests decoded one or two, the rest were indecipherable. I brought you here and I told you our secret because they say you are fluent in the script," she said. "That you can read the ancient language of the Soleri, the forbidden tongue in which these marks are written."

Noll looked as if his answer might anger Sarra. "No one can read all of the old symbols, Mother Priestess. Even during their time, the keys to the ancient language were kept hidden. The gods did not share their tongue with their subjects, but I've pieced together a skeleton of sorts, an inventory of the old characters."

"Good. This is an antechamber, nothing more. But through that passage"—Sarra gestured—"there is a larger chamber, one carved entirely in these same symbols. We've seen hundreds of storehouses, but only this one carried the markings. I need to know why this site is different." Sarra coughed, pushing dust from her lungs. "I want to read the symbols."

Sarra led Noll through the gradually narrowing passage, cool air rushing through cracks in the stone. The passage widened into a brazier-lit room. Miniature symbols covered the chamber walls.

At first glance, the marks resembled the scratches of a caged animal, but they were characters in a forgotten script. "Do you recognize it?" Sarra asked, gesturing to the marks.

"It's hieratic." Noll squinted at the wall through the flickering light. "Derived from the old pictographic language of the Soleri."

"I know what the word means, it's the symbols I am interested in," Sarra said. "Others tried to decode the inscriptions, but the language was beyond their ability. I've summoned priests from all over the kingdoms, but none of them could read the marks. We asked the Harkans to send us scrolls from the repository in Harwen, but the parchments were of no use. I'm hoping you will have better luck."

His eyes darted from symbol to symbol. "The walls contain prayers, wards of protection, curses against those that trespass."

"*Wards* you say?"

Noll nodded without turning from the inscriptions. "Yes, wards. This is a forbidden place, a chamber meant only for the Soleri," he said, walking deeper into the room, up a step. Noll kneeled before a column and traced a circular carving, an ornate ring incised at the base of a pillar. Upon closer inspection, faint indentations, markings that resembled scales, dotted the ring and what seemed to be a chip at the circle's top was actually a snake's head carved in the act of consuming its own tail.

"What is it?" Sarra asked.

"The snake is the symbol of Pyras."

"The firstborn of Mithra-Sol?" Sarra asked.

"Yes. The snake's head circle is an ancient ward, placed here to frighten looters. The mark warns that the eye is watching."

"Whose eye, the eye of Pyras?" Sarra asked, looking askance at having to say his name. She knew the myth well.

The story of the first of the Soleri cannot be told without Pyras; the two were entwined from their beginning. Pyras was the progeny of shadow, Re the child of the sun. The children of Mithra were birthed in a place beyond the heavens, in Atum, the domain of Mithra-Sol, the land beyond the sky, the home before time.

Atum. A world fashioned for Mithra-Sol's children. A world that after a time seemed too small for the sons of Mithra. So Pyras, firstborn of Mithra-Sol, searched for a land that he alone could rule. He found none that were worthy, so he devoured what he discovered and fashioned a new world from the remains of the old.

But Re, seeing this new world and wanting it for himself, pricked a hole in the sphere of Atum, so its light could shine upon this new land. That pinprick became Sol; the land became Sola. Through the fissure, Re plummeted to the earth.

Mithra's child touched the desert sand, and his essence poured into the land, the amaranth bloomed, and life blossomed across the desert. Mithra granted Re a wife, Rena, and together they gave birth to ten children. These were the first of the Soleri, but they were beings of Atum, made of pure light. To more fully experience their new world, they took on new forms, bodies born from the creatures of the land, shells made from the stones of the desert and the light of the stars.

The Soleri made a new home, a new perfection, and claimed it as their own. But the stars and the stones and the desert sand did not belong to the Soleri—they belonged to the Pyras and his progeny. Pyras made this world. He was the first.

A great conflict erupted between the two families.

Seeing his children quarrel, Mithra-Sol devised a solution to their conflict. He gave his children both darkness and light in equal amounts. To accomplish this feat, he set the sun and stars into motion. He made the world spin. Day and night were born, and the children of Mithra-Sol were once more at peace.

But the Soleri did not want peace. They wanted the world for themselves and so they tricked the firstborn of Mithra. In secret, the Soleri gave birth to Luni, the moon, and placed her in the sky so even at night Mithra's light would shine upon the land.

The light defeated the endless night and the domain of shadow. The strength of Pyras and his children waned and the firstborn children of Mithra were turned into slaves—witches and dogs whose only purpose was to serve the Soleri.

"Yes." Noll's bright eyes pulled Sarra from her thoughts. "The eye of the snake is the eye of Pyras. The slaves of Re and their powers were likely a myth, but the fear they inspired was real." His finger hung on a carving. "You spoke of other storehouses, was this symbol found at any other site?"

"No—the other storehouses are utilitarian, they bear no marks or decorations. As I said, this chamber is unique."

"If the eye exists here and nowhere else, we can assume this storehouse contained something absent from the other sites. Something of importance."

"I see. Why place wards unless you have something to guard?"

"Yes." Noll cocked his head. "But what were Pyras and his symbol protecting? What is here that we have not yet found?" Noll traced more carvings: a circle in a square, a column filled with rows and rows of grain-sized markings.

As Noll worked, the morning turned to noontime, the brazier dimmed. Priests brought cool amber and salted meat. Sarra chewed the hard strips. Her acolytes fetched Noll's inventory of symbols, a roll he kept safe in an oilskin sack.

Sarra stoked the brazier's flames as the boy hunched over the scroll, poring over the carefully noted markings, holding the roll to the ceiling, to the light, making notes in the margins as he scratched his brow.

Sarra finished the amber. Tired of watching the boy work, she found a spot where she could observe a crack of sunlight as it moved across the chamber's entry. She used the changing light to gauge the hour. When that orange glow failed, when the flames guttered out and evenfall approached, she gathered her things and made for the way out, but Noll halted her retreat.

"Wait," he said, an outstretched arm pointing to the ceiling.

"What is it?" Sarra asked.

"The light changed."

"Why would that matter?"

"Normally the light would not affect the reading of the symbols, but in this case it has. I ignored the ceiling at first, because the symbols were illegible, there were too many marks in each arrangement. I assumed the ceiling was written in a script I did not understand or that it was somehow coded so as to make it unreadable. Apparently it was the latter. The raking shadows of the late-afternoon sun are concealing what I now realize are extraneous marks. In this light, with those marks removed, I can finally understand the words," said Noll. "Do you see it?"

"Where? I see the hieratic characters, but they are not ordered in columns as is customary."

"If it were a story or a tale of some kind it would make no sense, but this ceiling is neither. It's a map. Look to the walls, then study the ceiling."

The markings above were indeed different from those on the walls and floor—those marks were arranged in neat columns. But the markings on the ceiling were ordered in clumps. Sarra had noted the discrepancy upon entering but had not understood its meaning. "It's a map carved in words."

"Yes," Noll said, indicating a mark. "Rather than a picture of a mountain, it uses the Soleri character that depicts a mountain: two lines slanting left." He leaned his head from side to side and cracked his neck. "The markings could not be seen in the lamplight, only the dark brought them out."

Sarra was at once fascinated. She took a step back so she could gaze at the whole of the ceiling. It was a map, and a hidden one at that, but what did it describe and where did the road lead? "If they wanted to conceal the map's contents, why did they carve it into stone?" she asked. "Why not parchments or tablets—they are easier to conceal."

Noll shrugged. "Such is the arrogance of gods," he mused. "Sometimes they leave their secrets in the open."

≥23≤

Ren breathed deeply, tasting his freedom, his horse galloping across the wilds of Harkana. The wide blue expanse of the sky above filled him with awe. He had lived underground for too long, he could not stop staring at the vastness of the heavens. That the two soldiers with him barely seemed to register its presence was all the more remarkable. How could they stand it, all that openness, all that space? At any time, he felt the earth might let him go, let him float away into the blue, up and up, as if he were not flesh and blood but a spirit ready to disappear, unseen, unknown.

He flung back his head, craning his neck and closing one eye as he turned toward the clouds, toward the sun that burned on the desert plants, the rocks, and the shoulders of his gray tunic. The sun warmed everything it touched. He would never be cold here, he would never be trapped. He breathed in once, deeply, and felt how fresh the air was, how sweet. At the edge of a small oasis, the rich smell of loamy earth and growing things reinvigorated him, and when they came to a creek, little more than a thin trickle of water running through stones, the water was so clear and bright that Ren stopped his horse, slid himself down, and plunged his face into the cool stream, opening his mouth and drinking until he could not breathe.

When he sat up again and looked around, the water dripping from his hair onto the shoulders of his tunic, he felt changed, charged with something electric. He was a prisoner no longer. He was a free man, a king's son, and he would prove to his father and to his kingdom that he was worthy of the throne he was born to inherit. The king had asked him to take the hunt, had said that it would enable Ren to prove his worth to the kingdom. *I've already proven my worth. I survived the Priory and the Sun's Justice.* But the hunt was important to his father, so he would do his best to see it done.

Ren and his Harkan escort climbed their way up the rocky trail that followed the bank of the creek, skirting the rocky lowlands for the hills, when one of his companions spied a horse tied to a tree—a saddled destrier, as if its rider intended to come back at any time. They approached the horse, Ren following his escorts until they stopped. "Look," the younger soldier said, pointing at the richly ornamented saddle.

"Harkan?" Ren asked.

"I cannot say. Perhaps it belongs to the warden." The soldier shook his head and motioned for Ren to follow him. They swung wide to avoid the horse and nearly trampled a still-smoking campfire.

Ren placed his hand on the hilt of his father's dagger. "We're not alone," he said, and guided his horse down the path. The Shambles was a place reserved for the king's family and their escorts, their servants and messengers. No one else was permitted to enter the sacred grounds. He worried that he was being followed, that the gray-cloaks had found him once again.

As the sun failed in the west, Ren and the Harkan soldiers reached a stone gate marked by an eld-horn totem—the threshold of the hunting reserve—where an old man, his bronze skin deeply wrinkled by time and sun, stood awaiting them, a dog at his side. "Dakar Wadi," he announced, tipping his head ever so slightly toward Ren. "Warden of the reserve. You the king's son?" He chewed a blade of grass as he appraised him. "A messenger arrived, said you might be coming." He rubbed his forehead.

Ren offered the man his hand to shake, but Dakar shook his head: as a man of low status he couldn't shake hands with kings. Ren was embarrassed, as he was not king yet. Not until the hunt was complete. He still felt like nothing more than just a ransom—despised, injured, afraid. It might take him a long time, he realized, to get used to better treatment.

"You know what you are here to do?" Dakar asked.

Ren nodded.

"A man can't rule Harkana without claiming the eld's horns. He makes his sword with the horn, and that sword becomes a symbol of the king's power for the rest of his reign."

"My father explained the custom to me. Like killing a deer, I suppose."

"The eld is no deer. It is unlike any creature that lives outside the reserve. It is an ancient breed, a fierce creature of immense proportions, and rare as well, living only in the high canyons, among the narrow streams that fall from the high cliffs. Along the rivers grows a withered-looking plant called smoke grass. Look for the marble-white flower; then you'll know you've found the plant. The eld is always close by there."

"Gray grass, white flower. Easy enough."

"Not easy at all, I'm afraid. The eld is clever. The eld *chooses* the king, and only a king can tame one, but in my experience, only a king should try." He fixed Ren with a penetrating look. "You'll need to keep your mind on what you're doing, son. The Shambles is no place for daydreaming."

Ren inspected the old man more closely. The truth was, he *had* been daydreaming. But a creature of hideous size was something entirely out of legend—old stories meant to frighten children, like those they told at the Priory. "I understand," he said, even if he didn't. "How do I go about it, then?"

Dakar smiled, as if he had been waiting for just this question and was pleased Ren had asked. He regaled the company with a long story detailing the creature's habits, how it fed and nested, how it lived and died. "It's a solitary animal." Dakar gnawed at the straw that hung from his lip. "The eld follows its stomach and you should do the same—look for the smoke grass, it worked for your father."

"What was he like?" Ren asked.

The old man paused and handed him a hard cake of bread. "I remember the king's arrival for the hunt. He was a tall boy, far thinner than his current bulk would suggest. He could command a pack of dogs with the tone of his voice and could wield a bow better than any man I've met. He killed an eight-point buck on his way back from the hunt. We cleaned and roasted the deer and got drunk on amber as we picked through the meat." Dakar's voice went quiet.

Ren realized the old man thought Arko was dead, as there was no other reason for Ren's presence in the reserve.

Arko was as good as dead, and I am not ready to be king.

Dakar handed Ren a sack of provisions containing flat bread, honey, two jars of amber, and some salted venison. "Take the dog," the old man said. "He knows this land better than I do, but you must leave your escort behind," he said, turning to the king's men. "You cannot accompany the heir."

Ren nodded and dismissed the men. He knelt, letting the black-haired mutt wet his face with slobber. He had never had a pet before and welcomed the company. While the little dog licked his cheek, Ren gazed up at the mountain; the tip was white and the cliffs were near vertical.

"That food'll last a week," Dakar said, pointing to the parcels. "No king has needed more time, but if you do, I'm here." His eyes narrowed. "Be careful, boy." He bowed his head respectfully, but his words were edged with warning. "The cliffs are a dangerous place, and the eld can be ferocious; it can come from nowhere to attack and you could be dead before you spot it—"

"Don't fret," Ren interrupted, his father's dagger in his hand, the provisions slung over his shoulder, the small hunting dog by his side. *I've stood beneath the sun, felt the sting of a cane, the bite of a whip. No hideous deer will get the best of me.*

Ren would return with his horns. It was the least he could do for the father he never knew.

≋24≋

First they'll bludgeon me. Kepi saw the outlines of their clubs, whirling in the darkness. *Then they'll kill me and feast on what remains.*

Gray ribbons of stone jutted above the sandy earth. The rocks were as high as her knees, her shoulders, a few steps more and the stones stood above her head. As Kepi fled deeper into the stone forest, away from the San warriors pursuing her with nips and howls from Dagrun's carriage and the scene of battle, she tried not to think of Seth, how she had been forced to leave him alone and outnumbered. She'd fled across the bridge and into the Cragwood, a place many times the size of Harwen, a forest of rippling stones. She had a chance here—a chance to hide, a chance to strike at her attackers if she was careful. But what chance did Seth have, ten against one in the open?

Kepi darted from one stone to another, keeping to the shadows, keeping hidden. The stones towered above, their shadows overlapping in the distance. *Breathe.* She pressed her back into a rocky concavity, felt the stone cup her shoulders. She had been here before, long ago, with her father. She was young enough at the time to share a saddle with Arko, who held her close and told her about this place. "The Cragwood is Feren's sacred ground," her father said, "home to the Waking Rite, the place where

Feren kings have earned their crown for untold centuries. The rite tests a king's strength, and his heart too."

Thinking of Arko made her feel melancholy. *I want to see him one last time.*

An angry bark shook Kepi from her thoughts. The sun had begun its descent and the stones were growing dark. She should head due north, deep into the slanting gray rocks, to the stone circle where Seth had bade her to promise to meet him. It would be safer to flee the forest, but she had left Seth behind once already and would not do so again. So Kepi kept running, the voices of the ash-covered warriors coming closer, their grunts and barks sounding at times as if they were right behind her. She was on foot, alone, and still wearing the brightly hued gown that Dagrun's soldiers had insisted upon, along with the light slippers of a lady. The San were fast-moving, a pack of wolves driven by hunger and blood. Glimpses of ashy-white skin flashed between the rocks; her foes visible for fleeting moments. The men carried crudely forged blades, their edges dull and ragged. They cudgeled their foes rather than cut them—it was a brutal death. Kepi had seen the remains of their victims with her father, the skull smashed in, the rib cage crushed.

She ducked as an ash-covered arm passed to her right. Then another. A flash of iron, a blade glinted in the darkness.

Hide. She was not going to outrun them much longer.

Kepi came upon a clump of stone shards three times her height, gray with flecks of pink that gleamed in the fading sunlight. Inside was a hollow crevice, accessible only by a crack barely large enough for her to squeeze through. She pushed herself into the ragged fissure, crouched on her knees, and waited.

Voices echoed between the rocks. The men from the High Desert spoke a crude tongue that bore little resemblance to the emperor's speech. Their words sounded like curses, strings of consonants, hard on the ear. Her father knew their tongue and had taught her, and so she understood the gist of their conversation.

"Where's the bitch?" one grunted, and another answered, "I can taste her stink. She's not far."

She pressed her shoulders against the stone, knowing what was in store if they found her, her memory of the night with Roghan vivid in her mind. *They'll take me. Or one will take me while the other cudgels me with his club.* She saw a soot-smeared leg between the stones.

With a shout, Kepi drove her blade low between two stones and cut the man's ankle, severing the tendon that connected the foot to the leg in a gush of blood and sinew. He collapsed, screaming for his companions, and she squeezed out of her hiding place, running as fast as she could while his cry reverberated through the stones.

She went twenty steps and found another small shelter, wedging herself inside and listening the way her father had taught her, counting footsteps: *one, two, three, four.* She waited. The outlanders twice passed her without catching her sight or scent, and she remembered what her father had taught her: *When you're outnumbered, draw your opponents apart. When you're outmatched, tire your opponent before you attack. Don't forget, Kepi.*

I won't forget.

Kepi slipped from between the stones, following far enough behind them not to be seen. She cursed her brightly colored dress, how visible it was against the gray, but she managed to stay behind the men, hiding whenever they stopped, throwing a stone the other way to divert their attention, trying her best to tire the men by making them chase her. She went ten paces and hid, then twenty more and hid again. They heard her running, heard her breathing, but could not catch her.

At a large clump of stones she was able to split them up, taking the north fork while throwing a fallen branch into the south fork and hoping the sound of the wood striking the stones would make them think she had gone that way. She hid behind a wall of stone. One followed, his skin sparkling with ash as he emerged from the shadows, a cloak of bones jingling on his back. The second, a taller man with scars wrapping his arms and face, went the other way. Kepi's chest heaved with exhaustion. If she kept this up much longer, she would be too tired herself. *Strike now. You can face them one at a time.*

"Do you see the bitch—" The rest was unintelligible. She could no longer translate; her mind was a gray cloud of fear. She heard the fatigue in their voices, the frustration.

It was time.

The bone cloak rattled in the darkness. The ash-skinned warrior tore through the rocks, his breath coming in bursts, coming closer. Kepi cupped her hands around her mouth, turned in the opposite direction, and gave a cry that sounded like a raven. The call echoed off the stones, confusing her attacker.

When the San turned to look, Kepi struck.

The echoing birdcall cloaked her footsteps as she raced forward and swung the mighty Feren blade. The sword was made for a man twice her size, and it cleaved the man's arm in two.

He screamed. The air was full of ash as he fell to the stones, struggling for a moment before his limbs went soft and his eyes closed.

Kepi spun, tried to flee, but the scarred man was upon her now. She started to lift the blade over her head once more, but it was too heavy, and she was too slow. Weaponless, the outlander clobbered her forearm with his fist. She had trained for this moment; she knew what to do. Kepi thrust her heavy sword at his chest. The blade nipped his skin, and his eyes went wild. His scarred face furrowed as he grabbed for the sword and with bare hands tried to wrest it from her grip. Blood poured between his fingers. He grunted and cursed, his teeth glowing blue in the moonlight, his eyes yellow, his breath stinking like spoiled amber. He thrust the sword's tip between two stones and wedged it tight. Kepi pulled, but the sword stayed fixed. *Gods!* Her body was electric, her heart a hammer in her chest. She was defenseless, unarmed. *What now?*

He hit her twice, once in the head, opening a gash over her eye, then again in the chest, a hard blow that took her breath away. She let go of the hilt of the sword as the force of his blow sent her tumbling onto her back. The outlander cried out, his hands dripping with blood, the scars on his body animated by his every movement.

Not like this. Not here. I'm not meant to die here.

He fell toward her and Kepi planted a firm foot on his chest and kicked with all her strength, but he remained where he was, a sickening smile on his ash-dabbled face.

Kepi winced, preparing to die.

Wings rustled in the distance, a gray flutter passed overhead.

A shadow blackened the sky as a large bird with a wingspan greater than the height of a man crashed into her attacker. Its sharp, curved beak dug into his eye, ripping through the lid as it bit the flesh.

She thought of her father one last time: *Never hesitate,* he'd told her. *Opportunities in battle last shorter than breaths.*

Kepi lunged for her sword. She turned it roughly, snapping the blade free of the rocks, breaking it about halfway down. Still sharp, still usable. Before her enemy could recover, she used the sharp edge of the blade to slice across his gut, spilling entrails and gore onto the rocky earth, his blood red and viscous. His intestines slithered out like a nest of snakes, which the great bird snatched at and ate with relish.

Coils of viscera hanging from its beak, the kite fixed its gaze upon her and Kepi found herself momentarily transfixed. She gaped at the creature, the kite beating its wings, rising into the air, its dark silhouette vanishing into the night sky.

Awestruck, Kepi threw down the sword and fled deeper into the stones.

She ran, following the rocky terrain upward to a high point, where she cocked her ear to the sky and listened for more shuffling footfalls, for grunts and curses. She listened, but heard only the wind whistling between the crags. She was alone in the forest of stone, but her heart would not stop pounding and her limbs would not stop shaking. She wandered the tall rocks exhausted and thirsty, nursing her bruised forearm. After a few paces, she collapsed, but forced herself to stand, to keep walking. The grade changed, the earth sloped upward. She moved from stone to stone, resting when she could, exhausted, out of breath, but determined not to stop.

The moon circled the sky, the air cooled, and she lost track of time.

Heartsore, stumbling, and feeling closer to death than when she had been attacked, she fell down among the tall rocks. Darkness. Pain. Silence. She could not give in to it. Her head jerked back and her eyes flew open.

The darkness resolved into gray columns. A circle of stones stood not more than ten paces from her spot. The King's Throne. The meeting point. Seth. She scrambled up the slope, the grassed-over ruins of an ancient castle, to higher ground where the stones had been arranged in a wide ring.

A sculpted gray monolith stood in the center of the circle, a throne carved into the stone. The sun was going down, and the last rays lit the middle of the throne like an ancient fire. But there was no Seth, not that she had truly expected him, she had only hoped.

Still, it was a good high place from which to keep watch, so she settled into it and waited all the rest of that evening and into the night, which was cold and dark and full of the rustle of the wind down the stone canyons. Kepi was too frightened for sleep, and so she sat there on the stone, shivering under the stars, waiting for Seth.

She was still alone when the first rays of the sun illuminated the forest, when she heard a long, piercing cry coming from somewhere overhead—the same cry she had heard in the forest.

A large bird disappeared behind the tall rocks, a familiar shadow fluttering across the stones. She turned and caught sight of it approaching from behind.

It was beautiful but unnaturally large, gray, and fiercely clawed.

It circled—over and over until it wound a broad arc around the throne—its small eyes tilting toward Kepi.

⇒25⇐

The hunting grounds were dense with rocky hills and sharp, broken outcroppings that provided little shade in the noonday sun. It was his third day in the reserve, but he had not yet seen the eld. Ren searched for the wispy grass with the white flowers Dakar had described, but found little in the blighted landscape that was alive. As he climbed, he thought of Tye, and the Priory. And Adin . . . he would find out what happened to his friend, if he was dead or alive. He wanted his friends to find their freedom. For his part, it felt strange to acquire his independence and at the same moment lose the only life he had ever known and the friends who had surrounded him. It was as though he were moving between two lives, but neither one had yet taken hold. The Priory was behind him, but he was not yet a Hark-Wadi, he had not met his sisters, nor had he stepped foot inside the Hornring. *Why must I pass one more test? Was the Priory not enough?*

He spent the day hiking up a steep and narrow mountain trail, chasing after his black-haired hound, following the spine of an ancient path that led to a row of narrow, rotting wooden stairs. A rope handle fastened to the rock with iron rings allowed him a little balance, and he felt the air become cooler as the slope went higher, up toward the clouds. Pausing now and then to look down into the valley, he saw nothing of the eld. *I'm alone here.* He'd once seen a herd of deer, but they were gone, and he'd seen nothing since.

Ren reached a narrow ledge. He made his way along the flat rocks, sliding with one foot in front of the other. A tree blocked the path, so he grabbed a branch and swung himself around the trunk with the dog leaping behind him. Ren's foot landed on a loose plank and he teetered before he caught his balance. The dog whimpered, his big brown eyes looking to Ren for reassurance. "I know, I know," Ren said, to calm the dog as much as himself. "I'm nervous too, boy." On the far side, there was a gap in the planks, a void that stretched to a bottom that he couldn't see. He leapt across the gap, falling clumsily down to the other side. The dog jumped as well, tongue wagging in exhaustion. "Good boy," he said. "Stay close now."

Beyond the gap, the planks angled upward, the wood wet in spots—remnants from the morning. He placed both hands on the guide rope, holding tightly, skirting the mountain and looking for some end to his climb. The guide rope was so old and worn that he dared not use it in some spots, and the planks were not in any better shape. Dust thick enough to grow moss covered the wooden surface, and in the middle was a sandal print. Someone had walked this path before him. *I'm not alone after all.* The mark certainly didn't belong to Dakar; he was too old to make the climb. So who made it? He recalled the horse he had seen tethered to a tree. Were the gray-cloaks still following him?

Ren couldn't guess, so he moved on, the plank walk continuing around the sharply curving cliff face. He followed the path, resting in spots, catching glimpses of the view, the distant mountains and the barren landscape. He had never imagined that the world could hold such vastness, such expanse. The sky stretched to infinity, the desert disappeared into boundless dunes. *If I die on this hunt, at least I saw this.* He stood with his back to the cliff, eyeing the gently changing clouds till the wind started to blow, and he feared it might topple him. *It would be a terrible shame if I survived the Sun's Justice but let the wind blow me from a ledge.*

Ren gripped the rocky face of the precipice, taking one or two more steps before coming to the end of the path, which opened onto a wide plateau. He made camp in the embrace of an ancient cypress, hoisting the dog and himself up into the branches for safety. A light rain fell, but the wide canopy of the tree kept them dry. Still, Ren was not able to sleep, and he again stared back down toward the desert flatlands he had left, the long, low darkness of the horizon ending where the stars began. On the other side sat a high plateau filled with hills and canyons, green and cold. The mongrel whimpered and moaned for a time, as the lowing of a deer hunting in the darkness kept them both awake.

Clouds concealed the moon, the temperature dropped, and the light rain that had been falling turned into soft, white flakes. Ren had never seen snow before but had heard of it, how it would fall and cover everything like a white blanket. He held out his hands to catch it, though as soon as it touched his skin it melted away. It felt like his freedom—a delicate, destructible thing that vanished the longer you tried to hold it.

Even when the snow faded and the dog's whimpering quieted, thoughts of his family kept him awake. He'd always understood that his father would be dead the day he was sent back from the Priory, and it had been a welcome and unexpected surprise to realize he would be afforded a meeting with the man who'd sired him. Arko was taller and stronger than he had imagined, yet also absentminded—as if the old king were only half there when he spoke. But then, Ren supposed that was to be expected, as he too had just been pulled from his life, summoned to Solus to face the emperor, and gods only knew what else. He knew his mother no longer lived in Harwen, and he had not expected to see her. Ten years in the Priory and the Mother Priestess of Mithra-Sol had not once visited. She was a mystery to him, nothing more. He wished he had been able to meet his sisters, at least, before being sent away to this hunt. He wanted to see their faces, but there had been no time for a reunion. Merit and Kepi were an empty spot in his memories. He knew only his father's face, but the king must be dead by now, or he would be soon enough.

Unable to sleep, Ren washed in the stream, drinking long and deep, before walking off to piss. He ate Dakar's bread and finished the amber. He found what he thought was the smoke grass, but he saw no flowers. He waded through the thin gray stalks. The grass grew to knee-height, pale and wispy, like a cloud frozen among the rocks. He stood among the wispy stalks, inspecting the foliage. Was it even the smoke grass? He wasn't sure. *This is folly. Damn the hunt, damn Arko Hark-Wadi and the crown of Harkana.*

It was nearly morning and if he couldn't sleep, he might as well make his way back down the mountain. He walked backward along the trail and then he saw them—white blooms where there had been none. In places, where the moonlight struck the grass, it had blossomed into patches of bright flowers. The smoke-grass flower was night blossoming, its white petals glowing blue in the moonlight. The warden had skipped this fact, or left it out on purpose, or did not know about its nocturnal nature.

The dog barked sharply.

Ren stopped. Turning, he heard a rustling in the brush, saw a shadow moving toward him in the moonlight, looming large and breathing heavily.

≋ 26 ≋

"Kepi, wake up." Seth's voice.

She blinked and opened her eyes. The gray bird was gone and it was noontime. She stood from her perch in the circle of stones, threw down the broken sword, and embraced him. "I thought you were dead."

"I—" The words caught in his throat. His hair covered his eyes and there was dirt on his chin and on his arms, scrapes on his hands and on his cheeks.

"I'm so sorry I lost you at the bridge," he said, his voice strained.

"We're together now. That's all that matters." She beamed at him, feeling relief wash over her. She was free—free of the San, free of Dagrun. Seth had saved her at the Rift valley, and what was more miraculous, he had found her in the Cragwood, found her amid a forest of stone.

The sunlight on the stone circle was like the first day there ever was.

"We should go. We'll need food, water. Horses if we can get them. If we can find our way to your family, everything will be all right," Kepi said.

"My family?"

"Yes, of course. Dagrun's caravan was attacked; I'm missing, most likely killed by the San. Don't you get it, Seth? I'm free. You can go home, to Barsip, and I can go home with you." *As your wife,* she thought, but was too shy to say, remembering the wedding cake they had shared.

"Right." Seth nodded, but he was looking at the stones, over his shoulder.

"Are you all right?" she asked, finally noticing how nervous he was. It was natural, they had both just survived the outlanders' attack.

He smiled and shook his head. "No. I mean, yes. I mean, I'm fine. It's good to see you, you're alive and that's all that matters."

"Let's go," she said, linking her arm in his.

For the first time in years she breathed deeply, comfortably. She had no sword in her hand, and she had no need for one. She felt safe. *When we reach Barsip I'll never need to wield another weapon.*

They left the throne and fled deeper into the Cragwood. The only direct route out of Feren was the way they had come, but there would be no way to cross one of the bridges over the Rift valley if Dagrun's men were holding them. They decided to head east, to take the long route along the valley toward the lowland passes, west of the Harkan Cliff, where the rift grew shallow and easier to cross. "Come on," Kepi said, practically pulling him by his tunic. After the trials of the day before, she felt nearly intoxicated, not quite believing in her good luck, almost singing as she dashed between the stones and scrambled over fallen logs.

"Slow down," Seth called. "Slow down, will you!" He sounded almost angry.

Ignoring his request, she leapt over a rock, tripped, and fell hard on the earth, nearly landing on her face. The gash over her eye, a present from the San warrior who had tried to kill her, tore open once more, blood leaking down the side of her face. The wound on her neck ached.

Seth caught up, helped her to sit up and calm down. He took the hem of his tunic and wiped the blood at her temple. He shook his head. "I told you to slow down," he said with an unhappy tone to his voice. "You, with all of your bruises, you're are always getting hurt."

She shook her head, still feeling exuberant, liberated. "I'm fine," she said. "I'm dead and I've never been happier."

He frowned. "We're not free yet."

"But we will be soon. Thanks to the San, I've finally found a way out of my marriage. If the Ferens think I am dead, they will finally leave me alone." Kepi would have the freedom she desired.

She took the piece of bread he offered her and devoured it. How clever of him to pack food. How resourceful he was, this boy she loved, so unlike Dagrun, who was used to having his way as he wanted, when he wanted.

Seth was the son of a crofter, and had once apprenticed with a physician. He understood herbs and tonics, and he was used to making do with little, used to caring for others. Even now, tending to her wound, he'd torn his tunic to bind the gash. It felt like the first day they had met. "When we get to the farm," she said, "do you think your mother would teach me to be a seamstress? I'd like that, I think. Learning to sew. To do something useful."

"My mother isn't much of a seamstress herself," Seth said, tying the ends into a firm knot. "But I suppose she might show you what she knows."

"My mother wasn't around to teach me to sew." Kepi picked at the torn place on Seth's shirt. "Maybe I'll fix this for you, when we get there."

"Hmm," Seth said, and then he was quiet.

Kepi was rubbing the torn fabric between her fingers, thinking of Seth's mother—would she teach Kepi to cook, to care for goats?—when underneath his tunic she saw a fresh cut arching across the smooth skin of Seth's belly. The gash was newly sutured, the stitches as small and neat as a physician's.

"What's this?" she asked. She had seen the outlanders draw a blade across his chest, but how had he managed to bandage the wound? Alone in the forest with no needles, no thread?

"Oh that," Seth said, tucking his shirt into his breeches now. "It's old. Yesterday, before the San attacked, I had a skirmish with a Feren soldier in the camp. He thought to best me in the ring, but I got a piece of him too."

He glanced to the side. The buzzing in the back of her head grew louder. Kepi had tried not to pay attention but there was something wrong here. Seth was edgy, unhappy, and unable to meet her eyes. He glanced behind them, at the way they had come. She realized he was waiting. But for what?

The bread. The stitches. At last she understood. "We're not escaping, are we?" she asked, all the joy gone from her voice.

Seth closed his eyes and took her hands in his. His face was long with anguish, his hands cold. "They're coming," he whispered. "The Ferens. They're following me here."

Kepi pulled her hands from his, disbelief etched all over her face.

"I had no choice," he told her. "They captured me as I entered the forest to find you. Dagrun said he would kill both of us if I didn't help them. I had to. I'm so sorry. I had to," he confessed, tears in his voice. "I'm so sorry, Kepi, I'm so sorry."

"No, no," she muttered.

She could have made her way out; she hadn't had to wait for him, she did so only because of love, but now her love would bind her to her enemy. Seth had sold them out for a threat. If it had been her who had been caught, she would have fought—she would have died fighting—so Seth would be able to live.

Instead Seth had chosen his life over hers.

The buzzing in her head exploded, burning and white with anger, anger that congealed like sour milk in her stomach along with the pain of sadness and disappointment. He was gentle and he was also weak. This boy she loved.

"We'll find another way to escape. We will, Kepi, I swear it," he cried, trying to reach for her hands again.

Kepi turned away from him; her vision had narrowed to a thin, dark tunnel, and at the end of it she saw not the boy she loved but a servant, a servant who had betrayed his mistress to save himself.

"I did what I could to keep us both alive. They said if I took their soldiers to you, all will be forgiven. Dagrun would stop hunting you, he wouldn't hurt you for running. And he'll allow me to stay on as your master-of-arms in Feren. He doesn't know about us."

"Seth—Dagrun wants me alive, I am no use to him dead. You did not buy my life, only my imprisonment," she said softly, as if explaining to a child. Kepi shook her head. Was it possible he was so simple? That he had not thought it through at all? "I should have died last night in the forest, let the San take me rather than live to see this day."

Seth shook his head desperately, but it was too late, they heard the Ferens approach—a clank of gauntlets, of swords.

Four men dressed in silvery armor, their chest plates bearing the Tree of Feren, appeared out of the mist and surrounded the couple. "Good work, boy," one of them said with a laugh.

Seth took a step back, his face red from weeping.

Kepi lowered her head as the soldiers bound her hands, and though she told herself she would not cry—not for Seth, not for herself—she cursed and swore at the Ferens, and in the struggle to hold back her tears her vision blurred as they led her back to the carriage.

⇒27⇐

The shadow and the rustling in the brush revealed an ordinary man and not the eld. The stranger was alone, dressed in gray robes, and he held a curved dagger in front of him, but loosely, as if he was not certain if he planned to use it.

He did not move. No wave. No greeting.

As Ren approached he saw he was a man of middle years—handsome, with dark hair and eyes, muscular, nearly as broad as Arko himself, with his chin raised as if he saw something in Ren he did not like. His thick black hair was silver at the temples, but there was no denying he was still in his prime, or that he seemed reluctant to greet Ren, waiting until the boy was an arm's length away before giving him the slightest nod.

"Your sister Merit sent me. I'm her husband, Shenn Wadi. I hope you don't mind, but it's long been practice for the heir to bring a man or two along to watch his back. Your father did it. Your grandfather too, from what I hear. It's just not sung about in the King's Hall." The man gave another barely perceptible bow as he stowed his knife and offered Ren his hand. The warden had told Arko's soldiers to leave the reserve, so how was it that Shenn had been able to enter it? Was it because he was married to Merit, his sister? Shenn was a member of the king's family.

Ren took his hand. "I don't need help, but I might like the company."

The man's grip had been cold and wet. Shenn was nervous, and his tone was overly bright. Ren had observed the same behavior in the priors when they were about to do something unexpected or unwanted. He hoped he was wrong, he hoped his sister was being overprotective, but his gut told him otherwise. "Thank you, brother."

Shenn folded his arms. "Don't thank me yet, I've heard the eld are bloody difficult to kill."

"If you say so," Ren replied absently. Who knew if the man was even telling the truth about who he was? Ren was all alone in the Shambles and he knew no one in Harkana. From what he could see, this man was clearly Harkan. He lacked the sophisticated manners and opulent attire Ren was accustomed to in Solus, the way the traveling lecturers in the Priory smelled of fresh cardamom or sweet cassia, their hair glistening with wax. The Harkans had none of that, even Shenn—who was well mannered and well dressed—looked common compared to the men of Solus, and he reeked of old castor oil. Still, Ren wanted to know more about his family and his people. He wanted to embrace the kingdom he would one day rule.

"Can you tell me about my sisters?" he asked. "I was sent away before I could meet them."

"If you wish," Shenn said reluctantly, as if the topic bored him but he would do it anyway. He spoke at length about his wife and her sister, about the clothes they wore and the place where they lived, how they looked and how they spent their days, how Kepi enjoyed sparring with her trainers while Merit managed the affairs of the kingdom. Each description, each detail—no matter how brief—made Ren eager for more. He wanted to fill the blank spot in his memory, the place where his childhood and his family should have been.

Impulsively, Ren thought to ask about his mother. Sarra Amunet, who was once Sarra Hark-Wadi, had left Harkana at nearly the same time that Ren had left the kingdom. The timing had always made Ren wonder if he were the reason for her leaving, if his exile in the Priory had somehow been the cause of their parting. He needed to know more. "Sarra Amunet, the Mother Priestess, does she visit Harkana—do you know her?"

Shenn shook his head. "She has little or no contact with the kingdom, and your sisters don't speak of her. I know as much as you, maybe less," he said, his tone telling Ren that he had nothing else to say on the topic. Surely that wasn't true, but Ren decided not to press him.

This man was his brother by custom of marriage, but Ren knew nothing about him. His accent and his manner were as strange as his face. He once more felt the urge to distrust Shenn, but he fought it. *I must forget the customs of Sola and embrace what is Harkan.* But he knew this would not come easily. *If a thing seems foreign we assume there's something wrong with it.* Without him knowing it, the Soleri had trained him to mistrust his people, to think of them as nothing but savages, barbarians at the walls. To assuage his uneasiness Ren kept up his inquiries, asking about Harkana, what the people ate, and how they lived. Shenn did his best to comply, but his answers were always too brief for Ren's taste.

As he asked his questions, the trail wound higher up the mountainside. The morning had come and the white flowers had disappeared, the buds closed once more in the warmth of the rising sun. Around them waves of steam rose off the rocks, making the air shimmer. Ren recalled his lectures in rhetoric, the way the priors would ask the boys seemingly simple questions, although the answers they were seeking were far more complicated. He wondered if it would work on Shenn, or if the man was too clever, or too experienced, to fall for such a ruse.

"This grass," Ren said, turning to Shenn with wide-eyed innocence. "What's it called?"

Shenn gave a slight smile. "Smoke grass. Didn't the warden tell you?"

"Not really. Maybe he did. Maybe I wasn't paying attention. Does the eld eat it, the grass, I mean?"

"No, it feeds on the rodents that eat the grass. The eld has a taste for their sweet blood." Shenn picked up a dead branch and thrashed the smoke grass, flushing out a medium-sized rat, a fat, furred creature that scampered away with a squeak. "There's more at the higher altitudes," he said. "The eld hunts them. It'll scoop up ten or twenty in a day, given the chance."

"So many?" Ren asked. He had starved in the Priory but would eat his fingers before he ate one of the skittering creatures that filled the wispy grass.

Shenn shrugged. "We should be grateful the eld has a taste for rats rather than men."

"Maybe I will be, if I ever get off this mountain."

They spent the afternoon following the smoke-grass trail, resting, sharing provisions. Later, the trail ended at a stream and a slim waterfall. "We'll need to climb," Shenn said, shading his eyes and looking up. Ren did not like being alone with the man, especially on the more treacherous cliffs, but he had no way to get rid of Shenn, so he tried to put some distance between himself and his brother.

They traveled up the path that ran alongside the crashing water, the dog close at Ren's heels. The path led away from the stream, up the sheer side of the precipice. To double back around to the smoke grass, they skirted along the cliff, though this time there were no planks or ropes, just a slender ledge and some wedgelike handholds carved into the cliff face. How he would get back carrying the eld horns, even if he were to kill the beast, he couldn't imagine.

It was then, with the dog barking and fear in his throat, that Ren saw his so-called brother tear one of the handholds free, cracking the ancient stone. Shenn continued ahead, without warning him. Ren would have to continue moving without the use of the hold. Shenn watched and they locked eyes. Ren stretched his arms, feeling them lengthen as he reached around the splintered rock to the next hold. He balanced, his hand in the air as he grasped for, then gripped, the next handhold. He teetered and nearly fell, but his grip held and he was able to gain his balance. A few more steps and he reached the end of the narrow passage.

Shenn kept his distance, moving ahead, not looking back.

Had his brother tried to kill him? Had he fractured the handhold on purpose? It had happened so quickly Ren had not had time to process what he'd witnessed. Again, he wondered why the man was here. What were his true intentions? Ren didn't know, but he guessed they were not good. At the ridge he caught sight of a stream and more smoke grass, and he used it as an excuse to pick up the pace.

"Slow down, boy," Shenn called. "What's the rush? The eld will come when it chooses. The hunt is about waiting." He quickened his pace. "Come, let's find a perch and wait for the animal. An eld is trapped, not hunted."

Ren would not listen, nor would he allow Shenn to draw any closer to him.

His brother by law smiled too broadly, his voice was too loud but trailed off at the end of each sentence. "Did you know that your grand-father lured the eld into a pit? And that your father trapped his between a pair of rocks?"

Ren did not answer, struggling to keep the distance between them as his suspicions about Shenn multiplied, but the stones grew denser and he was forced to slow his pace.

Shenn approached, his breath quickening, and Ren thought he saw his hand reach for his dagger.

But just then the dog began to bark, running up the trail, and from far away there came a great howl, long and low and angry—the eld. Ren gave Shenn a questioning look, and the two of them turned and pursued the animal, following the dog's yelps as it went deeper into the woods.

Along the narrow steephead valley, at the source of the clear spring that had carved the ravine into the rock, they found the dog circling, pant-ing, sniffing the air. The peaks rose in a sheer cliff above their heads, but there was nothing there.

No eld. The sun was setting, the air once more growing cold, the smoke grass undulating in the wind.

The dog looked up at the edges of the valley and gave a quick bark.

"Don't worry," Shenn murmured to Ren, coming up and taking the boy by the elbow, his eyes never leaving Ren, the knife in his hand.

Ren's suspicions were correct: Shenn was not there for the eld.

"What will you tell my sister?" Ren asked. "After?"

"That the job is done," he said, "that I did what her boys failed to do in the Hollows or in the bordertowns."

So that was who wanted him dead. His own kin. His own sister had sent the gray-cloaked men who had trailed Ren since his release from the Priory. His own family was behind it. Ren had been too eager to trust the Harkans, to be their king. He had tried to befriend Shenn, but it had clearly been a waste of time. It was true what they said back at the Priory, that ransoms were seldom welcome back home. He had pushed

the thought from his mind, but he could no longer deny it. The truth lay
in the dagger Shenn held in his hand.

What was family when you were taken from them at three years
of age?

Ren had no family.

He had no one but his fellow ransoms. Adin. Tye. They would never
break his confidence or turn on him.

They were all he had left.

"It'll hurt more if you fight me," Shenn said, lunging with his knife—

Ren twisted away from the killing blow just as the eld leapt from the
outcropping above, its hoof and horn hitting Shenn flat in the chest.

The creature trampled over him, screaming its outrage as it pounded
on Shenn's chest with its large hooves while the dog snapped at its heels.
The eld's front hoof caught Shenn's cloak, and dragged him for a few paces
before his shoulder hit a large stone, wedging him there while the animal bucked and screamed, shaking its head violently and laying down its
horns, aiming them at Shenn's throat. A lunge, a scrape, and Shenn's blood
poured out—but from his shoulder, Ren saw, not the throat, as the horns
had nearly missed him.

Shenn fought back; he slashed at the eld with his dagger, but Ren could
see that his strength was already gone. The dagger severed the hide, but
the wounds were only glancing and did little to deter the eld. The creature smashed Shenn against the rock, then retreated, craning its neck, dis-
playing its mighty antlers in all their glory, the white bifurcating tusks
glistening in the light.

Then the creature bent its horns toward Shenn once more.

Ren hefted a mighty stone and hurled it at the eld, knocking the animal
hard on the skull, just above the eyes. The eld roared, doubled back, and
paused, its attention turning toward the new distraction.

Ren froze, his mind spinning. He was shaken by the sudden appearance of the eld, the trampling of Shenn, but most of all his words—*the
job is done.* His own family, his sister wanted him dead. What sense was
there in any of this, in trying to win his horns and the throne of Harkana
if the family he had suffered for was as ruthless as the men who had kept
him locked in the Priory?

In his anger, he locked eyes with the eld and the creature bellowed,
mist rising from its nostrils, the antlers glistening like a crown of thorns.
The eld bent its head and charged. The creature swept its many-pointed
antlers from side to side, scraping the earth. Ren sidestepped the antlers.

He hit the ground rolling and landed in a cloud of sand not far from Shenn. The man was spitting blood, his hands shaking, trying to find the wound, the gash that was leaking blood onto the sand. Shenn's face was white, lips purple. Ren glanced from his brother to the eld and back. *I should help him.* Assassin or not, Ren didn't like the idea of leaving his brother to bleed out while Ren pursued the hunt. So, he hurled a stone at the eld, then another. The creature retreated, then circled, giving Ren time to rip a piece of cloth from Shenn's tunic and place it on the wound.

"Hold it here," he said. Ren took Shenn's hand and showed him where to apply the pressure, but his brother's arm fell limply back to his side.

Just then, the eld charged. Ren grasped Shenn's dagger and threw it at the creature. The blade struck the eld's right flank, digging into the muscle. The creature roared its fury, charging past Ren, shaking wildly and trying to dislodge the blade.

"I've bought us some time," Ren said as he tore more cloth from Shenn's tunic. He wound the fabric around his brother's chest, passing it beneath his shoulders. "Here," Ren said, taking Shenn's hand again and pressing it once more to the wound. Behind them, hooves clattered on the earth.

As the eld bore down upon him, Ren managed to throw himself mostly out of its path, but the eld's horns caught his foot, sending him tumbling to the earth. *That's what I get for helping Shenn.* He scolded himself for aiding his brother, even though it was the right thing to do.

Ren leapt to his feet, his clothes matted with dirt and dashed with Shenn's blood. He held out his father's dagger as the eld circled, coming around for another attack. It wasn't until he saw the slender blade silhouetted against the mighty eld horns that a thought occurred to Ren: *Why such a tiny knife?* The dagger was simply too short to wield against the eld. Each of the eld horns was about the length of his outstretched arm, while the dagger was not much longer than the width of his hand. *I need a bloody two-handed sword.* The dagger might as well be a sewing needle for all the good it would do him.

The eld advanced and so did Ren. He took two great strides forward and ducked when the creature raised its horns. He came up behind the mighty tusks. Instinctively, his hand shot out, and his fingers wrapped the nearest eld horn, holding tightly around the burr as he pulled himself up onto the creature's back. The eld bucked furiously back and forth as it tried to knock him to the ground where it could trample him with its hooves.

Ren struggled as best he could, finding strength where he thought he had none. His grip was iron and he held on with everything he had. The creature kicked again and he caught sight of something odd, a section of horn that was shorn off at the base. A flash of inspiration struck him: There was no need to fight the eld, no use in it whatsoever. The dagger Arko had given him was too short, and its serrated edge was not meant for stabbing or cutting flesh.

He put one hand to the eld's forelocks and gently caressed the gray tuft of hair. "Easy," he whispered as he tightened his legs around eld's flanks. "Easy," he repeated as he coaxed the creature to sit. The wild beast should have thrown him to the ground, but it didn't.

The eld kneeled, folding its legs beneath it, its muzzle coming to rest on the earth. When the eld was at last still, Ren noticed something else. There were narrow slits above the creature's eyes and when the eld sat they winked open. The creature had four eyes, and all of them were trained on him. *This is no deer. What is it?* he wondered, unable to breathe, gripped by awe.

The great eld horns rose up on both sides of him, and among the forked tines of its antlers he saw two or three more places where a section of the horns had been shorn off.

It was never my task to kill the eld. Ren recalled his father's words when he handed him the knife: Use this to *claim* the eld horns. He'd never asked Ren to kill the creature. The knife was made for sawing, so Ren put the blade to the horns.

The creature shifted beneath him. He feared the eld would resist, that it would throw him to the ground, but it made no effort to dislodge him and Ren worked as quickly as he could. "Be still," he coaxed the great eld. "Be still, you magnificent creature, and I'll be done in a flash."

The severed horn came loose and Ren took it in his hand. The other sections of horn were cut with the same serrated edge as the one he held in his hand. *My father once sat here with this same blade and sawed a horn from this very creature.* Arko had sat in Ren's place and his father's father and his father before him had done the same. Each man had taken his horns from the great beast—each had discovered how to subdue the eld without killing it.

This was the gratifying secret behind the king's hunt, one Ren hoped his own son would one day discover.

He dismounted, took two steps backward, and faced the eld. The creature stood gracefully, its four eyes winking. It bowed its head as it disappeared into the dark of the wood. *Is there only one eld?* he wondered, but quickly realized he might never learn the answer. *No wonder the peasants still worship it.*

Excitement shivered through his body. *It's done. The hunt is over.* He felt not only satisfied but also fulfilled. When the eld bowed its crown of horns, when it at last submitted itself to the king, Ren had felt a connection to something primal, a thing buried deep within all living things, a resonance that now echoed from within him.

It's as if I've touched Mithra Himself.

Shenn saw Ren return holding the white horns. "You have the horns; you are king of Harkana. Is the beast dead?"

Ren shrugged, holding the eld horn in one hand like a cane. The secrets of the hunt belonged to the kings of Harkana.

"Help me," Shenn whimpered, his face smeared with blood—his own, the eld's. "I can't breathe. Help me . . . brother . . . king . . ."

Ren clambered to Shenn's side. He eased him to the ground, supporting his back as he laid him flat on the earth. Shenn clutched his stomach, still desperately trying to stanch the bleeding.

Ren bent over Shenn and put a hand on his chest cautiously, and determined that his ribs were probably broken. "You're lucky it wasn't worse," he said, his hands soaked in Shenn's blood.

"I'm lucky you're fast," he gasped. "That could have been the end of me."

"I'll bandage your wounds," Ren said. Shenn had a little water in an oilskin and Ren poured it over the bloody spot. The wound was not as bad as he had originally thought, but the man still had a pair of broken ribs. He took a clean piece of Shenn's robe and wrapped his chest as best he could. *I'm not a physician. For all I know I'm hurting the man, but I doubt that's the case.* He thought to tie him up, but he doubted Shenn could move, not yet.

"What are you going to do with me?" Shenn asked.

Ren wasn't certain what to do yet, so he made a fire. He found dried strips of meat tucked in Shenn's robes and took them. The dog whimpered and Ren tossed the pup a stick. The two men sat in silence, Ren warming his hands against the flame, the older man moaning over his wounds. Every now and then Shenn would speak to him, his voice fading in and out. The bleeding had stopped, and although he looked weak his brother would live.

"I don't even know Merit," Ren said aloud. "And she doesn't even know me and yet she wants me dead rather than alive." Ren brooded. He felt numb, cold. "I've never even met her," he said as he stoked the fire.

"Nor should you." Shenn coughed blood and winced at the pain. "Few people in Harkana have seen your face. I know I am the last person you trust right now, but listen. Use this to your advantage. Flee. Otherwise, your sister will never stop hunting you. Everywhere she has eyes and ears. The crown Arko wishes to place on your head offers little protection. If you seek the throne of Harkana, you'll spend your life looking over your shoulder, watching the shadows. You won't even dare to eat your morning meal without someone tasting it first. She will fight you for her kingdom. The people respect Merit. She has been queen in all but name until now.

"But if you leave us, if you go peacefully, I'll return and tell her you're dead. It will buy you some time. You've spent ten years watching over your shoulder in the Priory, why spend another forty doing the same? Run. Go away. Make a new life for yourself. I have provisions. In time I can offer you coin. I can help you." He tossed a bag toward Ren.

Ren picked it up. It held salted meat, a few coins.

"You'll need this if you want to live." He threw the bag back to Shenn. "I'm certain the warden will help you return to Harwen."

Shenn shook his head, as if that were not a possibility. "What will you do? Where will you go?"

Ren doused the fire with a handful of sandy earth but gave no reply.

"I shall tell your sister you are dead," called Shenn as Ren walked away.

Ren shuddered inwardly. Without a name, without a home, he was nothing. He would not give up his birthright so easily. "No. I'm done playing dead. Tell my sister I live, and I will take what is mine." He gripped the eld horns. He was the true heir of Harkana and he would claim the horned throne and rule his father's kingdom.

Without looking back once, he left the man, alone, in the dark, with no fire and no food and only the bitter cold of the mountain and the lowing of the eld to keep him company.

⇟ 28 ⇞

The Repository at Desouk was the largest building in the city of priests, superior in size and importance to any structure within the city, its great hall like the vaulted half of a gigantic barrel full of echoes of sound and dust motes and the smell of time. Sarra Amunet, the Mother Priestess, spotted Noll, waiting for her on the repository steps. Nearby, Ott sat on a low stool, engaged in a game of Coin with another young priest. A crowd of beggar children had gathered around him, watching the match and listening to Ott as he gestured to the various pieces, moving his good arm about in the air. Between turns Ott fed the children with cakes of bread, ensuring that he had an audience.

Noll waved to Sarra. "I've been watching your scribe," he said.

"Have you?" she asked as she joined him on the steps.

"He comes to the plaza every day and feeds the starvelings, teaches them Coin and chats with them about God-knows-what. Sometimes I think he feeds them from his own allotment."

"The boy can't help himself, he's thinner than a beanpole, but he gives his bread to the blind children and the buskers in the plaza," she said.

"He has a kind heart and keen mind, but surely the Mother Priestess could find a more suitable scribe?"

"Let me know if you find one," said Sarra. She made her words sound like a jest, but her face held no mirth. "You must know a few things about beggars, Noll. Your accent is Wyrren—isn't it?"

"Yes, my humble upbringings betray me." The boy clutched his oil-skin sack.

"Where in the southern islands are you from?" Sarra asked. It had been years since she had seen her home in the south.

"Vimur," Noll murmured, his accent suddenly strong. "I was raised in the northern reaches, but when I became a hierophant I asked to be posted in the southernmost islands."

"The Stone Reefs? Scargill or Thurso?"

"A bit of both."

"Why would you go—"

"There? I had my reasons. In the Stone Reefs, there are temples and towers that no scribe has seen in centuries. In the untamed islands there are many relics a scribe cannot find in Desouk or anywhere else. From my earliest memory, the gods have fascinated me: their sacred language, their golden masks, the way the Soleri shelter behind the Shroud Wall. I wanted to read their language so that I might understand a bit more about our unseen rulers."

"And you found that knowledge in the reefs? I was told you found a great number of ancient scrolls, and that you used those scrolls to some-how decipher the Soleri symbols."

"The reef folk use the parchment scrolls as bedding. The men sleep on them, the women sew clothes from them. When the locals held up the parchments, they saw only goatskins."

"I see. And those scrolls were the keys used to understand the old sym-bols?" Sarra asked.

Noll nodded slightly.

Sarra stood. "Show me what you have found."

They walked up the stairs and through the arched doorway into the repository. Inside, the priests and priestesses went about their business, lighting the alabaster lamps, laying out offerings to the statue of Mithra. Acolytes wandered the stepped platforms, arranging scrolls on tables and stands. Priests held amber parchments up to the lamps, straining to read ancient markings while all around them servants rolled carts and brushed dust from the many racks. Priests talked and argued, their voices mingling with the sounds of rumpling scrolls and birds fluttering in the vault.

As they made their way, Sarra told Noll about the repository, describing the many tunnels beneath the stacks, the organization of the scrolls, and the archives on the upper level. She detailed the repository's rare collections and treasured artifacts. From the Salt Barrens, there were parchments fash-ioned from human skin and inked in ochre-stained fingerprints. From the Wyrre, the archive held oracle bones made from the plastrons of great sea turtles, carved in bone script by shamans of the old faith. There were the butterfly manuscripts from Zagre with their long, spindly leaves and elaborately carved symbols. And, from the Riksard, the repository base-ment held sandstone tablets chiseled in a forgotten tongue, lumps of stone so great they had not been moved in centuries.

A priest approached Sarra, then another and another. As Sarra walked, as she guided Noll through the hall, priests trailed behind them. Since her return from Solus and her escape from the riots, her priests and acolytes bowed a little more deeply and approached her a bit more often. Each time they were eager to inquire about her time in Solus, to hear how the Mother was touched by Mithra and spirited through the crowds. Always she refused these requests, hoping her reticence would add to her mystique, and it had.

At the far end of the hall, a white-robed priestess greeted Sarra and Noll and led them down a stair to a closed chamber beneath the great floor of the repository. Inside, a pair of scribes wearing the simple wrap of the acolyte—a robe cinched beneath the arms and wrapped into a tight roll across the breast—was kneeling on the floor, eyes deep in thought.

Sheets covered in charcoal impressions blanketed the chamber floor. The mountain chamber Sarra had visited with Noll two days prior had proven a difficult worksite. To make the work easier, Noll had ordered the scribes to make rubbings of the marks they found in the old grain silo and to arrange those rubbings on the floor of this chamber. The priests had carefully marked all of the extraneous symbols with an *x,* making the text legible without the aid of the late-day sun.

Sarra knelt alongside the scribes.

"Some symbols defied translation," Noll said, kneeling as well. "The carvings were either damaged or worn. Perhaps one in eight was illegible. In another week, I can finish. Look at this," he said, retrieving a drawing from the floor.

"What is it?" Sarra asked.

"A map of the empire's storehouses, dating to the reign of Den."

"And?" Sarra asked eagerly.

"Ott confirmed that most of these were previously discovered and emptied."

"Useless."

"Wait, there's more. We found a series of characters labeling a road. When transposed the symbols read 'Amaran Road.'"

"A road to connect the storehouses?" Sarra translated.

"Maybe. This is the character for house." Noll drew the symbol on a tablet.

"And this is the character for storehouse." He drew another.

"Except for the gap, they're nearly identical," Sarra observed.

"That's the issue," Noll said. "Dozens of symbols share the arrow shape—in many cases I cannot be certain which variation we are reading. The structures might be storehouses or they could be any kind of house—goat houses even."

Sarra groaned.

"But there is hope. At the road's end, we found a third symbol." Noll scratched the mark on the tablet with chalk.

"The symbol combines three ideas: house, stone, and stars. The order dictates the overall meaning. When drawn in this configuration, the symbol reads 'house of stone, house of stars.' We found instances of this same mark in the documents loaned from the Harkan repository. We were uncertain why the Harkan literature referenced the symbol until we found the road."

"The road leads to Harkana?"

Noll nodded reluctantly. "To the Shambles. We could send priests, but the Shambles is a forbidden place. Only Harkan royalty are permitted to enter the sacred grounds."

Sarra knew the prohibitions attached to the Shambles. She was once Harkan royalty herself, and since Arko had stripped her of her title but had never disowned her, she was still due the benefits of the king's wife. But she had not stepped foot within Harkana since she left her husband ten years prior. The Shambles was a dangerous place, filled with reavers and outlanders from the High Desert. She risked her life by going there.

Sarra leaned over the drawings, studying the symbols and considering her options. She had searched for storehouses all over the empire and had found success, but more often than not she had found only failure, tombs and caverns that had long ago been emptied of their grain by thieves or animals or the elements. In the past, she had sent only acolytes to search for the grain, but now she must make the journey herself.

Is the amaranth worth my life? Maybe. A new storehouse might put off the impending crisis, buying her a few more years. If the shortage were discovered, the rabble would tear her apart, just like they did with Garia on the last day of the year.

In the end, she had little choice in the matter.

"I'll go to the Shambles. I was once their queen," she said. "If I make the journey, the Harkans will not block our convoy. As a member of their first family it is within my right to request an escort and entry into the Shambles." She would send word to the Harkans, requesting soldiers and horses to aid her on their journey.

Noll looked uncertain, but Sarra saw no other way. "You'll come along as well," Sarra said, urging him to stand. "We leave in two days' time."

⇥29⇤

"Why have *you* come?" Arko said to the slender man who stood in the doorway. Groggy from sleep, he remembered only vaguely what happened the day before, the tour of the Empyreal Domain, and the bloody spot Suten left when he fell dead on the stones. Afterward Arko had stumbled back into the Hollows of Solus. He had not wanted to slumber in the domain of the Soleri. The thought of sleeping there gave him a bitter chill, so he had sought accommodations elsewhere. In the many waiting rooms outside of the Shroud Wall he had found this small chamber with an unused pallet, and had made his bed.

Now someone had come to wake him. The man was short and slender, robed in gold, his skin as dark and wrinkled as a sun-dried date, his bald head stippled with silvery hairs. The man did not reply to Arko's question, which had long since passed. He only waved his hands in fawning motions as he knelt before Arko, his forehead touching the stone as he bowed to the new Ray of the Sun.

"Up," said Arko. And the man stood, slowly.

"My lord," the man said, "I am Khalden Wat, the servant of the Ray.

I've been looking for you. It's my duty, my master, Suten Anu, bid me to serve you."

"Your master is gone." Suten Anu was rotting in the throne room of the Soleri, but this man didn't know that; he could not enter the domain of the emperors.

The servant nodded. "He bid me to guide you in the ways of the Soleri and the customs of the court. That is why I am here."

"Well, what is it then?" Arko asked impatiently.

"It is time," said Wat, "for the new Ray to perform his first and most important duty."

"What's that?"

"Letting them know you exist."

Arko raised an eyebrow.

"It is time for the people of Sola to wake up to a new Ray. The light must shine upon the mountain, then the people will know that a new Ray wears the Eye of the Sun."

"Give me a moment," Arko grumbled. His muscles ached and his head throbbed. He pushed himself up onto his elbows and swung his legs over the side of the bed. A deep sluggishness had settled into all of his limbs, so that it took him a great deal of mental and physical effort just to move his arms and legs. Lying on the bed far belowground, crouching in the meager chamber, he had the feeling of being buried alive—a not entirely unwelcome sensation, given the magnitude of the task that Suten Anu had left to him. In many ways he wished the old man had simply taken his head, rather than the other way around. No. Arko took back his wish. He did not regret what he'd done, the task he had accepted, the life he had taken. He felt sick, dizzy. There was blood on his hands and he needed a drink. He had grown accustomed to starting his day with an oilskin of amber, sometimes two. *How shall I eat? Who will feed me?*

Wat glanced at his bloodied hands, but he made no mention of them. "There is a tower at the far end of the Empyreal Domain, a structure set apart from the others. The men and women of the Kiltet service this place; go there and they will provide you with food and clothing, anything you require. Once you are Ray, when this day is finished, you will have no need to visit this place." He wiped a strip of dust from the wall. "This is a place for ghosts, come here too often and you might scare them away." Wat rubbed the gray dust from his finger. "The tower was Suten's home, and now it is yours. You may go there when we are finished. Today we travel to another place, to a chamber buried deep beneath the mountain."

Arko stood, brushed the sleep from his eyes, and pushed his hair back behind his ears. When he was ready, Wat lit a lamp and led him out of the room, following a path different from the one Arko had taken the previous day. Wat guided him through underground chambers of mag nificent size. The halls here were brightly ornamented. Slabs of calcite, lapis, jade, and alabaster painted the walls, each stone emblazoned with the symbols of the forgotten tongue. *These passages belong to the Soleri. These halls are meant for gods.* Indeed, he noticed the exaggerated height of the ceilings, the preposterous width of the corridors. This was a space built for beings whose proportions, or at least their egos, must have dwarfed those of normal men.

"All this was theirs?" Arko asked. "They lived here once?"

"A long time ago," Wat said, pointing to the shallow grooves in the floor. "A hundred generations of Soleri walked these corridors before they sealed themselves behind the Shroud Wall. Now only the Ray may gaze upon their likeness," he said, reaching another door and pushing it open. "Come." Wat beckoned. "The people await their new steward."

Arko followed the old man through a warren of long corridors—some brightly painted, others flecked in silver and electrum—keeping his eyes on the lamp that Wat held the way he had kept his eyes on the lamp the emperor's blind women had used. It was unexpected to learn that so much of life in Sola was lived underground. This was the city of the sun, and yet since he had arrived, he was constantly in darkness. Could he possibly get used to it? Living buried in the earth like a mole? These brightly colored walls were no substitute for the sun. As king of Harkana he had lived entirely in the open, his successes and failures all perfectly clear to both his friends and his enemies. This was something new; now he would have to get used to the shadows.

Down they went, into the bowels of the earth far below the city of light, far below the city of darkness even. They walked in a place beyond the Hollows, journeying past caverns of glittering black stone and dried-out caves of water. Stalactites dripped stone from the ceiling, forming little hillocks and hollows and tunnels, sometimes narrowing to dark passage-ways, sometimes opening up into great halls many stories high. For hours they journeyed in near silence, only their sandals breaking the quiet.

After a time, the rough stones gave way to a smoothly carved floor.

"Above us, on the surface, it is afternoon and the sun is low in the sky and this part of the mountain is cloaked in shadow. Time to begin the rite," Wat said without explaining himself any further. Listening to the old man speak, Arko barely noticed that he had stopped walking. They were in front of a door, one that appeared black at first but as the two men came closer and the light fell across it, it bloomed into a glossy amber, the color of the sky at the edge of morning. The stone was veined with white and brown streaks, polished so that the flames, and the men, were reflected on its translucent surface.

"Here's where I leave you," Wat said. He reached down and lifted the bronze ring, and the door swung open easily, as if it had been opened just yesterday instead of half a lifetime ago. "Your passage starts here. You will do as all have done who have taken the Ray's seat, you must walk alone, deep into the mountain. You must find the Ray's staff and fit it with the glowing citrine that Suten Anu pressed into your hands. The Eye of the Sun."

"Then what?" Arko asked, but Wat would not explain further.

Sighing, Arko took a lamp from the wall and pushed through the door. It shut behind him with a barely audible *click*.

When he was alone, Arko took a moment to take stock of where he was. The chill he had felt outside the door seemed to dissipate almost immediately, replaced with dense, humid warmth, making him break out in a light sweat along his hairline and across his upper lip. The floor was smooth and worn, the space dark, though he could see a hint of light on the edge of the wall along the chamber, a fleeting glimpse like a shooting star, a spark caught by the lamp and winking back at him. The echo of his footsteps and the eddies in the air gave him the feeling of being inside a great space, though the dark pressed in, pressed down, until he almost felt as desperate as the blind men who begged at the gates of Harwen, except instead of food and water all he sought were answers and a sense of purpose to this journey.

He was meant to find a staff, of all things, in which to place the great jewel. *Then what?* He knew the answer as well as the old servant: then he would be the Ray of the Sun, the most powerful man in all of Solus. Arko had come to the city expecting to meet the divine, and instead of seeing the face of god he was shown his own face in the mirror. *This is all that is left of the Soleri,* Suten had told him, *and so the First Ray of the Sun continues the tradition; we serve an absent emperor, and with our service we preserve the peace of all the kingdoms.*

Arko wandered the dark passageways until he found the door of a small anteroom, a tiny chamber carved into the stone at the far edge of the cavern. He bent down and ducked inside. In a narrow space, a small round room carved with the names of the dead Rays—Ined Anu, one said; Heruhirmaat Anu, said another—and at last he found the staff, bronzed and polished and balanced upright in the middle of the floor. At its head was a golden circle carved with symbols he could not read, and in the middle of that, a small recess just big enough for a single yellow jewel.

He laid down the lamp, took the jewel from his pocket, and placed it in the hollow, but nothing happened. He picked up the staff from its resting place, but when he closed his fingers around it, he was not transformed. He was alone in the dark with a staff and a jewel and no idea what he was supposed to do with any of it.

Arko muttered a curse, frustrated. Picking up the lamp once more, he spied a pair of doors at the far end of the cavern, their surface cast with images of the rising sun, a radiant landscape soaked with the golden light of Mithra-Sol. He pushed open the doors and stumbled forward, but still there was darkness, nothing special about it except for a ray of light that came in from someplace up on the surface, a pinprick really. He eyed the staff. *Perhaps I'm supposed to use it as a blind beggar uses his cane.* Another thought occurred to him just as quickly: *lift it up.* Taking the staff, he raised it high above his head. The Eye of the Sun seemed to seek the shaft of light of its own accord, grabbing the light as a lodestone grabs a lump of iron.

With a flash—

The light exploded from the Eye of the Sun in infinite multiplication. Out and out and out it flew into the vast blackness that surrounded Arko Hark-Wadi, gathering strength and growing in intensity until it was so bright that it seemed Arko stood inside a flame—a bitterly cold flame that made him want to shiver. The room was full of crystals, great yellow crystals of the same shade as the Eye, the finest quartz and citrine in the entire world. When at last the light seemed to peak, Arko lowered the staff, sensing the glow would not fade, and indeed it did not. Light continued to shine all around him, twinkling and pulsing.

The passages he had walked had taken him deep within the heart of the mountain. He had sensed that the cavern was large, but now that he could see it clearly, the cave was so vast that any notion of size or scale was subsumed by the space. The crystal formation captured the single ray of light that had come from above and multiplied it endlessly. It was like witnessing the beginning of the world, the birth of the universe, a thing so new it did not cast shadows.

The light that reflected in the cave could be seen through a breach in the shadow-drenched mountain, sparkling like a star in the heavens. When the people of Solus saw the cavern's light shoot through the twilight sky, they knew that the Ray of the Sun was dead, and a new Ray of the Sun had been chosen.

The light reflected from the cave was the light of Mithra-Sol.

A new Ray of the Sun glowing in the darkness.

Blessed by the gods of the Soleri.

It was impossible to measure distance in that strange pulsating space, Arko tried to count his steps but lost track after two. There was no way he could concentrate. He felt his hands shaking and gripped the staff as tightly as he could. The room seemed to grow colder and colder as he approached the far end, and he seemed to grow older and weaker with each step. Without realizing it, he began to lean on the staff. Never mind how holy it was—without its support, he would collapse. The weight of the light was too heavy for any man to bear.

When Arko was sure he could no longer endure the exhaustion, Khalden Wat entered the chamber. He met Arko's gaze and nodded—the task was complete. The empire knew of the new Ray's ascension.

Arko dropped his staff and it rolled to the floor.

I am the First Ray of the Sun.

I have to send word to my family that I am alive.

THE NIGHT WEDDING

30

The blackthorn tree shivered in its death throes.

Deep in the Gray Wood, slaves wearing little more than breechcloths scurried up the winding scaffold that ringed the tree, making the ancient wood shake with motion. Merit followed the busy workers as they surrounded the trunk, scraping at its tough bark with sharpened flints till the gnarled black hide gave way to pale sapwood. She counted a hundred men involved in the felling, maybe more. The sun was nearly set and, although the work had begun before dawn, the workers were only now reaching the tree's lower sections. The first rite of the Feren king's wedding, the felling of a blackthorn, was nearly half complete. Merit had hoped to avoid the long ceremony, but Dagrun had insisted she join him.

On the roads between the kingdoms, she heard rumors about the fate of the Mother Priestess during the Devouring that never came. Some said the pilgrims dragged the Mother from the wall and tore her limb from limb. But others swore her followers had shepherded her through the city unharmed. Merit didn't know which was the truth and which was the lie, perhaps neither was true. The riots in Solus made communication with her emissaries in the capital nearly impossible. She would have to wait to know the truth, which left her feeling cold and uncertain. She never knew what to think of Sarra Amunet. *You are the Mother of the faithful, the mother of thousands, but you never took the time to be my mother, to be a mother to your own family.* Merit did not even know why her mother had left them. It was Sarra's choice, Arko told her again and again, but he offered no further explanation. Merit had her suspicions, she guessed Ren was the cause—that Sarra could not stand to lose her son to the Priory. But the loss of one child was hardly reason to give up on the rest of the family. *Why not stay with your daughters?*

The sound of wood breaking caught Merit's attention. Presently, she stood atop a hastily assembled platform, the king at her side, along with a host of other dignitaries, all of them gathered to watch the Feren rite. A branch fell from the upper half of the trunk, its thorny pods showering the platform. She snatched one of the pods and held it up to the light. The shell was as hard as iron; a needle pricked her thumb. The blackthorn was named for its spiky seed, but she could not help but think the empire's name for it was more appropriate. In Solus, they called it ironwood; there the wood had been used to make mighty barques, trestle bridges, and breaching towers of exceptional strength and longevity since the earliest days of the empire. The blackthorn trees stretched two, sometimes three times the height of a desert palm. And while the Feren commoners fashioned their homes from the smallest trees, the king reserved the cutting of the largest blackthorns for royal events: funerals and coronations. For his wedding, the king ordered the felling of several of the oldest blackthorns as well as his birth tree, the one that was planted on the day he left his mother's womb. The Ferens called it Cutting Day. An honor Merit guessed her absent sister would neither care for nor appreciate.

The bride had not yet reached Rifka, but preparations for the wedding continued apace. Nobody seemed much concerned, least of all Dagrun. "We found her in the Cragwood," he said as the slaves swarmed the fallen trunk with their axes and picks. "We caught her servant escaping into the stones, and he led my soldiers to her," he said with a confident shrug before returning his attention to the felling. "She'll be safe in Rifka in a few days' time."

"A relief," said Merit. And it was indeed a relief. She had sought only to marry her sister off, not to see her set loose among the outlanders. Immediately, it felt as though a weight had been lifted from her shoulders. When she'd first heard of Kepi's escape, of the battle at the Rift valley, Merit had briefly doubted the path she had chosen. She feared she had gone too far. But now that Kepi was safe once more, Merit's confidence had returned.

"Your husband," Dagrun said, without looking at her, "have you heard from the man?"

"No. Shenn will join us when he is finished." She hoped he was finished, she hoped her husband had done what her men had failed to do in the Hollows and again in the bordertowns. *It is mercy,* she told herself. *It is better if the boy never reaches Harwen—better if I never see his face.* She'd spent years telling herself the kingdom was better off without a ransom for a king. But in truth, she had gotten used to the throne and had no intention of giving it up, least of all for her father's true heir.

Dagrun and Merit were not alone. For appearance's sake, an emissary from Rachis and three warlords of Feren had joined them on the ceremonial platform. The man from Rachis, Kal Bendal, dressed in the deep purple of the mountain lords, occupied a folding stool, while Ferris Mawr of Caerwynt and Deccan Falkirk of Caerfrae sat on blackthorn stools and chewed nuts as the slaves sawed at the tree. Each man wore the colors of his clan. Deccan wore the gray and white, while Ferris donned the green and black. The last of the tribal warlords refused to sit. Brock Sutharian of the Northwoods—the land of the graythorn, the forest beyond the Gray Wood—paced, looking uncomfortable. Merit guessed he was unused to ceremony. The men of the Northwoods were said to live within the trees themselves, in great hollows carved in the ancient graythorns. Brock wore clothes of his own making and did not offer a greeting when Dagrun introduced him to Merit. She guessed he was not rude but rather not fluent in the emperor's tongue, although looking at him she decided that perhaps he was not fluent in any tongue.

As with the other lords and grandees, Merit was an honored guest, nothing more. She kept her chin up and her face impassive as they watched the slaves work. The process fascinated Dagrun and she tried to share his interest. Above, on the scaffolds, slaves chipped at the hard, spiky bark like quarrymen. When they had opened a furrow wide enough to work, the men lifted saws. It took four of them to draw a blade across the tree and another four to pull the blade in the opposite direction. They heaved one more cry and the log tumbled to the ground.

When she had first thought to marry her sister to her admirer and co-conspirator, she had not factored in any jealousy on her part, but she could not deny that the elaborate preparations for their new queen were making her heart ache a little. As always, she felt slighted. In more ways than one, this was her wedding—her day and her tree. This was her triumph, but she had to pretend she was nothing more than an observer. She had to act as if the whole affair were a bore, rolling her eyes and heaving great sighs of exasperation.

Dagrun called out instructions as another section of trunk thundered to the ground. The wood caught on one of the tree's lower branches and crashed awkwardly against a neighboring blackthorn. The king of the Ferens took the overseer by the neck and turned him around, patiently detailing the man's error until he was interrupted by a shout. A young man rushed the platform, brandishing a blackthorn spear. "False king!" the man cried at Dagrun. He hefted a long and sharply pointed stave.

The king of the Ferens ignored his heckler, pointing to a winch that was poorly placed, a knot that had slipped. Dagrun coolly went on speaking to the overseer as a pair of soldiers cut the protester down with a couple of bloody swings from their swords, the body falling in three pieces, four.

Dagrun brushed a gray needle from his tunic as he ushered the overseer from the platform. Behind him, the seated warlords folded their hands uncomfortably but said nothing. Brock Sutharian gave a smirk, but only Merit acknowledged the incident. "Walk with me," she said, leading him down the platform steps and away from the ears of the others. She gestured to the fallen man as they passed. "After all this time?" she asked. "They still do not accept you as king?"

Soldiers followed Dagrun at a distance. He waited till the clinking of their armor ceased. "It's the damn Night Vigil."

"I thought you underwent the Waking Rite."

"No. Didn't bother," he said as the soldiers collected the protester's remains.

"Why not? A single night in the Cragwood? You've survived worse." She glanced at the forest floor, where only a bit of red remained in the place where the young man had fallen.

Dagrun grimaced at the bloody spot, his brow furrowed in dark ridges not unlike the rings of the trees around them. "No, it's more than a night quarreling with outlanders in the forest. When the king wakes, he is supposed to find a kite circling above his head. *The kite chooses the king.* It joins him on the throne, like some kind of great bloody turkey." The king of the Ferens shook his head. "I *took* my throne. I earned it with blood and coin. I don't need a damned symbol—I have an army. But some think that without the kite, I have no right to call myself king. Superstitions and nonsense is what it is." A flurry of silvery branches crashed one after another to the ground. In the distance, his soldiers maintained their guard.

Merit crossed her arms. "People live and die by superstitions and nonsense. It might be to your advantage to go through the rite, if only to put an end to the people's reason to oppose you."

Dagrun shrugged. He bent, as Merit had, to recover a spiky blackthorn seed. His callused fingers squeezed the thorny pod and it popped open. "Even if I did undergo the rite, there would still be opposition and strife in the kingdom," he said, plucking out the soft nut and crushing it between his teeth. "The kite is just the latest excuse for their unhappiness." He chewed. "If Barrin were still king, they would oppose him. I've made changes, I've helped my kingdom, made the crofters and foresters profitable." He collected a pair of seeds, bunching them between his fingers. "Feren is blessed with great resources. But in other ways they curse us too. Blackthorn foresting requires legions of unskilled workers, slaves. We need these men and women to harvest the trees, but we cannot feed them. Many starved under Barrin's reign; others were sold off to Soleri traders. Feren has half the workers it had a decade ago."

"How is this possible? Is the forest not plentiful?"

"The forest is not the issue, the empire takes half of what we grow. Each month Tolemy asks for more and Feren must comply." They walked deeper into the forest and Dagrun motioned for his soldiers to stay behind. He cracked the second nut and raised a finger to indicate the forest, the infant trees struggling upward around the old giant, now missing its top branches. "This is what we earned for betraying your grandfather. When Dalach abandoned Koren Hark-Wadi in the Children's War, the Ray swore to him that no imperial solider would ever set foot again in the Gray Wood, that Sola would leave our blackthorns alone. We keep our trees, but the empire takes our crops. We have an army, but not the resources to feed that army." Dagrun shook his head, leading her into a grove thick with blackthorn trunks. "If we had joined Koren, it might have ended that day." His eyes hardened. They were alone now, standing in a forest of tall bracken and spiky trees. "*I'd* have joined him. I would not have left your grandfather holding his cock on the battlefield." Dagrun glared at Merit, his eyes black, his face colored by regret.

"If only you were king then," she said. "If only Dalach had been as strong as you."

Dagrun brooded on that. His voice fell nearly to a whisper. "I will not see it happen here, the way it's happened everywhere. Dalach was a coward and a weakling; he gave his boy to the emperor. Barrin gave his son to Tolemy."

"You can give Kepi's to the emperor. And one day, after we've overturned Tolemy, we'll have a child that no one can take from us."

"One day?" he asked. "Isn't the wedding all but finished?" His hand brushed against the neckline of her dress and pulled at the fabric gently, so that his finger brushed her nipple until it stood firm.

"Not now." Merit's whole body flushed as she pressed herself against him, against the heat at his core. Dagrun groaned against her neck, his hand still cupping her breast, the other one impatiently lifting her skirt to touch her underneath. The trees and bracken sheltered them on all sides.

"I'm nearly through waiting, Merit."

"You will not have to wait much longer," she whispered, taking his hands away from her body and kissing the tips of his fingers. His soldiers were not far and she did not want to be seen standing so close to the king, so she took a step back. "But I cannot be yours. Not until after your wedding night, not until I see the bloody sheets."

⋹31⋺

The carriage followed a road that led slowly up into the mountains outside Rifka, the air cooler, wetter, the land greener. Kepi held the shutter open. Refusing to speak to her captors or to Seth, she focused on the workers streaming toward the High City: slaves in rags, burly woodworkers with their tools on their backs, tired-looking boys half-asleep on their feet. The Feren soldiers forced the workers away from the road to let the caravan pass, holding them away at sword point. If this were Harkana, Kepi would have said something to them about their roughness with the workers, that there was no reason to terrify them on her account. But this was not Harkana, and Kepi was not yet their queen. At the moment she was no better off than the workers shivering under the glare of the soldiers—none of them were masters of their fate.

When she and Seth were captured in the Cragwood, the Feren soldiers had pinned Seth to the standing stones at sword point and searched him. Seth had seemed to think the soldiers would thank him—he kept talking to the one in charge, a broad-shouldered man with a gray beard, as if they knew each other—but they tied him with ropes and kept warning him to stop talking. When he refused, they knocked him on the head, and he fell to the ground like a bag of old linens. *Like a fool,* Kepi thought sadly. *Don't hurt him. He's just a boy.*

The soldiers had not tied Kepi, though they had kept her closely and respectfully guarded as they led her to the Rift valley, where a vast contingent of Feren soldiers held the border. Dagrun was not present at the camp, though she knew his men sent a messenger to the king who was attending the Cutting Day ceremony with her sister. The felling of the blackthorn honored the new queen, but it was Merit who would enjoy the pageantry. Kepi was not bothered—in some ways she guessed this marriage was more Merit's than her own. Leaving Kepi to brood over her second wedding, the soldiers gently led her back into the carriage, locking it once more from the outside. Seth had come and knocked on her door once, but she hadn't the heart to answer. "Talk to me, Kepi," he begged. "I promised you we'd be together. I saved you, Kepi. That was all I did." Eventually he went away.

The caravan continued over the high mountain pass, drawing ever closer to the High City, the horses climbing slowly into a green meadow with rocky, crumbling sides, the roads growing more and more crowded with workers, with traders and soldiers traveling to Rifka. Once, she thought she saw the great gray bird, the kite, but she could not be certain. She saw its shadow among the crowds, but the narrow carriage window prevented her from seeing the sky. Afterward, the caravan descended into the cover of trees, passing into shadow, the roads thick with carts and wagons, the world closing in around her small carriage. She lost track of the sky and the kite as the forest's cool air wrapped her skin like an unwelcome hand. She longed for the open desert plains of Harkana, for the dust of the Hornring, even for the amber house in Blackrock where she and Seth had met in secret.

No, not Blackrock, she thought with a pang, and not with Seth. She should have ended it a long time ago. He was soft, unprepared for the harshness that was her life. She would try to help him as best she could. Perhaps he could find meaningful work for himself in Feren.

A shout rang out as a soldier announced their arrival in Rifka. The carriage stopped and the door opened in front of the gatehouse of the caer, a round fortress surrounded by a high stone wall made of the same granite as the Cragwood, the solitary fortress into which the people would scurry in times of war. Soldiers approached. The men led her out of the carriage and across the blackthorn bridge. Above, logs hung from chains— the Chime Gate, they said, named for the forest chimes the hanging logs resembled.

When she passed beneath that gate, so like the mouth of a hoary beast swallowing her alive, Kepi knew she would not be able to leave, not this time. This was not Roghan Frith's shabby village in the woods. There would be no locks in her chamber, but she was a prisoner just the same; the men who stood at her door would not allow her to pass, and everywhere guards would be told not to trust the Harkan woman, the woman who would be their queen.

"There is news from Desouk," said the tall Feren who walked at her side.

Kepi was uncertain of how to react, news from Desouk meant news from her mother, Sarra Amunet.

"This morning we received a missive from the Mother. She wrote to inform the faithful that she survived the riots on the last day of the year."

"Riots?" Kepi asked as they left the bridge behind. She had heard whispers about unrest in the capital, but she hadn't stopped to consider what that might mean for the Mother Priestess. "What happened?"

"After the sun failed to dim, there was chaos on the wall and in the Waset, burning and rioting, but the Mother was ferried safely through the crowds by her followers. She is out of harm's way, in Desouk, where she will remain. I thought you might want to hear the news."

"Thank you. That was kind of you," Kepi said. The soldier must have known that Sarra was her mother. She supposed everyone knew. He was trying to be kind, to bring good news to the girl who would soon be his queen, but his message had the opposite effect. It reminded her that her father was gone, and she had not seen her mother in ten years.

The soldiers led her across a great yard, to a fountain where slaves dressed in homespun wool greeted Kepi with sober eyes and folded hands. Their thin woolens, open at the chest and neck, revealed scrawny torsos and protruding ribs. Over the left breast of one she saw a scar in the shape of a tree. She had heard the Feren soldiers, on their journey, refer to these slaves as plodders and drudges. From what she knew, most Feren slaves were neither property nor prisoners, though now and then a few were culled from the prison ranks. Instead, servitude was a station they inherited and kept for life—the lowest caste in the kingdom, and hence the whole empire. *Barbarous.* Even in Harkana, where life was rough, people were not bound to one class.

In the yard, the servants and slaves came out to watch Kepi's arrival. A whisper echoed among them and grew and grew until it was all that she could hear—words like "captured" and "survivor" and "fugitive." Perhaps they had heard of the night she had spent in the Cragwood, the sacred forest. During the long ride from the Rift valley to the High City of Rifka she had heard that Dagrun had not suffered the Waking Rite. She knew he had taken his kingdom by force, but she had not known that he had neglected to complete the Feren custom. More than one soldier had muttered that the king of the Ferens was cursed for not having undergone the ritual. She hoped the soldiers' words were true, she hoped the man who had once held a sword to her throat was cursed, but doubted the truth of what the soldiers said.

She spent a restless afternoon alone in a vast, drafty bedroom of the caer, a room with a single well-guarded door. A great fire roared at one end of the chamber. She pulled the feather-stuffed bed toward the flames and basked in their warmth. Feren was said to have great stores of wood, forests packed with birds and small animals. She hoped she would find more wealth in Rifka than she had found in Roghan's hovel. She hoped the forest's abundance was not just one more lie told by the men of the Gray Wood.

The fire was warm and its constant crackle rattled in her ear, but it was Seth who kept her feeling uneasy, or rather thoughts of Seth. She remembered the way he had come to the carriage window and begged for her to speak with him.

A knock at the door startled her. She stood up, expecting to see Dagrun, or at least one of his sworn men, perhaps even her sister, but instead a group of slave girls, their faces unfamiliar, stepped inside. "Where are my waiting women?" Kepi asked. The girls had accompanied her from Harwen.

"Gone," murmured one of the slave girls. "Taken by the San," said another.

No one had bothered to tell Kepi. Shocked, she bowed her head as the Feren girls filled the room. Her waiting women had been servants, not slaves. They were free women and her friends, but the Ferens acted as if they were nothing, as if their loss was of no importance. Kepi blinked back tears as the slaves surrounded her. They carried a simple dress, its white fabric a textured linen woven from flax and sewn into a single long piece of cloth. It appeared simple to her eyes, severely plain even, but she'd noticed almost every other woman she had seen in Feren wore little more than a rag at her waist or neck and a necklace of wooden beads, so she supposed she should have been grateful.

The girls unrolled the dress; they held it up for Kepi to inspect.

"What is it?" she asked, and the girls told her. "Your wedding dress, mistress. The king had it made specially for you."

"Wedding?"

"Yes, mistress," said the eldest girl, a dark little sprite not much older than Kepi herself.

This is my wedding dress? She sighed and took the slip of linen in her hands. The fabric snagged on her bitten-down nails. She had lost her friends, her waiting women, her possessions. And now she must marry a man she hardly knows? She thought of her father—he had been with her the first time she came to Feren—and longed for his companionship. She wondered if he still lived, if he had met the emperor yet. Would she ever know what had become of him? Or was her father just gone, without a funeral, without closure, without the courtesy of a day on which she could mourn the end of his life?

"Shall we dress you, my lady?" the sprite was asking.

"Now? It's nearly night."

"Don't worry. We're just going to fit the dress. It won't take long. But we'll need to scrub you clean first. Come," said the slave girl. "We've got work to do. We need to get you ready for the wedding. The king has felled his tree, and the construction of your chamber is under way." In fact, Kepi could hear the sounds of sawing and nailing taking place somewhere in the distance, but she could not see the chamber. She saw only a little bailey, the stone wall around the caer, a thin, dirty-looking trench, and the poor, scrubby burg surrounding it all.

I won't marry Dagrun. I won't stay here.

She knew she told herself lies, if only to comfort her nerves. And yet, she wondered how the people of Feren could stand to have as their queen a woman who disliked them all, their king especially? Once again, she longed for a blade, for the feel of cold iron in her fist.

"Come now, step into the tub, my pretty lady," said one of the slave girls as the others bustled around her chamber, setting out pots of ointment, filling the tub with water, unaware of the struggle that raged in her heart, in her trembling hands.

"I've brought you something to eat. The queen mustn't be hungry. No, no," said the black-haired sprite. She offered chips of salted quail and a crock of amber.

"Thank you," Kepi said as she took the cup and drank.

The slaves stoked the fire and pushed her bed into a corner.

"Take off your clothes—hurry, hurry," the sprite told her, but the others were already stripping Kepi bare, motioning for her to her stand in the wooden tub as they readied themselves to pour water over her shoulders. They washed her with a yellow cream that smelled of salt, and rubbed her skin with a sweet oil. All the while they chatted with her about the king, their silly girlish voices joking about the wedding night, about how fine-looking Dagrun was. "A man like that," the sprite said, "could keep any woman happy."

Kepi could not hide the bitterness from her face. "If he's such a prize," she said, "perhaps you would like to marry him."

The girl gave a slow, curling smile. "Perhaps I would," she said, "if I were a king's daughter from a far-away land."

A kind but clumsy girl, with one eye brown and the other gray, gazed at Kepi with sympathy and changed the topic, "But anyway, you'd have to deal with his temper, he's a difficult man, they say. Moody, angry at times, and . . . violent, some say."

"Shut up," hissed the sprite, but Kepi told the gray-eyed girl to continue. "Violent?" she asked.

The gray-eyed girl frowned at the sprite—clearly there was some old tension between these two.

"Nonsense," said the sprite.

"It's not nonsense," the gray-eyed girl said. "I heard you telling old Halsie about it last month."

The sprite shook her head. "It was not the king but the guards who beat those girls. When the king found out, he put the guards in shackles."

Kepi stared at the two girls and was uncertain which, if either, she could trust. In truth, she knew Dagrun no better than his slaves. He was a mystery to all of them.

When the gray-eyed girl saw concern on her mistress's face, she smiled her clumsy smile and gave Kepi a sympathetic look. "This poor thing needs to know what she's facing." The girl moved to spread oil on Kepi's arm, but dropped the jar. Kepi wondered if her gray eye was blind, if her disfigurement had set her apart from the others, had made her the object of their scorn. "Do what the king asks," the girl said. "Do as he says and you'll be better off."

Kepi went cold. Something in the girl's tone made her think of Roghan. She gulped amber.

"Is something wrong with my pretty queen?" asked the gray-eyed girl.

"I'd ask for a blade," Kepi said, "but I know you can't bring me one."

The slaves all shook their heads and went about the rest of their work sullenly, the tension between the girls making them silent. She could not imagine these slave girls as her waiting women after she became queen, but then she could not imagine being Dagrun's queen either.

"Eat," the gray-eyed girl said. "You are so very thin, my lady."

The slaves wrapped the dress around Kepi. She was embarrassed when she realized the dress left her breasts exposed, coming up just to her waist.

"It's the tradition," said the gray-eyed girl, nodding as she fitted the dress beneath Kepi's breasts.

Even Merit's most tasteless gowns cover more than this. She cast about for a shawl, a cloak—but no, nothing.

"We just need to stitch you up, nice and tight, yes," said the sprite. "You're a slender one, but we can't have you looking like a boy. No, no— we need to make you nice and pretty for your king," she said as they stitched the fabric to her form with thick wooden needles. Kepi could barely contain her disgust. *I wish I were a boy.* She no doubt had the body for it.

Once the dress was properly fitted, the slave girls removed the white slip and Kepi donned her old clothes. A thought occurred to her as she pulled the fabric over head. "The wedding—when is it?"

"Three days," said the sprite.

Three days, thought Kepi. She had hoped for three months, three weeks even. Time to escape, or to hurl herself out the window.

She'd do either before she'd marry Dagrun.

≢32≣

Ren saw the horned totem gleaming like a thorny branch in the morning light. The pole, carved with the outlines of eld skulls, one stacked atop the other, marked the edge of the hunting grounds. Ren was nearly free from the reserve, but he paused. There were bits of pale skin showing between the grass and rocks. A body lay awkwardly at the totem's base, one arm fixed at an unnatural angle, a red puddle turning black against the pale sand. The head was turned and he recognized Dakar's face, his gray hair and wide eyes. The warden of the Shambles. The one who had given him his hunting dog and his provisions. Ren knelt down and pushed a strand of hair from the warden's face. His skin was cold and Ren closed his eyes. He guessed this was Shenn's work. Now Ren knew why Shenn had looked at him oddly when he made mention of the warden.

He found tools and dug a grave.

The rocky earth was difficult to move, the digging slow, but he didn't mind. He needed time to think and plan, to comprehend what had happened on the hunt. Merit, the sister he had never met, had sent a man to kill him. And now her husband, Shenn, was up there on the mountain, wrapped in bloody bandages. Ren wondered if he'd been too lenient with Shenn, if he should have ended him. *What if I've saved my brother only to face him again? Will I wake with his dagger at my throat?* Ren didn't know, but he was certain of one thing: He didn't want to be like Merit—he would not kill his own kin. If he had to face Shenn again, so be it. Until then he had more pressing concerns.

Ren knew what he should do next. He had left the Priory. He had performed the hunt—he held the eld horns. He had done what the empire asked and what his father requested. It was time to return home. He would go to Harkana and take his throne, but there was little sense doing it right now. *If I march straight into Harkana, Merit will poison me at my own coronation, or her archers will shoot me down at the wall and call me a beggar or thief.*

Ren would go home, but he would go there with allies. After what he'd learned—the way Merit had first sent her gray-cloaks, then her husband, to kill him—Ren knew he could not walk into Harkana alone. There was no one there he could trust. His father was dead and Merit was not family—not the kind he pictured, at least.

When I walk into Harwen, I'll do so with Adin and Tye at my side, and their kingdoms' armies too. Perhaps Tye's father could assist them. It was the only sensible thing he could think to do. Right now, walking into Harwen felt like suicide. Ren would take his father's throne, but he'd find his friends first. It was what he wanted anyway. *I promised Adin I would find him when I got out. I'm free and I want to see my friend. I need his help.*

He recalled how, when he was younger, Adin had stood up for him against Kollen and the older boys who constantly teased and harassed the younger ransoms. Adin had more than once offered Ren his meal when Ren was sick or feeling malnourished. And once, when Ren knocked over the kettle in the refectory, it was Adin who took the blame, because he hadn't wanted to see his friend suffer. Ren thought he owed Adin something, so he would head to Feren first. If Adin were still alive, he would need all the help he could get.

Ren took what provisions he could find in Dakar's cottage, a few crescents, and headed north, toward the woodland kingdom. He took the eld horn and covered it with red clay, disguising it. He tied a leather thong he found in Dakar's cottage to both ends of the horn and slung it over his shoulder. Leaving the cottage, he tried to entice the dog to follow, tossing it a strip of meat, but the servant would not stray from its master's grave.

Not far from the warden's cottage, he heard a distant whinny and followed it until he found a horse tied to a broken tree. He had seen the creature once before, with his father's escort. It was likely Shenn's mount; the saddle was richly made, the horse well groomed. He pulled himself up onto it, gripped the reins, and with a kick bid farewell to the hunting reserve.

Ren traveled north toward Feren, following an uneven trail, hoping to catch sight of the forest but finding only sheer cliffs he could not scale and rocks too ragged for his horse to climb. More than once he got lost and had to double back or follow a different path. Later, the terrain grew so dense and rocky he had to free the horse and continue alone on foot, heading north and looking for the Rift valley. Soon after, he spied the deep but slender rift. The great gap marked the edge of the desert, a dark gulf from which mountains rose to form the granite face of the Feren kingdom. The sides of that gulf were jagged, the edges cracked like dry desert mud. He traveled the rim, skirting the deep ravine. The gap was often wide, always impossible to traverse. He found a spot where the Rift narrowed and a bridge spanned the gap. Long lines gathered at the passage. From their tools, he guessed the men were craftsmen. A lumberman with a pair of axes walked alongside Ren and a woodworker of some type with a pack full of chisels walked ahead of him. Something was happening in Feren, a gathering of some kind, an affair that required a great number of tradesmen.

He overheard a gray-haired man talking about a set of chambers that would be under construction for the new queen of Feren. From what the men said Ren gathered that the king of Ferens was marrying in a few days' time.

"Who is the king to wed?" Ren asked absently, not really caring about the answer.

"A Harkan girl, Kedi?" The gray-hair scratched his head, uncertain of the name.

Kepi. My sister. Kepi is engaged to the king of the Ferens. Ren wasn't certain what to think about this revelation. He did not know if she was friend or foe. Was she Merit's ally? Or was she allied with his father and would she assist him?

The workers kept up their banter. "Kepi's her name," said a man whose skin and hair were darker, possibly Harkan. "I saw her once in Black-rock, cloaked atop her horse. They say she's a wild one, always riding out at night."

Ren listened closely, but the shouts of the Feren soldiers on the bridge drowned out the rest of the conversation. If Kepi hid from her family, if she ran from them, perhaps she was not allied with Merit, maybe she was more like him and maybe she would aid him. A queen could be a powerful ally, but that wasn't all he cared about. He still wanted a family. If his father was gone and his mother had left them, if his elder sister was his adversary, Kepi was all he had left. She was his last chance at a family, so he decided to seek her out when he reached Rifka. *I need to know if she truly is family—if she'll welcome me.*

Ren crossed the Rift valley with a band of woodworkers, staring down into the depths of the chasm, smelling sap from the freshly cut wood. Soldiers guarded the bridge and the pathway, directing the tradesmen, making certain no one strayed from the trail.

"When is the wedding?" Ren asked aloud.

"Three days," he heard someone grumble. "Three days to make the platform, three months to build the Queen's Chamber—we'll be lucky if we get any sleep."

Little by little, as morning passed into afternoon, as the mountain pass gave way to a deep valley, he entered the Gray Wood, where Ren encountered a sight he had heard about, dreamed about, but never seen— the blackthorn trees of legend, thousands of years old, more massive than any structure on Earth. Soon there were no more stones at all, only a cathedral of ancient trees and the soft underbrush, and the smell of wet earth and plants growing in the moist, rich soil protected from the sun by the thick canopy overhead. He passed carpets of small white flowers shaped like stars, great fragrant bushes of honeysuckle, of jasmine. Ren passed berry patches bursting with ripe fruit and stopped to stuff himself, leaving only seeds for the birds. He stumbled on a patch of wild onion and stopped to gather the plant, tying the green tops together and hiding them in his tunic. It was marvelous, he thought, to be in a country where wild things grew, where the desert had not shriveled every living thing. A green country, and lush, so different from the deserts of the south.

Soldiers at their back, Ren and the woodworkers came upon a great village where hundreds of slaves gathered between stacks of blackthorn logs, sawing, stripping bark, carving pegs and holes that would all be necessary to create the great house for the queen. There was a second village, he heard, where the king held the Cutting Day ceremony, but Ren didn't know where it was or how to reach it. The men here were prepping the wood and sending it to the caer, where a second camp took up the finer work. An enormous undertaking. No wonder they needed so many men. The Ferens had slaves, but they lacked craftsmen. Ren hoped he could pass as one.

"You," barked a foreman, pointing his whip at Ren. "Yes you there, runt. Where'd you come from, boy?"

"From the Wyrre," Ren said. He knew his pale hair would appear strange to the Feren's eyes. "I was born in Barham, but I grew up in the mountains near the Rift valley," Ren lied—it seemed easy enough. "I'm just here to split wood." Ren labored to conceal the accent he had learned in the Priory.

"Another fluke from the south? What's wrong—did your island sink?" He motioned toward the saws. "See that you get out of the way when the trees fall, boy." With that he let Ren pass. There was work to be done.

Ren picked up a bucksaw and joined the others. He relished the moist, fragrant scent of the forest, so unlike the desert, where the air was dry and lifeless. Alive with sounds and smells, the forest moved always around him—the men cutting, sawing, swearing, hoisting. He was getting more used to being outside now, and yet sometimes when he would wake in the morning with nothing but the sky overhead, he would have a moment when he was not certain where he was, if he was even alive still. If the world outside the Priory was real, or if the sun beating down on his head was the face of Mithra, welcoming him into some other life. But then he would breathe in and out, and feel hungry, and his legs would ache, and he would know once again that he was alive. Alive and usually in urgent need of taking a piss.

The soldiers fed Ren cakes of crushed potato and strong amber, and he felt for the first time how good it was to work, how useful work was to the mind of a man.

All that day the glade filled with the sounds of sawing, of nailing. The scrape of wood, the ring of iron, the voices of men telling stories to pass the time. Ren listened to all of it. They might tell a story of the former king's son, Adin, if Ren were careful enough and paid attention.

"Seen the Harkan yet?" one of the grunts asked.

"The wildcat? The witch who killed Roghan?" Another spat. "What he wants with that bitch the gods only know."

"Thin as a board and as hard to nail," someone said, and laughed.

"Too bad Dagrun didn't bag the other one." The man nearest Ren leered. "What I'd give for a piece of that ass."

The one-eyed man made a puckering sound and drew a curvy silhouette of a woman with his hands in the air. "Tits for days and wasted on Shenn—everyone knows he'd rather have Dagrun."

Cruel laughter followed that joke.

"Shut your mouths!" Ren said, inserting himself into their conversation. They were gossiping about his sisters and it angered him.

"What's gotten into you?" said the one-eyed man, taken aback, a little frightened. "We're just havin' a bit of fun, boy. What do you care about the Harkans? Ya look like you're from the Wyrre, anyway."

Ren stood up. He was taller than the others and young and perhaps a bit intimidating. The one-eyed woodworker's fingers began to shake from fear or just old age. Ren had the mud-covered eld horn at his side and, likely, the man feared Ren would beat him with it.

"Nothing," Ren said, and in the silence that followed he recounted their words, comparing them to what Shenn had said in the Shambles. Merit, they said was beautiful, her hair as lustrous and dark as the kohl beneath her eyes. Kepi, if the men were right, was not a beauty like Merit. Kepi was only a few years older than him. Was she once his friend, his playmate? Who was this girl now betrothed to the king of the Ferens? He wondered if she would find happiness in her marriage, but doubted it. The house of Tolemy arranged most marriages and the matching of the bride and groom, beyond the marriage's political ends, was seldom considered. The women were not treated much better than the boys sent to the Priory. Except perhaps Merit. He wondered about her, about what the men said about her husband. Merit—he knew little of her, save for her desire to keep him out of Harkana. He thought he should hate her, but somehow he guessed he should just pity her. She seemed like one of the older boys in the Priory—sad and desperate, trying to hold on to a power they could not quite grasp.

Talk resumed—there were rumors that Barca had conquered the Wyrre, that the general had slaughtered the royal families of the southern islands and named himself ruler of the kingdom. This last news gave Ren pause. If the royal families were dead, Tye's imprisonment in the Priory was done. With Ren, Suten Anu had forgone the usual procedure, but it was tradition that the ransoms who were released from the Priory were let go when the moon disappeared from the sky each cycle. It was called the new moon, or Thieves' Moon. It was a time when boys became men, their childhoods stolen away in the night.

That night, exhausted but awake, Ren gazed at the half disk in the sky and guessed Tye had a pair of weeks, maybe ten days, before the Thieves' Moon and her release. He tried wandering off into the woods, hoping to escape, but found guards blocking his path, guiding him back to the camp. Ren was not a prisoner, but he was a foreigner, and he guessed the Ferens didn't want him in the kingdom. If he did not find Adin soon, Ren decided, he would return alone to Solus for Tye's release from the Priory. She meant something to him. He could not push her from his thoughts; he didn't want to imagine her alone in the Priory, without his protection, or running through the darkness of the Hollows, alone and vulnerable.

The next day he woke with thoughts of the wedding and his sister. The Feren slaves had spent a day loading the wood for the Queen's Chamber onto dozens of carts, and now they hitched up their horses and headed north, toward the High City, where the wedding would take place. Ren found work with the carters, helping clear brush as the carts moved through the dense forest.

Whenever the caravan stopped at a town or a settlement, Ren asked after Adin, the presumed heir to the throne until Dagrun had taken it by force. Had anyone seen him or heard news of him, did anyone know what had become of him? No, no one had seen him, no one had any news of him. The Ferens scowled and shook their heads at the mention of Barrin, Adin's father. They called him the Barrin the Black, the Worm King of the Gray Wood. Ren knew little about Feren, but he guessed the old king was not well liked. After a few conversations Ren began to think Adin's father was not the good king his friend had always imagined and he wondered if Dagrun was not the tyrant Adin had blamed for his father's death.

Dagrun had taken Adin's throne, and was now betrothed to Kepi, his sister. Which meant Dagrun was in one way a foe and in another way family, a description that now seemed all too familiar. Perhaps the bonds of family were not what he thought; they seemed now more like chains, links that were unwelcome and hard to break.

When night fell, he slept with the rest of the company, taking space in an abandoned barn and sleeping restlessly in an otherwise empty stall.

As the sun rose the caravan set out for Rifka, but they did not arrive at the Feren capital until the day was nearly spent. In the fading light, they passed between cottages with straw-thatched roofs and walls woven from blackthorn twigs daubed with reddish clay or smeared with brown, hay-speckled dung, the place stinking of garbage, a rumbling sound in the air. The city was dark, and the noise seemed to come from everything, from the very walls of the place, as if the whole city were trembling. When the caravan passed under the gate of ironwood logs, he was struck by a strong urge to turn around and go back. But he passed beneath the gate and into the walls of the fortress nevertheless.

Inside, the sound was stronger and he realized it was actually a song, a keening without words. It was there, within the wall, amid the chaos of the day, that Ren slipped from the company of woodworkers and disappeared into the narrow streets of Rifka.

He followed the rumbling noise through the alleys, past towering war machines, shabby inns, and a torchlit marketplace that sold little but hard strips of dried goat. A group of Ferens in their thin rags was rushing toward the noise too, clutching bouquets of the small white flowers Ren had been seeing in the forest for days. He followed them, not wanting to get too close.

Soon the city opened up into a grassy yard, where a great platform had been erected, a wooden stage held up by columns carved with vines and flowers. Reached by a tall set of stairs, the platform was topped with a smaller central dais on which a man wearing a thorny crown stood waiting amid a ring of torches. A white-robed priestess waited at his side. Alongside her stood a second, younger girl dressed in a muddy gray robe, a Feren priestess of some type.

He elbowed through the crowd, the song growing louder, the mob growing denser, the hymn like a dull pounding in his ears. A long line of slaves, their necks collared, blocked his path. All around them the hymn rang out, but these slaves acted as if they could not hear it, as if they were not present. Why? What was wrong and who were these people? None of them looked up, none of them so much as made eye contact. Women and men, children and babes. He heard them referred to as gifts, these men and women were gifts to the new bride and groom, slaves of exceptional worth, he heard said. *What slave could carry such worth?*

In the center of the line kneeled a tall boy whose skin was paler than the rest, his body thin and malnourished, his ribs so visible that Ren could count them. His long hair fell into his eyes, but then he raised his head slightly and Ren recognized him. Adin.

≋33≋

There was a struggle, jarring her from her stupor, sounds of screaming, battle. Kepi opened her eyes blearily and turned to the girl at her side.

"A slave, my lady."

"What of him?"

"He has broken his bonds and fled."

"Fled?"

"It is of no consequence." The air outside was once more quiet. "There is no escape from the caer, the soldiers will find him. They find everyone." Kepi was uncertain how to interpret the scuffle.

The slave girl offered her another drink and she gladly accepted.

She'd been drinking since early that morning, trying to calm her nerves. But there was something odd about that last sip. Her head spun as if she had drunk too much amber. Had she had too much? Was the amber here so much stronger than what they served in Harwen?

She peered down and grimaced at the drink. A milky wisp ran through the golden liquid, laced with some opiate, probably. She had thought of running, of fleeing the ceremony, but she was suddenly so weak she could barely stand. She wondered if she would still be conscious when the wedding took place. Her head spun, the opium coursed through her veins, and the tent obscured her view of the gathering outside. Dimly she heard the servants bickering, blaming one another. *Didn't you tell her?* said one. *No,* said another. *It's tradition,* said a third. *The queen drinks opium before the Night Wedding, didn't she know?*

No. Kepi shook her head as her eyes closed and her head swam.

A low hum broke the stillness. The hymn had started again. Dissonant chords filled her ears as her handmaids carried her out of the tent. Kepi flinched at their touch, at the strange noise and the flickering torches. The hymn was hummed, not sung. It had no words, and its vocalists did not stand in a choir. The men were spread throughout the crowd, as if the song emanated from the forest itself, surrounding her in a single, mighty sound. A sound whose power seemed amplified by the darkness. It occurred to Kepi that the hymn was not quite music but was the sound of the trees themselves, a song of the forest, a rumble like thunder that pounded the listener's chest, that rattled the earth.

Leaving the tent, Kepi's thoughts wavered and her ears pounded. She was barefoot and cold, naked from the chest up, a crown of lavender hanging on her brow. Slaves wearing woolen mantles, their hair braided and wreathed with wildflowers, held her arms while she struggled against the opiate, her vision wavering, her head throbbing. The ground was uneven beneath her feet, and she kept stumbling, and when she looked up she saw a priestess in a white robe, a member of the Desouk cult standing alongside what Kepi guessed was a priestess of Llyr, the forest god. The girl wore a gray robe caked in the red mud of the forest floor. It was an ugly gown, a matted, tattered robe. She had heard of the priestesses but never seen one; Roghan had not bothered to find a priestess to seal their union. Now Dagrun, her second husband, peered down on her from atop the wedding platform.

He wore clan stripes, gray and black and green. The Feren crown sat atop his head. The bronze circlet, cast in the image of blackthorn twigs and woven with curling barbs, drew slender shadows across his face. His nose was broken, slightly, at the ridge. In the past, she had not noticed this detail. Perhaps it was the firelight that highlighted the wavering line. The torchlight illuminated the upper half of his face while leaving the rest cloaked in shadow. She could not see if he was smiling or frowning, nervous or angry. His features were masked, an illusion that made him appear all the more intimidating.

She had been dreading another Feren wedding for years, but now there was little she could do to stop it. Memories of her first nuptials returned, of that cottage in the woods, of the fog and murk, the way the guests had stared so sadly at her as they stole food from the small feast and left without bidding her goodbye.

If I had a blade in my hand, I could end this wedding, and Dagrun along with it. But she had no blade and no armor, and she was barely clothed. She shivered, wanting to cover her breasts, but decided that would be seen as a sign of weakness and so she kept her arms held tightly at her sides.

The slaves urged—no, pushed—her forward, their arms locked around hers, Kepi's feet barely touching the ground. Higher voices joined the hymn, passing the melody through the crowd, echoing the song from side to side, voice to voice. The whole city was in attendance, gathered around the large wedding platform in a grove of trees, a miniature forest in the heart of the caer. The grove's sloping ground enabled all in attendance to see the king and his new queen, the dazed girl at whom the people were throwing star-shaped white petals, carpeting the forest floor in white like falling snow. They stuck to her made-up face, to her hair and her hands, and Kepi reached up to brush them away with shaking fingers. *Let this be over soon.* The beauty of the forest and the white flowers made the ceremony somehow all the more terrible.

The people were gathered in circles around the platform, Feren warlords nearest in their colored mantles, sworn men at their sides. The freemen of Rifka next, then vast rows of slaves, bare chests and knotted hair, everywhere that the eye could see, and all the while the hymn grew louder and less intelligible. *How can they all just stand and watch as I'm forced to marry against my will?* She wondered how they could smile at this misery. Kepi wanted to hear beauty in the song, but she couldn't: it sounded like a dirge, like grief, like a slave's song. Appropriate, perhaps—but no less painful.

Now she stood at the base of the platform. The slave girls clustered around her. Up the low steps they went, then the staircase, a rain of white blossoms falling from some unseen hand. She shivered in her wedding dress, her chest bare, so cold. *I won't do this,* she thought. *I can't do this.*

Kepi kept her hands at her sides, clenching and unclenching. Her ladies had powdered and dressed her face and breasts with gold flakes that now and then caught the torchlight. The image was no doubt stunning, but Kepi had never felt less like a bride than she did at that moment. She felt like a sacrifice. How she longed for her armor and sword. *I want my freedom.*

The song stopped and the girls parted. Slaves lit braziers on all sides of the platform and the blackthorns came alive with flickering lights. Dagrun spoke to the crowd—words that rang out in a voice that might have been stirring had Kepi been capable of being stirred by anything Dagrun did or said. Either way she did not bother to listen to the content of the words—she had no interest. Across from her she saw Merit, wearing their father's double crown, their mother's short sword, and a dress of sheep's wool, warm and long-sleeved, a look of naked triumph on her beautiful face. *Why does she hate me so?* Kepi wondered, not for the first time.

The hymn stopped abruptly. Kepi struggled against the slaves and the opiate, stumbling as she tried to free herself from their hold. Dagrun caught her before she fell to the ground, but she pushed herself up, pushed him away. *I need no help.*

The priestess in the gray robes picked up Kepi's cold hand and placed it in Dagrun's large, rough one. She wrapped their grasped hands with the sleeve of her muddy robe. The gesture was symbolic. Feren handfasting— the girls who dressed her had explained—bound the wife to the husband and the wedded couple to Llyr. The Feren priestess, her skin caked with mud, spoke in a language Kepi could not understand, her prayer a single, unaccented stream of words. *"Tha-llyris-colla-han-fere-an-Dagrun-inne-Kepina-shri-bal-tanne,"* she chanted, then spoke in the common tongue. Kepina Hark-Wadi, she announced, was now queen to Dagrun Finner, first of that name, king of the Ferens and Lord of the Gray Wood.

Bells chimed in the distance. The warlords of Feren scaled the wedding platform. Feren had twelve clans, and the head of each clan gave a speech in her honor, rambling on about her unparalleled beauty, her unequalled worth. Each wore their respective clan colors, gray and green and black strands woven into their mantles. Ferris Mawr of Caerwynt spoke first, then Deccan Falkirk of Caerfrae, Seken Anders of Caerkirk, Arni Faerose of Caerspirren, and Cowen Ulli of Caeriddison.

For each tribute Kepi wanted to snort in laughter—surely they weren't talking about her, the youngest and least attractive, the least worthy of the females of the house of Hark-Wadi. Her sister would have glowed under such praise; to Kepi, who recognized them for the false accolades they were, they felt hollow.

When he was done speaking, each warlord presented a slave to Kepi, a gift from the clan to the new queen. Eleven now sat before her, and one was missing, but no one seemed bothered by the slave's absence. The girls who dressed her had described the ritual: After each clan offered a slave to the queen, she was to pick one slave—a slave who would be sacrificed—an offering to Llyr, the *kitefaethir.* Llyr's followers named him the mud god, the lord of chains, deity to all who served and suffered in the Gray Wood. The sacrifice of the slave sealed the marriage and brought good fortune to the couple.

Silence.

She had only to lift her finger and the task would be done, but Kepi did not move. One to kill and ten to consign into her service till the end of their lives. Another barbarian practice. Her arms at her sides, her mind frozen with rage and fear, Kepi remained silent. *I will not choose.*

Merit cleared her throat. "Choose," she hissed. "Choose one and be done with it."

Dagrun nodded, waiting. "Whatever my queen desires, she will have."

But still she did not move.

Choose one.

"I have no—" Her mind went blank; the opiate still pulsed in her veins. "I have no need for more waiting women and no desire to see death on the day of my wedding." Kepi heaved a long breath. "And as for tradition, perhaps, since it is the first union between a Feren king and a Harkan king's daughter, may I suggest a new offering?"

Dagrun raised an eyebrow.

"I choose to give them all their freedom. The Harkan gift."

For a moment, she thought Dagrun might slap her. Merit took a deep breath and her eyes blazed. *Foolish girl.*

But the king of the Ferens only laughed in amusement. He clapped his hands. "The Harkan gift of freedom. A worthy gift." He gestured to his men. "Whatever my queen desires, she will have," he said. "Take your freedom as a sign of good faith from my new bride."

Kepi flushed, her chest a rosy pink, and for a moment she was as beautiful as Merit, if not more beautiful. She felt Dagrun's eyes on her face, on her body, and saw the slow curve of his smile and returned it with one of her own. Next to her, she felt Merit's anger, coiled and ready to spring.

But there was nothing her sister could do about it. Merit was only queen regent of Harkana.

But today, Kepi was queen of the Ferens.

≋34≋

Ren shouldered through the noisy streets of Rifka, blood on his hands, fingers gripping Adin's wrist as he pulled him through narrow alleys and courtyards where packs of beggars roamed like sheep, past a gate of dangling logs and the blackthorn bridge. All the while, they saw soldiers searching the crowds, soldiers on the walls and in windows. "Find the boy," shouted one. "Capture or kill the filthy little bastard," said another. If the streets were not dark, if the crowds were not so dense, they would surely have been spotted. Ren pictured himself in Feren chains, kneeling alongside Adin, explaining that he was heir to the Harkan throne. *No time for that. Adin's a prisoner and I need to get him out.*

Ren had struck at Adin's guard when all eyes were on the wedding platform. He'd pierced the man's silvery mail with his father's blade, freeing Adin, the two of them stealing away into the crowds. Ren had wanted to find his sister, the queen, but after he'd seen the way the Ferens treated Adin, chaining his friend like a common slave, Ren had lost all interest in Kepi. *Why bother; she must be just like Merit, ruthless and unkind.*

Past the gate, they hurried through the thronged streets, over the newly poured sand that covered the muddy roads, past the herds of peasants bearing white flowers. Beyond the densest parts of the city, they stumbled into a wide, lightless field. Drunken woodsmen and skinny dirt-farmers filled the dark, muddy pasture, men who had come not for the wedding, but for an excuse to drink and brawl while their children ran wild through the fields. Ren and Adin pushed through the revelers, their hearts pounding, wind in their faces.

"Mithra's burning balls," Adin said as he ducked halfheartedly to avoid an amber-filled mug. Sour-smelling liquid splashed over the boy's shoulders. Adin shook, his breath quickening, a flush returning to his hollow cheeks. "Dammit, Ren, it's really you."

"Real as your mother's stink." Ren caught a spatter of ale on his cheek. Blood still covered his hands, so when he moved to brush aside the amber he smeared red viscera across his brow. "Dammit," he cried as he struggled to clean the blood from his face and arms.

Adin stole an unattended tank of amber from a tree stump. Stumbling in the darkness, he gulped it down in a single mouthful, holding the downturned vessel over his lips as he savored the last drops. Ren knocked him lightly on the jaw.

"Don't worry, Ren, next one's for you." Adin drew an amber-soaked grin.

"I'm not worried about my next drink." Ren was worried about soldiers, they were everywhere in the city, but they had managed to get this far. He wanted to keep moving, but Adin seemed unaware of the tenuous nature of his escape. Ren glimpsed iron helms in the distance. "Let's go," he said, still walking, tugging at Adin's shoulder. "You won't be safe until we've left Feren."

They ran, past the grubby, unlit cottages on the outskirts of the city, the hawkers of pots and blackthorn trinkets, past the wagons piled high with logs, only stopping when the crowds started to give way to farmers' crofts and hunters' lodges, to the dark quiet of the Gray Wood. At a crossroads where the path diverged in four directions, they waited on the road, looking through the darkness at the way they had come. Hooves beat in the distance. Soldiers approached, riding horses, moving faster than before. The boys hurried from the road, sloshing through ankle-deep mud and waist-high bracken, the green fronds brushing their arms, catching their tunics' loosely woven fibers. Huddling behind the spiky trunk of a blackthorn, they collapsed aside each other, heads spinning, their breath coming in gasps. They were malnourished, bone-thin, exhausted, but alive. Just as they had been in the Priory.

"Pain makes the man," Adin murmured. Ren wanted to laugh; his belly shook but he decided it was better to keep quiet.

As they sat in darkness, horns blared and hooves clopped. Ren exhaled in relief while Adin slumped in the pine needles that skirted the blackthorn's bell, his body so emaciated he looked like a reed bent in the wind. The smell of the starving was everywhere on him: His body was eating itself. Adin was in such poor condition he made the Feren slaves look healthy. *He would not have lasted much longer.* Ren immediately reached into his pack for a little bread and meat, handing them over to his friend.

"I could kiss you—you lovely bastard," Adin said, eating greedily but swallowing with difficulty.

"Hush," said Ren. He checked, but the soldiers were gone. "Save it for the whores." Ren covered Adin's mouth to avoid the boy's stink. "On second thought, start with the slaves. Have you smelled yourself? I sniffed horseshit at the Dromus that was less ripe."

Adin nearly choked on a bite of bread. "You would know." He cocked his head. "Prisoners don't meet whores, though I did smell a horse or two on the road." Adin exhaled into his palm. "You're right. Smells like turd. In fact, I smell like turd." He brushed dirt from his fingers. "Ren." Adin sobered. "Remember how we thought the Priory was the worst thing that could happen to us?"

Ren felt a chill.

"Well, after a day with the fucking slavers, the Priory felt like a bloody paradise. I ate beetles and bristles in the desert, a rat in my cell. They gave me a bucket to shit in, but they never emptied it." Adin's words went quiet, his gaze distant. "It feels like decades since Solus, how long has it been?"

"Weeks."

"Fuck. I thought it had been longer." Adin brushed back his hair and raised his eyebrows; he tried not to look weak or sad, though he looked both. "So your father—he's dead, then?"

"No, the king is not dead . . . but he may as well be. He was called to Sola, to appear before the emperor." Ren sighed.

"*To gaze upon the Soleri is to gaze upon the sun, and no man can survive that light,*" Adin quoted. He bowed his head. "I'm sorry, my friend." He put a hand on Ren's shoulder and gripped it manfully.

Ren shrugged. "I barely knew the old man. I cannot say I am sorry, or not sorry. I never expected to meet him. I suppose . . . ." He searched for words. "I suppose I should be happy I had a chance to know him."

"So you are the true heir of Harkana." Adin changed the subject. "You actually killed one of those oversized deer?"

"No need." Ren held up his walking stick, brushed the dirt from it, and revealed the eld horn.

"You're a king, then? So, why'd you come for me?"

"Are you that fucking dumb?" Ren asked.

Adin shrugged. "Maybe—care to enlighten me?"

"The eld—it's just some deer. It doesn't make me a king, not yet, not until I've taken my throne. In the meantime, I saved your ass—now, *that's* something, isn't it?"

"So you're really here by yourself? No kingsguard? No black shields?" It took a while for Ren to figure out that Adin was joking. "Mithra's ass, Ren. I thought you were leading me to a Harkan legion. We're really alone?"

"Just you, me, and that piss-soaked rag you've got tied around your waist." Ren stood. "I'm sorry I wasn't able to take the damned throne of Harkana before I came for you, so for now you will have to suffice with my help and no one's else's."

"Fair enough," said Adin, shivering in the night air. The boy was almost naked. Ren offered his tunic, but Adin just shook his head. He was half-starved and half-clothed, but he still had his pride.

"We should keep moving." Ren walked to the edge of the trail and glanced in both directions, but saw only darkness. "Which way?" Ren said. They stood at the crossing of three roads. "This is your country, isn't it?"

"You'll excuse me if I've forgotten the way." Adin's voice caught. "I was only eight when I left and I've spent the last few weeks in chains." When he saw the look on Ren's face he snorted. "I was only pulling your leg, old man. This way." He pointed down the dim road that led south.

When Ren still looked doubtful, Adin cocked his head in the opposite direction. "Soldiers're coming from the north—we're certainly not going in that direction."

Voices rang in the darkness, men coming down the Rifka road. His friend was right.

"Hurry." Adin pushed Ren in front of him.

Down the road and past a shabby wreck of a farm they ran, talking as they stumbled through dense bracken and gray trees. "How?" Ren said. "How did this happen—the chains, the soldiers. What happened when you left the Priory?"

"Well . . ." Adin nearly knocked into a blackthorn. "They caught me in the Hollows. Dagrun's men surrounded me before I could leave the city, before my father's loyal men could reach me. They put me in a cage, but my father's men infiltrated their camp. One of his soldiers passed me a message. My father was dead, but men loyal to him were maintaining the *tulou* at Catal. There were loyalists in Rifka too. My uncle by marriage, a man named Gallach, worked in the caer and would help me if I could find him. My father's soldier told me to seek out Gallach, but I had no opportunity, I saw nothing but the four walls of my cell, and spoke to no one."

"Have you had word since then?"

"No, nothing. I can't go back to the caer, so I need to find Catal." Adin ducked into the shadowy gap between two trees. The city was long gone. Darkness covered all of the wood, the trees turning to stone once more. "Should we make camp?" Ren asked, but Adin shook his head. "I don't want to stop."

Reluctantly, Ren agreed. Even if he had wanted to he knew they would not sleep tonight. There were soldiers in the forest; he could hear their horses and laughter. "All right." The shadow-drenched road lay ahead. "I suppose being lost in the woods is still preferable to Feren prison."

The two boys walked, side by side, Adin talking softly of his life since they had last seen each other. Ren was glad for the companionship, for a familiar voice to keep him company, though sometimes Adin's voice was like the sighing of a spirit coming in the night, the darkness so thick they could not see each other.

"I thought I had been there for months, Ren. I thought I had gone from one Priory to another. Aside from that first message, no one spoke to me—no guard said my name. Nothing.

"I thought they had left me to starve, then a pair of guards unlocked the door, bound my hands, and led me to the wedding platform. They tied me to the other slaves and left me. I was part of the bridal offering. I was to be a slave, a servant of the bride."

The bride. Dagrun's wife, my sister.

Ren shushed his friend: He thought he had heard something, a noise behind them—a twig snapping. But there was silence again, enveloping them in its cold comfort.

"I would have strangled Dagrun had he come close enough."

"The soldiers would have slit your throat before you reached the platform," Ren said.

"I don't care. That prick who murdered my father and stole our kingdom. The bastard did not even bother to suffer the Waking Rite. He's a thief—nothing more. I'll kill him."

"You will," Ren said, trying to sound hopeful, "but you're going to need help to manage that. Besides, what do you know of Feren? What do any of us know of our kingdoms? Perhaps your father was a tyrant and Dagrun did the Ferens a favor when he took the throne." Ren recalled the woodsmen's stories, how they had feared and reviled the old king.

"I'll find help at Catal," Adin told Ren. "You'll see."

"Catal?" Ren asked. "How can you be certain Dagrun hasn't taken the fortress and killed your father's men?"

"They live. My father's men will be there. And they'll help me, they'll know what to do."

Ren shook his head. "No, that's the hunger talking. Dagrun would not allow your father's men to live."

"So what would you do?"

I'd go to Catal. They needed soldiers.

Ren shifted uneasily in the darkness. He was still getting used to the sound of Adin's voice. He'd missed his friend. The tall boy was kin. Tye. Adin. They were the only ones who cared about him. He had no one else. It was why he had come back for Adin. If one did not have any family, what did one have? He thought of asking Adin to go with him to Solus, to wait for Tye's release, but he put the notion aside. He had another week, maybe ten days, before the Thieves' Moon. He could go to Catal, then Solus, and still arrive before the new moon. It seemed the best course. Adin's family could provide weapons, provisions, and perhaps a few men. Ren did not want to return to Solus unarmed and alone, not unless he had no other choice.

He thought of his sister Merit, who had sent soldiers to hunt him down, her own husband to cut his throat. There was no family there. For ten years he had dreamed of his kingdom, he had known the path he would take outside the Priory. That path was no longer certain.

He stood up, brushing the needles from his tunic, offering his hand to Adin. "We head to Catal," Ren said, ready for the journey. "Do you know how to get there?"

⇒35⇐

The wedding done and the dress removed, Kepi's servants washed and perfumed her, dressed her in a silky frock, this one even smaller than the last, a slip of fine muslin that hung from two straps, open at the chest, the younger girls blushing and giggling as they went about their work, the elder looking grim. Kepi yawned. Her head was only now clearing from the opiate. The servant who had pitied her—the half-blind girl, Dalla—dressed Kepi's hair with oil and said that she would check on her in the morning, that she would come at first light to see what her queen needed from her. The girls took their time and Kepi did not rush their preparations. They fussed and fretted. Dalla was the last to leave, her bony shoulders disappearing behind the blackthorn door as it closed.

Alone, the cold chamber brought back memories of her first wedding night. Kepi gnawed at her bitten-down nails. *In the morning, Dalla, will you find me cowering in some closet? No.*

In the hallway she overheard Dagrun's voice, the sound of his footsteps. "I want Barrin's heir found," he said. "Bring me his head, or offer me yours," he said, dismissing the other man. Footsteps thudded in the corridor. The door opened. She cast about for a sheet to cover herself, then realized she was being silly. He had already seen her. All of Feren had.

"My wife," said Dagrun, not unkindly. His expression bore something strange in it, something she could not quite read. It was kindness—or at least it was trying to be.

Kepi was unmoved.

"Are you all right?" he asked.

No words formed on her lips.

He came nearer. He was so close now she could feel his warmth against her breasts, against her belly through the fabric of her dress. He picked up her small wrist in his large hand, encircling it completely.

She tried to calm herself, but she could not keep the servants' gossip from her thoughts.

"There's no need to be frightened of me. I hope you haven't listened to the girls' stories." He cast her a doubtful glance. "And you were never so scared to meet me in the ring."

"We were both wearing armor then," Kepi said dryly.

Dagrun smiled. "Shall I fetch your sword? Will that bring you comfort?" he asked. "Don't believe the servants' chatter. Scandal is their currency—am I wrong?"

No. Kepi swallowed. He was right, of course. His words rang true, but did it matter? Dagrun and Merit had tossed her in a cage and ridden her to Rifka without any care for her comfort, or her pride.

When she once more refused to reply, his smile flattened, his teeth abruptly looking strong and white against his face and the darker stubble where his beard had grown in four, five days' growth, the crook in his nose that had looked menacing in the torchlight now giving him a rough, mannish air. "We are married and might as well speak to each other."

"We did not *speak* as we rode to Feren. You locked me in a carriage."

"The war carriage was made for your protection. If you had stayed within it, you would have been safe. My soldiers told me what happened, how you fought the outlanders. It was *unnecessary*. The carriage was black-thorn and sturdy. No arrow could breach its walls."

She nodded ever so slightly, acknowledging that he spoke the truth. "Why was I kept isolated?"

"My men," he said. "I don't trust all of them, not yet. On Cutting Day, in the forest, a man armed with a spear rushed the platform. He was trying to kill me. The dead king has loyalists, still. And his heir escaped during the wedding. There are traitors everywhere. In the forest, in the company of soldiers, you were not safe. Kepi, I meant you no harm."

"I don't know," she said, finding it hard to believe him. She retreated, thinking, considering his words. Upon reflection, the carriage, its armor and slotted windows were justified, but those facts hardly mattered. She was here, in Rifka, against her will. Even if he cared for her safety, he ignored her happiness, her freedom. It was Merit he wanted, not her. "Why was I not told any of this?" she asked. "Why was I kept uninformed? Do you know how that felt, and what I thought of you? You protected me as you would protect your property, nothing more. And besides, I know it's my sister you want."

He took a step, then another, moving Kepi back and back until she felt the cold of the wall behind her. "Your sister?" he asked.

"It's the talk of the empire. You and Merit."

"You know a lot of gossip."

"Is it *true*?"

"About Merit?" His brow furrowed. "I have not bedded the woman, if that is what you ask." He was so close now that Kepi could smell the amber on his breath from the wedding feast, strong and sour. Her heart thudded in her ears. *He's lying. He has to be lying. Everyone in Harwen knew Merit and Dagrun were lovers.* "I don't believe you."

"Ask her yourself." He pushed up against her, pulled her close so that he could whisper in her ear. His hands on her shoulders were firm, warm.

Her stomach clenched with revulsion, with confusion. His other hand slid down her back and up her dress. "Ever since we sparred, since I felt your strength, I have wanted you, Kepi. Why do you think I spared you in the ring?"

His hands were on her nipples, brushing them so lightly she was not quite sure they were real. They felt soft, and strong, and sure. Not like Roghan, who had clawed at her body like an animal, who had cared nothing whatsoever for her pleasure. Not like Seth, even, who had been so shy and uncertain that he had hardly touched her. Dagrun moved his hands in little circles down her belly, up the soft insides of her thighs. Her muscles were so tense they were shaking. Her breath came in short bursts.

"No, stop," she said, and Dagrun's hands fell from her body.

She looked up wonderingly at him. "You stopped."

"You asked me to," he said reasonably.

"But it is our wedding night."

Dagrun leaned back on the bed. "And?"

She stared at him. "You will not . . . force yourself on me?"

"I can't think of anything more distasteful," he said. "I told you not to believe the stories they tell about me. They *are* only stories."

"My first husband, he—" She wavered, wondering how to begin her story. His unexpected kindness compelled her to tell him who she was and what she had endured, so she told him about her first wedding: the cottage in the blackthorn grove, the brief wedding ceremony, and the sad little feast Roghan held after it. She told him how Roghan drank and the violence the drinking brought out in him.

He listened, patient and observant, his eyes never leaving her face.

She told him about her year in Feren, her story, but not all of it. She was not yet ready to share the whole truth, to tell her new husband what she had told no one, so she waited for him to speak, to see how he would respond.

"Roghan was a drunk, a crass and drunken fool. I knew you were imprisoned, but I didn't know that he had abused you. I am not surprised though. I knew Roghan Frith, but he was no friend. I knew the kind of man he was and how he was with women. I have known animals more clever—kinder too," he said softly. "I am sorry you had to live through that, sorry that I said kind words about the man at our betrothal in Harwen." Dagrun lowered his voice and continued. "I am no Roghan. I am not even Feren, not wholly. It is not well known, but my blood is half Rachin. The mountain lords raised me in the highlands beyond the Harkan Cliff. Their ways are harsh but honest. They live by a code, the Chaldaan. They value merit, not birthright. A man must earn his wealth as well as his title. I am a half-blood. By Feren law, I am unworthy of the throne and yet I am king. I earned the blackthorn seat; I fought for my place in the Chathair. I did what no other Feren was willing to do: I killed Barrin and took his throne. The man was hated, despised by even his sworn men. He bankrupted his kingdom and made slaves of those who opposed him. He was Roghan's cousin—*did you know that?* The pair were well matched, their appetite for debauchery well known. Neither deserved their power or position." He squeezed her hand and asked again, "Am I wrong?"

"No," she said. "You are more right than you guess."

She drew up close, her lips nearly touching his. She would tell him now. She would tell him everything.

"I killed him," she whispered, her eyes dark and fiery. "I watched him die. When we were alone in his cottage after the feast, when it was just the two of us in his bedroom, he tried to hurt me. He threw me down on the table and ripped my clothes. He meant to take me by force, but I struck him with a kick before he could put himself inside me. I sent him rolling to the floor like a drunken fool. He hit his head. Unconscious, he choked on his own vomit while I did nothing. He drowned in his spit. I've told no one the truth. For three years I've told no one. I think about it every day and I am glad. His people believe I killed him and they are right. I was only ten and three and I didn't know what else to do. I didn't know what *he* would do when he woke, so I did nothing. I killed Roghan Frith."

Dagrun did not respond, and the silence between them grew. Kepi shivered, uncertain of how her new husband would reply. Would he send her to the gallows? She had confessed to killing a man.

"Say something."

"There is nothing to say. You did not kill Roghan. It was his drunkenness that led to his end. You only did what you had to do. We are not so different, Kepi." He folded her short locks, cupping her neck, her cheek. "At our wedding, during the offering, I was glad when you freed the slaves, happy to see the tradition ended. It's a barbarous practice—a wedding sealed by a sacrifice."

He placed a woolen mantle on her shoulders to cover her. "I will not take what is not given freely and I will not hold you in Feren against your will. In the trunk there is a dress, sandals, and a cloak. Go, out the door, past the wall. Leave if you like." He gestured to the door. "My guards will not stop you."

Then he was gone, and Kepi felt curiously bereft. A small part of her thought it might not have been so terrible if he had stayed.

36

Sarra's caravan left Desouk on horseback, riding in a thin wisp of smoke just after dawn, riding hard and making camp outside the Dromus, on a strip of land that straddled the Harkan border. The escort she requested while still in Desouk arrived as her priests pitched tents. The Harkan soldiers dismounted and their captain announced himself: "I'm Sirin Dasche." He told them that Barca, the Soleri traitor, was approaching at a terrific pace from the south, the San from the north and west. "You'll have no more than a week in the Shambles before you'll need to turn back. If you stay any longer, Barca or the San will block your retreat."

Sarra considered her situation. Wars were unpredictable things, but the Shambles was a desolate place. It held no strategic worth. She had to hope the outlanders would ride around the barren land and not block her path.

Her eye caught something odd: Dasche wore a strip of black fabric wrapped around his arm. Black was the color of Horu. Sarra had worn it in Desouk to illustrate her grief. "What is it?" she asked. "Why do you wear the black?"

"It's . . ."

"It's what?" she asked. "Is it the king?" Her husband was aging, perhaps something had happened to him.

Dasche nodded. "He was summoned to Solus, to meet the emperor."

"'To meet the emperor.'" She repeated his words. Immediately, she wondered why her informants in Solus had not relayed this news prior to her departure. Perhaps the riots were to blame, or Barca's army.

"When?" she asked. "When was he summoned?" Sarra doubted much time had passed or she would have heard the news.

"The call came just after the Devouring," he said, spitting when he named the high feast of the Soleri. "An entire legion of the Alehkar arrived in Harwen. I heard the king slaughtered a dozen soldiers before they took him, just to show the men what he was made of. He left Harwen some time after the Devouring."

"Then it is done," she said, her words a whisper. The march from Harwen to Solus was not long. Arko had met the emperor when she was still in Desouk. He had seen the face of the god and perished.

She walked to the edge of the camp, motioning for Ott to attend to the men.

Arko is dead.

A meeting with Tolemy had no other outcome. No man entered the Empyreal Domain, save for the Ray, and survived.

Sarra cursed.

There was something she'd wanted to say to Arko before he died, a matter she had kept hidden for a decade—one that would now stay hidden. That realization hurt her more than the news of her husband's death.

She rubbed her sandals against the rocks. *Damn you for leaving like this, Arko.*

She pictured the king of Harkana, the rough beard and hulking shoulders. The white stone he wore around his neck. She had begged him to discard the thing, but he refused. She wondered if he kept it still, if he wore it on his neck when he met Tolemy. Was the stone burned to ash just as Arko was surely turned to ash when he stood in the emperor's presence? Were the stories even true? Perhaps Suten's guards had simply cut off Arko's head.

"Are you okay, Mother?" Dasche asked, looking concerned.

Sarra tried to smile, but her lips would not move. "Yes, of course." She ground her teeth. "I'm fine—just feeling a little regret," she said. "Tell your men to pitch tents and prepare the camp. We leave at first light," she said sternly, not wanting to look weak as she had a moment prior. She turned from the others, leaving Dasche to direct the men while she took a soldier aside to help her raise a tent so she could sleep.

She made camp, but found little rest.

The next morning, while the desert hills were still black with shadows, Sarra and her caravan set off with their Harkan guard, moving fast, resting little, up from a dry creek bed into a brown landscape of sandy cliffs pocked with small holes where sacred statues of ancient gods had once sat, then down into the dry, sandy valley.

This part of Harkana was desolate in a way that had always depressed her, as a younger woman, as a queen—it was nothing but rocks and sand. When she was a child in the southern islands there was always the water, the movement of the sea, the endless blue horizon, the pale clouds, and gray, fog-hooded mountains, the chirping of birds. The island kingdom had not yet fallen to squalor and poverty then, but was a place of peace and relative plenty. Harkana had none of that. When she had first seen the north, the desert plains and the Shambles, when she had crossed the land as a young woman, it had made her heart sink. She saw neither homes, nor herds, nor any other sign of settlement. Even the buzzards had abandoned this place, moving on years ago to the more fertile hunting grounds of Feren. There was some life in the lowland plains and in the hunting reserve, in the high mountain pastures where trees and grasses grew and the eld hunted, but there was none here. Nothing moved and nothing lived, and the bareness of the landscape did little to improve her mood.

"Noll," Sarra called to the boy as she rode up alongside him. "Pass me your map." Noll drew forth the parchment, pointing out a few monuments to help Sarra orient herself.

The drawing described the country through landmarks: the mighty cliff with its pockmarked face, the absent statues, the long plain running parallel to the cliffs. The monuments that time could not wither, the mountains and plains, remained for them to see, but the Amaran Road was hidden, covered in sand and rocks. They knew where the road would have been, but they could not find it. They combed the rocky desert, shading their eyes against the sun, their progress slow and exhausting. Her caravan had to stop often to water the horses, water themselves, the Harkan soldiers snorting as they took long gulps of amber and laughing at some unheard joke.

The sun ground its circle into the horizon; they made camp and rose early the next day. At midday they passed a line of standing stones, small totems that marked the edge of the Shambles. Not longer after, a sizeable Harkan patrol blocked their path, but when the soldiers recognized her Harkan escort and saw the woman who was still their king's wife, they quickly let her caravan pass. Sarra had known the Shambles was well guarded, but the size of the force surprised her. Aside from the Elden Hunt there was no reason for anyone to come here—no life, no resources. Nothing anyone wanted. They found only half-buried rocks, stones whose skin was mottled and black, coarse sand, and lifeless plants.

"Perhaps the road is buried underground," Sarra said.

"Maybe it was covered, concealed by someone," Ott said. "Perhaps the road's surface lies just below the sand." Ott rode astride a low hill pointing to an uneven cliff, its face oddly vertical, like a loaf of bread with one side removed. "The Soleri built their roads from local limestone," he said. "The wide, flat stones made a cart's passage smoother, but the large pieces were difficult to transport. So the paving stones were often quarried from cliffs that ran alongside the road." If they could not see the road, if the trail were buried beneath centuries of sand and rock, they might at least spy the quarries from which the stones were taken. Ott pointed to a cliff. The sheer face seemed too flat to have been carved by nature's hand. He stopped the caravan and slipped from his horse.

"Dig here," he said.

The Harkans drove their spears into the hard-packed sand until their points clinked against a layer of stone.

"Shovels," said Sarra.

The men brought out their digging tools. Clearing away the sand and rocks proved difficult, so much so that Ott suggested that perhaps the road was not covered by windblown sand but had been deliberately buried. Sarra glanced at Noll, who nodded. Perhaps that was why the Amaran Road was so difficult to uncover—it had been buried, concealed by someone beneath a layer of earth.

Shadows drifted across the sand as the soldiers cleared away rocks and hard clay. When their work was done, Sarra walked upon what she guessed was the old road, the trail they had sought. Standing on the stones, she saw the road's direction and shape. She noted where the hills had been cut and altered, where the road swung to avoid a cluster of stones or a cliff. "So this is it, the Amaran Road, a path once walked by the Soleri," she said.

They rode on through the rest of the afternoon, passing a circle of rocks where a tower had once stood, a groove left by ancient wheels, a trench where a wall had been. Wind and war had long ago destroyed the buildings and left nothing in their wake but ruin. The ground grew rockier, the road faded in and out, the sun dimmed. Sometimes they saw only gouges in the cliffs where the stones were once quarried; sometimes they saw nothing at all. More than once they lost track of the road completely and had to double back to where they had last caught sight of the trail or its quarry. Up ahead, the day's last light lingered along a distant ridge. Sarra shaded her eyes and watched a line of dust on the horizon: San warriors moving northward. Sarra needed to hurry.

Near dusk they came upon a shallow hole in the earth that once must have been the cellar of a mighty stone tower, now filled in with sand and rock. A half-collapsed stair led downward from the tower's base, but rocky debris blocked the remainder of the passage.

Noll pointed to a symbol on his drawing, one of the arrowheads that indicated a house of some kind, a storehouse perhaps, then glanced at the distant landscape. "Those cliffs are on the map, the dry lake bed too. This place, the tower, once sat astride the road."

"Then we will stop here." Sarra nodded toward the stair. "Dig."

The soldiers dug until past dark, until their shovels met stone. They lifted the stones out, one by one, pulling them from the earth and passing them from soldier to soldier in a chain. By morning the soldiers had cleared the rocks from what now appeared to be a subterranean stairway. By afternoon they had found a passage beneath the tower, a door half-buried in sand revealing a set of stairs spiraling downward, and beneath that a well-preserved corridor, its floor only partly covered with sand. The tower they found astride the Amaran Road concealed a warren of underground tunnels. A stout Harkan led them through the passage, a torch held high, its flickering light dancing on the walls.

The walls were black. "Mold?" a soldier asked.

"No. There is no rot in the desert." Sarra ran her finger across the rumpled black surface. "Ash." The markings turned to dust at her touch, the air filling with a faint cloud. *What happened here?*

A snapping sound echoed through the corridor. She saw Noll bending to unearth a broken arrow from the sand. *A battle,* thought Sarra as she brushed more ash from the wall. Deep grooves marred the stone relief.

Ott ran his fingers through the dust.

Sarra gave him a questioning glance, but he only shrugged. He had no idea what they were looking at either.

The Harkans pushed onward toward the as-yet-unexplored end of the corridor, their black leather blending with the darkness, leading Sarra and her priests deeper into the passage. The corridor widened, and rows of statues flanked the passage. Long folds of drapery hung from the statues' shoulders, a snake coiled into a circle graced their chests. It was the same symbol she had seen in the map chamber. *More wards.* Statues and murals built to scare off looters. She brushed her shoulder against a stony hand, its touch feeling like a piece of the past reaching out to contact her, to speak to her.

They found chamber after chamber, destroyed, soot covering the walls, doors broken, tables shattered. "They were beating out a retreat," one of the Harkans spoke out from the back of the line, a boy named Taig. He froze when the Mother Priestess and former queen caught his gaze.

"It's a retreat," he continued. "They were fighting as they retreated, blocking passages, locking themselves in rooms. They were trying to escape."

"Who? Who fled and who chased?" she asked, but the boy had no reply.

Ott seemed unconvinced. "Where are the victims, their bones at least? Our desert loves its corpses—the sand and salt will keep a body intact for centuries, sometimes longer."

Taig stammered until his superior clipped him on the head. The Harkan captain, Dasche, finished for the boy, "Isn't it clear? They escaped."

The passage led to a wall of sand. The Harkans brought spades and shovels. They found stones beneath the sand, chunks too large to dislodge.

They collapsed the passage. In desperation they sealed the stones behind them and continued onward. Who were they? Who chased and who fled?

"Gods," Sarra murmured, Ott at her side, "what happened here?"

≩ 37 ≨

The crack of iron cleaving wood shot through the open window of Merit's chamber. Outside, sullen-eyed slaves chipped at the wedding platform, splitting the logs and carrying them away. The Night Wedding was over and the platform was nearly half disassembled. Two days had passed since the ceremony. Kepi had married Dagrun; their kingdoms were united. She had waited impatiently for Dagrun to come to her chamber, or to summon her to his, but there had been no sign of him so far. Perhaps he had heeded her words too deeply and was intent on making certain his new bride was with child before he laid his hands on Merit. Perhaps she had been too restrictive. No matter. She would remedy the situation soon enough and erase all memory of her sister in his mind. It was doubtful that Kepi had even made an impression on him. All Merit needed now was news from Shenn—word that the deed was done and Ren's claim to the throne was ended.

But that news had not arrived.

More than a week had passed since Shenn had left for the Shambles, but she had not heard from her husband. There were Feren outposts along the northern edge of the Shambles and Harkan outposts along the southern. When her husband left the sacred hunting grounds, he could send word to her. But he hadn't.

She wondered if he had failed her.

The door creaked open.

Ahti entered without knocking. "Dagrun called for you—he requests your presence in the Chathair."

"The Chathair? Why?" she wondered aloud. And if Dagrun wanted to see her, why not just arrive at her chamber as he had in the past? Why did he need to speak to her in a formal setting?

"I . . . I don't know," Ahti said, her face blank.

"He gave no reason?" Merit asked, but the girl only shook her head.

Sensing that she would learn no more from her waiting woman, Merit thanked Ahti and went out, shutting the door behind her. Why would Dagrun summon her to the seat of power?

Unfamiliar with the corridors of Caer Rifka Merit lost her way, but only briefly. Stumbling down a corridor she caught sight of a tall and soaring chamber, a space so vast that it could only be the Chathair. Slipping between the open doors, smelling fresh pine and lotus, she entered the vast hall, a round space of indeterminate depth, cluttered with statues and carvings. Past a block of stone she gazed up at a sight that took her breath away: blackthorn columns whittled to an almost ethereal thinness filled the hall. They were not ordered in neat rows like the monuments in Harkana but staggered almost at random, giving the effect of a finely carved forest, gleaming in the torchlight. Merit pushed through the columns and caught sight of the Chathair itself. It was a simple stool carved from the same silvery-gray wood as the rest of the chamber, its four faces inscribed with strange characters. Behind the stool, in a place where the slender columns parted, stood a thing that appeared, at first glance, like a dead tree, but was in fact a monumental sculpture. It was the Kiteperch. She had heard of it, but never imagined it would be so enormous. A proper king of Feren held the kite as a symbol of his throne and his power. When he sat upon the throne, the kite roosted above him on the perch. In Feren legend, the kite was joined on the perch by all of the forest birds. They cried a great and solemn song, the Dawn Chorus, to announce the reign of a new king. Dagrun had no kite, he had not undergone the vigil and so the perch was empty. As far as Merit knew, no kite had sat upon the perch for fifty years. The previous king, Barrin, had earned his kite, but the creature had quickly abandoned the king, casting doubt upon Barrin and his rule.

"Is this your first time in the Chathair?" The words belonged to Dagrun. He emerged from behind a spindly white column. "I first saw the tree when I was a boy. There was no kite upon it, the Kiteperch was empty then as it is now," he said, moving closer to the tree and touching it. "See that opening?" He pointed upward, to a place where the thatched roof parted to reveal a blue patch of sky. "It's called the Wind's Eye, it's where the kite enters. In past days, the birds of the forest would descend through the Eye, swarming the chamber, alighting on the great perch, cawing wildly. It was a gruesome sight, or so I am told. I rather like it without the creatures."

Merit nodded. While she shared some interest in the superstitions of the kingdom, she was more interested in why Dagrun had summoned her to the throne room and not his bedchamber.

"I haven't heard from Shenn if that's why you summoned me," she said, thinking that perhaps he too shared her worries. He had asked about Shenn once before, at the Felling.

"This isn't about your husband. I'm certain he will be successful in his endeavor—no, this is about Barca."

"The rebel?"

"He has changed course. He is not yet ready to strike at Solus, but he *is* strong enough to strike at a less formidable opponent."

"Harkana?"

Dagrun nodded. "Are your men prepared?"

"Of course we're prepared. From the moment he breached the Coronel, we guessed he might advance on the Hornring." It was true, they had anticipated Barca's actions, but she had not guessed that he would move with such swiftness.

She understood now why Dagrun had not summoned her to his chamber. This was a matter of state, about the safety of her kingdom. He had summoned her as a fellow monarch to discuss their common enemy. "Why haven't my messengers reported this news?" she asked.

"Barca is using an army of outlanders to attack from the north while his troops approach from the south. The outlanders may have captured your messengers."

"Are the roads blocked?" she asked, her voice raised just a little.

"No, the ways are clear, but they are dangerous," he said quietly.

"I must go then," she said, knowing she had no other choice. Harkana was without its ruler. "I must leave immediately, and arrive in Harwen before Barca. I cannot be trapped on the wrong side of his lines."

"Of course."

Her thoughts were spinning. "Harkana will take the rebel with ease. He will find our troops are not as soft as the Protector's guard. Even now I'll wager that our troops are testing him."

"I have no doubt," he said. "But must you go so soon?" he asked, his voice lower, and he moved closer to her, whispering in her ear. "Can it not wait until tomorrow? Perhaps, after tonight."

After tonight and the promises they had made each other would bear fruit.

She had waited for this, had wanted this ever since they had met a year ago. Why had he not come to her earlier? It was two whole days after the wedding. Why had he not sought her out before now? He had wasted time and now she was out of it.

Merit shook her head. She had duties and responsibilities to her kingdom. War was afoot. The rebel was upon her land. She could not linger here, not with him, not in his bed. Her desires must wait, as must his.

"I want nothing more," she said. "The roads are clear now, but they may be blocked soon enough. Each moment I delay leaves my kingdom in danger."

Dagrun drew her close to him. "Do what you must, then return to me." His tone and the strength of his voice told Merit that she had nothing to fear, that their union, though unconsummated, was strong. They had waited for so long to be together, surely they could wait a little longer.

She sighed in his arms. Yes, of course. She would return to Rifka. He would find no comfort in her sister's thin arms, she was sure. Dagrun's desire for Merit would only flourish in her absence. "I am yours," she whispered. "I owe you a wedding night. Wait for me."

"I have done nothing but, Merit," said Dagrun, resigned.

She nodded, satisfied.

He released her from his embrace. He cleared his throat and spoke to her as a king and not a lover. "See that your guards speak to my man-at-arms and the stable master. You should take fast horses and arm your guards well. I have a contingent of soldiers who will escort you safely to Harwen."

"There is no need. My guards will suffice. Sevin and his men are as fierce as they are loyal," she said, too proud of her Harkan men to accept any of his. "Barca would not dare strike at my caravan. A Harkan regent travels under Harkan guard—I need no chaperone."

⇥ 38 ⇤

"The bright fire that blazed on the mountain now shines upon the city of light." Khalden Wat forced open the doors of the Cenotaph, proclaiming the glories of the new Ray. The Mouth of Tolemy had lit a star upon the cliffs and told all of Solus that there was a new Ray of the Sun. The assembled grandees of Solus shuffled inside in their glorious finery, in their diaphanous cloaks of fine muslin, in their jewels and gold, to find the Harkan king, Arko Hark-Wadi, half-drunk and leaning on his elbows at a table that filled nearly the circumference of the Cenotaph. *Let them scoff,* he thought. *Let them whisper and hiss.* He expected no less.

Arko studied each as they entered, eyeing them closely, judging them as they no doubt judged him. He could see the generals and viziers, the priests and merchants, attempt to conceal their surprise when they realized who the man was in front of them, who it was that the emperor had chosen.

The young Protector, Amen Saad, made no effort to contain his disrespect, refusing to bow and clearly finding displeasure at having to celebrate the ascension of another man to the Ray's position. A man whom the empire had believed was called to his death. Saad carried a cheated expression, looking as if Arko had stolen the Eye of the Sun from him. *Maybe I did steal it,* thought Arko.

He gave the young Protector a second glance, looking him up and down. So this was the ambitious young man who desired to rule the empire, thought Arko as he took the measure of Saad, and watched the way he shouted and slapped his generals and advisers on their backs. Untested warriors, men like Saad, were often overconfident—their ignorance made them proud. Seeing the way Saad stood, the way he smiled, Arko already knew how he would dispatch the Father Protector.

They settled into their chairs one by one, and in their pointed glances at one another and shocked whispers Arko could already see his future. He would never please them. He would never manage to give them what they wanted, which was a Ray who was one of them—not this outsider, this Harkan, and one who had never even seen the inside of the Priory either.

This was his second week in Solus, though it seemed as if he had been here for ages. He had spent his days conferring with Khalden Wat, discussing Arko's role within the empire. He had toured the House of Ministers and seen the great hall where a thousand scribes hunched over trestle tables, scribbling out decrees and other mandates, copying and translating scrolls from every part of the empire. The mechanics of it all were mind-boggling at first sight, but Wat had told him to be patient, that it would take time for him to learn the ways of Solus. For now, he needed to attend to his formal duties. This banquet was his first task.

Wat took his place at Arko's side, standing atop a wooden stool, introducing the gathered dignitaries to Arko Hark-Wadi by name and title: Cheneres Haas, Vizier of the Southern Nomes; Geta Entefe, High Priestess of Horu; Bern Serekh, Keeper of Days; Mered Saad, Keeper of Seals, Overseer of the House of Crescents . . . the list went on. The new Ray poured himself another drink and raised his glass, but he saw little use in flattering them—he had never been good at it anyway. He had always left such duties to Merit, who had reveled in them. He felt another pang of homesickness and wondered how his daughter was faring. She was wrong to say that he only loved Kepi. While his youngest shared his interests, he relied on his eldest to run the kingdom. Though he had shielded his first daughter from the burdens of power, he trusted Merit, and perhaps the next time he saw her he would tell her that. He thought about Ren too; he was eager to know the boy's progress. He had ordered messengers sent, but had not yet received replies.

While Wat droned, Arko took another drink. He started to feel warm and tipped his head back to look at the broad sphere of the Cenotaph, lit from outside at the moment by the midday sun. The dome above was dotted with tiny perforations, holes that let in the daylight. Against the black inner face of the dome, these points of daylight resembled stars in the night sky—one star for each of the Soleri who once lived in this city and ruled over the empire. The Soleri had no other graves, no burial monuments of any kind. They had only this chamber, dotted with these points of light. Gazing at those lights, Arko realized what the Cenotaph really was: a tomb with no body. He guessed the building was just another ruse, an elaborate deception, designed to conceal the absence of the Soleri. It made him wonder if the Soleri had ever existed, but he quickly took back the thought. Surely the gods were not a myth. A distant forebear, many generations removed, Sarren Hark-Wadi, had seen one of the twelve, roaming the markets of Harwen, wearing his mask of gold, in the time before the War of the Four. His grandfather had passed the story down through the family, and his father had often told it to him as a child.

In a far-off niche, a girl sang a hymn. "The Song of Days," Wat called it. It accompanied the meal and was sung from sunrise to sunset. *Beautiful but pointless,* Arko thought, his mind starting to turn hazy from the alcohol. *Like everything else in Solus.*

As the girl crooned and the dome faded from darkness to light, the Feast of the Ray would be served in twelve courses, spanning from sunrise to sunset, so that all who attended could observe this cycle of the sun and stars. "Like some damned torture session," Arko had moaned, but Wat had turned up his nose and said he hoped not. At the cycle's end, Arko would perform his first public duty as Ray: a simple address thanking the gods, the emperor, and the highborn citizens in attendance. Arko was looking forward to his address. He wanted to show the gathered priests and viziers, dressed in their colorful silks and muslin wraps, how a man from the lower kingdoms spoke, how a king from a rebel land commanded his subjects.

A bell announced the start of the feast.

Wat stepped down from his seat and raised his hands. The doors opened at the far end of the hall, admitting priestesses in white robes, their arms filled high with greenery. They came first with bundles of palm leaves, then rushes wrapped in date twine and poppies. They laid out strings of vine woven with golden safflower, wreaths of acacia, and heaping olive-leaf bouquets that overfilled the table. In a tribute to the kingdom of Harkana, they had woven garlands of willow leaves over gnarled ram's horns and hung the bony festoons among the wreaths.

A priest brought out a horned glass and filled it with date wine.

Arko downed it in one long gulp, then signaled for another. It wasn't the good, strong amber of Harkana or even the sweet wine of the southern islands, but he could get used to it.

While the priestesses adorned the walls with garlands of cornflower and softy polished beads of carnelian, Arko again emptied his cup and asked for another. The women lit dim fires. The stars above burned brightly in their mock nighttime display, adding glimmer to the beads and dressings. The priestesses carried deep-blue faience bowls and poured water to the vessels' rims. The white-robed women placed a bowl at each setting and gestured for the dignitary to rinse.

Arko gulped another cup of wine.

A tall priestess with fiery eyes caught Arko's gaze as she laid a floral collar over his head. The smell was overpowering, but Arko saw only the woman in front of him. Something in her eyes reminded him of his wife. He hadn't seen Sarra in a decade, but he knew she came often to Solus. He realized he had been expecting to meet her at nearly every moment since he had been named Ray. He murmured to Wat, "Where is the Mother Priestess, Sarra Amunet? Is she in the city?"

Wat shook his head. She had gone to Desouk, he said, after the Devouring, and no one knew when she might return. He told Arko what transpired on the last day of the year, how some said the crowds had torn the Mother from the wall, while others said the pilgrims had shielded the Mother from the rioting. Sarra herself had sent news to Solus telling her followers that she had emerged unscathed from the riots.

"A hoax then, that was not Sarra Amunet on the wall," said Arko, dismissing the story with a wave of his hand. A shocked look crossed Wat's face, but the man gave no reply. Perhaps he felt Arko's accusation was sacrilege, but Arko didn't care. He knew the woman well and understood how her mind worked. "Tell me when you hear that she's returned to Solus. She is . . . unpredictable, remember that." Arko touched the white stone at his neck. He thought of his childhood, the time before he was king, before he truly understood the concessions his kingdom had made to keep him out of the Priory, before he felt the weight of his position, of his father's decisions. He remembered his tutor, Magnus, and the girl his tutor brought with him from the Wyrre. Arko stroked the white stone and breathed a little deeper.

Wat rumpled his lip, a sign of disapproval, but Arko paid him no attention. His thoughts were on Sarra. A confrontation with his wife was inevitable. If he knew her like he once did, he guessed she would seek him out when she returned to Solus, and he wanted to make certain he was ready. Arko emptied his cup in a single draught and pushed aside his plate.

"Did Suten Anu go through all this misery," Arko asked Wat, "when he was made Ray?"

"He did and he saw to the details himself," Wat replied with a faint smile.

More dishes arrived—candied citrons and cherries, cakes of dried dates and figs. In the gap between plates, Arko insisted Wat speak to him. His mind was on his family. "Have my letters," he said in Wat's ear, "reached Harkana yet?"

Wat replied that it was too soon, that in another day or two, word would come.

"I hope so," he said. "It's not like my daughter not to answer." Merit would know what to do, he knew. He hoped she would visit Sola as he had requested. "One more thing. My good friend and captain, Asher Hacal, accompanied me to Harwen. The soldiers sent him home, but he stayed outside the city walls, said he'd camp there till I was gone. Can you search for the man, see if his tent still sits outside the wall?"

Wat agreed, motioned for a page, murmured in the boy's ear, then sent him away.

When they cleared the plates, the last pinhole of light faded from the dome and a eunuch lit the mighty brazier at the center of the Cenotaph. The room came alive with dancing flame. The girl who sang "The Song of Days" emerged from her niche to wander the dark chamber, humming her tune, hearing the words echo across the dome.

To an appreciative roar of the crowd more men carried immense beasts—the horned oryx and addax, roasted whole on a spit—into the chamber to be sliced and served. They brought slabs of wild oxen and cakes of black pudding, reminiscent of a Harkan favorite Arko had loved as a child. The black and bloody dish brought back memories of his father, of the war he had fought with this very empire, with the Ray of the Sun.

Such power in my hands now, Arko thought. *I shall reshape the empire. I will ease the tributes and end the practice of sending ransoms to the Priory.* Arko swore that there would be no more marriages blessed by Tolemy, and no more slaves across the empire, that all citizens would be free men and women as in Harkana.

Arko had asked for a gathering of the highborn families, a congress with the viziers, as well as a meeting with the Protector, but Wat had told him to wait. The city was on holiday due to his ascension as Ray. There would be no meetings, and when the holiday was over a series of rites and initiations must be observed before he could hold office. Arko had grumbled loudly. The position was all ceremony—he yearned for action.

"It's nearly time for you to speak." Wat interrupted his thoughts. He cautioned him, indicating the cup of wine with a slight wave of his finger, begging Arko to cease his drinking, but Arko ignored the old man.

The servants came to take the plates while the viziers and generals stood, soaked their hands, dried them, and waited for the next plate. Arko, head spinning wildly, turned to Wat, who shook his head and laughed. Was his unease that obvious? "Thank Mithra for the dimming fires," Wat told him. "Otherwise all of Solus will know that you despise them as much as they've guessed."

Arko laughed at that. Indeed, the room was nearly dark and Arko had had more than his fill of wine.

"Is something funny, Harkan?" a voice growled. "Do you find our ceremonies amusing?"

Arko leaned forward, but he could not see who had spoken—all the guests had the same unpleasant looks on their faces. Only Amen Saad set down his cup, wiping the dregs from his beard. He raised his eyes to Arko's. "Not at all," said the new Ray, pushing the plate aside. "I choose not to indulge myself while there is war in the kingdoms. A regent suffers the same hardships as his soldiers. That's what a Harkan king would do and what a Ray ought to."

"The customs of Harkana won't hold here."

"True," Arko said, unexpectedly. "Those customs don't hold here—they haven't for some time—a deficiency our emperor has chosen to correct." He said no more, but his implication was clear. Change had come to Solus, the Anu family was gone and a Harkan wore the Eye of the Sun. Surely more changes would follow.

The Father Protector opened his mouth to speak, but no words came forth. His uncle, Mered Saad, put a cautioning hand on his nephew's shoulder. Saad bit his lip and turned to one of his generals and laughed at some joke he had probably not heard. The young commander was brash, crude, but still uncertain. He did not yet know what to make of this new Ray.

A finger tapped Arko's shoulder. Wat, who had heard the whole exchange, leaned over to whisper, "The new Protector is still feeling threatened in his position. He takes every word as a slight."

"Good," Arko said, sipping his wine. "He should." The room went quiet and for a moment all eyes were on Arko. He shrugged and took another drink.

When the next plate landed, the great brazier burning dimly, he realized the night had passed into day—the cycle was done. Before departing, the eunuchs served walnuts and fresh dates, raw honeycombs stacked on bright-green leaves, hard cakes of emmer and dried apricots mixed with red berries Arko had never seen before, small and tart. It was time for him to stand, to address the grandees of the feast, to show his strength to the men and women who would be his subjects. He motioned to rise, but when the doors opened, he paused, waiting for the final course to be served. The priestesses who had begun the meal carried in the final offering. The women arrived once more in long lines, this time their robes black as night. A cold evening wind flooded the Cenotaph. The same bright-eyed priestess he had noticed before placed another collar on his neck, this one woven with smoke grass, the marble-white flowers blooming in the late night air.

Arko smelled the smoke flower. The Elden Hunt. How long had it been? And now he was an old man, and all his mistakes still lay on his shoulders. But it did not have to be that way. This was another beginning, another rite of passage into a new and different life. He was the First Ray of the Sun, the right hand of the emperor. As good as emperor, in a world without a center. *Time to stand, time to speak.* He was going to address the drought, make them see their ceremony as the excess it was. This would be the first of many addresses, the seed of something larger. Arko moved the cup to his lips, but it was empty and he dropped it. He motioned to retrieve the cup, but faltered.

Darkness obscured his vision and he fell to the ground.

When Arko regained his sight and his wits, his head was spinning and Wat was gesturing to a servant, urging him to bring water. The boy set two cups on the table, then retreated. The music was gone, the girl had wandered out into the streets, and the murmur of the crowd had vanished. The room was cold, and a night wind whistled through the open doors. Arko saw the great table, the chairs, and a scattering of garlands, but no generals or priests, no Saad, no one but Wat and the servants of the Ray.

"What happened?" he asked, but his adviser's shaking head and disapproving glances told Arko all he needed to know. "How long was I out?" the Ray asked.

"Long enough for the wellborn and wealthy to lose patience." Wat tapped the table with a wrinkled finger, his eyes downcast. "Long enough to offend the men and women of our city."

Arko stood up and sipped the water.

The drink was cold and it made his skin prickle. He felt sobriety return to him. There would be no speech, no opportunity to show his strength. Arko masked his disappointment with a hard cough and a grim smile. He stood straight and walked to the door. He kept his chin up as he exited, but his fingers were trembling.

⇒39⇐

"The San," said Ott. "They've lit fire to the desert scrub."

Sarra saw an orange glow against the black horizon, columns of gray-black smoke swirling in the air. She'd spent days tracing the old road and all she had found was an ashy corridor and a few abandoned towers. She still did not know what to think about the burnt-out chambers she had found below the first tower. Robbers might have lit the fires, but she doubted that was the case. The road concealed something of importance, she felt it, but she did not yet know its nature. So she continued onward, following the map, searching for the symbol at the end of the road, hoping it would lead to some discovery that would justify the journey.

As morning turned to afternoon, the burning desert scrub blocked out the sun, making it difficult to tell where they were going or how much daylight was left. They searched for landmarks, trying to stick to the old road, but they kept getting lost, taking a wrong turn at an old creek bed, a crack in the earth they mistook for a rut. They pushed on, but the trail grew fainter with each step. When the last traces of the path disappeared, they dismounted. The soldiers cleared rocks and pushed away tumbled boulders, but it was no use—the Amaran Road was lost.

Sarra forced the Harkans to reverse course, to scour their tracks, to see if the path branched or turned, if they had missed a fork or overlooked a trail. Hours passed, the light faded, but they found no trace of the road. The Harkans looked to Sarra, and she told them to halt their search while she considered her next move.

She turned to Ott for advice and found him sitting on a rock. He was bent over, back arched, head pressed awkwardly close to a hand-inked drawing. He turned as she approached, his face wrenched into an unfamiliar look—confusion, she guessed.

"What is it, Ott?"

"The map's last symbol, *House of Stars,* there is no precise way to locate it—no landmarks aside from the cliffs and the trail. We know the cliffs' location, but—"

"The cliffs are as big as the Shambles, it is the road we need." Sarra had not meant to cut him short, but the revelation was unsettling. This was quickly becoming a pointless endeavor. She could not be caught wandering through the scrub when Barca swept the territory, or worse yet the San. If she were captured, the Mother Priestess of Desouk would fetch a considerable ransom, but Noll would likely be killed. If Ott were captured they would gut him on the spot. The outlanders feared the deformed and would likely think him cursed. She had no desire to leave, but Sarra knew she had little choice if she wanted her priests' heads to remain intact.

"They are close," a soldier interrupted, calling to them across the plain. "Those calls . . ." He paused and Sarra heard a faint whistling. "The outlanders approach, we should—"

"Go. I know," Sarra said. "Time to leave the Shambles." She glanced once more at the parchment in Ott's good hand. The map showed a steep ridge, a place called the Harkan Cliff—a rock wall that had, since the kingdom's birth, protected Harkana from a northern attack. The slopes above were too steep to scale and the lands beyond too rough to traverse. Her husband had once called this place the end of the world—the end of Harkana, at least. According to the map, the last symbol lay at the base of the cliff, but as Ott had noted, there was no clear indication of where the symbol stood along the cliff—no monument or marker, except the Amaran Road. And Sarra had lost the trail.

Even in this desolate place, the Soleri had gone to great pains to conceal their road.

Ott glanced at the map, his face again cluttered by uncertainty.

"Noll, I'm trying to decipher your notes, what is this?"

The boy's attention was elsewhere, his eyes distant, but his head jerked around when he heard his name. He glanced at the spot Ott had indicated. "The last symbol. I thought it read *House of Stones, House of Stars.*"

"Yes, you explained," Ott said.

"I know, but my translation was incomplete. In Desouk, we worked from a charcoal impression. At this spot," he pointed, "the rubbing was not made with the proper pressure so I could not tell if the marks alongside the inscription were symbols or just cracks in the ceiling. I am now certain the additional marks were symbols. The second set of symbols adds to the meaning of the first, an annotation. The complete phrase reads: *House of Stones, House of Stars. Through darkened stone, Mithra's light will shine.*"

"It could mean anything, any light, any stone," said Sarra as she motioned to the soldiers, her hand gesturing to the west, toward the setting sun, indicating the direction of Desouk. Her shoulders sagged. "We are out of time. I was willing to risk lives when we had the trail, but without the road, without a path forward, I cannot proceed."

Ott scratched his head. "Wars aren't tidy things, Mother. It could be years before the way is clear, maybe longer—are you certain we should leave?"

"The San approach from the west, the Harkan Cliff stands in our path—what more certainty do you require? We have no options, no way forward, no path to the last marker. At the moment we are fortunate to have an escape route, but if we linger we will lose that as well. A bit of poetry is not sufficient cause for us to proceed. We must go."

So they went, faster than before, riding hard, unencumbered by the need to search for trails or artifacts. They rode toward Desouk, Sarra's heart heavy with regret. The Harkans were loud, they drank, happy to be rid of this desolate place, eager to return to the safety of the larger army. War was near and the soldiers knew the Shambles was no place to be stranded when Barca's riders arrived.

As the caravan prepared for the long ride, Dasche ordered a brief pause to feed the horses. He gathered his men and rode to a crop of dry grass. Sarra led her mount to a low ridge, her horse beating its tail, swatting flies while she studied the cliff.

Stars peeked through the murky sky; the cliffs below were nearly black. Sarra crossed her arms and gazed at the rocky precipice. This was not her first defeat, not the first time she had gone looking for the grain and come back empty-handed. She would continue her search, but the map and its last symbol would remain a mystery, for now.

She turned to go, but Noll's horse blocked Sarra's path. The boy pointed to the cliff. Sarra turned and saw it then, shining on the mountain, a confection of light and shadow. *Through darkened stone, Mithra's light will shine.* She had mistaken the lights, at first, for low-hanging stars, but quickly realized that the flickering did not come from the stars above but from *below* the horizon—like a reflection cast upon the cliff. The amber lights pulsed like coals stoked within a fire, shimmering for a hot moment before vanishing.

This was it. Sarra ordered the men to ride. Their grumbles were loud, louder than before. The soldiers looked to Dasche for direction and the man wavered. He stared at the cliff, then his eyes darted toward the setting sun, toward Harkana. Sensing the men's hesitation, Sarra swatted her mount and rode out. Ott and Noll followed, but no one else. No matter. She was so close now, so close to discovering the last symbol. She rode hard and though the glow faded, she kept her eyes fixed upon the cliff, her gaze never wavering. It was not long before she heard the knock of heavy hooves, one horse, then another, as the Harkans followed.

As they drew closer to the cliff, she saw the flickering lights resolve into a curious arrangement of niches in the stone: a ladder carved into the cliff face. She ordered Dasche to climb and he did so, his footman Taig following, the others waiting at the base of the cliff, protecting the horses.

"There's a passage," Dasche shouted when he reached the ledge.

"I want to see it," Sarra said, and so she climbed, her fingers and feet navigating the tiny niches, scaling the rocky cliff. Head pressed to the stones she saw now that the inner face of each toehold was made from a smoothly polished stone. The rock was translucent, and unlike anything she had ever seen. Sarra guessed the shimmering surface was angled to catch the sun's last rays. The footholds would glow for a moment each day, then vanish.

The light had nearly died when she reached the ledge; darkness was upon them and they lit torches. The fire, brighter than the failing sunlight, illuminated an opening in the cliff where moments earlier she had seen nothing more than cracked rock. For an instant it appeared as if the passage was just another trick of the light, but Dasche sent his footman forward and the boy disappeared between the rough stones. The ancient builders were said to possess exceptional skill; perhaps they possessed long-forgotten techniques—tricks that could make an entryway appear as if it were just another fold in the ridge. Sarra waited for Ott to scale the cliff, the soldiers half carrying him up the precipice. When he stood once more at her side, she slipped through the curious opening—not an arch or a passage, but a breach, a wound, she thought, as she slid between the carefully hewn stones.

Inside, by the glow of Dasche's torch, she found an arcade. Dense carvings covered the walls, inscriptions similar to those she had seen in the map chamber. The columned hall opened onto a round-shaped room with a vast dome. Crumbling frescoes covered every column and alcove: a jungle, a forest, a panorama depicting wild beasts of unimaginable shapes—tiny exotic birds, gray-winged kites, a horned panther, the eld. Sarra pressed onward, she was close, she could feel it. There was something here—*but what?*

In a far alcove, Ott found a spiraling stair. They stumbled down the sand-covered winders, Dasche's torch extinguishing as cool air whistled from the stair's depths. Sarra reached the chamber floor in complete darkness, her hand clinging to the rail. Dasche dripped oil on the smoldering torch head, making the flame burst back to life. The room came alive with the crackle of fire. The spiraling stair had deposited Sarra and her party at the center of a round space, a disk encircled by arched openings. Sarra gazed through one after another of the arches. *Darkness, nothing but darkness.* She glanced from arch to arch. Which opening led forward? Which way should they go?

At the far side, through a distant archway, she saw a faint yellow light. Sarra stepped toward the light and motioned for the others to follow. They passed room after room, a bridge between, a pit below. Cobwebs filled the passages and the bridge's wood planks crumbled as she dashed across the narrow channels. One chamber folded into the next, each passage wider than the last. Arrows littered the floor; tables sat overturned atop smashed urns and dented shields. Through archways she glimpsed towers and walls, a city beneath the mountain. Sarra urged the men onward, her heart quick, her breath short.

They drove through a small chamber, then a larger anteroom, another and then another, a long series of rooms that led to progressively larger ones, each one growing in size and grandeur. Gone were the tight corridors and narrow bridges; they were inside a palace. Flower-topped columns flaked in gold formed glistening archways. Alabaster slabs adorned the floor and everywhere there was gold, in the walls and in the columns, in the ceiling and floor—an opulence she had seen only in the Waset, in the Golden Hall, and the temple of Mithra at Solus. Here there was furniture left intact, tapestries and urns. The air was cool and moist, a light wind brushed her face. The sun had nearly set, but there was light ahead, the same illumination she had seen in the archway—a dim light leading her forward. *This is it. The map leads here.* As the light grew more intense, as Sarra's eyes adjusted and the walls of the chamber became visible, she saw the same dark soot she had found in the underground passage. The fire must have been more intense here. The damage was hideous; the stones were wrinkled and warped.

Passing beneath a crumbled arch and out into a grand chamber, soaring in height, with a light reflected through long tunnels in the encircling rock—Sarra entered the final chamber. A grand solar, a throne room. Buried within the Empyreal Domain, in the forbidden palace of the gods themselves, there was said to be a chamber of pure light, the grand solar of the god-emperor. Could this be its twin? Was this the hidden palace of the Soleri, the place where they sheltered in times of war? No living man, save for the Ray, had seen the solar, but the room matched the descriptions she had read in the repository. The throne of the god-emperor. A place that only the ancient Soleri could have crafted, its dome so tall and thin that no craftsmen, save the gods of old, would have dared attempt such a structure. So smooth were the walls, so glorious was the height of the structure that Sarra imagined herself standing within a space made from nothing but the sun's light. *A chamber of rays.*

In an instant, everything was light and they could see what remained in the chamber.

Ott gasped and the soldiers stepped back, mouths gaping. Only Sarra stood calmly, her face a mask of tranquility. "It's them," Taig blurted out, staring at the still, silent figures in the room. "It's them, just as the old words described."

Every child in the empire was told: *Before time was the Soleri, and after time the Soleri will be.* The phrase referred to a story about the Soleri's creation and destruction—a myth that linked the two events. The story described the birth of the Soleri—how, after the gods plummeted from Atum, they forged earthly bodies from the same elements as the stars, the same grains that made the rock beneath their feet. They were made from things so primitive, so pristine, that the Soleri could not die, they could only revert to the elements from which they were made—that once the Soleri perished they would become the stones, the stars, the fabric of the world.

Truly this was the House of Stones and Stars.

In the middle of the room stood a ring of glistening statues, figures contorted in grotesque postures, figures that stood as if cowering from some unseen force—fire, she guessed, but what fire could kill a god? The room was burnt black; soot covered the floor. A flame as hot as the sun had scorched this room, as if Mithra Himself had reached out and filled the chamber with His searing light. The statues—which seemed not like statues at all, but like living beings frozen in place—were obsidian in appearance, like the black, glossy stone that came from a volcano—glistening like stars, hard like stones.

This was death. The end. Twelve figures crouched in a circle, arms raised, burnt black, scorched till their forms became rock—twelve monoliths poised in their death throes.

"The Soleri," Ott said.

Noll gawked.

The Harkans stood silent.

Sarra circled the ashy ring, her heart pounding like a child, like someone who still believed in myths—in things she could not see. She took deep breaths, in and out, her lungs cold with agitation, her skin wet with perspiration, tingling with excitement and confusion. She felt that burning, the feeling she sometimes experienced when she came upon a great idea, a revelation like the one she'd had with Ott below the Desouk Repository when she learned that the sun would not dim.

The massacre of the Soleri. This was all that was left of them, this ghostly ring of figures—Mithra-Sol's last light reflecting off his dead children. She saw the outlines of their grand costumes, medallions and collars burned into their flesh, their desiccated faces screwed in odd contortions, their once-golden masks and headdresses mottled and dripping.

Ott broke the silence. "The pendant around that neck, it bears the sign of Sekhem Den, last of his line, the last to pre-date the line of Tolemy in the time of the old war, the War of the Four, the moment, two centuries ago, when the Soleri walled themselves off from the kingdoms."

The emperor did not hide within the Empyreal Domain. He was hounded. He was hunted down and killed, along with all of his family. Twelve figures, the emperor, his wife and their five daughters and five sons. Ten children. Always ten for the Soleri. One of each, as the Soleri married each other. This was the last remnant of the ancient divine race.

"They did not wall themselves off after the war, they were driven here, away from the Empyreal Domain. They must have used their sacred road, the Amaran Road, to flee the capital. We thought we were following the grain, but we weren't. Without knowing, we were following them, following their road to the place where they perished. It was here that they made their final stand."

You cannot kill a god.

To look into the face of the emperor is to face one's death.

Before time was the Soleri, and after time the Soleri will be.

Lies.

For two hundred years the Soleri have knelt here, frozen in death's contortions while in the capital, in the empire, things went on as if they were still living, as if they were still in power.

For two hundred years while they were frozen here.

A thought occurred to Sarra. Two centuries ago the amaranth seed lost its fertility.

The gift of the Soleri was rescinded.

When they died, so did their flower, the amaranth. When the Soleri perished so did their land. The life-givers were gone. Sarra understood why the seeds of the amaranth no longer grew, why only the ancient seeds blossomed. The amaranth was born of their power—it said so in the sacred texts. When that power died, the amaranth died. For two centuries the empire had coasted on the remains of the once-great kingdom of the Soleri, but that time was at an end. The ancient amaranth was gone and the flower that gave life to the desert would not bloom again.

The Ray of the Sun, the emperor and his domain—all of it was nothing more than a clever ruse—a façade.

There was no emperor and there had not been one for two hundred years. The Ray of the Sun was the true ruler of the kingdoms and his power was nothing more than a farce.

How could she judge? The priesthood had concealed the amaranth's infertility just as the Rays had concealed the emperor's absence. It was all lies; they had deceived one another. This is the secret of the empire, the secret of the Soleri, the secret from which they had drawn their power and position. With a start, she realized they were not alone.

Dasche and Taig waited for orders.

Noll kneeled alongside the statues, carefully studying them.

Sarra looked at Ott.

He uncapped a wine sack and offered the soldiers a drink, then Noll. They drank and Sarra waited. In a moment the poisoned wine would take their lives. She had enough to poison the soldiers who waited at the base of the cliff as well.

Secrets were power.

Sarra Amunet did not have to be the First Ray of the Sun to know this.

THE DAWN CHORUS

⇛40⇚

Dirty and thirsty and longing for her own bed, for a long and detailed game of Coin with an inscrutable Ott on the other side of the table, Sarra returned to the city of light, the secret of the Soleri's demise burning within her. She cantered through the eastern gate, the Rising Gate, and recalled her hasty exit from the capital just a few weeks past, the day she stood in the Protector's Tower and watched the eclipse fail and the crowds riot. The sky had been black with smoke, the walls splattered with graffiti, the air loud with the cries of pilgrims and priests alike.

And I nearly lost my life.

Now the white-walled towers were newly plastered, flags waved above the circus, and a plume of white smoke billowed from the temple of Mithra. Deeper into the city, past the outer districts, she saw banners swinging in the wind—gold and white bunting stretched between hastily set poles. The statues in the garden of Amen Hen were newly polished. And at the steps of the Waset, flowers littered the streets, cassia and milkweed, their petals mashed to the ground by the footsteps of a celebratory crowd. The rioting was over; the city was changed. Renewed.

But why? Sarra slowed her horse so she could take in the scene. The white smoke. The gold-trimmed bunting and yellow flowers. Sarra tugged the reins, stopping the horse. Solus had more festivals than the calendar had days, but this was no common holiday. It could only mean one thing: Suten had left his post. The light had shone from the mountain, and a new Ray had been appointed. The white and gold were his symbols. Up ahead, men and women in saffron colored mantles gathered at the Shroud Wall, at the veiled window of the Antechamber.

A shadow loomed behind the screen, a tall, broad-shouldered man. The figure was too large to be Saad. *But who?* Sarra tapped the helm of a nearby soldier. "Who is it, boy? Who is the new Ray?"

"The enemy. Mithra sent a traitor into our midst," the boy said.

"His name?" she asked, her voice filling with impatience.

"The Harkan." His words were like spit. "Arko Hark—"

Wadi. Arko Hark-Wadi.

She wanted to ask the boy if he was certain, but she caught herself. There was no mistake. In the Shambles, the Harkan soldiers told Sarra that Tolemy had summoned her husband to Solus. She had thought Arko a dead man then. With a start, she realized her mistake. *There is no Tolemy, no emperor.*

"I assure you this wasn't Mithra's doing," she said as she rode off. *This is Suten's work.* Sarra understood why the Ray had refused to meet with her during the Devouring. He had already chosen his successor, and it was Arko.

Arko Hark-Wadi is the new Ray of the Sun. He held the seat she desired. Arko Hark-Wadi, her former husband. No, he was her husband still, for they had never said the words that unbound one from the other. She had simply left. Arko had never remarried; he had been loyal to her in name, but never in practice. Especially not during the marriage.

So that had been Suten's final move, to name a successor before Saad or Sarra could move against him. The old man was too nimble by half. Where was he now? Suten had a vineyard in the Denna hills. She could imagine him underneath the vines, sipping the latest vintage.

Arko Hark-Wadi. Did it have to be you? The news made her bitter. To think that she now answered to her husband, that he held sway over the priesthood and all of the empire. It was galling. She had come here to confront Suten, but he was gone and now her husband sat in his chair. *Solus is changed, but not for the better.* This news colored everything. It made the buildings frown at her, and every archway looked like a grimace.

Sarra guided her horse down the long ramps that led deep into the Waset—down the wide streets, past temples fitted among spindly obelisks, alabaster coffers, and crumbling statues—till she caught sight of her temple.

A priest greeted Sarra at the steps, his eyes darting.

Sarra dismounted, handed the animal to a groom, and strode up the stairs. Picking her way between the lotus-topped pillars of the columned hall Sarra saw what had unnerved the young man—what she had expected to see since she rode into the city. Soldiers. A group of armed men brandished spears in the hall. Saad had told her not to return until the last day of the year, when her duty bade her to do so. But she was back in Solus and not even a month had passed since their quarrel. Saad was letting her know that he was watching, that her return was noted. Sarra had expected as much.

"Out," she said, "out of my temple. Go!"

"Will do, Mother," said the man. "We were just keeping an eye on all your pretty statues."

"I'm sure you were, now leave," she said, walking toward him, heading straight into his path without pause. The man stepped back and the other soldiers parted, clearing a path like contrite children caught playing dice. Then—behind her back, laughter. She kept going, ignoring their taunts.

She passed through bronze doors into the sanctuary, catching the first notes of Ott's voice. He had ridden ahead of her, on the Harkan's fastest horse, to prepare the Ata'Sol. Now her clever friend was pacing at the birthing pool, mumbling, the golden statues of the Soleri towering above him, his weak arm hidden beneath his robe, a soldier shadowing him, aping his awkward movements. Behind half-open doors her priests were standing back, whispering to one another, not daring to interfere. The soldiers were trespassing on sacred ground and her priests were unsure of how to react. Custom dictated that when the toe of Re, first of the Soleri, touched the desert floor, a spring bubbled forth from the sand, and the first amaranth plant sprung from the pool.

That pool was located at the temple's center, in the heart of the sanctuary, where currently one of Saad's soldiers stood with legs spread, relieving himself in the water.

"I saw your pool looking empty," the solider said, "so I thought I would help fill it up, Mother."

Sarra paid him no notice. She inserted herself between Ott and the soldier who was mocking him, the sound of piss hitting water reverberating throughout the sanctuary. "Out," she ordered. "Out of my temple!" she said. "Both of you! Now! Your weapons and your boorish humor can find the door. Leave us—stuff your cock in you breeches and go!"

Or what? she thought. *What can I do against these men?* It was Saad's duty to guard the priesthood and the temple. He was the Sword of Mithra, but now he'd turned that very blade against the people he was sworn to protect.

"Saad sends his regards, Mother," said the soldier standing in front of her.

"Give him mine." She drew herself up to her full height, her eyes flashing.

"We will, Mother," said the soldier at the pool. "And we'll leave you in peace. I only needed a bit of relief and now I've had it," he said, shaking himself dry. The two of them laughed as they went out of the inner sanctum, the air behind them smelling like piss.

Sarra went to Ott but refrained from putting a hand on his shoulder. "It's all right. They're gone."

His fingers twitched, but he nodded that he understood.

"Are you okay?"

He shook his head, no.

"When did they arrive?" she asked. She knew this would happen when she returned to Solus, but she had not expected Saad to act so quickly. Slow, she was too slow. She had to move—faster. Especially with her newly acquired knowledge.

"Not long before you, they forced the doors, snapped the bolt, and let themselves in. . . ."

Sarra came up alongside him and stood by his shoulder. This was the way Ott liked to speak with her: standing side by side, so he would not have to look in her eyes. She saw Ott relax when her shoulder came alongside his, and Sarra felt a new wave of affection for him.

"Mother, I have news. The new Ray of the Sun is—"

"Harkan." She nodded. "Yes, I know," Sarra said, brushing perspiration from her brow. Exhausted from the long ride, she needed cool amber, a rest, and a bath, but those things would have to wait.

"His presence will make matters difficult. I had expected to deal with Suten and not my former husband." She paced. "The new Ray has much to hide."

Ott tapped. "He hides nothing from us, Mother. We know his secret. We know that Tolemy is a fabrication, that the Ray is the mouthpiece of a man who does not exist. With this knowledge, we can control him— we can own him," he said, his voice still shaking a bit.

She turned. "I don't want to own him, I want to ruin him." She smiled, as she knew how she would do it. Yes, she would demand an audience with Arko. *But not yet. Not until I have prepared.* She wrapped her robe a little tighter around her shoulders.

"You will reveal him then? Expose the lie of the Soleri and expose him to all of Solus as a fraud?" asked Ott.

Sarra shook her head. "If we revealed the Ray's secret, Saad would declare Arko a traitor and a liar and the matter would be quickly resolved in Saad's favor. Saad would take Arko's life and the Amber Throne. Fear of the emperor is the only thing that keeps Saad in line right now. No, I have something more subtle in mind."

"Before you settle on a plan, you should know that we lost two priests this morning. Taken by the Protector, most likely, incarcerated for some minor crime they did not commit."

"Who?"

"A boy and a girl, from Rachis. I knew them. We played Coin every now and then. They were simple lectors—they knew none of our secrets. Still, the act itself is telling. Should I send an offering of grain and ask for their release?"

"No. Do nothing." She brushed a hand through her hair. "Friends of yours?"

"Yes."

"I am sorry." It was her fault. She had been unable to tame the boy, unable to protect her people, unable to make Saad cower. Sarra gritted her teeth. "It's a fresh game of Coin." She paced, glancing at the pool, the statues, wrinkling her nose. "Why is he trying to pick a fight so openly? On the last day of the year, why did he murder a priest on these same temple steps?"

"Maybe he wants us to retaliate. Think on it, Mother. Picture the conflict and how it might unfold: a pair of priests disappear, then a general is poisoned; three acolytes fall from a wall, then four officers die in a brothel. If we retaliate, if it looks like the priesthood is at war with the army, Saad will have his justification to act against us—if only to restore the peace. But if he attacks without provocation he risks the ire of the highborn families, or the emperor and his Ray." Ott tapped at his palm feverishly.

"We'll tread lightly then. I won't give Saad cause to attack us."

"He already has cause. He bid you not to return to Solus," said Ott.

"I know—I was there when he did it. We must hope my performance in the Protector's Tower will give him pause."

"Doubtful," he said.

"Doubt is all I have of late."

"Do you still doubt the Soleri?" he asked, changing the subject. Behind the pool, golden statues of the twelve Soleri stood upon a plinth of black granite. Ott walked toward it. "It was a vision—seeing them in that circle and knowing that they are real, that they exist."

"They *did* exist," Sarra added. "Until someone snuffed out their light."

"Was it the Anu family?" Ott offered. "Suten's family benefited more than any other from the absence of the Soleri. They took control of the empire and held it until now."

"No." Sarra flattened her lips. "Suten's family did not assault the Soleri. They concealed the emperor's absence, sealed the Shroud Wall, and seized the empire for their family—I see that now, but they did not murder the twelve. In the Shambles, we saw stone turned to ash, the bodies of the twelve reduced to obsidian. Could the Anu family produce such fire, such heat—could anyone? No. The one who did this, whoever it was, wielded a strength as great as the Soleri—who else could kill a god?"

"I don't know, but I'm eager for answers—aren't you? Who murdered the twelve and why do they remain hidden?"

She had no answer for him and so she turned her back on the twelve and walked to the edge of the pool, the place where the Soleri first touched the desert floor. The water was now yellow. The spring was nearly empty. It had been years since anything much had bubbled forth from it. On most days, her priests had to add bucketful after bucketful of water to the pool, just to keep it from going dry.

"I had hoped that one day the amaranth would again blossom, but I fear it will not. The gods are gone and soon the last of their precious gift will be gone too. Someday soon after that, all of this"—she gestured to the sanctuary, to the city beyond—"will be gone. Saad senses this. He feels the end. That is why he is nervous—desperate to hold on to power, why he haunts our temple and steals our priests, why he seeks the Ray's seat. He feels the desert closing in on Sola. Everywhere in the empire, it is felt. The drought, the wars. The scarcity of the amaranth. The failed eclipse. The outlanders swarm in the west. Barca marches in the south. For three thousand years the Soleri held back the sand and the wind and the sun, but that time is ending. The gods that held this empire together are dead," she said, stepping away from the pool. "We must prepare for what comes next."

⇥41⇤

Unseen and unheard, unable to leave his post, Arko Hark-Wadi paced in the shadows, prowling like a dog in a cage, one impatient for its supper. *More ceremony, more tedium,* he thought, swigging wine and watching the procession of highborn citizens through a screened window, one that hid all but his shadow from view. He did not see why he actually needed to be present for the ceremony when no one could really see him, but Wat had insisted that the ritual was vital to his new position—that he must regain what respect was lost during the ceremony in the Cenotaph. "If you do not attend," Wat had said, "the priests and viziers will know. If they do not see your shadow through the veil, they will take offense. If you want to rule the empire, sir, you must demonstrate your understanding of the empire's customs."

Arko smirked. "Are you sure you're not having me on, Wat? Making me sit through all this nonsense just to watch me squirm?"

Wat had almost smiled. "No, sir. It is simply an advantage of my position."

So Arko prowled the dim chamber alone, only statuary for company—one female figure in each corner, arms raised, hands open, each balancing a disk upon her head that bore the weight of the ceiling above. Their faces were cloaked, hidden from view as they stood facing the emperor's empty throne. Arko picked at the stone-carved shroud, tracing the folds that looked like cloth but were made of stone. Even the sculptures were not permitted to gaze upon the emperor's face, the emperor who did not exist.

Arko drew a slip of parchment from his pocket and read it over. Ostensibly, the parchment was a transcript, a record of a conversation with Tolemy. It was, of course, a fabrication. There was no Tolemy, and he'd had no conversation. He read the words one last time. When the people of Sola heard that Tolemy had named Arko as his Ray, they must have feared that change was coming and now they would have it. Flowers blanketed the streets, banners hung at every intersection. Solus was quiet, it had accepted its new leader, but the calm would not last. When the proclamation was posted, their anger would begin anew. The people would comply, he hoped, but he doubted they would do it gladly.

In the meantime, he had other concerns. Arko had sent for his soldiers, his men from Harkana, but they had not yet arrived. He had sent word to his children that he was alive too, but he had heard no reply. The traitor, Barca, was ravaging the areas to the south of the wall, and his cohorts were running amok in the north, killing messengers and scouts, making communication difficult. Arko had called for an audience with Saad, but the Protector was busy preparing to engage Barca and kept putting it off. Even if the Protector had made himself available to Arko, it seemed impossible to conduct business in the capital. Nearly every other day was a holiday. In the last week Arko had suffered through the Coll of Bes and the Tubidam. And there were more festivals in the planning. In the weeks to come, the city would celebrate the Opening of the Mundus and three or four other festivals. He'd forgotten all of the names. On the day Arko took the Ray's chair, the city had witnessed the Lermur Al'Dab. He was not able to observe, but the festival—a holiday for the dead—seemed an appropriate choice for his first day in the Antechamber. *Maybe I am dead and this business of being Ray is just my punishment in the afterlife.*

Below the high window, in a broad court lined with buttery yellow stone, the wellborn and wealthy of Solus processed down a long avenue lined with yellow banners, and white and gold flags hung on posts. The streets were strewn with palm leaves and milkweed. Chins raised, the highborn of Solus—the overseers, nomarchs, and viziers—strode as if they owned every rock beneath their feet, every statue and gold obelisk they passed. As they entered the courtyard, Khalden Wat announced them: Amen Neko, Bek Serekh, Sekhe Rah, Nikan Anun-Han, Meren Ini. As Wat called the names, the highborn men and women came forward. Wat presented each with a collar knitted of gold, a gift from the new liege. They would kneel, and Wat would bestow their title. All titles came from the First Ray of the Sun and would have to be restored with the establishment of a new reign. A scribe recorded the title on a wax tablet. With the coming of each Ray, the names and positions were shuffled according to the will of the new Ray. Wat had seen to the appointments, assuring Arko of the necessity of each.

Arko had laughed when Wat told him about the ceremony. "Isn't the word of Tolemy—the god-emperor—enough to make me Ray? Why all the fuss?"

Wat had shaken his head. "These men think they *are* Tolemy, or at least they act that way. The emperor's influence has waned over the years. Some viziers support their own private armies, tend their own livestock, and trade with the priesthood. They can make life difficult for you if they think they are going unappreciated. And you have already offended many of them."

Arko made no attempt to disagree. He remembered all too well the banquet in the Cenotaph. If only the Mother Priestess and the Father Protector were required to beg for their titles as well, his troubles would be far fewer.

He shook his head, took a long drink of wine and then a second. He tried for a third, but the wineskin was empty. Through the screened window he caught sight of a single rider, a white-cloaked priestess with incandescent red hair. Was it her? He checked again. Red hair, white robe. *Sarra Amunet,* the name wound through his stomach like a coiling snake. It had been ten years since he had seen his wife. Ten years since she had turned her back on their family. *So you came back, Sarra. Here you are, in Solus, where the pilgrims tore you from the wall.*

There was a knock on the door.

Arko groped for a weapon, but he wore none. Unprotected. The First Ray of the Sun was protected by the Soleri and hence was the only man in all of the empire who did not carry a sword. He hoped he wouldn't need one in the future. No one but Khalden Wat was supposed to know where he was. "Who's there?" he asked, sounding more anxious than he liked.

"It's Asher. I have news, sir."

His friend and captain of the kingsguard, Asher Hacal. Wat's boys found Asher camping outside the walls of Solus, exactly as Arko had described.

Arko tucked the parchment into his pocket and opened the door to find the man looking grim. Asher was a large man, bearded, and solid; like most Harkans he was deeply tanned, sharp-nosed, and longhaired. He surveyed the chamber, asked if the room was secure, if he could speak candidly, and when Arko nodded he shut the door.

"What have you found?"

"Nothing good, I'm sorry to report." Curious why he had not received letters from his children, Arko had given Asher a mission. That morning he had sent an imperial messenger to Harkana. Asher trailed the messenger. "The man made it as far as Darene—only an hour's ride—when he stopped. I watched him find an inn and ask for a bed, though it was only midday. He said he would be there for a few days."

Enough time to pretend to have gone to Harwen and back, Arko knew.

"I saw him throw a piece of parchment into the fire."

"My message," Arko said, his words a long sigh.

"It appears so."

He sat on a wood chair across from the throne and sighed, rubbing at his forehead. *Think.* He closed his eyes, picturing the Shambles, the herds of deer. He saw again the eld he had trapped in the vale as a young man, an enormous creature with dripping tusks. He would give anything to be back there right now, his mind clear of anything but the hunt, the smell of an animal being pursued, the beauty of the bow as it flew from the quiver. Not this—dusty rooms, whole kingdoms of bruised feelings and ambitions to appease.

"Asher," he said, his eyes closed still, the Shambles still a shadow across his mind. "Do you ever wish you'd had children, a family? Would that have meant something to you, do you think?"

The captain shifted in his chair. "It might have. It's difficult to imagine a different path for myself."

"Sometimes I'm certain my life would have been better if I'd had no children at all and no wife. I would have been happier, I think," said Arko. *I've made a mess of things, my marriage and my kingdom.* Arko thought about the woman he had loved, the one he wanted to marry. He stroked the white stone at his neck.

"My king?"

"Never mind, Asher. I'm just rambling. I'm tired, that's all."

He crossed the stone floor to the place where his friend and captain stood. "I need you to deliver a message to my daughter."

"Alone?"

"If possible. You must travel in secret. Make sure only my eldest daughter receives this missive."

Arko wrote on the scroll in code. A child's code he had taught Merit once, a secret only she could decipher. "When you've delivered this message to my daughter, go to Harkana and call for my guard. I fear my first message was waylaid." Arko handed Asher a second scroll, detailing his needs.

Asher left, leaving the door open behind him. The corridor was dark for a moment, then Wat appeared, eyes grim. "There's an issue that needs your attention," he said.

Arko shook his head and fingered the slip of parchment in his pocket, but did not yet draw it forth. "Right now we have more urgent concerns." He told Wat about Asher's story of the messenger burning his messages. "This is untenable," Arko said, "a grave disrespect to my position." He ground his teeth. "I look to you for advice on how the empire deals with such matters."

Suten's old adviser bowed his head. "Forgive me, but I am at a loss for the moment. Suten Anu never had this problem. His line ruled for two centuries. No one would have dared."

"Lucky him. You suppose one of those wellborn bootlickers is behind this? Playing with me?"

Wat grimaced. "That's what I've come to tell you. A few of the richest and oldest families who have been loyal to the empire and the Ray for centuries have refused their titles."

Arko tightened his hold on the parchment.

"This act is unprecedented," Wat continued. "The highborn of Solus are refusing to accept title and position under your reign. My ears in the White-Wall district say the viziers and nomarchs are still chafing from the . . . lack of respect you showed in the Cenotaph."

"Then let them lie with the rabble."

"That's not how it works," Wat said.

"Mithra Himself lit my way, I carry the stone that sat on Suten's head. Do they dispute this? They dare to refuse the emperor's wishes?"

"Not quite. It is the Ray who grants their titles. Suten's great-grandfather was the first to arrange the naming ceremony. He did it to bolster the Ray's position, and it was a good move for his family—they were the most powerful in Solus at the time—but times have changed, and so have their fortunes. Suten's line has ended, his family's gold squandered. They owe no allegiance to Suten anymore, and these families are formidable in their own right. Mered Saad, the brother of the former Protector, is the wealthiest among them and he has declined his title. Others have done the same."

"So they refuse title and will not bow to my position because I failed to honor them at a banquet?"

The old adviser nodded. "It is one reason. Still, I doubt these nomarchs and viziers are the cause of your troubles. They lack faith, but I don't believe they are bold enough to attack you outright."

"It's the Protector then."

"I'm guessing this business was orchestrated by Amen Saad."

Arko rubbed his forehead, rubbed at the yellow jewel that sat uncomfortably just above his eyebrows. *This damn thing.* Everyone in the empire had a reason to oppose him, for power, for position. For revenge. It was like walking into a snake pit, this business of being the Ray.

Arko needed to take control.

"Tolemy has spoken," Arko said as he drew forth the proclamation and handed it to Wat.

The old man pored over the transcript. "'From this day onward,'" he read aloud, "'Tolemy V, lord of Sola and Emperor of the Five Kingdoms, halts the collection and sequestering of the noble sons of the lower kingdoms. He declares the tributes of grain and meat to be cut by one-half, allowing all of the kingdoms to share in the burden of the drought . . .'" Wat lowered the parchment. "This is unprecedented," he said, pausing, seemingly unable to speak.

The empire will no longer collect ransoms. Arko had wanted to release all of the ransoms, but he had not yet thought of a way to do so. Each of the noble-born children in the Priory was there because Tolemy commanded him to be there and the emperor never reversed one of his commands. Arko knew enough about imperial politics to understand this. Gods did not err. An emperor might alter an existing policy, he might stop the collection of tributes, but he would never release the boys he had already imprisoned, not without a compelling reason. Arko was confident that he would soon have such a reason, but he could do nothing more until he found it.

For the time being, it was enough that he had halted the taking of ransoms. This practice, which had so tormented the noble families of the lower kingdoms, was ended. With this simple proclamation he put an end to the fear Tolemy had instilled in the heart of every regent, king, and lord. He put an end to the dread that haunted him still, the terror of not being able to protect his family, his son and his daughters, the horror of not being able to protect himself. As a king, even as Ray, that fear haunted him still. He sometimes felt it at night when he awoke, alone in his chamber in the impenetrable dark, thinking, *I'm dead. The emperor's killed me. I've died, and everything else is a dream.* But then the truth always closed around him once more, like a suit of armor that fit too tightly. There was no emperor. It was all a lie, all madness. *Madness seems to be our only occupation in Sola,* Suten had told him before he died. *Sanity, on the other hand, is a tremendous weight.* Arko looked once more at the proclamation, pondering Suten's words.

"Take these directives and have them formally transcribed. I will tell you when to post them," Arko said. "And as for these other matters, Tolemy has no interest in the politics of Solus and neither do I. Let Saad play at his petty games. Let the nobles refuse their titles. We have more pressing matters to address." He glanced at the slip of parchment and knew that it would change the empire forever.

Wat gave him a slight nod, his face uneasy, his fingers jittering. "I'll do as you say."

He took a step backward toward the door. "Is there anything else?"

"Wat." Arko affected his most kingly voice. "I don't care if the city is on holiday. Send for a messenger. Tell Saad that Tolemy calls and the Protector must answer. It is time that boy learned some respect." Arko faced the courtyard. "And one last thing. Damn your traditions. Find me a sword. Something heavy and long. It rattles my nerves not having a blade at my side."

⇛42⇚

Kepi dreamed of a storm, frightful cracks shattering around her all through the night, but when she woke to blue above the trees and heard the tearing of wood, she realized it was only workmen splitting blackthorn timbers outside her window, the *rap-rap-rap* of the spike going into the wood, the long ripping sound of the ancient timber peeling apart. Then the *rap-rap-rap* would come again, and the whole process would start over. A busy place, Rifka. *My home*, she thought briefly, and then just as quickly banished the word from her mind. The Ferens were not her people, and Rifka would never be her home.

She sat up slowly and looked around. She was alone, as she had been for the past week. Dagrun had left no guards outside or in her room. She could march right out the door, out of the caer, and into the Gray Wood without anyone trying to stop her.

She stood, crossed the room, and as she did each day, she put her hand on the ring pull and gave it a tug. It opened with a soft whine. Unlocked. She could open the door and leave.

Take her sword, take a horse, and go.

Yes. And then?

Where would she go, and to whom? Back to Harkana, to Seth and his family, to poverty and desperation and disgrace? To Blackrock, to be a laundress or a scullion, a shepherdess? To the Hornring, to sit and wait for another husband? No. Each day she considered her situation and made the same decision.

Kepi shut the door.

She returned to her bed, thinking again of how small she had felt beside Dagrun on their wedding night, how she had told him her secret. He had left her alone then. *I will not take what is not given freely.* She was the queen of the Ferens, wedded to Dagrun. His wife, but not yet his woman. Just like Merit, if she believed him. He had never bedded her sister, he'd sworn. And now Kepi didn't know whether she wanted him to be telling the truth or not.

She had believed him to be a liar. The girls who dressed her had said that he was a violent man, but he had been gentle that night. Not the man she had expected him to be. So much of what she had thought of him was based on rumor and presumption. A week had passed since that night and she had hardly seen him.

Why was she still in Feren if the door was unlocked? What was keeping her there?

It seemed impossible, all of it.

A knock startled her. It was Dalla, her servant, bustling into her room wearing a brown cloth draped around her waist. "Good morning, mistress," she said, looking at the floor, as a good servant should, to protect her mistress's modesty. "Did you sleep well?"

Kepi shrugged. "Lift your eyes from the floor, Dalla, and tell me why you're here."

The girl composed herself. "Yes, yes, of course. Forgive me." Over one arm Dalla had a new dress, a woolen gown for Kepi. "The king sent this for you. Pretty—isn't it? He asked that you dress and meet him outside of his chamber."

Kepi took the gown and ran her fingers over the wool, fine and soft but plain, as all Feren clothes were.

"The king had it made for you. Picked out the cloth himself."

Kepi doubted that, but she let Dalla dress her anyway. With the girl's help, she combed her short hair and dressed quickly, tugging the fabric into place. At least this one covered her breasts. She did not like gowns, even for daily use; they flowed around her ankles, threatening to trip her, making her feel foolish and clumsy and frail. In Harwen, she had usually worn an old set of sparring clothes left behind by one of her father's footmen, or a simple tunic and breeches. But a queen of Feren, even a reluctant one, would have to make an effort to look presentable or risk more trouble than she wanted. Kepi groaned—another bit of herself she had to give up if she were going to stay here.

She was tripping down the passageway, trying to free her feet from a bit of wool, when she caught sight of Seth coming up the stairs from below. She tried to hurry past him, but he blocked her path. "Are you all right?" he asked. "Are they treating you well?"

"I am their queen," she said simply. Her heart ached at the sight of him, as she realized whatever love she had once felt for him had fled when he betrayed her. "Excuse me, I have somewhere to be."

"Wait," he said, catching her arm. She looked down at his fingers wrapped around her wrist as if not quite believing what she was seeing. He blushed and took his hand away.

"Is there something you need, Seth?"

He leaned close to her, putting his mouth on her ear. "I've got somethin' planned for us," he said. "There was a battle in the south, at Catal. People here are angry about what happened. They want to help us. The master physician, Gallach, is one of them. He offered me work and he gave me access to his herbs."

"That's nice," she said, cutting him short, not wanting to hear any more, but Seth persisted.

"I have an idea," he said. "Wait here." Before she could tell him she did not want to listen to whatever it was he had planned, that she no longer thought of him as highly as she once did, he disappeared back down the stairwell, into the darkness.

Kepi looked around nervously. *What if someone had seen them?* Whispering in her ear like that—it was too familiar, too intimate.

"Kepi." A voice startled her. She turned, seeing Dagrun come out of a room at the end of the hallway, looking bathed and shaven. Fresh.

She glanced down into the dark well of the staircase where Seth had disappeared, hoping he would stay down there. When he did not return, she squared her shoulders to face her husband and walked toward his outstretched hand. He reached to put his arm around her shoulders, but she shied from his touch. He only smiled and led her through the doorway to the courtyard, where the noise of sawing and hammering was even louder than it had been in her chamber.

"Morning," he said. "I hope the noise did not trouble you last night."

She tried on a bit of a smile, but it felt crooked on her face, awkward. "A little. I thought it was a storm. I thought I was dreaming." She felt warm inside.

"Did you dream morning meal?" he asked.

"No, I'm not hungry," she said quickly, then added, "thank you, though."

She followed him down a single narrow staircase to the courtyard outside, where the workmen were erecting the Queen's Chamber, which would be her home in Caer Rifka. Workmen sawed and chiseled the tough gray wood. From the width of the cornices, they were crafting a chamber larger than the Harkan King's Hall, and more finely made. Woodcarvers used hand tools to chisel elaborate forms into the stony wood, blackthorn nuts and needles, and—she noticed it now—the Tree of Feren, entwined with the Harkan ram's horns. She felt a quick stab of homesickness and tamped it down again. *Is this all for me?* she wondered, even though she knew the answer.

Surrounding the Queen's Chamber on all sides sat temporary workshops where workmen crafted furniture and fittings: bedposts, chests, cunning little stools like the one in her bedchamber but more beautiful and intricate. Enough for an army, she thought, not just a girl from Harkana with scabby knees.

Dagrun pointed to a set of large wooden panels and told her these would be the doors to her chamber. He indicated a set of chairs, and a stack of wooden plates. He took a delicately carved stool and placed it before her. He said all of these things were cut from his birth tree, and would be the most precious items of the house. Kepi sat on the stool, her hands woven into the folds of her dress.

Dagrun knelt, taking one of the sculptor's tools and tracing the outlines of the new chamber: here were the outer and inner halls, a bedroom, a cellar, a shrine to Llyr. "What do you think?" he asked, with such earnestness that Kepi threw him a suspicious look.

"I oversaw the work, approved the composition of the rooms and their elements. But it's not too late to make alterations."

She composed herself once more. "It's fine. I mean . . . it's beautiful really."

"Is there something you want to change?"

Nothing, it's perfect, she thought, but held her tongue as he led her onward. She was shy around him now, ever since their wedding night.

He was the first to hear her story, all of it, and the intimacy she felt from that encounter made her feel exposed. Since that night, he had not come to visit her in her chambers, and she had felt a strange mixture of relief and disappointment at that fact.

I will not take what is not given freely, he had said.

Recently she had been imagining what that might be like, if she did welcome him into her bed. If she gave herself to him out of her own free will. If she wanted him.

Her breath caught in her throat at his nearness, but she tried to ignore it. Where was the girl who valued nothing more than swordplay, she wondered, the one who wore her bruises as if they were badges of honor? All of that seemed childish now.

In the shadow of the Queen's Chamber a silvery-gray tent had been erected, where slaves ducked in carrying bundles of shavings and small twigs. Dagrun went and stood in front of the flap and held it open for her. "Here," he said. "I have something more for you."

Inside, when her vision adjusted to the dim light, she saw priests sitting at long tables, white robes gathered around them in the chill and the damp. Not slaves, but scribes from Desouk, copying passages from scrolls onto parchment. "What's this?" she asked.

"A chamber for books."

In spite of her best efforts to keep ahold of herself, Kepi turned and gave him a broad smile. "You're joking."

"Not at all. Where better? We have enough raw materials in Feren to re-create the entire Desouk Repository twice over."

"What do you mean?"

"Look." He held up a mottled gray sheet.

Not parchment, then, but something different. Dagrun explained that while the empire and even his kingdom had long used the ironwoods for military purposes, he had found another use for the strong wood: he indicated a jar of ironwood pulp, softening in water, and sitting next to a copper screen. The wood fiber was mixed with water, then spread over the screen, pressed, and then dried. The process resulted in a flat, grayish sheet with a deckled edge.

"Does it work?" she asked. "I mean, it doesn't fall apart when they write on it?"

"See for yourself."

Alongside the sheets sat copper vessels containing pads of minerals: black kohl, red ochre. The scribes were dipping their brushes in water, swirling them on the cake, then painting words on the blank pages. The paper, despite her concerns, seemed no more likely to dissolve than parchment. It was a novel use for the wood, she had to admit.

She went close to one volume and read the title: *The Birth of Solus*. "Quite an undertaking," she said, unable to keep the admiration from her voice. "Didn't know you were interested in such things."

"I want to give the people something other than the army, the caer. I said as much on our wedding night." He took the bound pages from her hand and ran his fingers over the gorgeously rendered title. "When I told your sister, she laughed. She believes Feren is nothing more than slaves and soldiers, she believes the stories, but if we are ever going to stand up to the emperor, we must have knowledge too." He set down the fragile book, picked up her hand, and brightened immediately. "Now, about morning meal. They should be ready for us in the dining hall. My baker makes the best brown bread in the lower kingdoms."

"Really?" she asked, tipping up her face to look at him. "That good? I will have to see for myself. Though we *did* have an excellent baker in Harwen, if I may be allowed to boast."

"If you don't swear you love it, I'll send my baker away and hire yours," he said.

"Done," she said without thinking.

Dagrun reached out his hand to seal the bargain, but she withdrew, her expression shifting from eager to reluctant. She wasn't certain why, but she could not take his hand quite yet. Was she so afraid to touch him? Or could it be that she feared she might like it too much?

Embarrassed, she retreated from the king. "I . . . I'm sorry but I didn't ask for this." She gestured at the books, the tent, and the Queen's Chamber. "It is too much." Her smile faded, her posture stiffened. "I cannot accept."

⟫43⟪

"There's still a ways to go," Adin said. "I don't know if I can make it."

They had climbed without pause since daybreak, crossing the highlands southwest of the Rift valley, moving toward Catal, always looking over their shoulder for soldiers. They had seen two patrols the day before, but none since. Perhaps they were clear of Dagrun's soldiers by now, but Ren could not be certain.

"You'll make it. I'm not hauling your ass to Catal," Ren said. "Besides, isn't this what the Priory prepared us for—pain? Have you forgotten their mantra—pain makes the man?"

"I'll never forget it, but if the priors were telling the truth, I think I'd rather stay a boy. I'll skip manhood."

"Well," Ren said. "It did teach us humility. That must be worth something."

"If you say so. In fact, if I fall, just leave me behind," Adin said. "Come back for me with my father's men." Adin was weak, his arms and legs rubbery, his eyes glazing over and then focusing once more. His weeks in captivity had caught up with him, but when the mountain's edge resolved into a drum-shaped bulge, revealing the distant outlines of Catal, his friend must have found some hidden reservoir of strength. Adin broke into a run. "It's too far!" shouted Ren, but his friend would not listen: Adin was already stirring a cloud of sand as he hastened toward the fortress. Ren followed behind him, glad to be in sight of civilization. There were tracks in the sand, many sandal prints, pointed in opposing directions, as if a large army had come and gone using this very road. *We are not the first to come this way.*

The sun was nearly gone when he caught up to Adin. The great drum of the *tulou* sat just outside the southern edge of Feren, along the border with Sola, where the Dromus sprang from the mountains to touch the edge of the Rift valley, forming one enormous barrier—high wall here, deep gorge there. The drum-shaped fortress sat in the knuckle. "This was the home of Feren's first king," Adin told Ren, waving his hand at the *tulou* like it was the grandest of imperial palaces. "Its walls are stronger than the cliffs and thicker too. They made them round like the sides of a drum to keep out intruders." Adin's eyes followed the long curve. "No army has ever breached these walls."

"Who would bother, way out here?" Ren asked.

Adin shaded his eyes and waved. Ren searched the horizon. There was no watch visible on the walk, no guards standing at the gate, the only way in or out. But the sun was in his eyes, hot and orange. "Maybe they are at evening meal," Ren said.

Adin kept moving. "I'm sure that's it."

When they came closer, holding up their hands to show they were no threat, still no one called out to them and no one came to meet them.

There was no gate at the *tulou*'s base. They saw the spot where the hinges once stood, but the metal was torn from the stone. Ren knew what had happened here. The torn hinges and broken gate told the story plainly enough, but he kept his mouth shut.

They passed through the gate, down a dark passageway, and out into the center of the drum. "Hello!" Adin called out, but heard only an echo. "I think I see something," he said. There seemed to be people moving inside the fortress, shadows that flickered and shifted. Adin dashed along the ringed wall. "Is anyone here?"

As a cloud drifted out of the sun's path, Ren realized that the movement Adin had mistaken for inhabitants was merely bits of cloth blowing in the wind or tattered flags stuck to spears. The *tulou*'s walls were crumbled at the top, the bricks shattered in places. The cooking fires were cold, the animals killed or carried off. Here and there dead limbs poked out of the soft dust, human and animal. In places, the flesh was still raw, the damage recent. Everything was as Ren had feared, but Adin would not relent. He rushed to the inner gates, to the burnt wood doors hanging half-open on failed hinges. He was desperate, eager for any sign of lost relatives. There was none. The ringed interior was destroyed—everything was burnt. Adin fell to his knees. No family, no soldiers, no glory was here.

Ren pulled his friend from the wreckage. "I'm sorry." He had tried to warn Adin.

"Where are they? I don't understand—where did they go?"

All dead, Ren thought. He had seen the tracks left by Dagrun's army. So much hope lost.

They scoured the inner chambers, looking for parchments, hoping they might find a message from his family, a name, a scroll. They found nothing. The inner chambers were burned, their contents turned to ash. What was not consumed by flame—the shields and swords and copper vessels—was broken or mangled. The Feren Army had not simply murdered his family, they had destroyed every trace of their occupation, every weapon and provision, every person and animal. Adin's family might as well have not existed.

When they were too tired to search further, and the sun had faded from the old stones, they found a chamber that was free of soot and ash. They slept on the stones, not a word passing between them. The other boy's sadness and frustration was nearly a palpable thing, a ghost moving from room to room asking where everyone had gone.

Ren woke when the sun rose, his belly grumbling again. He caught sight of Adin sitting atop the outer wall, smoke rising from a fire.

"What're you doing?" he called out, but Adin gave no notice. *He'll make me climb.* So up he went, climbing the steep wooden steps, then scaling the crumbling face of the wall. He reached the wall walk, where he saw Adin balancing a pot above the flames of a small fire.

"What's this?" Ren asked.

"Morning meal," said Adin as he took the old pot from the fire. "I found a little amber, some meat, and a pot. It's been a while since either of us had a decent meal, so I thought I'd make us one." He placed a burnt piece of meat on a clay dish and offered it to Ren.

Ren's stomach groaned at the sight of it. He ate greedily as the sun rose across the desert. They nibbled at the food, sipped their drinks, and laughed, Ren cherishing the moment, Adin's eyes growing somber as he talked about his family and all that he had lost.

He told Ren how he had dreamed of the great Chathair in Caer Rifka, of a bride, and of a kingdom to rule. "I wanted to stand beneath the Kiteperch, to spend my night in the Cragwood, to roam the ancient Chathair and study the monuments that pack the throne room. I remember so little of my home. Do I have a birth tree? How would I even find it?"

Ren did not interrupt; he let him ramble. Adin needed to talk and it was good to have his friend back. Ren had suffered plenty, but his spirits were high. *If only Tye were here.*

As the sun rose higher in the sky and the boys finished their meal, Adin poured the last of the amber. "I don't know what to do," he said, his voice low, his gaze distant. "I don't even know where to go for help. Perhaps it's time we went to Harkana. We'll be safe there."

Ren choked at Adin's words. He had not yet told Adin about his sister, the queen regent. He doubted they would be safer in Harkana. He wondered if they would be safe anywhere. The two boys stood shoulder to shoulder, watching the distant horizon where what looked like a crowd had gathered at the Dromus gate.

"I don't want to go home, Adin—not yet."

"Then where?"

"Tolemy's house."

Adin watched the horizon turn from soft purple to amber. "Why? Who else is left?"

"Tye. I heard stories in the Gray Wood. The lords of the Wyrre are dead. If it's true, she'll be set free on the Thieves' Moon."

"How long?" Adin asked.

"Four or five days—maybe less. If we leave now, there is enough time for us to reach Solus before the arrival of the Thieves' Moon."

Adin's face flattened into a frown. "Fuck, Ren—the Priory? It's the one place I don't want to go, the one place I never want to see again."

"We're not going back—at least not all the way back. We can wait at the gate—"

"And if she does not appear?"

"She will." Ren nodded. "I'm no more eager than you to return to the Priory, but—"

"I know." Though they had never spoken of it, he guessed his friend knew how Ren felt about Tye, the affection he harbored for the girl.

"But I still don't want to go there." Adin massaged his forehead, looking as if the very thought of the Priory made his head hurt and his thoughts spin.

"It's not a matter of wanting. I have to go back there for her," Ren continued; he would not be dissuaded from his task. "When I left the Priory, I thought I was returning to my family, to a crown and kingdom. You thought you would find your father's soldiers. We were both wrong. Nothing is as we imagined it would be, but I'm not ready to give up, not yet. If we don't have families or kingdoms, at least we have each other.

"Do you remember the way Tye made us all laugh? Even the priors would crack a smile when she told a good one. She almost made it all right that we were locked up in that hole in the earth."

"Ren, do you really think we'll find her? After what happened here, I just don't want you to be—"

"Disappointed? Fuck. I'm past all that, Adin. I just need to know that I tried."

"And if that gets us killed?"

Ren bit his lip. "I don't think it will come to that. Besides, I wouldn't have made it in the Priory without Tye."

"It's a risk," Adin said.

"I found you. Saved your ass. "

"I was in bloody chains, shackled to a bunch of slaves."

"And about to be executed."

"Well, that's true. You always did have a good sense of timing."

"So trust me. Come with me to Solus. Adin, this is about more than just our freedom. There is a reason why we ransoms are so often feared.

We are strangers to our kingdoms, but comrades to each other. We are three regents with an alliance that runs deeper than blood. Two kings and a king's daughter. Between us, we hold the claims to the thrones of Harkana, and Feren. Can't you see it? A pact between the lower kingdoms? A chance to take back what is ours. Isn't that worth risking our lives?" he asked Adin, kicking sand to extinguish the flame, making his way toward the ladder that led down to the base of the wall.

Adin glanced at his family's broken fortress, wiped his tears, and hurried toward the ladder to join his friend.

⇥44⇤

Merit crossed the Rift valley in her *calash,* the wheels rattling, the tarp whipping in the wind, a bright wedge of forest framed between granite cliffs. Her caravan wound down the mountain trail and out over the first low hills of the desert plain. She sat with her back facing the horses, her eyes fixed on the Feren wood as it disappeared behind a stand of gray-leafed willow. Merit watched the forest for as long as she could. *I should have waited a night, I should have stayed with Dagrun.* One night for the two of them. It was all he asked and she had refused him once again.

For two days her caravan skirted the basin of Amen. She pursued a long but safe route, hugging the Shambles as she made her way toward Harwen. At night her soldiers made camp with the horses huddled between the tents. Merit and the soldiers lit no fires, ate dried meats, and drank tepid cups of amber. They woke and rode out again. By noontime on the third day, the sun was hot and the sweat on Merit's neck and back was mixing with the dust, making her itch. Her caravan had not stopped since morning meal, riding hard through the desert to reach Harkana. Now the soldiers were coated in a mud made of road dirt and sweat, the *calash* groaning. She needed air. Pushing open the tarp, she called Sevin Mosi, her captain, and ordered the caravan halted. The wheels ground to a stop. Merit stepped out, her waiting women, Ahti and Samia, following as she went a few paces up the trail. Ahti moved to dab the sweat from Merit's brow, but she brushed the servant off. "It's no use," she told the girl. "The dust will be back in a moment, and the sweat too."

A little hiss of wind preceded the *thunk* of metal striking rock. A long black dart shattered against the stones, then another, its loud whistle dying into something soft. Ahti was clutching the shaft of a blackwood dart that had pierced her through the neck. Already her limbs were going slack, her body slumping to the ground. Merit remained calm, but Samia gave a little strangled noise of mute horror. Then battle cries, shouting.

A dart sailed past Merit's ear, nipping the flesh. They came from behind, the sun at their backs, their skin mottled in ash. Men with slings and blowguns dashed through the caravan. Darts flew through the air, and two of the four geldings fell. A cold hand gripped Merit's shoulder. She reached for her mother's short sword, but the blade was gone, lost in the chaos. She turned, seeing a warrior in chalk-white desert robes slipping past her in the dust. He stared at her with strange golden eyes, put one hand on her shoulder, and the other on his lips—*shhh*—and disappeared. Spooked. Like a ghost in the darkness.

"Did you see that?" Merit said. "Did you see him?"

"Where?" Sevin shouted, and without warning he was there, holding Samia with one hand and his sword with the second. He either had not seen the outlander or had not reached him in time. Merit had seen the man and she recognized his strange golden eyes. The Hykso were traders and slavers from the Salt Barrens. While they shared much in common with the San, they were a more civilized tribe. They valued life, if they thought it could fetch a price.

The dull clinking of swords rattled the air. Two horses remained, their bodies shielded by a ring of Harkans.

"You take one, Sevin, and I will take the other. The soldiers will stay with Samia. We'll ride hard for the Hornring. When we are safe within the walls, I'll send the army to fetch the others." A hail of stones struck the *calash*; a blackwood dart scraped the nearest horse. The creature turned violently, knocking two soldiers to their knees. A second dart whistled past the horse's head. They didn't have long. Merit grasped the horse's reins and moved to pull herself up, but Sevin blocked her with a cautioning hand. "The horses are already at their limit. This one here," he said, indicating one good-sized gelding with foam on his flanks, "he won't make it. He's done. We'll be stuck on foot and forced to walk." Merit cursed, her fingers turning white as they tightened around the reins. Risk the road or wait here while the outlanders wore them down—neither was an acceptable option.

Before she could consider the matter further, a piercing whistle broke the silence. From high on the cliff the hiss of darts sliced through the air, howling war cries echoing from all sides. Merit dropped the horse's reins, but she would not hide from her enemy. She stood tall, commanding the soldiers. A blackwood dart struck the man standing in front of her, the shaft, thick as her thumb, broke through his chest, through armor and flesh. The tip sprang from his back, shedding blood on her blue dress. The wounded soldier collapsed, but she pushed his body aside, knocking him into Sevin. Beside her, Samia was screaming, the blood pounded in Merit's ears but she stayed calm, trying to find the archers' location. The outlanders were firing high, their projectiles often sailing over her men's heads. *What are they doing?* Too late, she realized their true target: the horses. "Raise shields!" she cried, but the darts and stones were already arcing over the soldiers' heads and finding their targets. The horses collapsed. The raiders had done their work: Merit's company, what was left of it, was trapped.

As the cries of the Hykso faded into the hills, as the soldiers fanned out to form a protective ring, Merit remained standing, her guards clustered around her. She searched for her mother's short sword, spotted it on a pierced seat cushion, and pulled it forth. She sent out a soldier to test the perimeter, to see if the Hykso were watching, if they were truly trapped, but when her man stepped beyond the ring the Hykso leapt from behind the rocks, hurtling spears and loosing darts. The soldier fell dead on the ground, a black stave protruding from his chest. They would not escape on foot.

"Why?" Samia called from behind Merit. "Why have they trapped us like this?"

"Because," Sevin spat, "they're not savages. The Hykso are traders, hunters. They're a careful folk. They'll wait till we're out of water, exhausted and wild with thirst. Then—"

"Enough." Merit brushed Sevin away as she surveyed the mess of broken armor and dead horses. Sevin was right, but he did not have all of the answers. It did not explain why the ash-skinned man had not killed her. Clearly he had been close enough to cut her throat—she could still feel the cool touch of his hand on her shoulder.

Sevin ordered his men to raise tents. The outlanders had retreated from sight, but she could hear their cries, voices that imitated animal sounds: a hawk's screech, a coyote's snarl. The outlanders were letting them know they were close, they were watching, waiting to attack.

Merit cursed. She should not have left Feren without Dagrun's soldiers, his horses, and their fortified armor. She needed a larger company, an army for an escort, she was queen regent, but she had only a small entourage. In Rifka, she'd let her pride interfere with her judgment and now she was suffering because of it.

With his men standing at attention, or patrolling, Sevin and a few others set camp. He ordered the dead girl dragged from the wreckage. Through the bustle, Merit watched the men wrap Ahti in the lap blanket and bury her in the sand. Samia stood, sobbing quietly, too afraid to make a noise. In a few days, maybe less, wolves and wild dogs would come to dig for Ahti's corpse, and vultures would pick her bones—the second death, if the Hykso did not unearth her first. It was a good reminder, Merit thought, of all that there was to lose.

She sat down next to her captain, watched him stare into the fire as he called out orders to his men. His face was worn, eyes red. *I should have ridden out while the last two horses stood. Damn you, Sevin, if you've cost me my life.* When he was finished with his men Sevin turned to Merit. "What do you think those outlanders are doing on the Feren border?"

"Does it matter?" she said. "Start thinking of how you'll sneak me out of here." Merit left the fire. The daylight faded. They spent the night huddled in tents and the morning crowded around the fire. Merit found Sevin and ordered her captain to send messengers: one toward Harkana, a second toward Feren. "Perhaps a lone soldier can elude the Hykso," she said, her eyes tracing the distant cliffs.

Sevin gave her a doubtful look, but he brought forth soldiers, gave them amber and bread, stripped them of their heavy armor, and told them to move as quickly as they could toward the respective kingdoms. "There's a Harkan outpost a day's walk from here," he said. "Davo, you head in that direction, toward Harkana. Cerrik, you strike out toward the Rift valley and surrender to the nearest Feren soldiers."

"Sir," the soldiers said, and, looking warily at Merit, they started off on foot.

The first had scarcely disappeared when a chorus of animal cries bounded from the high cliffs. The snorts and howls echoed like boos from a crowd. They had found her man and were mocking her efforts.

"Should we go after him?" Samia asked.

Sevin gave Merit a cold look: the boy was dead.

Merit searched for the second messenger, the man headed toward Harkana, but the soldier was gone. She waited, eyes wide, skin cold. She listened for the howls that had accompanied the first kill. She stood, heart beating, but heard only her breath and the distant cawing of a crow. No sounds of battle. An hour passed, then a second. Merit sent out a third soldier to survey the canyon, to see if the Hykso had taken her man and left. The soldier wove through the rocks and scrub, his black leather mixing with the dark rocks as he disappeared over the ridge. She waited for the clink of iron, for their captors' cries, but heard neither. Flies buzzed and hawks screeched. Merit retired to her tent. Sevin lit a fire and the nervous Harkans gnawed at what provisions they had.

Just after midday Sevin's voice resounded through the camp. "Gather your arms," he said as Merit pushed open her tent flap. An outlander had crested the hill and was moving quickly toward them. Her captain took three of his strongest and marched toward the man, stopping just short of attack. The men converged, raised their swords, but came up short. The Harkans sheathed their blades and the ashen warrior lowered his spear. The five men stood together and talked for a tense moment, then turned and hastened together toward the camp.

"What's happening? Are they going to kill us?" Samia asked, panic rising in her voice, and Merit answered, "I don't know, but keep your voice down. They might kill you just for panicking."

When they came closer, Merit saw the ash-covered man was too tall to belong to an outlander tribe, his bearing too stiff. He was Harkan, and Merit knew him well. His name was Asher Hacal, a close ally of her father's, his friend and his captain. Merit immediately stood to greet him.

"Queen Regent," he said, and bowed.

"What brings you so far from Harwen?"

He told Merit that he had intercepted her messenger en route to Harkana, given the man his horse, and told him to ride hard toward Harwen while Asher continued on foot, following her man's instructions to reach Merit's camp. When Asher encountered the Hykso, he had killed one, stolen his guise, and slipped through to the encampment.

Merit stopped him. She was confused—Asher had been escorting her father to Solus, not Harwen. What was he doing on the road to Harkana? "What's wrong, Asher?"

He caught his breath. "I have news, it's from Solus. Something only you can hear."

She brought him to her tent and stood under the billowing blue cloth, where Asher's face, long known and trusted, looked haunted, bruised. "Well?" she asked. "I assume you have come to tell me my father is dead."

He swallowed, looking at the cup and clay vessel her servant had set on a narrow table. "May I have a drink of that?" he asked. "I've ridden so long, I'm absolutely parched." Merit nodded. Asher went over and poured himself a drink, then drank it all in one long, smooth gulp. "Better," he said. "Thank you."

She folded her arms in front of her. "Don't make we wait, Asher."

He shook his head. There was something oddly sorrowful in his face, something hollow. What was it?

Asher told Merit all that had happened to her father in Solus.

"My father is the Ray?" Her mind spun. Asher cleared his throat. Merit was so dazed by the news she had almost forgotten his presence.

"Merit," Asher continued, "this new position, it's left your father isolated in the capital. He's been eager to get through to you." Merit started to speak, but Asher held up his hand. "I have other news, a matter of much greater importance," he said, and swallowed hard. "The capital is a perilous place, and your father is uncertain of his safety. If anything should happen to him, there is another matter he needs you to understand." He produced the small note, written in a child's code, one Asher could not read. Recognizing her father's blocky script, she took the note and read its brief contents in a single glance, her eyes working more quickly than her mind, her fingers nearly dropping the note when she understood its meaning.

There is no emperor. The throne room sits in ruins, the Amber Throne smashed. Smashed long ago, centuries, probably. There has been no emperor in the living memory of anyone in the empire.

⇒45⇐

The soldiers of the Protector's Army arrived in columns at the Antechamber of the Ray, filling three adjoining halls, a wide vestibule, and the entirety of the courtyard beyond. More than five hundred well-armed, well-fed soldiers of the Alehkar assembled outside the Antechamber. From the look of them, all muscle and sinew, Arko guessed they were chosen from among the strongest and healthiest of the Protector's sworn men. Behind the courtyard's ring stood a second group, the Jundi, in their kilts and leather breastplates. Saad had spared no effort assembling this show.

When the last man stepped into line, the soldiers nearest to the Ante-chamber let out a shout, stomping their feet like fools, beating their bronze-tipped sandals in time with their war songs. A core of flagmen held red banners and waved them in time to the chanting. Saad would not come until Arko had had his fill of pomp and ceremony, the knock of spears, the stamping of feet shaking the ground. Like a herd of elephants out his window, Arko thought, or an army marching to war.

Earlier that day, as he waited for Saad's arrival, he had asked Wat to post Tolemy's proclamation. At the time, Wat had urged Arko to hold off until after his audience with the Father Protector. Arko had accepted Wat's counsel and now he understood the wisdom behind it. His pres-ence in the Antechamber, a rebel king ruling at the center of the empire, had obviously unnerved the young Protector, so much so that Saad had assembled five hundred of his best troops to stand at his side. If Arko had posted the decree that morning, Saad might have brought the whole army with him and Arko wasn't ready for that—not yet. If it came to a fight, he would rather he had his loyal Harkan soldiers at his side, and since they had not yet arrived, he needed to bide his time and try to force Saad to leave Solus peacefully.

Presently, a noise went up from among the soldiers outside, a mur-mur either of approval or despair, Arko could not tell which. He went to the screened window and saw Saad crossing through his men, who parted to let him by. He had seen the boy only once, in the shadows of the Cenotaph, and was uncertain if this was the same man. He called Wat over and pointed to the figure coming toward the Antechamber of the Ray. "This man is the one who killed his own father? He looks barely old enough to hold a sword."

A young man, bull-necked, his chin thrust out, Saad elbowed aside anyone who did not move fast enough for his taste. "He has the look of a second son, one who's decided the throne should have been his all along."

"That might not be too far off the mark."

Arko watched Saad fling a young soldier to the ground and push his boot in the boy's face. More than anything, Arko hated a bully, a man who ruled by force or fear. "Maybe he needs to remember his place."

"Be cautious, sir," Wat said. "Antagonizing him here and now might be costly."

"I'll keep that in mind."

A knock at the door announced Saad's arrival at the Antechamber, followed by two servants in yellow cloaks. "Now comes Amen Saad, Father Protector of the Dromus, Binder of the Circle, Guardian of the Walls and Keeper of the Chant, the son of Raden who twice vanquished the outlander horde—"

Arko smirked. Banners and chants he could understand, but the last was a stretch. When it came to the outlanders, Saad's father had taken more hits than he had given. Arko stopped listening, but the list of titles and accolades continued. When he could bear no more, Arko held his hand up, interrupting the litany. "Thank you for informing me of the Protector's might, but if he's not planning on coming in soon, I might need a break to take a piss."

Wat wrinkled his lip, knitting his brows together in concern.

The chanting grew to a crescendo as Saad's men stomped their final beat and the Protector entered at last, taking his time still, his chin raised a finger's width in a gesture Arko recognized as common to short men who built their muscles with intense exercise and diets of bull testicles, feeling they had something to prove to all the world. Arko disliked him immediately.

The customs of the place dictated certain formalities: Saad greeted him with a curt nod, then had his servant recite his own list of greetings for the Ray: "Hail Arko Hark-Wadi, First Ray of the Sun, Eye of Tolemy, Light of Mithra-Sol, the Brightest Star in the Heavens—"

Arko interrupted. "I think we can forgo the usual," he said. "Welcome, Saad. I've heard much about you, and none of it has been exaggerated."

Saad was too dim to understand when he was being insulted. "Thank you, sir. I welcome you to court. Suten Anu's exit was long overdue." His voice was higher than Arko would have imagined. A boy's voice.

"I hope we may be able to work together," Arko said. *I doubt it, but I can hope.*

He saw equal misgiving on Saad's face. "We share the same hope. I am told you are a soldier-king, a man who leads from the front lines. My father was such a leader, and I intend to be one as well."

When you grow a little taller. He was glad the boy showed some sense of honor. Or was Saad just telling him what he wanted to hear?

"It is a shame my father left the empire in such a mess," Saad continued. "It will taint his legacy, I fear. I have spent some time reorganizing his men, promoting where needed, trimming where necessary."

Murdering your father's loyal generals, bribing the rest.

"It has . . . kept my attention at home."

"I trust that is all over now?" Arko asked, more hopeful than confident.

"For now," Saad said. "There may come a time when I need to revisit the matter. At the moment, though, all my thoughts are on the rebel."

"Good to hear it," Arko said, though in reality he did not have the slightest confidence in this pup to defend the empire from a seasoned leader like Barca. Saad had spent his time in office bartering with generals and waylaying messengers. The boy had his eyes on Solus; he cared nothing for the lower kingdoms, the cities beyond the capital. Arko wondered if Saad would attempt to bait him, if he would ask about the messages that went missing. Arko decided to avoid such topics; they would serve only to highlight his weakness.

"What plans have you put in place?" Arko asked.

Saad went on to deliver a record of the army's status and positions, bringing maps to show greater detail—how the still-loyal men of the Protector's Army had moved to the Dromus to take up the positions Barca used to occupy, how Saad had positioned provisions and armaments for the coming conflict. It was all done with great pomp and ceremony, the colorful maps and figures laid on the table, the armies of the Protector represented in yellow, the army of Barca in red, the outlanders in white. Saad knocked them about with the tip of his sword, showing the movements of threat and counterthreat across the empire like some kind of elaborate game of Coin. Arko grumbled—he was a king, he wanted to remind Saad, one who for decades had commanded his own army. Arko knew and understood Barca's strategy, its shortcomings and its strengths. But for a change he held his tongue. However silly it was, moving toys around a board, the message was the same: Barca was moving closer, using the outlander tribes to pillage while he moved around behind their lines, masking his movements and his strength.

"Thank you for that report, Protector," he said. Then he waved a hand to dismiss the Protector's men. "Leave us," he said. "We have matters to discuss."

The soldiers looked at Saad, whose face was darkened by the shame of having his own men dismissed by the Ray, but he wisely nodded his assent and the men left the Antechamber. Then Arko told Khalden Wat to close the doors, leaving the three men alone. The Antechamber sat astride the Shroud Wall, half inside and half outside the Empyreal Domain. Wat opened a pair of shutters, revealing amber windows. The windows faced the Empyreal Domain, but the amber slabs prevented a visitor from seeing directly into the emperor's precinct; only shadows passed through the honey-colored resin. Men from the Kiltet stood on the far side of the amber windows, their hazy silhouettes falling across the amber panes. To report back to the emperor, Arko wanted to say, but Saad did not ask. The shapes of the men were enough to let him know: the emperor was listening.

"Tolemy commands you to send a legion of men to the Dromus," he said, explaining that the Protector's Army was to reverse Barca's progress through the Wyrre and Harkana, capture the rogue captain, and rebuild the Outer Guard. Barca's trained soldiers would be reintegrated into the new Outer Guard, and the farmers and fishermen whom the traitor had drafted into his service would be sent back to their homes. In truth, Arko didn't care about Barca attacking the empire, but he was worried about *his* kingdom. The rebel had already moved against Harkana and was even now advancing on the Hornring. Arko needed to block that advance, but also wanted to get Saad out of Solus, and war was the best way to make the Protector leave. The campaign against Barca might take years to complete and Saad's absence would give Arko time to cement his power and make changes to the empire. *I need to get rid of you, Saad. And this is the best way to do it.* Arko faced the amber windows. A shadow fell through the resin, giving an eerie sense of movement beyond.

"What of Barca?" Saad asked.

"What of him?" Arko asked. "You'll take his head or he'll take yours. Let's hope it's the former," Arko said, smirking. "You will need to leave Solus in one week's time." Arko held out a scroll with the emperor's seal— gold, shining with the rays of the sun. Saad accepted the document silently, his anger already visible in his face. *His temper may yet get the best of him. That is, if Barca doesn't kill him first.*

Saad had five hundred men at his back; he could easily strike now and take the Eye of the Sun from Arko's brow, but he did nothing. The boy straightened his back. Khalden Wat led Saad to the corridor, where the sounds of soldiers beating their feet echoed once again in the stony vaults. Their chants grew louder when they saw their leader approach. The soldiers raised their spears as Saad passed into their lines.

Arko circled the empty chamber, listening to the chants fade as the last soldier left the yard. He spoke when the yard was empty. "He's not leaving Solus. I saw it in his face, Wat."

"You might be right."

"If he doesn't leave Solus, I'll need options—ways to defend myself."

"What would you like me to do?"

"Find some men."

Wat narrowed his eyes.

"Men that are good at killing," Arko continued. "I assume there is no shortage in the capital. I'm sure Suten employed more than one during his reign."

"I'll find what I can," Wat said, looking uneasy. He seemed accustomed to the intrigues of politics, but not the ways of war. Arko, on the other hand, was well accustomed to such things. He had more than once fought the outlander tribes and was each time victorious. If a fight were inevitable, he would not shrink from it. He found politics vexing, but a war he could manage.

"Do you still want me to post the proclamation?" Wat inquired. "The boy waits with the parchment."

"Yes, do it now," Arko said, but there was no need.

Below him, in the empty yard, a door opened and a boy appeared with a large sheet of parchment in his hand. The page held Tolemy's decree—a brief but eloquent proclamation detailing the amendment of the imperial system of tributes that was initiated two centuries prior by Tolemy I. Wat had asked him to soften the language and to post each amendment separately with a long interval between each, to lessen the shock, he said. But Arko would not hear it. If his directives caused unrest, he would embrace it. He would not shrink from his responsibilities. Suten had not offered him power so he could squander it.

The boy held up the sheet and hammered it into the wall.

≋46≋

"Stay close," Sarra said as she led her priests into the Hollows of Solus. She was searching for a particular passage—one that the priests of old, in the time before the sealing of the Shroud Wall, traveled to enter the Empyreal Domain, a passage known as Mithra's Door. She needed to confirm what she had found in the Shambles, to make certain the throne room was empty and the Soleri were all gone—a daunting task, but not one she could ignore. *I need to know if the gods are truly dead.* Mithra's Door was said to lead from the Ata'Sol, through the Shroud Wall, and into to the throne room of the emperor. Sarra had read about the passage but never searched for it. Prior to her encounter in the Shambles, it had never occurred to her to seek out the door. Opening it would expose her to the emperor, to certain death, to the immortal and intolerable light of the god. But there was no Tolemy. The gods were dead. They were stars and stones. Ash and obsidian. The Empyreal Domain was empty—or so she hoped.

Sarra traveled the corridors with three priests. One read from a scroll, following an ancient set of instructions, while the second held an oil lamp, the third tools—a pick, a hammer, a few chisels, and an adze.

She slowed her pace, allowing the men to move a little ahead of her. Over morning meal a scroll had arrived from Rifka. Her daughter had wedded Dagrun Finner, the king of the Ferens, which meant that she had left Harwen. Kepi was in Rifka now and Sarra tried to picture what she might look like, the woman she had become, but too much time had passed since she last laid eyes on her daughter. In truth, Sarra knew about as much about Kepi as she knew about Dagrun. They were both a mystery. She only hoped the rumors about Dagrun—that he was a violent man, a brutish smuggler and thief—were untrue.

Sarra nearly collided with the wall. The light was gone, her priests having left her behind. She rounded a corner and caught sight of the lamp.

"A bit slower," she said. "We don't know what's down here."

Indeed, the dust here was finger-deep and the cobwebs were everywhere. No one had come this way in a very long time.

They edged around corners, making certain they were alone and the way was safe. Even if the Soleri were gone, their shadow lingered over the Empyreal Domain, following her every step, making her startle as they lit each new passage. Up ahead, the lamplight illuminated ornately patterned walls. Star and palmate motifs embellished the ceiling and walls. Rendered in bright lapis and dotted with shades of umber, the many small stones reflected circles of light in all directions. She guessed, by the character and quality of the designs, the tunnel dated to the Middle Kingdom. Only the emperors of the Amber Age, the great builders, would dedicate such opulence to a subterranean corridor, a pathway traveled only by priests.

"The door is up ahead," the man holding the scroll announced, his voice wavering a bit, with expectation, perhaps, or dread. "Open it," Sarra said, not hesitating, not wanting to pause for fear that she might lose her nerve. Her priests laid down their wares. They put their palms to the door and pushed. The great bronze door, its face crusted with verdigris, squealed on its hinges. The men shook their wrists, adjusted their footing, and pushed again. The door creaked open by degrees, slowly revealing a dark space beyond.

"Lamps," Sarra said.

Her priests raised oil lamps, but the light revealed nothing more than a wall of roughly set stones erected only a few paces back from the bronze door. At the edges of the barrier she saw magnificent decorations. Chips of agate sparkled on the ceiling and the walls were clad in bronze, the surfaces adorned in the curling symbols of the hieratic script. Sarra had crossed into the Empyreal Domain—she knew it. All that stood in her path was the stone wall.

"Remove a stone," she said, quickly gesturing to one of her priests, who lifted a slender pick and began digging at the top of the wall. "Quietly," she said, though she guessed the task could not be accomplished without making a bit of noise.

Her priests grunted as they removed a round boulder about the size of a man's head. The opening revealed a second wall, sitting directly behind the first. There was a snake carved in the shape of a ring incised in the stone. *Someone was awfully thorough,* she thought, though the precautions did make some sense. The builders didn't want anyone to wander into the throne room of the dead Soleri, after all.

"Keep going," she said, encouraging the men, but with all their labors it still took an hour to pierce the first wall. Her priests had to carefully and painstakingly remove each stone, chipping at the grout between them, prying at the rounded rocks with picks. In the meantime, every sound, every crack of stone or iron rattled her nerves. If they were discovered, this breach would cost them their lives. But no one came to arrest them, no guard approached. No one had come this way, she guessed, for many years.

The digging revealed that the second wall was newer than the first; its stones more carefully laid, the coursing more regular, and the blocks were larger too and they took more time to dislodge. They had to push the first stone into the corridor beyond to dislodge it. It landed there with a mighty thump, cracking the tiles inside and making an awful racket.

She cringed again, listening to see if anyone was there, if a bell rang or a shout echoed. She waited, but no sound rattled the corridor. They were alone, so Sarra lifted one of the lamps and peered through the opening, past the wall and into the corridor beyond. Dust choked the passage, but the way was clear and the corridor was empty. The only signs of life were the tracks left long ago by mice, shallow indentations that were themselves covered in a layer of dust. *Nothing,* she thought. *There's no one here. The throne room's as empty as this passage, as barren as the solar I found in the Shambles.*

"Clear the way," she said. "I will send provisions and more lamps. Open the corridor, but do not venture into the domain." She was already re-treating toward the Ata'Sol. When sufficient time had passed for the men to clear the passage, she would send a single priest, one loyal to her alone. He would carry cool amber and bread, both laced with strychnine, or mandrake root. She cringed at the thought, but saw no other option.

Sarra left the workers, carefully considering her next move, how she would use her newly acquired knowledge against Saad. Deep in thought, she retraced the path she traveled with the three priests, moving more quickly now. She was no longer afraid of the Soleri, their guards, or their ghosts. She had not yet seen the throne room, but she would soon, and she guessed it was as empty as the passages she had just explored.

She made her way out of the Hollows, eager to find Ott. But when she closed the door to the underground passage she did not find him waiting outside for her as she had expected. A girl Sarra did not quite recognize greeted her at the door.

"Who are you?" Sarra asked. "I've seen you before."

"I'm Ott's scribe, Kara," the girl said, her voice trembling, her eyes red and swollen.

"What is it—where is Ott? I was expecting him."

The girl peered nervously at the Mother Priestess, as if she were afraid to speak.

"Go on," said Sarra. "Tell me what's on your mind."

Still the girl would not speak, something had clearly rattled her.

"Get on with it," Sarra said.

"Ott's gone."

"What do you mean?"

"Earlier this morning on the temple steps, while you were in the Hollows, soldiers in bronze mail confronted Ott. They led him away."

"Where?"

"To the tower, he is with the Protector's men."

She did not trust herself to react to this news. She pressed her back to the door, running a hand through her red tresses, thinking. Saad was testing her again, but this time he had taken someone of value. A jolt of fear struck her, but it quickly faded. Ott knew the secret of the dead Soleri, but that did not mean her secret was lost. The Protector would not ask if there was a Tolemy, just as he would not ask if there was a sun in the sky. Saad would likely concern himself with the secrets of the priesthood. He would ask about Sarra's intentions in Solus, her plans to confront Saad, and her weaknesses. In these matters, Sarra felt secure. She had shared her plans with no one—not even Ott. She had revealed bits and pieces, but only as needed.

The girl interrupted, "Mother Priestess, what should we do?"

"About what?"

"Ott," the girl said. Perhaps she was close to Ott; Sarra didn't know. She didn't care. Ott was more important to the Mother Priestess than to anyone else, yet Sarra could not waver from the course she had chosen. If she wanted to see the boy again, she needed to stick to her plan. She would use her knowledge of the Soleri against Arko and Saad, manipulating the two like marionettes on a string.

"Nothing," she said. "At the moment, there's nothing we can do for him. We must be patient. For now, I need you to find a messenger. Tell him to arrange a congress between the Mother and the Father. Go now—leave me."

When she was gone, Sarra faced the door that led into the Hollows. Her eyes were stinging and she didn't want anyone to see her. Over the years she had lost much: a husband, her daughters. *Ott saved my life on the last day of the year, but can I save his?* She could not bear to lose anyone else. *I need to end this conflict and I need to do it now.*

Saad was forcing her to act and Sarra would do so. She was ready; she had found the door to the throne room. She could access the empty chamber without using the formal entry and the Hall of Histories. Now she just needed to lead Saad into that room. He would go if she gave him the right reason, the right incentive.

He would come alone, without his swords and his soldiers. After all, no man may enter the Empyreal Domain with a weapon—unless they found a back door.

⇥47⇤

There is no emperor.

Her father's message burning within her, Merit lifted the hem of her dress and climbed the sandy cliff till her eyes crept above the canyon's shadow. It was late in the day, but the sun was still bright and hot; she winced and made a visor of her hand, scanning the sun-drenched canyons, searching the horizon for the Dromus. She caught sight of its curving line, traced the distant barrier until the canyon's edge eclipsed her view. In Sola, the sun did not set upon the horizon; it dipped each night below the Dromus and rose from its far edge the next day. The wall was Sola's horizon. Walls within walls—who would have thought that their center was empty, that the throne was unoccupied? Her father's message was simple: *The throne room sits in ruins, the Amber Throne smashed.*

This changes everything. If there was no emperor, her children were no longer subject to the Priory, and she was no longer bound by the marriage Tolemy had arranged. There was no Tolemy. Merit was free. This news had the power to unmake the empire, and she alone held it. Arko had sent his messenger to *her* instead of Kepi or Ren. The emptiness at the heart of the empire was too important, too dangerous, to share with anyone but the ruler of Harkana, and for now, at least, the ruler of Harkana was still Merit. Her father was alive and he trusted her. The man who for so many years had shielded her from the burdens of power had now placed the empire's greatest secret in her hands. She held a truth that could cripple Solus, words that could remake her kingdom. He had denied her power for so long that Merit feared she would never have it, but now it was here and it was hers. He loved her. It sounded silly, but Merit had often felt cheated of her father's affections. She had thought the king of Harkana had no love for anyone but Kepi and his absent son. He certainly had no love for his wife, the one who left him, the woman Merit had so often imitated when she was young. Now all of that was in the past. Merit was his daughter, loved, and more important, *trusted.*

The sound of sand grinding against stone drifted into her ear. *Where did that come from?* She caught a terrible stench, the smell of ash-soaked sweat.

"Sevin!" Too late, she called out to her soldiers as she caught sight of the spear. The outlander crept between the stones, clutching the blackwood, feet lifting silently, his eyes narrow and focused.

"What do you want?" she asked as she settled her shoulders against the tall rocks.

The outlander raised his sharpened stave, his fingers tensing on the shaft, but he made no move to attack. His eyes seemed transfixed by the deep blue of her dress.

"I have coin," she said, "and jewelry—gold." She raised her bangled arm.

The outlander lowered the spear.

"Is that what you want?" she asked as she slipped the gold from her wrist.

He held out a hand to Merit, palm facing up, fingers extended, his face a mask of white chalk, impossible to read. He shook his hand to urge Merit forward.

I have to stall, if only for a moment, she thought. *I can't die. Not now, when the whole world has just opened up to me.* She cursed herself for being foolish enough to wander off alone when their situation was still so perilous.

Her fingers brushed the outlander's. She offered him the gold, but he wouldn't take it.

"What is it you want?" she asked again, though she knew he could not understand her. "What are you waiting for? Kill me or capture me," she said, her eyes following her soldiers as they crept up the hill. Merit waited, counting the seconds. When the men were close, she threw herself out of the way. A Harkan spear whistled past the outlander, striking rock, sending sand into the air. Merit pushed forward, trying to sidestep the man, but the outlander was gone before she could act, scrambling silently through the tall rocks and vanishing.

Merit was left alone at the top of the cliff, wondering what had just happened. Why had he hesitated? Why had he not struck when he had the chance? The outlanders had twice left her alive, once when they slaughtered the horses and again just now. She understood their earlier tactic—she knew the benefits of starving your enemies—but this man had no reason to hesitate. She was his to kill, but he had stretched out his hand to her. He had wanted something other than blood.

"Queen Regent," said Sevin as he arrived at her side. "Now that you're done trying to get yourself killed, would you like to return to the camp?"

Merit smirked and Sevin grumbled something about foolish women and the problems of protecting a queen regent who wasn't anxious enough about her own head. Merit's waiting woman was as pale as alabaster when she saw her at the base of the cliff.

"It's all right, Samia," Merit said. "Get ahold of yourself, or they'll hear you." The girl settled back down on the hard sand, using her dress to wipe her face. Merit did her best to ignore Samia, but the man she had seen at the hilltop was clearly not alone. She heard animal cries echo across the canyon walls. Had her captors at last decided to advance?

Darts whistled through the canyon, a soldier fell. Merit drew her sword. Her captain came to her side and raised his shield. Loud cries bounded through the canyons. Blackwood staves raised to the sky, the outlanders crowded near the canyon's edge, approaching slowly, carefully making their way across the brown, hard-baked plains; through the scrub and the stones, they were coming.

The Hykso held back their attack for a reason. The man on the hilltop, his outstretched hand, he wanted a ransom, not a kill.

"We're not fighting our way out of this, Sevin. There is no need." Merit sheathed her mother's sword. She turned to the last of her soldiers, her hands raised over her head. "Put down your weapons!" she shouted. They looked confused, glancing from her to Sevin, to Asher and back. "Now!" she commanded, and they did, reluctantly.

Sevin sputtered. "You men, rearm yourselves," he ordered, but before they could pick up their weapons, Merit stopped them. "My orders stand. You serve the queen regent of Harkana and no other." The men lowered their weapons. The outlanders had not come for her head; she was certain of it—that was why the man had paused on the hilltop, why their darts had targeted the horses.

Merit Hark-Wadi stood tall and patted her captain on the shoulder. "It's all right, Sevin, Asher," she said. "Trust me." But her soldiers' eyes followed her, their expressions tense, confused. *Let them tremble,* she thought. The men's swords would not save them this time. They were outnumbered, trapped. If they fought they would perish, and Merit was not ready to die, not when she had just learned the secret behind the empire. She would rather bide her time as a captive than risk dying with her secret. So Merit strode to the edge of the camp, past Sevin, past the men hurrying to put on their armor, past the tents, past the little maidservant weeping into her hands that she didn't want to die, she wasn't ready to die, not today. Merit walked out beyond the stones toward the Hykso and held up her hands in supplication, in surrender. Her blue dress flapped in the wind behind her like a flag. What a sight she must have been to the fierce Hykso in their white ash, their mouths screaming for blood, to the Harkan soldiers sworn to protect her: a woman with long black locks surrendering herself to them, the queen regent of Harkana offering herself up as ransom.

<h1 style="text-align:center">⇛48⇚</h1>

Kepi startled when the door opened, the dress she held nearly falling to the floor. For a moment she had thought it was Dagrun. She had not seen the king since she left him in the tent filled with manuscripts. A week had passed since that day, but she still wasn't certain what had happened in the tent, why she had frozen in place when Dagrun held out his hand. Perhaps it was his generosity that startled her. She guessed that was why she had recoiled. No, it was something more. Something she could not admit to herself just yet. She had believed his gifts to be false tokens, a pretense of affection, but now, days later, Kepi wondered if she had it wrong. Perhaps he had put a bit of consideration into his offering, but *she* hadn't recognized it.

Dammit. Everything here was so foreign; she didn't know what to think.

Dalla entered with a crock of amber and cakes of bread for Kepi's morning meal. The girl kept her eyes properly lowered, but her presence was unnerving. Kepi had spent weeks in Rifka, her wedding was a fortnight past, but she was still getting used to her surroundings. She took the vessel from the girl and poured herself a cup, gulping it down, then took another. "Thank you. I didn't realize how thirsty I was."

Though indeed blind in one eye, Dalla's gaze was fixed on the floor. "Mistress," she said, "the king has made you some armor. You'll find it in that trunk over there."

Armor?

Kepi knelt and opened the trunk under the window. Near the bottom, she discovered a well-made set of leather breeches, a tunic, and a leather breastplate embossed with the tree of Feren in the center. All new, all done in her size. Kepi took them out of the trunk, pressed them to her breasts.

Sparring clothes. Dagrun had had his seamstresses make her a set of sparring clothes, so that she could practice in the ring.

In all her life, no one had ever understood how much she enjoyed the thrill of a sharp blade and the chafe of hard leather on her skin, how much it meant to her that she could hold her own in the ring against anyone, man or woman. Her sister had always discouraged Kepi's interests, and her father had always seemed amused and baffled that his youngest daughter was such a brute, wondering why she did not prefer needlework and dancing and other such girlish silliness the way Merit had.

But now here was her new husband, the man she had questioned above all others, presenting her with a set of sparring clothes, actually encouraging her to continue her swordplay after their marriage. *Odd,* she thought, *of all the people in the world, it is Dagrun who understands what I need. Or is he simply playing to my weakness?* Kepi could not be certain, but she thought she knew the answer.

"Mistress?" said Dalla, looking confused. "Are you all right?"

Kepi laughed. "I am," she said. "I've never been better."

Dalla helped her dress, though the servant was clumsy with the mannish clothes and had to be instructed how to properly tie the breastplate on, how to adjust the straps, and how to pull Kepi's hair away from her face so that it would not interfere in the ring. When she was dressed, Kepi looked down at herself clad in leather, feeling how soft the material was, how well worked. It all fit her too. With an imaginary sword in her hand she feinted and riposted. It was perfect.

Dalla smiled. "Are you ready?"

"Ready?"

"For the boy, your master-at-arms. He asked to see you for a training session."

Kepi's face darkened. She had no desire to see Seth. "He did? Where?"

"Outside in the yard. Mistress? Are you okay?"

"I think I will be, Dalla. Thank you for your help."

"It's all right. I hope . . . I mean, you are not like us. It's good. I'd like it if we could be friends."

Kepi smiled and patted the girl's arm. "We are." Like her father, Kepi had a way of making people trust her, making them loyal to her, simply by appreciating the kindness they wanted to give her. The girl gave her a quick squeeze and went back out of the room.

She found Seth waiting for her near the practice yard, weighing swords not far from the grove where she had joined hands with Dagrun to become his wife. It did not seem that long ago, and yet in many ways it was already a lifetime. In the distance she heard saws and hammers, the workers building the Queen's Chamber, the bed, the furniture, and the roomful of books that would all soon be hers. If only she would accept them as such. She shook her head again. The world was strange, and she was a stranger in it—new, even to herself.

When he saw her in the new clothes, the leathers and tunic, Seth was confused.

"Where'd you get that armor?" he asked.

"It is not your concern," she said. She would have him replaced, she decided. It was too dangerous for him to be so intimate with her.

"I need to talk to you."

"Not now," she said. She had avoided Seth with nearly the same vigor with which she had avoided the king of the Ferens. He was no longer quite a friend, she realized, and he had never been her lover. Though she had wanted to love him once, she had told herself she loved him, but that seemed foolish now, almost childish.

"Very well then, mistress," he said, his voice dull with hurt. Seth tossed her a wooden blade. "Shall we begin?"

She stood back and waited. He advanced slowly, kicking up a little dust. He tipped his blade at the last moment, feinting right, but not convincingly. The blade turned at the last moment, his arm too limp to make an effective strike at her. She parried, beating his sword into the dirt.

"Good work," he said, though she knew he could not tell good work from bad—his poor upbringing was showing. He wiped the dust from his blade. "Again."

She advanced, legs bent, back straight, feet perpendicular—right leg first, left leg trailing. She kept her practice sword low, her left hand held out for balance. He took her patience for sluggishness and lunged crudely. She stepped backward, and he missed. He recovered, took a step back and scowled, then started again, advancing with his sword held level. Seth feinted, but Kepi watched the direction of his eyes rather than his arm, anticipating the move, and countered in the opposite direction, touching him on the back of his thigh. He tried to parry, but Kepi stepped back, and when he lost his balance she caught him in the middle of his chest. "You're dead," she said.

His face reddened. "Again," he said, taking a deep breath and frowning.

Soldiers stopped to watch, and the slaves too paused at the field's edge—they had an audience. Seth appeared to take notice, his knees trembling when they bent. He steeled himself on his back foot and lunged at her. He was angry, embarrassed, not paying attention to what he was doing but determined to land a blow, to prove that he could. A moment before he touched her she stepped to her right, and Seth, hitting nothing but air, fell on his knees into the Feren mud.

Quiet laughter rang through the court. She pitied the boy and offered him her hand, but he would not take it.

"Once more," he told her as he pushed himself up with the wooden blade. He lifted his back foot as if to retreat but lunged forward instead. A clever trick—an advance disguised as a retreat—but he had forgotten that she had taught him the move. His blow struck her shoulder, but it landed too late: She had tapped him on the chest while his feet were still deciding which direction to take.

She heard a hoot, and then a round of chuckles. One soldier clapped, and the other slapped his friend on the back. "You are making a scene of yourself, Seth. Stop this," she said with a sigh. She did not want to humiliate him.

He shook his head. "Just once more. It's okay, I'm just having fun."

His face turned ugly. He was not having fun at all—he was competing with her.

He came at her with blade held high. His hand wavering, his grip loose. He was taller than she was, his arm longer, and he used his reach to his advantage, thrusting his sword at her from a distance. The dull edge caught her on the shoulder, the same spot as the last hit. The blow stung. Kepi beat the flat edge of his sword with hers, knocking the weapon from his grip.

From the edge of the yard a soldier came toward them, but Kepi gestured to stop him, "No cause for alarm," she told the man. "We like to play it rough."

"I see." The man snickered as he walked off the field. Their observers had doubled. In a moment half the guard would be watching. She hoped Seth was smart enough to keep quiet. She waited while he caught his breath, stood idle while he bent to pick up his sword.

"All right then?" she asked.

"All right?" he answered, his voice high like a young boy's. "What was that?"

"Sparring." She wanted it to end.

"If you say so." He gripped his sword, then threw it into the dirt. "I'm sorry. I didn't want this." He came up close so that only she could hear and breathed out his excitement. "I only wanted to meet to tell you I found us a way to escape. We can be gone by nightfall, Kepi. We don't have to stay here another moment."

"Maintain your distance, Seth." There were eyes wherever she looked.

His nose nearly touched hers and his breath was hot. "You think I care what Dagrun's soldiers think of us?" Seth whispered. "There are people here who will help us. Not everyone is fond of the king. It has something to do with the Waking Rite. He never completed the rite. His people don't accept him, not all of them. The master physician, Gallach, he's one of them and he wants to help us. They are planning something. They think Barrin's heir is alive and Dagrun is not the rightful king." Seth spoke so fast he was stuttering. "Kepi—"

"Don't address me by my first name. I'm the queen of the Ferens now." She took a step back, straightening her breastplate. What was he talking about? What was Seth planning with these people? She wanted nothing to do with it—these people were traitors, men loyal to the old king. Dagrun's men had routed a contingent of soldiers at Catal, but there were still men who did not accept her husband, who would never accept Dagrun. Dagrun's men had found a cache of weapons the day before, and that same evening they had arrested a band of slaves who had tried to steal swords from the armory. There were traitors everywhere. Kepi eyed the guards, who were all watching this exchange. *If they tell Dagrun, Seth will lose his head. Be quiet, or you'll get yourself killed.*

Seth's face darkened. He stepped forward, closing the distance between them. "It was only to save us, Kepi. You have to know that."

"Hush now," she told him. "If you know what is good for you, do not speak any more of this."

But he continued. "The Ferens would have killed me if I hadn't led them to you. But you can't seem to forgive me for that."

"I have forgiven you," she said softly. It was true. But what he did not understand was that while she had forgiven him, she no longer loved him, and she told him so.

"No—no. You are lying. You love me. You've always loved me."

"Leaving is not the answer, it never was. Not for us. We never had a future. It is time you accepted that as I have, Seth."

"Kepi, no—"

"We wanted to believe that such things were possible. But in my heart—in my heart—I knew I would never do it. I could not forsake my family or my name. Forget your plots against Dagrun."

She turned to leave, then came back around and stood next to him. Her heart broke for him. He had loved her, in his way. It was a foolish love, a boy's love, but she knew he had meant it. For consideration of that love, she decided to be gentle. "You go on, go ahead. Find your freedom, find your way someplace where you will be free. I release you from my service, Seth. Good luck to you, but I need to find my own way."

⇜49⇝

The outlanders took Merit on horseback, leading her with a goat-hide rope tied around her hands, the Harkan soldiers following on foot behind her horse. Sevin kept a strong face—he was stout-necked and accustomed to desert survival—but his soldiers had spent two days gnawing on leathery hides for nourishment and no longer had the strength to walk. One man collapsed on the road, stumbling into the dust, trying weakly to stand. The Hykso made no effort to assist the boy, and willing to make an example for their captives of what might happen if they walked too slowly or tried to resist, one of the outlanders slashed the boy's back, opening the wound to the sun and soaking the air with the smell of blood. The scent drew black-winged birds; they gathered upon the boy's back, pecking at the wound, undeterred by his cries as the riders moved off.

"Kill him," Merit said, craning her neck to look behind her. "For pity's sake, don't leave him like that!" But the outlanders paid her no mind, riding on as if they had not heard a thing. "Kill him," she cried again, angry and disgusted.

The sun beat down ceaselessly, the taste of sand in her mouth. Fearing she would join the fallen boy, Merit raised her bound hands, curving them into the shape of a cup to ask for water. A man with wrinkled skin and a twitching eye caught sight of the gesture, tracing the shape of her arms, the flow of her dress across her body. He shook his head—he would give her nothing. "Gods," Merit cried. She cupped her hands again. "If you want me alive, give me something."

Merit refused to be ignored. She kicked at the horse, tugging at the leather ropes, pulling the caravan out of order. Her mount tangled with Sevin's; the gray horse bucked and whinnied, and Merit lurched backward. She would have fallen to the rocks if one of the men had not caught her and helped her sit upright.

When she was securely in the saddle, one of the outlanders—making no attempt to speak, grinning madly, fingers shaking—offered her a cup. He wore a necklace of shattered skulls—gray fox, she guessed from the animals' wedge-shaped heads. He must be some sort of mystic. She took the brown cup and gulped its contents, then heaved when the bitter taste hit her throat—he had given her vinegar, or something worse. Her throat burned. The man beat his legs with laughter, jiggling the skulls like bells. The caravan halted, the rest of the outlanders eager to join in her humiliation. A toothless warrior, cloaked in a dirty robe, plucked off her golden earrings, took her necklaces and bracelets, putting on the pieces and swishing around, his face fixed in a comically haughty imitation of hers.

She would not be cowed. She looked to Sevin, but he shook his head. "Don't," he whispered. *Anger will only encourage them,* his expression seemed to say. She kept her eyes and her voice steady, and in words that they seemed to only half understand, demanded water, demanded her things be returned to her. The mystic paid her no mind, passing her jewelry to the others, pinning her earrings to their skin, laying the necklaces around their necks. A tall warrior with arms and legs dressed in ringlike tattoos swung her mother's short sword and chipped the blade on a stone.

"No!" she shouted. Sevin again flashed her a look of concern, but Merit saw nothing but red. She tugged at her mount, but the horse panicked, catching its hoof between two rocks and snapping its ankle in two. The horse fell, taking Merit with it. She lay under the beast, her leg pinned, unable to move.

The tattooed warrior stood over her, his golden eyes meeting her own. "Help me!" she cried, but he was unmoved. She spat at him, but he only laughed. His lips were red where the ash had worn away, and she thought for a moment that the man might simply take her right there on the ground while the others watched. Instead, he lifted the beast with his shoulder, then made two of her soldiers pull Merit free while he bludgeoned the screaming horse. She was alive, safe. *Barca must be paying a high price for ransoms.* Her worth as a ransom had saved her life, but the thought gave her little comfort.

To punish her, the outlanders forced Merit to walk. Closer to the ground, she could not escape the desert's inhabitants—the scurrying of a pocket mouse or the quick flash of a brush lizard darting between rocks. The desert was more alive than she had guessed, humming with insects invisible to the eye but buzzing in all directions, a frantic drone that followed her across the rocks. She wore only sandals, finely woven but not made for travel. They ripped on the rough terrain, flapping around her ankles and leaving her feet worse than bare. Eventually, Merit's soldiers had to help her walk. She started to thank them, parting her lips to speak, but her mouth had gone completely dry.

When the sand gave way to hard ground she curled her feet to avoid the hot surface, mincing painfully. One man saw her and stopped to give her his sandals. The leather wraps were too big, they chafed at her ankles and toes, but at least her feet did not burn. "Thank you," she croaked at the soldier, who barely raised his head and nodded.

The days dragged, one become two, the second stretched into the third. During the night, they marched. When the sun rose, they searched for shade and rested often. She tracked the movement of the sun, trying to determine their course, but they kept walking in circles. Were they lost? It felt as if she had spent weeks in the desert—the thirst, the noise, the pain in her heels. Her bones mashed against the soft balls of her feet, her every movement triggering some small ache. Her arches cramped and pulled as if they were about to snap. She felt the pain of her soldiers too, Asher and her waiting woman, Samia. Her father's message was her only comfort on the long nights and burning days. *There is no emperor. The throne room sits in ruins, the Amber Throne smashed.* With this news, she was free of Shenn, free of the marriage that had bound her, the union that had forced her to covertly pursue Dagrun. She could have him now— she need no longer fear the Priory or the emperor's wrath. Her father was emperor in any true sense. Alliances. Armies. She no longer needed these things. She had won. There was no battle to fight, no enemy; there never had been one. They had toiled beneath a shadow all these years, but no more. Shenn could have his freedom, his life, he could love as he chose and so could she. Merit need only survive and she would have all she desired.

Deep in thought on the sixth day of her captivity Merit fell again, her forehead mashing into the rocky earth, sand and pebbles clinging to her skin, falling into her eyes. Grass brushed her face. Not the bone-dry grass of the desert, but something softer. *Odd,* she thought, but gave it no further consideration. She pushed herself up on her elbows and paused there for a moment, gathering her strength, staring at the sand. Boot marks. They were fresh—a patrol had come this way not long ago. The soldiers must be Harkan or perhaps Feren. *This is good news. Perhaps an offer was made.*

The following day, the Hykso reversed their treatment of Merit and her entourage. They offered her strips of poorly cured meat and a pale, cloudy liquid to wash it down. The drink stunk of rotten amber, but it filled her belly. The horde thinned. Three times ten warriors had taken them captive on that first day, but nearly half those men vanished during the night.

The following day a second group departed and Merit, Samia, Asher, Sevin, and the six remaining Harkan soldiers were left with fewer than ten captors. She twice caught Sevin exchanging glances with Asher and his men, plotting some sort of rebellion, she guessed. But all of it was unnecessary. As the day came to its end, the Hykso warriors marched Merit toward a narrow gorge. Tall rocks surrounded her on three sides, making the stone hollow into a cage of sorts, a corral. Two sacks of rough linen stood within the hollow. The outlander with the gray-fox necklace grunted as he lifted them—they were heavy. He strode to where Merit stood and shook the heavy sacks. The tinny clamor of gold coins jingling against one another filled her ears. *The ransom. It is paid.*

One by one, the Hykso took their leave, following behind the man with his two heavy sacks. Hands tied, Merit stood, waiting in the shade as the Hykso fled into the desert, their ash-covered skins and hoary cloaks melding with the salt-gray sand. Sevin cursed as he struggled against his bonds, trying to break the goat-hide strands. His soldiers tore at their ropes. Samia kneeled, as did Asher.

But Merit stood tall and proud. Someone was coming—soon, she guessed. She scanned the jagged rocks. Whoever had laid out the coins was no doubt watching, waiting for the Hykso to disappear before coming to claim their bounty. *Where are you? Who are you?* Merit paced. *Who paid my ransom?*

⇥ 50 ⇤

Her ankles caked in dust, head pounding, Sarra returned from the throne room of the emperor. She had gone there alone, by lamplight, stealing through the long corridors that connected the Ata'Sol to the throne of the Soleri. She had seen the shattered chair, the burnt columns and empty pools, the fresh footprints in the dust. Suten's body lay amid the rubble, bruised and silent, rotting in the darkness. Only the Ray may enter the Empyreal Domain, so she guessed it was Arko who had done the deed and taken the revenge he had long sought. It was strange to see the old Ray dead, his regal attire soaked with blood. She had long coveted Suten's golden robe, and the sight of it, torn and bloodied, had shaken her more than she would have guessed. It reminded her of Garia Asni, the girl who stood in Sarra's place on the last day of the year. The whole scene—the burnt chair, the body—was overwhelming, too much to digest. She returned to her chamber, shaken but satisfied. She had seen the shattered throne and lived. Suten was gone and the Soleri were truly dead, their sacred domain abandoned. She slipped into a white robe and poured herself a cup of wine. Saad was already overdue for their congress, and she guessed he would not delay much longer.

The door swung open and she startled, dropping the bronze cup, spilling date wine onto the table and floor. The plum-red liquid dribbled around her toes. She lifted the cup and refilled it while a dark-haired priestess came close and bowed.

"Mother," she said, "Saad is coming. He passed the columned hall and should be here any moment."

"Then you should go," she told the girl, who went out and left the door open behind her. A priest entered bearing two scrolls stamped with golden wax. The sealing wax was still warm, the parchment crisp, ink bleeding through the page.

"Is everything in order?" she asked.

The priest shrugged. "I did everything as you asked."

"Good. Leave me," she said, holding the scrolls in her hand, setting them down when she realized her fingers were damp with perspiration.

Priests entered to prepare her chamber, cleaning the floor, moving fur-

niture around, pouring a second cup of date wine for the guest while
Sarra watched Saad come through the doors with a scowl on his face,
his scar red and pulsing, looking like a schoolboy summoned before the
lecturer. It took all her willpower to smile when he entered, lifting a
cup of the sweet wine and inviting the boy to sit in the ironwood chair
across from her, near the brazier. She settled into her own equally sturdy
chair. They were in Sarra's chambers in the Ata'Sol, her private rooms
beneath the temple—ones she was quite sure even old Suten Anu had
never managed to penetrate with his spy-holes and listening places.

Saad smirked, and for a moment she pictured herself cutting his throat
with the ceremonial sword that hung at his waist. Instead, she traded her
hatred for silence, forcing her muscles not to twitch, slowing her breath.
She waited, her smile as flat as her gaze, neither of them spoke. Saad had
come to the door with doubt on his face, doubt in his eyes, doubt in the
way he stood as Sarra's priests bustled around the room bringing them
food and wine, then bustling out again to leave them to speak in private.
When Sarra indicated that he should feel free to drink, he frowned, then
reached over, plucking the bronze vessel from the table by her side and
replacing it with his own. Only when he held her cup did he sit back
down, put the cup to his lips, and drink, swallowing it all in one long
gulp.

"You don't really think I brought you here just to poison your wine?"

Saad scowled. "I would not put it past you, god-lover."

Sarra's eyes bored into his. Had he come just now from wherever Ott
was held? She wanted to look at his fingernails, to see if there was blood
beneath them, red stains in the skin of his knuckles, but she resisted. He
had taken Ott to unnerve her, to toy with her, but he would not suc-
ceed. She had to trust that Ott had kept faith with all that he knew, that
Saad was still unaware of Tolemy's absence.

"Calm yourself," she said, pouring another cup for Saad and one for
herself, to show she had no ill intentions. "There are no weapons, save
yours, in the Ata'Sol. No poisons but the ones we feed ourselves." Sarra
drank the wine.

Saad reached for the cup, but this time he did not touch it. "Then why
have you called for me? Why are you in Solus? I ordered you to not return until your duty demanded it."

"You have no power over me. Tolemy himself bade me to return,"
she said, pausing, letting the words sink in. She knew of Saad's preparations for the offensive against the traitor, the orders Arko had given the

Protector to silence his former captain and put Barca's men once more under Soleri command. She also knew that Saad would not be able to carry out those orders, that the boy Protector—whose transition to power was still marked by suspicion that he had killed his own father, by murmurs of treason among his ranks—did not yet have enough authority with his own generals to go up against Barca. *That is why he is stuck here in the capital, taking innocents and torturing them in his tower.* If Arko could not dispatch the boy, she would do it.

"The emperor has spoken to you directly?" Saad asked. "Is this another ruse?" There was distrust in his eyes, the same distrust she had seen in his tower on the last day of the year. Saad did not believe her. He stood, knocking over the chair, backing toward the door. "I'm done listening to your fabrications. Leave Solus," he commanded, his hand reaching for the pommel of his sword. "Now."

Sarra remained calm. This was not the last day of the year. She'd had time to contemplate this meeting and was certain this time that she could convince the Protector to do her bidding. "Stay where you are, Saad. I'm not finished with you."

Anger rumpled his face, he motioned to leave, but Sarra kept on talking.

"I assume you have read the proclamation posted beneath the Antechamber window?"

Saad scoffed. He paused in the doorway, fingers rapping on his blade. "What about it?"

"That decree was not written by Tolemy."

Saad's eyes widened a bit. "Who then? The Harkan?" He took a step toward her, suddenly interested. He wasn't leaving.

Sarra nodded.

"And how did you come by this information?" His hand fell from his sword.

"Tolemy himself sent word to me. Mithra's Door is open. He called me to the edge of the Empyreal Domain, where his servants put these scrolls in my hands." She produced two scrolls and handed him the first—a small one with a gold seal embossed with the many-armed face of the sun.

"The Harkan is ignoring Tolemy's will. He is acting without the emperor's consent. The proclamation was not penned by Tolemy, nor was Arko's command that you should pursue the rebel. The emperor does not want you to pursue Barca, not right now, but to guard the city against any attack Barca might make."

"Then what was it that the Ray gave me?" he asked, moving farther from the door.

"Lies. Deceit. No doubt his little toad Khalden Wat devised the whole thing. But the emperor is not as foolish as Arko thinks. Tolemy wants our help, Saad, yours and mine. It is up to us to avert a coup that might wreck the empire."

Sarra followed Saad's face closely. Would he believe the story? Had he learned anything from his captive? Maybe, but maybe not. It didn't matter—not this time. She had learned her lesson on the last day of the year. She could not intimidate the Protector, but she could appeal to his ambitions. He did not need to believe her story—she knew he would accept the emperor's command if it served his interests.

Saad narrowed his eyes at her. "It's a risk," he said. "One way or another, I'm sticking my neck out, and I never stick my neck out for no reason, *god-lover*. What will the emperor offer me if I agree?"

Death. She pulled forth the second scroll and handed it over. Now was the moment when the boy would decide—now, and no other. He broke open the seal and began to read, but Sarra did not wait for him to comprehend what it said. "You've been asked to remove the Ray and take his post. Arko Hark-Wadi will receive judgment by Mithra's Fire."

"Me, First Ray of the Sun?" Saad smiled, then stuck out his chin. "Why? Is this your plot, Mother? If the Ray dies without naming a successor, the post falls to you. Does it not?"

She did not answer his question; she would not acknowledge his doubt. "Tolemy has decided, for reasons of his own, that you are the better one for the position. When the task is done, I will escort you through the Hall of Histories, past the statues of the emperors, and into the domain itself. There, in the throne room, Tolemy will speak to you through the protection of his holy veil and name you as Arko's successor. In the time between Arko's death and the naming of the Ray, I will serve in his post, but only briefly. This title will allow me to escort you into the domain, the holy precinct of our lord Tolemy. As I said in your tower, Mithra wants peace between the Father and the Mother. Our lord and emperor said the same words to me through the veil."

"Did he now?" Saad raised his hand and stroked his stubbled cheeks, his knuckles littered with small bruises and cuts. The hands of a torturer. He seemed to consider the offer, and then a look of satisfaction replaced the doubt on his face

He'll do as I ask and be grateful for the chance. Thinking himself worthy of the title and position, she guessed he did not stop to think too long and hard about the message, or the messenger. His greed, at last, made him trust the Mother Priestess. The boy could not be intimidated, but he could be seduced, and she had done as much with her offer.

Sarra stood, wrapping her cloak around herself. "I bend my will to the emperor's, and do as he commands. For his sake, Saad, not yours." She once again gave him her best imitation of a frank look, one she had used often on Arko, on Suten Anu, on Saad's own father, when needed: to look like she was doubtful, but doing as she was bidden anyway.

"Then it is finished." Saad approached. "I will go to the Ray. The task will be done by midday tomorrow," he said, adjusting the fit of his armor. She guessed he had resized the ceremonial armor since he wore it on the last day of the year, but the metal still didn't fit him. Saad paused, shaking his head. "All I needed was an excuse to get rid of that Harkan, and now I have one." There was pride on his face, triumph, just as she had intended. He poured himself another cup of wine, downed it, and took up the scrolls, one after the other. When he had secured the rolls, Saad turned and without speaking or acknowledging Sarra, let himself out of her chamber. It was customary to bow and bid farewell to the Mother Priestess, to wish her the sun's fate, but he did none of these things. *The man thinks himself Ray; he does not even acknowledge me. He thinks Tolemy is his only master.*

She waited until the Protector was gone.

"Scribe," Sarra called.

A girl appeared in the doorway.

"Fetch a messenger," Sarra said, and the girl dashed down the corridor.

At midday tomorrow, Saad would gather his men, he would light Mithra's Fire, and end the brief reign of Arko Hark-Wadi.

She must go to her husband, but not until tomorrow—just prior to Saad's arrival. Then she would tell him the secret she had been holding for a decade.

A boy appeared in the doorway, his feet covered in dust, a trace of perspiration on his brow. "I have a letter, but I don't want you to deliver it until the morning." There was no sense in giving Arko time to prepare for their audience. "When you wake, I want you to go the Antechamber and arrange a congress between me and the First Ray of the Sun. Speak to Khalden Wat and return with his reply."

51

"At last," Ren said, putting his foot on the parapet and looking out at the city of Solus, "a breeze."

"If you say so," Adin said as he lay on his bedroll. "I didn't feel one."

"You would if you'd bother to sit up a bit."

"You try to sleep sitting up."

"I can't sleep," Ren said. "It's useless."

"The Priory?"

"Yes. It's so close."

"You think too much. Tye always said that was your biggest problem."

Ren agreed, but said nothing. He had tried resting, attempted sleeping, but dreams of the Priory invaded his every imagining. Through sleep's eye he saw a prison made of sand. Every wall and every floor was hewn from sifting granules and when Ren moved, the walls collapsed, pulling him down into gray depths, suffocating him.

They had entered the city two days before, moving among the soldiers and refugees, blending in among the people asking for work, for food, for a few empty rooms. They looked like what they were: a couple of half-grown boys, refugees trudging the road from the Dromus, nothing more. War had come to the empire. They heard the traitor, Barca, was raiding all of the lands to the south and east of the Dromus. Everywhere they went, there were refugees, people journeying from the countryside to the capital, hoping to find safety behind the walls of Sola. There was much talk among the people, rumors that the new Ray had caused unrest by posting a proclamation. The people were clearly upset about it, but Ren and Adin dare not ask any questions for fear of revealing themselves.

In the dark of night, they had slipped from the crowd of refugees, past the long rows of tents the Protector had set out to house the crowds, and wandered into the city, reversing the route Ren had taken weeks earlier when he was freed from the Priory. The city was unfamiliar, but Ren remembered the gate at the entrance to the underground city, the place where he had first tasted his freedom. Who could forget such a thing? There they curled up against the wall and pretended to be blind, a couple of beggar boys whining for hard bread, largely ignored by the throngs of other desperate and frightened people streaming into the city.

In the morning they had looked for a room. They could not afford one, but they did find a man who would rent them his rooftop—nothing luxurious, just a place to stay where the city guard would not harass them. For the roof Ren gave his last tin crescent. It bought them a few loaves of bread and a place to stay, but they had no food for tomorrow and no coin to pay for another night, so they would have to make the most of this one or find another source of income in the morning.

From the rooftop, Ren saw the pillars of what he guessed was the temple of Mithra at Solus. Lamplight flickered between the stout columns. At the gates of Solus, he'd heard that the Mother Priestess had gone to Desouk after the riots on the last day of the year, that she was assaulted on the wall but had somehow survived. *Guided by Mithra's hand,* one woman had whispered. He guessed she would not return to Solus for some time. Nevertheless, he wondered what she would say to him if he confronted her, how she would explain why she never came to him in the Priory or used her stature as the Mother to lessen his suffering. Perhaps she was allied with Merit, maybe that was how his sister had learned of his release.

"Daydreaming again?" Adin asked.

"No, just thinking about Sarra Amunet. I saw her temple."

"Dreadful topic." Adin knew what Ren thought of the Mother. His friend broke another chunk of bread from the hard yellow cake and stuffed it in his mouth, his eyes on the horizon. The boys were not the only ones standing under the stars: Everywhere they looked, whole families lay on the mud-baked roofs, squirming in the heat, hoping for a breeze to pass as they pushed sweat from their brow. They shifted and settled as children leapt and played, waking sleepers, eliciting howls. Some roofs were so crowded the women were sleeping in shifts, some knitting while the others slept. There was no night here; the city was always in motion, always restless. He had heard only echoes from the Priory, distant barking, traces of laughter. He had not seen who or what made those sounds. Now he saw it all. The people of Solus were nearly as visible in the darkness as they were under the light of the sun: Torches hung from every roof, and oil lamps lit the streets. The city was bright, but the sky was dark. It was the new moon, the Thieves' Moon.

"Ren, can I ask you something?" Adin said, still chewing on the bread.

"Go to sleep."

"I can't—it's too hot."

"You'd be cooler if you stopped eating so much. You're going to get sick."

"Stop changing the topic. I want to know why you didn't go back to Harwen when you had the chance. Why come looking for me?"

"I—" Ren could not finish. Where could he start? With Merit, or Shenn? He still hadn't told Adin the truth about his family. "It's . . . nothing," he said. "I just thought I would help my friends first. You'd have done the same if you weren't locked in some Feren slammer," he said, not wanting to think about it.

"But the eld, the horns—why not go home with them?" Adin asked, not letting Ren avoid the subject. The horn slung over Ren's shoulder felt suddenly heavy.

"I wasn't ready," he said, a stab of guilt hitting as soon as he finished. He didn't like concealing things from his friends; he'd never done it in the past, so why was he doing it now?

"It's Merit."

"Your sister—what about her?"

He told Adin what happened in the Shambles. "I don't want to go to Harwen, not without allies," he said, and Adin seemed to understand. If he went there alone, he'd find his grave sooner than he'd find his throne. Adin had gone home and had nearly lost his life.

His friend listened without nodding or giving any look of pity. Adin's own story was just as painful. He had lost his family, lost his father without ever meeting the man, and from what Ren had learned about the old king, Adin was better off for it. The Ferens had spat when Ren spoke the name of Barrin and he guessed it was not without reason.

"We'll go to Harwen together," Adin said.

"But first we finish here," Ren said, watching the gate. "I can't leave this place without Tye."

"I know," Adin murmured, joining Ren at the ledge. Below, the gate banged closed and the torch above the archway flickered and died. Ren glared at the dark bars and the stairway that led down into the Hollows. He pictured Tye, lost in the darkness. In his mind's eye he saw the curve of her lip, the freckles dashed on her cheeks. *Come on, Tye. Come out. If you're not coming out, I'll have to come in. And what will happen then, I don't know.*

A soldier slid a key into the lock and the latch clicked closed for the night.

Ren gathered up the rags he meant to use as a pillow and tried again to go to sleep in the cold, yellow light of the city, but he lay there with his eyes open, staring into the darkness. He did not say what he was thinking, but Ren was all too aware that the gate below was closed for the night. The Thieves' Moon had come and gone, but the gate was locked and Tye was not coming.

⇥52⇤

Shouts pierced the walls of the Antechamber, disturbing the pleasant quiet. The city had read Tolemy's proclamation, and few were happy about it. They were used to their slaves and to grinding the noble families of the lesser kingdoms underneath their sandaled feet, but those days had ended. *Let them holler and break things. Let them cry out that their lord has abandoned them.* Arko Hark-Wadi had anticipated their angry reaction. Soon, the viziers would call for a congress with the Ray, but Arko would refuse them. The highborn families would cry at his door and the soldiers would curse him, but Arko would ignore them all. While Solus shouted out in rage, he would tear down the Priory, brick by brick, until only a great hole was left in the earth, a void like the Ruined Wall in Harkana—a monument to remind the empire of its past mistakes.

Arko stood alone in the Antechamber, in a room that sat astride the Shroud Wall, half in and half out of the domain, watching his servant, Wat, shuffle across the corridor, taking his time, pretending he did not hear the protests, though they reverberated all around him. When Wat came a bit closer, the light on his face revealed red eyes and a grin. He looked tired but hopeful, as if he were carrying good news.

"You have something to say?" Arko asked.

"Your soldiers are coming."

"When?"

"Midday. Your man Asher got through, or was at least able to pass your message to a soldier, who delivered it to Harwen. Asher went off to find your eldest daughter, Merit, but we don't know if he ever reached her."

"He'll find her. He's as loyal as he is resourceful. I have no doubts about the man. What else?"

"Your youngest daughter . . . Kepi, I believe?"

"What about her?"

"She is betrothed to the king of the Ferens."

"Dagrun, eh?" Arko frowned. "He's a good enough man. She accepted his proposal?" he asked, memories of her first wedding turning his stomach. He had left his youngest daughter to fend for herself without bidding even a last farewell.

"I don't know. There are no details, just a dispatch from Rifka."

"Send emissaries, immediately. Make my daughters aware of my position," said Arko. He needed to make contact with his family. Change was coming to the empire, and he wanted to prepare them. If Asher got through he would eventually find Merit and deliver his message. Ren would soon return from the hunt. And with Kepi in Feren, hopefully it meant Dagrun would likely join Arko's cause, brute or not. Patience was all he needed.

"What else?" Arko said.

"As you feared, Saad will not go after Barca," he said. "Most of his supplies are still in the storehouses, and only a small group of men are properly armed. Saad sits in his tower, though his soldiers began gathering in the courtyard outside this room an hour ago."

Then he's coming after me. The little shit. Arko took a long drink and wiped foam from his mouth. "Get my men in here. I need them now—see to it yourself, Wat." Arko took another drink. This imperial stuff was growing on him. "When is the Protector due?"

"Midmorning," Wat said. "He will come to present his final strategy for the campaign against Barca, just as you asked."

"Good. My men should be in place by then."

Arko reached for his wineskin, lifted it to his lips, and then set it aside. He needed all of his wits for what would come next. He sat in the chair that once belonged to Suten. It creaked a bit, as if the wood were made for a man of lesser weight—and it had been. Arko had never felt such pressure. All of Solus was weighing down upon him. He felt the city's anger but would not let it intimidate him. He knew what he needed to do.

Wat sat down across from him, making Arko consider the man. He was a good servant—as good as any he'd had in Harwen. The man's honesty made Arko feel hopeful.

"You know the story of my father, Koren Hark-Wadi," Arko asked. "The Children's War and Koren's handshake with Saad's father? Do you know what he promised my father?"

Wat bowed his head. "Suten was there. I know what happened that day. Raden Saad and your father were honorable men. Harsh in their ways, but honest."

"I had hoped that Saad might be more like his father. I had hoped he would do as he was told, that he might listen to me and stand against Barca."

"You dwell too much in the past, sir. Saad is not his father."

"That's for damn sure. What a miserable little pup he is. I would just as soon smash his head in as let him have the army."

Wat's mouth was set in a narrow line. "Raden was a relic. From the moment he shook your father's hand he was marked for death. If it were not for the power of Suten's family, the favor they showed the old Protector, his generals would have cut him down long ago. His honor never helped him—it got him killed."

"I thought as much." Arko rubbed the stubble on his cheeks. "Saad could not take his father's life without help. He isn't smart enough."

"Most of the generals wanted the old Protector dead for decades. He had a few loyal men, a few who have since resisted the son's control, but most of the military families were tired of Raden. They wanted a man who would make them rich, not safe. Saad is that man. He knows how to fatten their wallets and flatter their tempers, and they will support him to the very end. He won't help you."

"I know. I hold no illusions regarding Saad, or Sarra."

Wat swallowed when Arko said the Mother Priestess's name.

"What is it?" Arko asked.

"I have one last bit of news. Early this morning, the Mother Priestess sent a messenger. She requests an audience prior to your midday congress with Saad."

Arko thought for a moment. "The timing is no coincidence."

"If you say so. Perhaps our lord Tolemy should be made aware—"

"No," Arko interrupted. "There is no sense in disturbing the emperor."

"That's what Suten always said." Wat smiled kindly, knowingly.

"Return her message, tell her I will meet with her today, prior to my congress with Saad, as requested."

"Trying to accommodate the Mother Priestess?"

"No, but if Sarra or Saad want a fight, we might as well have one. Once my men are here, I am confident we can turn back any force. Have you found the hired soldiers I requested—the mercenaries?"

"Yes. I can bring them to you when you are ready."

"Do that. Do it now, Wat. Is there anything else?"

"There is this." Unwrapping a long bundle he revealed a two-handed sword, well forged but ancient. "It once belonged to Saad's grandfather. It has seen a battle or two, but you asked for a sword and this is the finest I could locate."

"Thank you, Wat." Arko took the blade. "It looks like a good sword." He weighed the blade and sighted down the edge, which had once been perfectly straight, now somewhat warped by age. In the distance, the people shouted their protests and something fragile shattered against a wall.

"I'll be going," said Wat. He seemed uneasy, perhaps he disliked the changes Arko had made just as much as the people outside. If he did, the old man didn't show it. He bowed politely and bid his farewell, "May you share the sun's fate, sir."

Arko rumpled his lip at the Soleri farewell. "No, if it's all the same to you and your god, Wat. One life is plenty for me."

⇒53⇐

Pale green tunics shifted in the tall rock. *Ferens. Dagrun paid the ransom.* There could be no other explanation. The king of the Ferens, not Barca or one of Merit's generals, had paid her ransom. Her messenger must have slipped past the ash-skinned warriors and walked to the Feren border. Soldiers bearing the blackthorn crest broke through the underbrush and rocks, confirming her assumption. One bowed to Merit, another cut her bonds. Three footmen lifted Samia from the rocks and gently untied her ropes. They freed Merit's foot soldiers, Asher, and her captain. The Ferens brought horses for her men, a carriage for Merit, food and fresh clothes. There was a physician in their company and enough water for her to bathe if she so desired. She thanked the men, but refused their offering of clean linen and salted meat—she even refused the physician and the bath. She wanted to ride out immediately. She would not stop to eat or re-dress, or to tend to her bruises. She was too eager to be free of this place, out of the desert and safe. The Ferens shook their heads but acquiesced. The Harkans sipped amber and chewed bread, laughing and shouting as they hoisted themselves atop the horses. With a bit more restraint, Merit and her waiting woman stepped into the blackthorn carriage. A whip cracked and they were off.

The Feren captain, a man who introduced himself as Keegan Stalls, rode alongside Merit's carriage, speaking to her through an open shutter. "We spent three days negotiating with the outlanders," he said, and then went on to explain the terms of her liberation and the process leading up to it. "We sent patrols, tried to locate the outlanders' camp, to free you, but the Hykso kept moving—they knew the ground and they knew how to hide. We found a dead soldier, his back slashed, but we could not find the outlanders. We had no way to locate you, so the king paid the ransom."

The story explained why the outlanders had forced her to march in circles, to hide during the day and move at night. It explained the tracks she had seen in the sand. Those marks clearly belonged to the soldiers who had pursued her—the men had been close by all along, but the Feren soldiers were unused to the desert. They were out of their element and had been unable to track her captors. Thinking back to her time in the desert, Merit recalled the tall grass she'd seen when she fell and wondered how close to Feren they were. "How long until we reach Rifka?" she asked, careful not to sound too eager.

"Three days' ride," the captain said.

Longer than she thought, but Merit only nodded, hiding her disappointment. She wanted to return to Feren as quickly as possible. She was eager to share her newfound secret with the king. Soon she would have everything she desired.

The small company rode a day before a large contingent of cavalry arrived, expanding their numbers, ensuring that Merit would travel unmolested to Rifka. The horses made a thunderous sound as they stomped the earth. They moved quickly, skirting the basin of Amen, crossing the Rift valley, riding through the pass and over the gray mountains that shielded Feren from the desert. They spent a night camped alongside the Cragwood, sleeping soundly, before rising again and at last entering the Gray Wood, the forest growing dense on all sides of her carriage as she passed beneath the first mighty blackthorns, the air cooler, moister.

As a heavy rain began to fall, Merit reached Rifka. The rain pelted her carriage as it rolled into the High City. The roof leaked; it let sheets of rain run through its cracked, knotty face. Merit was drenched, but cheerful. In the desert, a hard rain meant good luck—good fortune had come to her. Long, thunderous showers rarely struck Harwen, but when the rains did come to the desert kingdom, the downpours always preceded a good day, a lucky day. So as Merit's carriage crossed the bridge leading into Caer Rifka, as she passed the wall and the Chime Gate, she felt invigorated, she had suffered for a reason. She had learned the truth of the empire and had returned to Feren to undo the mess she had left behind.

Gray clouds pushed at the sun, obscuring its edges as Merit stepped from her carriage. The hour felt like twilight, though she knew it to be closer to noontime as she thanked her soldiers, then Sevin and Asher. She thanked Keegan and his company of Feren soldiers. The king of the Ferens was nowhere to be seen. He had not come to greet her, nor had he sent a messenger. She tried not to let it bother her; she told herself he was busy elsewhere, that it meant nothing.

His soldiers led her entourage to a set of interconnecting chambers within the caer. When they arrived at the suite of rooms, Merit made certain Samia was well cared for, was given clothing and blankets and food. She made certain that her servant and all of her soldiers were content before she allowed Dagrun's men to guide her to her chamber. The soldiers led Merit to the last door at the end of the hall. The room was sparse, but adequate. It was not a queen's chamber, but she guessed her presence here was only temporary. Soon Merit would sleep at Dagrun's side. She lingered in the room long enough to change her wet clothes, but no longer. Her feet felt too light to stand in one place, so she went looking for Dagrun. He was no doubt busy with preparations of some kind. There was war in the kingdoms and it was his task to defend Feren.

Merit strode from her room, down a corridor, and out onto the great lawn. She scurried beneath a dripping trellis, past pale-faced slaves and worried soldiers, some faces familiar, others new. A pair of guards trailed behind Merit. She asked one of the men where she might find the king. "Past the Queen's Chamber," he said, "in the Chathair."

He pointed, but she told him to lead. Her attention lay elsewhere. Everywhere she looked the city was alive. The rain made Rifka glow, the water washed clean the thatched roofs and soot-soaked chimneys, it washed the mud from the gravel paths and the stink from the sewers. Rifka was a green place. The city was full of life and energy. Even in the rain there was hammering and sawing, and the sound of workers talking as they went about their tasks. The Ferens hardly paused when the sky poured. Twice one hundred men labored in the misty square to finish the Queen's Chamber. The structure was larger than she recalled; it towered above nearly all others. Its blackthorn frame—arched beams topped by spindly purlins—rose through the fog like a skeleton, marvelous and gruesome.

They led her though open doors, deep into another part of the caer. In the corridor she heard shouts, iron breaking on wood, cheering. Then Dagrun called out something unintelligible, and the crowd roared.

Through the door to the Blackthorn Chathair she went, smelling earth and fresh lotus. A shifting crowd of slaves filled the entryway, jostling one another to get inside the inner chamber. She had not yet grown accustomed to the lack of clothing that was so common among the Feren slaves and recoiled from arms and elbows moist with perspiration pushing against her, trying to get a better view. What were they so eager to witness, she still could not say; too many heads stood between her and the spectacle in the hall, too many spears, too much noise in too cramped a space. On all sides the slaves wore necklaces of blue lotus, the fragrance mixing with their unwashed bodies, overpowering her senses. She pushed her way through, the clash of iron resonating from an opening somewhere up ahead.

A slave stepped back, crushing her toes, pressing his dirt-smeared body against her gown. The slaves and soldiers who filled the hall were moving backward, clearing a wider ring around their king and, Merit now saw, their new queen. Kepi and Dagrun stood facing each other across the ring. Then they bowed, tipping their swords to each other in respect. So that was the racket. Were they trying to kill each other? Had Dagrun decided he'd had enough of Kepi's scorn and decided to teach her a lesson?

No—he was smiling, and even Kepi showed a grin. Dagrun gave a thrust that put Kepi back on her heels, barely deflecting the blow, but his body language was loose-limbed, full of enjoyment. "Had enough yet?" he said.

Merit could not hear Kepi's response.

"Very well then," Dagrun said, and raised his sword again.

Kepi attacked, but it was without her usual ferocity—the last time, at the Harkan games, she had been all hands and blade, power and hatred—and Dagrun fought her off without difficulty. What was this? Some kind of public spectacle, a Feren tradition perhaps, meant to display the change in the couple's relationship since the wedding ceremony?

Row by row Merit pushed until her sister and Dagrun came into full view. They stood upon a simple platform, Kepi in tailored sparring clothes, the tree of Feren emblazoned on her chest. It was a regal set of leathers, expensive and certainly a gift from her new husband, as they carried his crest. Dagrun wore a woolen tunic and rough leather breeches, his skin even and smooth where the tunic fell open at the neck. How many times she had wanted to press her mouth to that place at the base of his throat. How many times she had stopped herself.

It had been fear, nothing more. She was regretting it now. Regretting that she had not made her mark on him before she left, that she had not given him what he had asked her for, many times over and over again. Merit had taken his interest for granted, it seemed.

But perhaps there was time yet.

She advanced until a soldier barred her path, blocking the way with his spear. She must have lost her escort at the door. In her haste she had forgotten about the men and now she was alone. Still, Merit was close enough to see Kepi's face, Dagrun's too—she could read the looks he was giving his wife. Kepi stood with her hands in Dagrun's open palms. Kepi laughed, her shoulders shaking, her face turning slightly red. When Kepi smiled she was beautiful.

It made Merit's stomach churn.

What was happening here?

Kepi was meant to be a proxy, a placeholder, but now she was queen.

A true queen.

A beautiful Harkan queen, who carried the same royal blood in her veins as Merit did. The same lineage that Dagrun had sought when he first came to her, asking for her hand and to dismiss her husband who could not love her.

Dagrun had his Harkan queen, and it was not Merit.

A young boy came in to carry away the swords, another bringing cloths wrapped in silvery leaves. Dagrun picked up one and used it to blot Kepi's face. The soldier at Merit's side, the man whose spear blocked her path, saw Merit's look and mistook it for confusion. "The king and queen had a duel. It's a celebration, I guess—something the king invented. Seems he met our new queen during a match in Harkana, or was it Rachis?"

"Harkana," Merit murmured, her mouth suddenly dry.

"If you say so."

Now Dagrun was asking his soldiers to take up swords as well. "Should we have another match?" he asked, and the crowd roared its approval.

"I seem to remember," Merit said, raising her voice to its public volume, "a bit more blood at your last meeting in the ring." *And a different encounter afterward, for all that.* How quickly he had come to her room after the contest, eager for Merit's embrace. She approached, but came up short. Dagrun's cool gaze told her to stay back, for now, to wait at the edge of the platform. Merit obeyed, standing at the corner of the dais, a few paces from the king and queen.

Kepi eyed her warily, confused at first. "My sister," she said. "I am glad to see that you are safe." Kepi returned the damp cloth to the boy, her face uncertain.

Merit did not reply. She cared only for Dagrun. The man who had begged her to marry him. But she had refused him. She had made him marry another. Merit told herself that it was the only choice she had. The emperor would not allow her to marry him. An alliance was her only option. Overthrow Tolemy and she could marry as she pleased.

But there was no Tolemy now.

Dagrun warmly cupped Kepi's shoulder, whispering something in her ear. He waved his arm in a gesture that told his servants that the games were ended. Kepi withdrew, the crowds flocking around her, slaves and servants alike.

Dagrun stepped off the edge of the platform.

Merit drew a quick smile as he approached, expecting him to return the gesture, but he did not. She tamped her expectations as he urged her to join him in the shade of the Kiteperch. She drew up close to the king. So much had changed since their last meeting, she was uncertain where to start. "Good to see you, good to be back," Merit said. It was all she could think to say, her excitement making it difficult to think.

"Your smile would not be so broad if you knew your price. The outlanders understand a queen's worth. Lucky for you, the rebel is short on coin and I have . . . no such difficulties."

"Am I not worth every crescent?" she asked lightly.

Dagrun appraised her, as one would study an item one had purchased from a merchant and not as a lover welcoming her return. "I would not have left you with the outlanders. I've bribed them for years with gold and grain, blackthorn and amber. The Hykso were eager to bargain." He inched closer to Merit, but did not embrace her. He looked to the crowds and the soldiers, to the generals who waited, their eyes darting toward them, just out of earshot. Fear and uncertainty were everywhere. There was war in the southern lands, and the king of the Ferens was distracted.

She had expected kinder words from Dagrun, a bit of affection. She had grown accustomed to his vigorous pursuit, the way he grabbed at her regardless of who was watching or where they were. Now he was cautious and she noticed that he made certain to stand at arm's length.

"I have news, Merit. You are not the only Harkan I've aided since your departure. We have your messenger and your husband too."

"What?" She had not heard from Shenn since he left for the hunting reserve.

"Shenn ran afoul of the Hykso when he left the Shambles," Dagrun continued. "He sought refuge in a Feren outpost on the north side of the reserve. Realizing his worth, my soldiers escorted him to Rifka."

"He's here?"

"Yes. When he arrived I sent a messenger to Harwen. As we speak, a legion of Harkan riders approaches Rifka and will be here by morning. They were sent to fetch your husband, but they can escort you as well." He offered a reassuring nod. "You'll be safe. I will send men to bolster their numbers. The outlander tribes cannot match a sizeable, organized force. You have only to fear Barca, and his army lies to the south of Harwen, outside of your path."

"My path? Where am I going? I have just arrived."

"Listen to me," he said, his voice raised. "Barca is still marshaling his troops, readying for another advance." Dagrun clenched his fist. "You must return to your kingdom posthaste."

She nodded. "Yes, of course." It was her duty to Harkana that had sent her from Feren before. But she lingered now and put a hand on his arm, stroking his skin. "But surely there is some time . . ."

He shook his head. "No. You have no time. We are burning the bridges, closing the Rift valley tomorrow. Leave Feren or you'll be trapped here."

He is dismissing me. Merit would not have it.

"No," she said.

"What?"

"I am not leaving. The kingdom can wait."

"If you delay, you may not have a kingdom. Your husband told me about your brother. Ren lives. Shenn bungled the job, nearly got himself killed in the process—he's a mess."

At that Merit stopped. *Ren was alive.* So that was why she had not heard from her husband.

Dagrun continued, "The boy has his horns and will return to Harwen. Ren will claim his throne."

"It is not his to claim." Her words were ice.

"He is Arko's heir and I will not fight a war for you."

"Dammit, why not?" she cried, losing her temper, which was unlike her.

Dagrun took a step back, his eyes narrowing. She thought for a moment that he would leave, that he would turn and go, but he stood there silently, pretending she had not cried out at him.

Dagrun. She watched him in the shade of the Kiteperch, the shadows of the great tree draping his face. The king of the Ferens. The man who had once promised to take on the entire empire for her love. The man who stole a kingdom. The king who had freed her from the Hykso. Now he offered nothing more than an escort, a few soldiers to ride along with her own. She reached out, tried to touch his cheek, but he moved deftly out of her path, circling the Kiteperch. She followed him, winding around the mighty tree, dodging branches, moving slowly, ever aware that they were not alone. She reached out again, tapping his tunic. This time he did not evade her touch. Hidden by the great trunk of the Kiteperch, unseen by the dwindling crowds, he clutched her hand, arresting it in midair.

She gasped.

The swiftness of the gesture caught her off guard.

She was queen regent and the king's daughter; she was not accustomed to such rough handling.

Merit angrily withdrew her hand. "You've changed. You've fallen for that little girl, haven't you?" she accused, once more in control of her voice, but not her emotions.

Dagrun would not reply. He would never reply. She saw that now.

Merit scowled. So be it. Dagrun was done with her; his desire lay elsewhere. He offered her no more attention than the serving girls.

Merit pressed her damp fingers to her dress.

She had wanted him once, she had wanted him for longer than she could recall, but that desire would not be fulfilled.

The king of the Ferens was no longer hers to command. She had pushed him into her sister's bed, believing Kepi was no match for her. But her sister had proven the more nimble warrior. The most fleet-footed warrior in the Harkan army indeed.

Merit took a step back from Dagrun. She would not be rejected. She was the prize, and always had been, not Dagrun, not his army. He was an upstart and a no-name. A brute with common blood.

And now the secret she held—*there was no emperor, no more Soleri*—was

worth more than any army or weapon, god or throne. With this secret
she could reverse Harwen's fortunes and marry whomever she desired. She
could even make a place for herself in Solus. Her father would need her
at his side.

Dagrun and his kingdom of slaves could do as they pleased.

She no longer needed him. She no longer wanted him. A lie, maybe,
but it would be true soon enough. Soon enough.

She was the queen of Harkana and no half-starved ransom from the
Priory would take that away from her.

She brightened and faced her former paramour.

"I will go to my husband. I will tend to his wounds and we will ride
out ahead of the bridge burning. Harkana needs me." She took one step
back, then another. "I am done here." *I am done with you.*

⹸54⹸

Kepi strode from the Chathair, fleeing the crowds of slaves, the servants
and the soldiers, wishing her husband had left Merit in the desert with
the Hykso. *No,* she thought, *I don't want that.* She simply didn't want her
here, in Feren. Her sister didn't belong—this wasn't her place and it never
had been. *This is my home.*

The rain was clearing—though she still felt it on her brow as she dashed
across the grass in the sparring clothes her husband had given her for a
present. She crossed the clearing with small steps so as not to muddy the
leather, then looked for cover. Finding none, she nestled against a wall
and closed her eyes, feeling the last of the rain on her face, dripping from
the eves, forming puddles, running through her hair, down her skin.
The rain made a sound like river rocks rolling underfoot, steady and
constant. It dulled her longing for Harwen, for home—so much water,
more than Harkana had seen in her entire lifetime, maybe. No wonder
Feren was such a green place, so much growing. *And I am queen here.* She
opened her mouth to let the water run into it, cold and sweet.

Eyes closed, she listened to the water falling, to the sound of her own
breathing, to the voices of the soldiers leaving the Chathair. She tried to
forget the scowl on her sister's face, the way she glared at Kepi in the

throne room. Dagrun had saved Merit from the outlanders, had paid her ransom, and now Kepi wanted her gone—back to Harkana, where she belonged. Dagrun said he would dispatch her, that her sister and Shenn would be gone before the bridge burning. She trusted him. At last she believed her new husband, but she was still eager to see Merit gone. She listened to the rain and tried to forget, but she could not push the image from her thoughts: Dagrun talking to Merit, the two of them together. It left an odd feeling in her stomach and she realized it was jealousy. Dagrun was her king and her husband. Merit didn't belong here.

A bird cried in the distance. She caught its shadow on the wall but missed the creature itself. Looking around, she saw only damp soldiers, a little sunshine, the blackthorn swaying in the wind. A group of slaves, ones she had seen in the Chathair, scurried through the courtyard. Up ahead, there was a hole in the clouds, a bit of sun, so she stepped out onto the wet grass. The warm rays were a welcome relief. Beams of light washed the field, not burning like the sun in Harkana but softer, the light green with leaves and damp with rain.

She felt a pang of longing for the steadier heat and light at home in Harkana and remembered the last time she and Seth had met in Blackrock, how sad and angry she had felt then. So much had changed since that night. Mithra promised His followers that everything taken from them would be restored, in this life or the next, and it was true—she had lost her father and Seth, yet gained a kingdom and perhaps a husband, as if in answer to a prayer.

Thank you, she said to the sun, though she had never been the praying type before. *Thank you for restoring what was taken from me. I don't know what I will do with this gift, but I accept it. I'm tired of running. If Feren is to be my home, if I am to be queen of the Ferens, I'll do my best to embrace what is given to me.*

At the entry to the caer, she caught sight of Dalla. The girl hurried toward Kepi, concern on her face.

"Mistress? May I have a word?"

"Speak, Dalla."

"Your master-at-arms, the boy, Seth? You asked me to look after him, to make certain he had a horse and provisions for his journey to Harwen."

"Yes."

"We couldn't find the boy."

"Did you ask the master physician?"

"He is also gone."

"What? Where are they?"

"I asked the guards. But neither one has passed through the Chime Gate. They haven't left the caer. There are whispers in the High City. Talk of traitors and men who are loyal to the old king."

"Find them. Find Seth, Dalla." Kepi heaved a fearful sigh—*What are you up to, Seth?* "The roads are unsafe. We should make certain he has a proper escort to Harwen."

Kepi didn't care about the roads—she was worried about Seth. The boy had clearly gotten himself mixed up with the old king's loyalists. "Hurry, Dalla," she said as she motioned for the girl to go. Dalla bowed her head and went, leaving Kepi once more alone, in the yard, a shadow interrupting the sunshine she had briefly enjoyed. It was the same shadow she had seen a moment earlier, the dark outline of a great bird. *It's the kite.* Kepi had seen it many times before. It had come to her that morning when Seth betrayed her, then again as the Ferens led her into the High City, and now here it was, watching her. The gray bird landed on a wood spire. She held out her hand, but it would not approach. It seemed to watch, its black eyes keen, following her as she crossed the yard. "Do I look tasty?" she said to it. "Think I'm the midday meal?" It had a hooked yellow beak and a long tail that had feathers of a reddish-gold color, not uniformly gray as she had first thought. It was beautiful in a fierce, uncompromising kind of way. Kepi decided she was rather fond of it.

She went around to the other side of the caer, circling the yard. Each time she disappeared from sight, the bird moved until it could see her again. What was it doing? It could not really be mistaking her for its prey, could it? The kite came to the king when he took his throne. Why had it come to her? She was not king.

She watched the kite, holding out her hand again to see if it would land on her arm, but nothing happened. She climbed the post wall to move closer, but the bird retreated to a higher perch. She followed the kite, moving closer then waiting for it to retreat—reversing the game they had just played. The kite was certainly not hunting her. It seemed to observe her, but only from a distance. She recalled now seeing it off and again on her journey from the forest. Several times the soldiers had taken note of the great bird, astonished not simply by its magnificent wingspan but by its ever-watchful presence, its clear and obvious pursuit of their caravan. They had seemed almost afraid.

"Why did you follow me?" she asked aloud, but the bird paid her no attention.

Now a gang of slaves scrubbing the post wall with knotted brushes of blackthorn twine paused when the great gray bird alighted on the wall. They dipped their heads in reverence, falling to one knee and laying down their brushes. *What are they doing?* She heard a low chant—a prayer, perhaps? She knew the bird was worshipped here, but she had not witnessed the practice. The chants were low and sonorous, spoken in a language she could not understand.

A Feren soldier approached the worshippers, knocking his spear on the wall, but the kneeling slaves did not move. When the guard lifted his eyes and saw the kite, he lowered his weapon and allowed the slaves to continue their silent worship. Then he too seemed to whisper, his mouth moving as if in prayer. Dalla had told her that in Feren legend the kite cried a great song, the Dawn Chorus, to announce the reign of a new king. It's a song like your wedding hymn, the girl had said, but deeper, and louder. They say the song is the voice of Llyr, of the forest.

Kepi retreated down the steps and across the wet grass, followed by the kite, who flew off the post wall and circled. Kepi was clearly not its prey, nor was it truly following her. She sensed the creature was watching, waiting—but for what?

She held out her hand once more.

The kite studied her. In its black eyes she saw an almost human intelligence, something older and wiser than anything she knew. She wanted to understand why it followed her, but the creature let forth a piercing cry and flew off, beating its wings until it disappeared above the trees.

When she went back inside and opened the door to her room, Dagrun was there, sitting across from the entry, his eyes fixed on the door, his expression hollow. "Where were you?" he asked. "I had my boys looking all over the caer for you. I was worried."

"I was outside," she said. "In the yard. Just getting a little air." She came closer. "Is she gone?" Kepi asked, referring to her sister.

"She'll depart in the morning." He took a step toward Kepi. "She . . . has no further business in our kingdom." His words were awkward, but she understood his meaning: Dagrun was done with Merit; their alliance was finished.

Kepi advanced, her head shaking. "Thank you . . . for paying her ransom."

He nodded.

"And thank you for sending her away," she said boldly.

"I will have no further contact with Merit . . . and all of Harkana for that matter. Feren is retreating from the lower kingdoms. We will shelter behind the Rift valley and wait out the conflict. It is what we have always done, and will do again. If you want to leave, this is your chance. You can ride out with your sister, her husband, and their entourage."

Kepi considered his offer but even before he had finished speaking she knew her answer. She moved closer to him, expecting him to touch her somehow, embrace her, to draw her close as he had done that first night, but Dagrun waited, his eyes hungry but patient. "You are my husband," she said, her voice knowing. "I'm not going anywhere." She wrapped a hand around his back. Her fear was gone, her anger too. She was done waiting and worrying, tired of keeping those she loved at arm's length. The warmth of his body pressed against hers and she knew in that instant that Roghan, her first husband, had kept her from loving a man, kept her from trusting a man, a good man. Seth was a boy, a foolish, childish infatuation. A pebble in the ocean of her feeling for Dagrun. Her husband. The king of the Ferens.

Dagrun was so close now. She could feel his breathing, heavy and thick. He grabbed handfuls of her hair, and he pulled her head back, pressing his mouth to hers, the door slamming shut as he laid her on the bed.

≋ 55 ≋

It was not quite midday when Sarra Amunet rode into the stony courtyard below the Ray's Antechamber, the bronze veil glinting as it had on the day she returned to Solus. Arko's shadow was absent this time, but she knew he waited within the chamber, or nearby. Her husband had accepted her request for an audience with an almost desperate haste. *He's all alone in Solus.* She guessed he had no allies in the city of the Soleri.

A soldier strode past Sarra, then another, their bronze armor clanking as they marched. Saad's soldiers were packing the courtyard, stamping their feet where the priests and viziers had once congregated for the naming ceremony. Two times twenty men assembled in the court and more stood in the distance, waiting out of sight.

Saad was moving quickly. *Good.*

She rode past the soldiers, past the lines of shining armor. She left her horse with the groom and climbed the Antechamber stair. *Say the words and go.* She interwove her fingers, forcing them not to fidget. *Tell him the truth and be done with it.*

Up ahead, the bronze doors stood open. Suten's desk waited in the vacant Antechamber, looking emptier than it had when she'd last met the man. She recalled his decaying corpse in the throne room and how she had left it there. Sarra crossed the threshold, the amber windows catching her attention.

"Trying to catch a glimpse of Tolemy?" A door opened, a puff of air hitting her face. Sarra prickled. Her husband stood so close she could feel the heat coming off him in waves.

"No." She retreated, taking a moment to observe the man who had once been her husband.

Ten years ago, on the day she left, when she found him asleep in their bedchamber with his mistress draped over him, he'd had the same rough, handsome features, his neck thick as a bull's, his shoulders broad enough to hold up the moon. Maybe he was grayer now, more grizzled, his face more lined, but otherwise he was the same, and she felt the same drop in her stomach when she stood now in front of him, the same hope. *Don't do this to yourself,* she thought. *Remember why you're here.*

Arko strode past her, not looking twice. His servant, Wat, followed. She noticed that Arko had forgone the golden robe that signified his power, his position—a mistake, she thought. He looked more like a common soldier, dirtier perhaps.

"So you survived the riots? You were torn from the wall, but escaped without harm?" The question caught her off guard. She was accustomed to formalities—the recitation of titles, ceremonial nods and genuflections. Sarra had forgotten the frankness of the men of the lower kingdoms.

"Were you even in Solus on the last day of the year?" He gave a sideways glance, but she resisted the urge to return it.

She smiled thinly. "The Mother stood on the wall," she said, glancing at Wat.

Arko gestured to Wat, and Suten's old adviser stepped from the chamber. She waited until the door closed before she spoke. "How have you fared in Solus?" she asked.

"Perhaps you can tell me. This is your place, not mine." Arko tapped his finger on one of the amber windows. "I'm starting to think all this"— he waved a hand around the chamber—"is nothing but a joke at my expense."

It was the first time they had been together in ten years, since the day Sarra had left her husband and daughters to join the priesthood, the only place a woman in her position—married but apart from her husband— could go. Arko was calm; perhaps the years had dulled his anger, or at least his resentment. At any rate he seemed unsurprised to see her here, almost as if he had been expecting her. As if they were simply continuing a conversation that had started an hour before instead of a lifetime ago.

"Like me," she said, her voice full of stone. "*I* was a joke at your expense, wasn't I?"

"You weren't my idea," he said. "Suten Anu was the one who arranged our marriage, not me. A punishment of sorts, for Harkana's rebellion against the empire. At least, I preferred to think of it that way." Arko met her gaze, his eyes repentant. "But you felt differently. I know that." So he knew she had loved him.

"Only at first. I learned my lesson."

He gave her an appraising glance and she drew herself up, her long red hair flowing over her shoulders, her chalk-white robe cloaking her like a suit of armor.

"You look well."

"And you look like shit," she said.

Arko left the amber window and slipped around the table, but instead of coming to embrace her, the way she feared, he walked around her and shut the doors through which she had entered. "You've done well for yourself, Sarra. I knew you would. You were always smarter than I was."

"Are you trying to make me laugh?"

"It's the truth. Your upbringing in the Wyrre may have been modest, but you have a gift for flattery, for knowing how to make people do your bidding, sometimes without even realizing they are doing so."

"Flattery never worked with you."

"It did sometimes. You know it did, especially when it came to the children. Telling me how much they loved me, how desperate they were for my attention and approval when what you were really after was keeping me away from—" Her old husband stopped, his eyes distant.

"I merely told you what you wanted to hear—that you were a decent man, a good enough father—and turned it to my advantage."

"I could use a bit of that cunning myself. It would be useful, in my position."

"Now you are flattering *me*. Learned a few things since coming to Solus, have you? Finally figured out that you cannot subdue a problem by hacking it to bits?"

He rubbed his forehead. "I'm an old man who's come up against his own regrets, that's all."

He never used to speak to her this way, never with such openness. Perhaps he was telling the truth, that he had grown something like a heart in the years since she had left him. "Do you regret me, then?" she asked.

He raised his eyes to look at her. His look was haunted, hollow. "I should never have married you. I should have dared Suten's disapproval and refused. It would have been better for you, for me. For all of us, if you had never come to Harkana as my bride."

Sarra felt the sting of his rejection once again. In spite of herself—in spite of all that had happened in the years since she had left him—it still hurt, that he did not want her, that he had never wanted her. The girl she had been, the poor, ignorant child who had come across the sea to marry the great and formidable king of Harkana, the girl who had wanted so badly to be loved—she was still in there, buried deep, and she still wept for what might have been. *Why?* cried that young girl, who despite everything was not dead yet. *Why give your love to that whore and not to me?*

"I know you never wanted the children," she said, keeping her voice steady.

He gave her a mirthless little smile. "You're right. But I loved them all the same. I tried. Sarra, have you ever thought that your own ambition took you from Harkana as much as my indifference? You were made for Solus, for Desouk. You would never have been happy in Harkana, ordering around waiting women in the scullery."

She started to feel her blood rise, the pulse of it in her ears, in her face. How she hated this man. Hated him because he was both right and wrong, because what he said made up for none of what he had done. She had never disliked anyone as much as Arko Hark-Wadi, claiming it was not in his nature to be a husband, a father, when the truth was he'd never even tried. He had been more interested in pleasing himself than seeing to his responsibilities. He hadn't changed, not in the ways that mattered.

He was only saying the truth out loud now, admitting it openly instead of pretending to be noble, putting on the face of a loving father and a good king.

"How are the children, by the way?" she asked through clenched teeth. She had been forced to leave Merit and Kepi behind when she left Arko. While they slept, she had kissed them goodbye before she departed. Sarra had known she could not take her girls with her. The heirs of Harkana remained with the kingdom, mother or no mother.

"Are they well?" she asked.

"Well enough, anyway. They've missed you, Kepi especially. She's turned into quite the tomboy. She would have done better with a mother's love than with mine, but she's a smart girl, tough as her father and clever too. Merit I think has not forgiven you for going, or me for being the cause of your going." He fixed his gaze on the ceiling, his thoughts moving toward the past. "Ren I can't speak for—I don't know. I'm worried for him, though. Whether he'll manage Harkana all right on his own."

"Has the Priory damaged him much?"

"I don't know. Maybe. Maybe not as much as I'd always feared." He gave a great sigh. "Is this what you came here for, Sarra? To have a chat about the children? What do you really want?"

"I wanted an audience with the new Ray. Suten and I used to meet often."

"So? If you have business, let's hear what it is."

"I wanted to ask if our lord and emperor is well."

He laughed. "That's what you want? To ask after the emperor's health? Want to find out how often he moves his bowels, whether his digestion is good?"

"Tolemy's proclamation has caused quite a stir. Has he offered any explanation for it?"

Arko just shook his head. "I couldn't say."

"No? Doesn't Tolemy confide in the Ray? You simply carry out his orders?"

"Sarra—"

"Did the emperor tell you why he had chosen a man from Harkana, of all places, to be his ears and eyes? Has he forgotten your father's war so quickly?"

"I can—I will not say," Arko said. "Dammit, woman, is there a purpose to this audience, or have you come only to badger me?"

"You haven't changed at all, Arko. Not even a little, not since the morning I found her name engraved on that white stone." Arko's hand twitched. Was the rock still dangling from his neck? After all these years, he still held her close? Serena. The girl her husband had loved. The girl her husband would have married if it weren't for the emperor's decree. If it weren't for her own arrival in Harwen.

Serena Dahl.

Serena had been sent to Harkana with her father, Arko's tutor. He had known the girl since childhood.

When she married him, Arko had promised Sarra that it was nothing but a childhood crush, a young man's folly, that it had ended long ago. He had pledged his trust to her, promised his love, but he had lied. He had loved Serena all along, loved her before and after Sarra.

"If you were as smart as you thought you were," Arko thundered, striking the arm of the chair now, the white stone falling out from his robe, "you wouldn't have asked me about her in the first place. Other wives learn to look the other way, Sarra. My own mother did it. Why couldn't you? Why did you always have to push, and push, and make yourself miserable, and make the children miserable, not to mention me?"

"Because I had a little respect for myself," she murmured. Her vision narrowed down to a single cold, dark tunnel, with Arko at the end of it. "Because looking the other way is for cowards and fools, and I am neither. I always knew the truth when it came to you. I wanted you to know that I knew. And that I was glad, I was glad when she died."

The whore had died in childbirth.

Arko had as good as killed her.

He approached as if to strike her, but stopped short.

Sarra gathered her white robe, but did not move. She would not shrink from his attack. She was no longer the silly girl from the southern islands, not his to correct or challenge, but a person who came to him now with her own power, her own worth. "You might learn to be a better liar in your new position," she said. "I wouldn't want the emperor to find out how badly you're keeping his secrets."

"Unlike you, is that what you mean?" he asked. "You trade in secrets. Tell me, has that worked out well for you, Sarra? You've lost your children, your family. They hate you—Merit, Kepi, Ren."

Sarra's eyes blazed. In the courtyard outside, she heard the Alehkar give a shout and stomp their feet; Saad was here. Arko's death was

approaching and she was glad. These would be their last moments together. She readied herself. *Let him have the truth now, the whole truth. Let
him choke on it.* "The boy who lives in the Priory was never our son! You
think I'd let my only son rot in that prison? Maybe you could live with
it, but I couldn't."

"My gods, Sarra, what have you done?" Arko gasped. "Who is he,
then?"

"Who do you think he is?" she sneered.

Serena, dead on the floor. The bloody bier. The other child. A boy,
born the same week as her own. A handsome little boy, perfect in every
way, with Serena's big eyes, and his father's handsome profile, so unlike
her own broken son, her own, beautiful but eccentric boy. She told Arko
about him now. "I knew you could never accept him, the way he was."
Arko Hark-Wadi could never love the boy with the withered arm. He
would have let the desert take him; that was their way. If you could not
survive, you were given back to the gods. That was what Harkans did to
boys like Ott. Renott Hark-Wadi. The true heir of Harkana. Who grew
up in love and seclusion, in safety in her priesthood, while Serena's son
starved in the Priory.

Her most exquisite revenge on the two who had wronged her most.

Bronze-heeled sandals echoed in the corridor outside the Ray's
chamber.

Saad was coming.

"Serena's boy . . ." Arko said, falling to his knees, ignoring the men
in the corridor. "They told me he was dead. That he was born dead. That
he died with her."

"They lied to you." Sarra smiled, the soldiers approaching. "It was
always so easy to lie to you, Arko."

"My son . . ."

"Your bastard!" She hissed, the shouts of the soldiers in the corridor
growing louder. "Let him rot in the Priory. Let them break him, let him
starve . . . let him burn beneath the sun. For all you know, he is already
dead." The soldiers formed ranks outside the Antechamber.

To her surprise, Arko began to laugh. He walked toward her, his shoulders shaking, his face red, but his eyes bright with triumph. "You never
knew me, Sarra. I would never have given our son to the desert. I have no
interest in those brutal traditions. I would have loved our broken boy.
You were wrong. You should have trusted me, but it matters not. Serena's

son lives," he whispered. "Suten freed him from the Priory. He came home to me and I named him my heir. Ren, *my Ren,* lives and has taken the Elden Hunt. You have lost, my love. Serena's son will be king of Harkana."

≋ 56 ≋

The Alehkar ground their spears into the stones, crowding into jumbled ranks outside the Antechamber of the Ray. The assembled soldiers were so densely grouped that Arko could not see the far side of the corridor or the stair beyond. He saw only their bronze chest plates, embossed with the fiery circle of the sun, etched with prayers and gleaming in the midday light.

Sarra took a careful step backward, as if his words had struck her down. She stumbled toward the soldiers, the white of her robes absorbing the amber glow of their armor. Arko savored his victory. Ren was the son of Serena; his boy lived. Serena's son. Our son.

I'll make certain Ren becomes king. No one must know he is a bastard. Arko followed Sarra out of the Antechamber, picking up the pace. She was trying to leave, but he would not let her. His fingers held the sleeve of her robe.

"Let go of me!" she snarled, pushing into the ranks of the Alehkar.

Arko tightened his grip around her robe. "You're not leaving—not until I command it." He raised a hand. Above him, wind whistled through gaps in the stones. Behind those holes, his men waited, bowstrings taut, ready to loose their arrows. Sarra must have seen the gesture and known what was coming next. "Do it if you must," she threatened, daring him to end her life.

Arko tightened his hold on her robe, ripping the fabric. Could he do this? Could he end the life of the woman who bore his children and who was once queen of his kingdom? He should. She knew that Ren was a bastard.

"Well?" she asked, daring him once more. "End this or release me." Her words were cold, her voice flat.

Arko kept his hold on her.

He did not take orders from the Mother Priestess. She could no longer tell him what to do, just as he could no longer tell her what to do. When she had first ridden into the Antechamber yard, on the day she returned to Solus, when he had seen her from behind the veiled window, he wondered how this encounter would play out. Was there some way to repair the damage done to their marriage? He knew there wasn't, but hope was a hard thing to bury.

She yanked her robe free of his grip. The archers were still poised, his hand still raised, ready to give the signal. He could take her life, just as he would soon take Saad's, but he didn't. Arko didn't have the heart. He would protect Ren from her; he was the Ray of the Sun now, infinite power in his grasp. And Sarra was still his wife—in name only, perhaps—but they had shared a bed, and children. She had left him to save her child, his child as well. If she had only told him the truth about the boy, if she had shared her worries with him and revealed the true nature of their son, perhaps they could have avoided all of this, but that was not what happened.

So he let her go. "Leave," he told her.

He needed all his wits to deal with the Protector, who was even now making his way through the ranks, approaching from the far side of the corridor. Arko's hand dropped to his side and Sarra fled, not looking back, scampered away like a child.

The last he saw of her was a shock of red hair vanishing behind the amber mail of the Alehkar, a red sun ground into a sea of yellow. He watched her leave, remembering that bit of red with more attention than it deserved. He had never wanted to marry her, had never had any need for the marriage or the responsibilities their union demanded. When he was young, no older than Ren, he had found the one he loved. Serena. He'd wanted to spend a lifetime with her, but Suten had other plans for him. And now those plans had led him here, to the Antechamber.

Arko searched for Sarra, but she was gone.

He looked past the lines of the soldiers to the city beyond and wondered if Sarra's son was in the capital, if she kept him close. Her family. Renott. Who was the deformed boy? Some priest, he guessed. He did not care that the child was deformed. He was Arko's blood, his son and heir to the kingdom. He would never have given the child to the desert. She didn't know him. She never knew him. That was why she had finally left him. It wasn't because of Serena after all, the one he loved—no, Sarra had suffered his mistress, she had stayed for all those years and tried to look the other way, tried to be a queen. She had left him to save her son. She must have hidden the boy on the day of his birth. Perhaps she had wanted to have a family of her own, a boy who was hers alone. He didn't know. He might never know.

At least his boy, Ren, was safe. He would find a way to the throne. Arko was certain of it. It warmed his heart to know that the boy survived, that some piece of the woman he loved persisted in the world. Arko took the white stone from his neck and rubbed the smooth surface. He traced the six letters with his thumb. *Serena.*

With a wave he motioned for the archers concealed in the ceiling and walls to stand ready. He hadn't had much time to position his assassins—the men Wat had brought to him—but he had done his best with the hours he had. The Antechamber, he found, was equipped with a number of hidden chambers designed for defense. Wat said the Ray required no protection, he was the mouth of the god and no one would dare assault him. Arko chortled at the notion. Clearly his predecessors had found the need to fortify their chambers and had done so to Arko's benefit.

A host of assassins hid at the far end of the corridor, and there were more stowed away in the closets of the Antechamber. Arko would not go easily. He had prepared for this moment, had guessed it was coming. He had done his best to arm himself, but he lacked Saad's resources. Arko needed his men, the five hundred well-trained Harkans. He took a long drink and waited in the doorway of the Antechamber, his eyes blazing as the Alehkar assembled in the corridor.

A boy entered from a side door, one of Wat's messengers.

"Where are my men?" he demanded before the boy could speak.

"Approaching the city gates."

"Get them in here!" he said, searching for the sword Wat had given him. He found it on the desk.

The messenger left and Arko stood alone in the Antechamber, the room unexpectedly filling up with quiet. The soldiers in the corridor had stopped their stomping. In the distance, Saad pushed past his men.

Arko picked up the sword and felt its balance, which was evenly distributed between hilt and blade but a bit lighter than he was used to. He would have preferred his own sword, which was heavier, sturdier, and had seen him through many fights, but he had left that one at the Ruined Wall in Harwen the day the Protector's men had come for him—he had given it up, thinking he would not need it any longer. How wrong he had been.

He raised the sword up and slashed the air. This blade would have to do.

Arko stepped through the Antechamber's open doors. Facing Saad's soldiers, he shaded his eyes and searched the horizon for the soldiers from Harkana. *Where are my men?* The gates were too far, though, the city too dense. *Hurry.* He looked in the direction of the unseen outer gate, past the Temple of Mithra where the tall columns shaded the dark interior, the secret goings-on of the priesthood.

She knows the emperor is a lie. Sarra's questions had made clear her knowledge of the matter. How she had found out, he wasn't certain. Sarra was clever though and it did not surprise him that she had uncovered the truth behind the empire. Had she known all along and simply chosen this moment to make her move? Or had she come to him to test some theory she held? Either way, she was using this knowledge against her husband, and using it well. Before his congress with Sarra, Wat had told him that she had requested an audience with Saad; the two were clearly working in tandem.

Dammit, where are my men? He searched, but could not see them.

Arko rubbed the gem on his forehead and longed for a drink. He wished he were not the Ray of the Sun. He wished he were back in the Shambles with a full wineskin and an entire afternoon to do nothing but hunt and burn the back of his neck in the heat of the noonday sun.

Footsteps down the hall, the clank of iron. At last, Saad had arrived fully armed, his bronze breastplate gleaming, his hair full of pomade, a pair of swords at his belt and his mouth set in a line of wry, amused arrogance. He was followed by five generals.

Arko looked past Saad to the long view of the city, the great walls, the vast labyrinth of the Solus, wondering if the Harkans were already too late.

When Arko looked down Saad was there, eyes raised, hand upon his sword. He nodded politely at Arko but refused to do more. *This is the man who will kill me?* What had Sarra promised him, if he took Arko's head? That he would himself be named Ray? *What are you up to, Sarra? If you think this empire will be easy to rule, separately or together, you are sorely mistaken.* The thought of his own death both irritated Arko—because of all the men he had ever faced, Saad was the least worthy executioner he could imagine—and left him feeling strangely elated, like at last he had found the answer to a long-sought question. Soon Sarra, Serena, Ren, Merit . . . all his regrets would be over.

Unless the Harkans arrived.

"Take a chair," Arko said. But the boy refused. His generals held maps, but they would not unroll them. Saad's eyes never left Arko's face. *What do you see there, boy, when you look at me? An old man, easy to defeat? Pick up your blade and find out. I'll die with a sword in my hand after all.*

"We are here to present our strategy," Saad said. His voice was oddly flat.

An underling stepped forward with a map. Arko did not look at it—no one looked at it. Arko's eyes were on the corridor, waiting for his soldiers.

Empty.

Damn the city, damn Saad.

He let them unfold the map carefully. They were taking their time. Did they know something Arko did not? Perhaps the Harkans were not coming at all, and the Protector knew it.

I need my men.

Saad let one of his generals detail the plans for arming the Protector's soldiers, for securing the supply lines back to the capital. When he finished, an older man with a strong accent described the route they would take to the Dromus, the points of weakness in the wall they would shore up with this company, with that battalion, but all the while Saad was sweating, his fingers fidgeting.

Arko checked the hall again. Nothing, still. *Where are you, where are my men?*

He watched the sweat grow on Saad's brow, trickling down the side of his face. His eyes rested lightly on Arko's hands. *Wanting to see what I'll do, Saad?*

As the general folded another map, Arko lifted his sword with one swift gesture, startling Saad, and making the generals take a step back. "It belonged to your grandfather and his son," said the Ray, holding it up so everyone could see the warped blade, the nicks and whorls in the metal.

"Looks it," said the Protector.

"Your father held it on the Reg, on the day Koren stood against the empire," Arko said. "Did you know I was there?"

"Didn't care to know. That's all ancient history." Saad leaned on the table. "My father could have crushed Harkana that day. Imagine how much trouble he could have saved the empire if he had just taken off your father's head?"

Saad's men gave nervous grunts, and the Protector smirked at their appreciation. The man should be an actor, Arko thought, and turning the sword on its side brought the flat edge of the blade down on the table with a loud boom. The sound made the generals wince. "Your father had honor. He respected my father's abilities on the battlefield and wasn't afraid to show it, for the sake of his men and ours. Five imperial soldiers died for every Harkan on that first day, did you know that? It's not written in your histories, or carved in your monuments, but it's true. I saw the carnage with my own eyes. Your father didn't put his boot on Koren's head—he shook his hand and called him an equal!" Arko glanced once more down the hall. Still nothing. "The Harkan Army was ready to fight that second day. Your histories say they fled, but my father's men were ready to take on the whole Imperial Army. My people stood shoulder to shoulder with their king, outnumbered but ready."

Saad shook his head. "Harkans, always thinking your bravery will be enough to save you." He glanced at Arko, alone in the chamber. "I see that hasn't changed."

"Things will change," Arko said. "Someday someone will come for your death, Saad."

"Not now." Saad waved his hand, signaling to his soldiers. "Not today."

At that, the Protector's men unsheathed their swords and slung their shields tight to their shoulders.

Arko took in a slow breath. *I'm ready.*

His assassins threw open doors and dashed into the Antechamber bearing wicked little swords, curling doubled-edged blades, one in each hand. Arko's men, while few in number, cut a path through Saad's soldiers, corralling them beneath the archers' sights.

Arko gave a sign and the archers loosed their arrows; black shafts flitted through the air. One, two, three of the generals fell. The fourth dove to save his master, throwing himself on top of Saad. Three arrows pierced his back; a fourth split his skull. The fifth general, thinking only of himself, flew toward the corridor, but knocked into two of the Alehkar. An arrow pierced his leg, pinning him to the floorboards. A second one stole his life.

Saad threw the dead general off of him, the body striking the floor with a thump. The Alehkar rallied around the Protector. Shielded by his soldiers, Saad retreated. He quickly passed the arrow loops, and was backing into the corridor. Arko gave another signal. The assassins at the far end of the hall threw open the doors and attacked, surrounding Saad's men.

Arko turned his blade into a battering ram, sticking it through one soldier's breastplate, then another, forcing them to the ground. He cut a swath through the Alehkar, advancing on Saad. He struck with such fury that he split the breastplate of the soldier who stood in front of Saad, rending the metal, sending the man crashing to the floor. Arko fought with two hands, striking a soldier with his fist while knocking another with the pommel of his sword. He moved with such fury that he did not breathe, did not think. He was all instinct, a soldier, moving faster than thought, faster than he had ever moved.

Bounding over the dead generals, he entered the corridor, arrows crunching beneath his feet. Already he noticed that only a handful of his men still stood, but it didn't matter, he had reached the Protector. *There is no one left to protect you, Saad.*

Arko leveled his weapon and charged. The Alehkar threw their blades at him, Saad slunk backward, taking a nip on the thigh, but he evaded Arko's blade by slipping behind one of his men. Arko knocked the soldier aside; he was face-to-face with Saad. But the Alehkar were packed so tightly Arko could not turn his sword to strike—only the assassins with their short, curling blades could move freely, could fight, and they did so valiantly, gutting the Alehkar with ease, slicing at the weak points of their armor. Grunts shot through the corridor, the sound of metal on skin.

Arko hit Saad on the jaw with his free hand, hit him again and again, mangling his face and nearly snapping his neck. He enjoyed Saad's every grimace, his every shout of pain. More than anything he wanted Saad to suffer the same fear Arko's family endured. He could have struck him down with a quick blow but instead he did it slowly. He fought with time he did not have.

A blade pierced Arko's calf, a second one cut him across the arm, and the Ray of the Sun faltered just long enough for Saad to retreat.

"I'm not letting you go, Saad."

He followed, but Saad's men were upon him. Arko hit two with his fist, told his hired men to hurry to his side. "Push back!" he cried, too late.

Saad was out of reach, backing deeper into the corridor. Arko met his eyes, saw that the boy was grinning now, his bloody face nearly giddy with victory. *Where are the Harkans?*

The courtyard was empty, save for the Alehkar; no one was coming.

His assassins' bodies covered the floor. Arko saw only the Protector's men, filling up the corridor. He was outnumbered. Surprise had been his only advantage, but it hadn't been enough. His men were falling and there were no more to replace them, no Harkans.

The Alehkar advanced, crowding the corridor, pushing Arko back into the Antechamber. They surrounded him, swarming around him like flies on a corpse.

A blade penetrated his left shoulder, a hot sharpness in his skin that grew and spread like the first drink of strong liquor. He swung his other arm, forcing his attacker backward, and punched, knocking the man over. The assassin at his left took a sword in the chest. One remained. He swung valiantly, clearing the path ahead of Arko, before taking a knife to the back.

"I'm not finished, Saad." Arko would not give up, he would not submit. They had forced him to retreat into the Antechamber, but he resisted—he pushed hard against the soldiers. One man at a time he fought his way back into the corridor. He caught sight of Saad, his armor, bright and yellow. The Protector was retreating, but Arko caught up to him, his sword held out. "Boy," he said, "don't even think of running away from me." The handle of the dagger still protruded from Arko's shoulder.

Saad shook his head, his eyes on the haft of the dagger. "You're finished, Harkan, one way or another," he said. "I'm under orders from the emperor himself."

The emperor? What the hell is this idiot talking about? So Sarra had not told the boy the truth. He didn't know. Arko pushed past the soldiers. He stood once more face-to-face with Saad.

"You damned fool!" Arko said. "You think Sarra Amunet will grant you power when this is done? That she will make you Ray? When she has coveted that position since she took the cowl of the Mother Priestess?" He pushed his blade into Saad's chest and staggered backward. Seeing the sword strike their master, the Alehkar slashed frantically at Arko, cutting his leg, his cheek. Arko ignored the blows. His eyes were on Saad. *Are you dead, boy? Is the task done?*

Saad cried out. His men caught him and carried him away. "Sir!" they cried. "Make way for the Protector!" they said as they made off with his body. They would try to save their master. They might manage it, but the look on Saad's face when he realized Arko had gutted him was worth everything else, almost.

With Saad gone, the men focused only on Arko. The Alehkar formed ranks, their captains calling out orders. They leveled their swords and pressed their shields into a wall, driving him back into the Antechamber.

The men forced Arko backward until he stood against Suten's desk, the chamber crowded with Alehkar.

A mighty crack, and the doors to the Antechamber started to close, wood splitting and bronze bolts screaming. The soldiers on the other side were locking the door. The Alehkar around him began to panic. Arko pushed forward, over the fallen bodies, but the door was already halfway shut, and though he tried to wedge himself between them, the doors ground to a slow halt. Then the sound of the bolt sliding home. Shut in.

The light dimmed. He was alone with the Alehkar, each of whom was as trapped as Arko himself. He turned, his body aching with every movement, his flesh tearing, ripping, heart pounding. He ducked behind the great table, his legs nearly giving out, his movements slowing. He tossed the table over to make a wall, to give him time to retrieve the shield from a fallen man. He was weak, but he could do this. He needed time.

His vision started to go gray: there was smoke in the chamber. A sickly odor, like the scent of a butchered hog. Arko beat back the approaching soldiers, knocking two against the wall. *Three more,* he thought. *Come on, then.* He composed his stance.

The floorboards were hot; he felt the heat through his sandals. Smoke whistled from between the wide planks, black soot winding its way around the face of the wood. The floor erupted into flame; the air turned black. A point pierced his belly, then another his back, another hot starburst of pain. He wrenched the knife from his stomach and forced it into the soldier's chest, kicking him to the floor, he turned to face the other, but the smell of smoke and hog fat had already gotten the better of the man, who collapsed at Arko's feet. Saad must be roasting a whole herd of pigs beneath him, their fat used as an accelerant. This was the old trial, the Emperor's Justice, Mithra's Fire—no enemy of the Soleri could survive it. Very clever, Sarra. Arko covered his mouth and nose with a cloth he tore from his bloody tunic.

Saad's last soldier approached, blade held high. *Why fight,* Arko thought, *when you're as dead as the man you seek to kill?* But the soldier came at him anyway, desperation in his eyes, as if Saad might still let him live if he performed this last task. Arko bested him with the dagger, jamming it into his chest, blocking the sword with his bare arm, then smashing the soldier in the jaw with a closed fist. The man tumbled backward, the impact of the fall shattering the weakened floorboards. A beam collapsed, taking half the floor down with it. Arko heard the man cry out, saw the outlines of the trap they had built deep beneath the Antechamber for the dying pigs, for the wood and oil. The stink of burning pig flesh was everywhere, the sound of the animals screaming. Arko crawled toward the shutters and managed to reach the window just before a beam gave way, carrying another section of the floor down into the flames. With what strength remained in his limbs, he pounded the amber glass of the Empyreal Domain, but the window would not crack.

Arko gasped.

There was no air in the room; the fire had taken it all.

There was only smoke and flame.

The boards teetered, suspending him above the fiery pit.

Arko Hark-Wadi thought of his children, his boy, his girls. He hoped his words reached Merit, he hoped Kepi was safe, he hoped Ren found the eld, that he would claim the throne before Sarra could move against him, he hoped and he hoped—but the moment had passed. The flames danced at his heels, angry and eddying. The floor collapsed and Arko fell into the fire.

⇒57⇐

Just after midday the gate to the underground city banged open and Ren rushed to the edge of the roof to see a hurried mass streaming out of the tunnel, followed by thick black smoke that swirled upward and finally left the passageway clear. Those who escaped coughed and spat. Ren grabbed his blade, shimmying down a narrow pillar to street level and sprinting through the open doorway, pushing through the crowd, turning sideways, shoving others aside, pressing his way down the long staircase, Adin at his heels, shouting, "Ren, wait! Not so fast, Ren!" From the rooftop Ren had seen smoke coming from the edge of the Shroud Wall, from what he guessed was the Antechamber, smoke pouring upward from the Waset. If Tye were not coming out, if she were still inside the Priory and the inner district was on fire, Ren would have to go in.

It felt like ages since his escape through the Hollows with Oren Thrako at his back. He remembered the gates, the narrow passages—the goose-necks, Oren had called them—but the two of them had moved so quickly that Ren did not remember the way anymore. In the dark, with the acrid smell of smoke in his nostrils, he felt a moment of panic: which way was safety, and which way was a dead end?

He struggled against the tide of bodies, battered by the people fleeing the fire, pushed and pulled in a hundred directions. A man carrying a filthy child knocked into him with so much force that Ren's teeth rattled. Three boys not much younger than Ren stumbled past him, screaming, their hair smoking, all of them going the same way, away from the trouble. Adin pushed him onward, elbowing the crowd aside. They passed into a wide sewer, the smell of refuse everywhere, so thick it made the boys gag. This was not the path Ren had taken to escape—he would remember this chamber, dimmer and dingier than the rest.

Adin uttered a long gagging sound, and the boy retched, splashing his most recent meal over his feet, last night's bread. Ren tore a strip from his tunic and gave half to his friend. "Cover your mouth and nose with this," he said, and tied his own face with the remaining half. *Where are the passages, the goosenecks—the long, dark corridors that pass between the walls?*

They searched for the door, for the path through to the next chamber, but they saw no gates save the one they had already entered. One by one people staggered past, tasting the air, pushing away the black smoke and the stink of human waste. Up ahead they found a long, wide stair that passed over a churning stream of black water and climbed up quickly. At the top, they staggered into a lightless chamber, stumbled into a wall, then inched through the darkness, following the murmurs of a distant crowd. They reached an archway and paused. Ren saw the sewer, the people running, covering their noses with one hand. The shouts of the crowd made it hard to think.

"Where are we?" Adin asked

"Lost." Ren tore a clean strip of fabric from his tunic and pressed it to his mouth. "We're lost."

"I noticed," Adin said, splashing filthy water on his face.

"We should go back."

"No," Adin said, grabbing Ren by the tunic as he eyed a sideways chamber. It was larger than the first, still choked with smoke but smelling less of sewage.

"Following your nose?" Ren asked.

"Better than following you."

"Let's hope."

Ren came around a rocky outcropping and caught sight of the chamber's full length, a long series of corridors packed shoulder to shoulder with the escaping masses. Behind him, Ren heard a scuffle. Adin had pulled a boy from the crowd.

Ren pushed him aside. "We have no time, Adin."

"But—" Adin pointed at the boy. Ren came closer, the strange boy's face settling into a familiar shape: It was Kollen Pisk, one of the older boys. Soot covered his gaunt features, but the long crooked nose, the black eyes, and beard were unmistakable. Adin had found one of the Priory boys.

"He's just come from Tolemy's house," Adin said. "He can help us find it."

The older boy laughed. "You two shits going back there?" He glanced from one skinny boy to the next. "Just the two of you? Good luck with that."

"We're lost," Ren said.

"No kidding."

"Will you help us, we need to find our way back. Were you the only one released?"

"You dumb prick. You think I was released?" Kollen raised a hand to his brow, wiping away sweat. "The guards fled. They saved their asses and left us to die. A few of us, the ones in the classrooms and in the refectory, escaped."

Ren felt a stab of anguish. "When did you leave?"

"Just now."

"Then there's still time."

"For what, crap-jaw? Time to get yourself killed?"

Ren smacked Kollen on the ear, but the older boy punched back.

"Kollen!" Ren said, putting his hand on his dagger and making sure the other boy saw. "Do it again and I'll cut your throat. Now, tell us the way back."

Kollen bit his lip. "King of Harkana, and you come all the way back here for the rest of us?" he asked. "For what? Oh I see. Your little girl is it? Tye?"

Ren flushed scarlet. "How do you know?"

"Everyone knows. After they took you to the sun, the guards stripped her down and searched her for weapons. They saw the truth."

"What happened—where is she?"

"That's the thing. No one knows where the guards took her, but I don't think it was back to her family." He leered.

Ren lunged at Kollen but stopped himself. The arrogant boy was his only hope for finding the Priory.

"You're a damn fool, Hark-Wadi. You always were."

"Maybe so, but that's my business. Show us the way you came."

The larger boy hesitated, looking over his shoulder, to the way the other two boys had come, but Kollen didn't flee. He righted himself and grunted a bit, pinching his nose to stop the blood, brushing his hair from his eyes. The crowd pushed, the smoke swirled around him. The older boy looked toward the gate, toward the route that led to the surface. He wasn't far; he could escape—Ren saw the thought flicker across his face—but he instead said, "Back there." He pointed to the far side of a massive turret and began walking.

"Come on," Ren said.

They followed the tall boy through the passage, Kollen telling how the priors had opened the gates when the fire started, how the boys had first been confused, then elated, then terrified when they saw the smoke and the flames. They had pushed for the door, toward fresh air, crushing one another in their urgency.

The older boy led them through a dim passage that curved to the west, behind the more well-worn routes through the underground city. Ren was thinking about Tye, hoping she was still in the Priory, that she was alive and unmolested. A sick feeling in his gut told him things had gone terribly wrong for the girl.

Up ahead stood a massive wall with a small black opening—a gooseneck. He took them through the narrow archway, past the gate, winding left, then right. The corridor was lightless and unguarded, the gates left open. In their panic, the people were avoiding the narrow passages in favor of the corridors that led directly to the surface. He guessed the older boy had come this way to get himself as far as possible from the Priory. He was an escaped prisoner and the underground city was a perfect place to hide as he fled.

The passage opened into a wide, smoke-filled corridor. The boys walked shoulder to shoulder, not wanting to lose contact with each other, Ren with a hand on Adin's shoulder, feeling the sweat drip off his friend's neck. The caverns were growing warmer, the smoke thicker. The crowds thinned as they pressed deeper into the Hollows. Ren and the two boys passed unmolested through the goosenecks, but the smoke at the end of the last was so dense they could hardly see. They clutched fabric, torn from their shirts and wetted, to their mouths and noses. They wiped their eyes, but the sting was maddening.

The smoke churned, caught in an unseen draft. Ren pushed onward, but something held him back: Kollen's arm across his chest. "There." The older boy pointed through a patch of smoke, across a bridge, at a doorway.

The path was unguarded, but smoke poured from the Priory. The darkness beyond the door flickered red and orange.

"Are we really going in there?" Adin asked.

"Do we have a choice?" Ren had to find Tye. He tore a fresh strip from his tunic and covered his face again. He put his shoulder down and barreled toward the door. It gave way, hotly, to a plume of smoke and fire. Ren was aware of Kollen and Adin behind him, dimly, the sound of their coughing cutting through the gloom.

Inside, smoldering embers and fallen beams littered the corridors and fire rippled across the ceiling, but the stones held. The Priory's walls were rock, but the substructures, the floors and ceilings, were wood. The boards were alive with flame, the heat intense. Up ahead, the body of a boy lay crushed under a fallen beam. Somewhere, from inside the Priory, a voice cried out, "Help!" followed by a single long shriek. A boy emerged from the smoke, his body black with soot, his hair on fire, skin peeling at the neck. He plowed directly into Ren, his hot breath exhaling into Ren's mouth as the two collided. The boy was unrecognizable—the fire had taken his face from him, robbed him of his voice—but Ren tackled him and beat the flames out as the boy screamed. A second shadow emerged from the smoke. "Kollen, get them out of here," Ren demanded. Kollen picked up the burnt boy and slung him over one shoulder while he pulled the other by the scruff of his neck, and led them both toward the entry.

Ren tried to orient himself.

The Priory felt alien, changed, but not only by the fire and smoke. Not even a month had passed since he had last been there, but the place felt different, the corridors smaller, the ceilings lower.

Down the hall Ren and Adin found two more boys huddled in their cells, Nix and Benk, neither boy older than ten. Ren pulled them out of their cells, and Adin started to ferry them to Kollen, who would show them the route to the surface. But both boys made it only a few steps before stopping. "You're looking for survivors?" Benk asked.

"As many as we can," said Adin.

"I'll help you," said Benk, and Nix nodded too. Four of them would be able to cover more ground. So they did, scurrying through the Priory's serpentine corridors, moving beams and leaping across gaps in the floor. They found Aric dead in his cell, only seven years old—choked to death on smoke, probably. Geb was dead too, his head crushed by a fallen door. A second body lay at his feet, the face burnt beyond recognition. *Is that you, Tye?* Ren couldn't tell. *Keep looking. Keep looking as long as you can.*

He found three more boys, including Carr Bergen. "Where is everyone?" Ren asked.

"The guards bolted when the fire started," Carr said. "They left us to die in our cells. Everyone in the refectory escaped." He scowled at Kollen, who joined them once more. "They left without opening our cells. He left." Carr pointed at Kollen.

"I saved my own ass," Kollen said. "Nothing wrong with that. I should have kept going when you two found me. Now we're all going to die in here, isn't that just roses?"

Ren pushed past the older boy, leading Carr and the others out to the hallways. They clambered up steps into the practice hall and found two more boys huddled in a corner, half dead from smoke. Ren could not recall their names, but he guessed they were nine or ten. The pair was sitting on a half-burnt rug, brandishing wooden swords. Ren reached out a hand to pull them up, moving more quickly now, not stopping to talk. They went up and down the hallways, beating down doors and freeing whomever they could. They searched the crypt and the passages beneath the Priory.

"We should leave," Adin said, watching the flames creeping down the hall toward them.

"Not yet. I have to make it to the roof; perhaps she was sent to the Sun's Justice."

The boys passed the crude lesson rooms, the scrolls now on fire, and then the armory, where the wooden swords were now embers, the racks turned to ash.

They found only dead bodies on the third level, a single living boy on the fourth. They climbed to the fifth level, running past the last rows of cells, all empty, or else their occupants were dead. They were twelve now in Ren's little group, twelve boys from how many he could not recall.

The refectory was empty, its stone construction and spare decoration saving the chamber from the flames. The great cauldron was still there, the long table and hard, flat benches, the bronze cups and wooden plates. He kicked a bench and watched it tumble.

"Tye's not here, not alive at least," Adin said, grabbing Ren's arm. "Let's go before the rest of us are dead too."

Ren searched the boys' faces. Some were scared, others eager to continue their search. "There's just the roof, let me look," Ren said, breaking loose of his friend's grip and heading toward the stair that was always guarded but now stood open. *Where did you go, Tye?* He dashed up the steps, skipping one, and then two at a time, stretching his gait as wide as he could manage. The door at the top was unbolted, the place where the guards stood now empty. He pushed the massive wooden leaf aside. Smoke whirled in the doorway, the sun illuminating the roof. He saw the place where he had stood in the light. The nest of shafts and wells that fed light and air into the Priory were empty save for columns of smoke and ash. Ren's heart broke at the sight of the empty roof.

No Tye.

Did she escape? Did the flames claim her, or did something else happen to his friend?

Ren hobbled, alone, down the winding stair.

"There's no one—" Adin started.

"I know," Ren said. "Tolemy's house is empty."

Ren led the survivors down the twisting steps, past the cells, through the training rooms, and out toward the bridge. He stood at the door, counting the boys, marking each as they left the Priory and crossed the bridge over the chasm. When he was sure they were all out, when he was certain they were all safe, he glanced one last time at the passage, his gaze fixed upon the corridor that led to the Prior Master's chambers.

It's time.

Ren lifted what remained of the great door and tossed it toward the opening, blocking the entry. It landed with a resounding *thud* that raised a cloud of smoke and dust.

"Ren!" Adin called, his voice already distant. "You're coming with us." His last words were barely audible.

Ren was not leaving, not yet. Not without her.

⇒ 58 ⇐

Over the city an acrid smoke rose, billowing up and up into the blue, cloudless sky. So it was done. Her husband was dead—not at her hands, perhaps, but through her will. Sarra Amunet was now the Ray of the Sun. And she shivered at the thought of it, at the achievement and what it had cost to accomplish it. Arko was gone and she had barely escaped the Antechamber. Her robe was torn and she had a bruise on her arm where her husband held her. She was safe from him now, but not from Saad. In a room, just past the Shadow Gate, Sarra waited for the Protector to arrive so she could escort him into the Empyreal Domain.

In death, it was easier to mourn her husband. Sarra closed the shutter, blocking the smoke from her sight. She thought of Arko, of the day they met in Harwen, his handsome face taking her in impassively as she stepped down from the carriage outside the city walls, surrounded by the entourage her father had arranged to bring her from the southern islands to the desert. He had taken her hand and led her inside the Hornring to the cheers of the people, had nodded and smiled and waved like a happy bridegroom. Once inside—once they were alone in her chamber, she trembling at the thought of him making love to her—he had bowed his head and bid her good night. Then he had turned, never once explaining, and left her alone to wonder when he would return.

All night she sat alone, waiting. When the torch had gone out and the chill had overcome her, she wandered through the unfamiliar corridors until she once more heard his voice. Stopping outside a closed door, kneeling on the hard stone, she peered through the keyhole to see her new husband inside, a woman between his legs. *Serena,* she heard him call the name.

There would be many more nights, many more keyholes, but that first time hurt her more than any other. She could still feel the sting of that humiliation, the new queen of Harkana on her knees outside a tiny chamber, watching another woman take what was hers. *If he'd loved you, would it have made a difference?*

It didn't matter anymore. He hadn't loved her. Whatever plan Suten Anu had had for the man, it had failed. She mourned for him as best she could. She had been his wife, but he had not been her husband. She had waited years to tell Arko the truth, to reveal to him that Ren was not her son. Her true son was Ott: her beautiful, perfect, but strange and withered boy. She needed Arko to know the truth before he died. To know why she had never visited Ren or never once used her position to lessen the boy's suffering. *I didn't walk out on my family, not all of them.*

Enough with the past. I am done with Harwen. Sarra wanted only to see her son, Ott—the boy who waited in the Protector's Tower.

A powerful knock startled her, and Saad swung open the circle-encrusted doors. She could tell by the Protector's swagger that he had been there when the deed was done: Saad still had sweat on his brow, his face streaked with soot and blood, a bruise on his eye, his cheek, and his chin, and a blood-soaked bandage on his chest. Bright-red circles blossomed across the linen wrap, and he spat blood as he approached. Despite herself, she hoped it was her husband who had gotten in that one good blow against the arrogant boy. A host of soldiers trailed behind Saad. All but one wore the armor of the Alehkar. At the back of the group a lone soldier stood with a cloak hung over his face, concealing his features.

The Alehkar closed the great doors, sealing the passage that led to the throne room, beginning their journey into the Empyreal Domain. Saad took his time crossing the corridor, stopping twice to take in the smoky air, his victory. The man walked with the confidence of an emperor, probably thinking himself already Ray, or as good as, but Sarra needed to be wary—she might not be the only one with a plan.

"Shall we go meet the emperor together?" he asked, making no reference to Arko's passing. "Or should I go on alone?"

"No elaboration on the death of my predecessor?" she asked. "Not a word of respect or regret?"

"Wouldn't that be a waste of time, *god-lover*?" His eyes sparked with bloodlust. "My soldiers tell me your spies watched every moment. I'm sure they've already described it to you in great detail."

He was learning. Too bad it wouldn't help him in the end. She straightened her robe. *Calm, keep calm.* She motioned to another door. "My predecessor named no replacement so I am Ray, though I do not wear the jewel and my light has not shone upon the mountain. There will be no need for me to do these things. As Ray, my only duty will be to escort you to our lord so that he may name you to the position." She led Saad and his men through the dark maze of corridors, the labyrinth of passageways that wove through the old buildings and half-buried temples preceding the Empyreal Domain. The passages were so narrow that Saad's men scraped their spears and bumped into walls as they thrust their torches into each corridor, clearing each passage before they would allow the Protector to proceed. Sarra waited silently at the corridor's end, feigning calm, smiling at the Protector as if his victory were her own.

Saad left his guards when the doors opened to the innermost chamber. His captain—the man who had so cautiously guarded his Protector's every movement—turned and nodded, leaving Saad alone at last. The domain was holy ground, a place for gods and no one else. The soldiers and their weapons could not enter the sacred precinct. Only the Ray could cross the threshold and return, so she did, beckoning Saad to follow.

At the door he motioned to the soldiers still waiting in the corridor behind him. They parted to allow the cloaked man to approach. Sarra had forgotten about the curious figure. Something about him gave her a chill.

Saad tugged back the man's hood, revealing Ott's face.

"What's this?" Sarra pressed her lips in a narrow line.

"Your priest," he said. "Did you think I would go alone with you, Mother? Who knows what traps hide in these depths. I will not travel into the Empyreal Domain unprotected. I can't bring my swords or my soldiers, so I brought something else. I brought your *son*."

"You're mistaken," Sarra said without thinking. "My son is in Harkana."

"No," said Saad. He took Ott by the arm and thrust him toward her. The boy stumbled and fell to the floor, weeping, his body shaking uncontrollably. "This is your son, the boy you keep at your side, the one who is the same age as the other, as Ren. He told his secret to the Rachins."

The Rachins. The two priests Saad had taken. Ott had told them his secret. She hadn't known he had shared his parentage. She'd told him to tell no one, to never speak of it, not even in private. Even we must not speak of it, she had said. The secret must be absolute, she had told him again and again. But Ott was no ordinary boy; his mind didn't work like hers. He was special, different.

"He is just a priest—"

"No," Saad interrupted. "Don't toy with me or I'll snap the boy's neck while you watch." Saad pressed his hands into fists, tensing his muscles, the scar on his face glowing red, the ugly bruises throbbing on his face and his neck, the wound leaking blood.

"He cannot enter the domain," she said flatly, refusing him.

"He can and he will. You said Tolemy would speak through the veil, that I would not yet meet the emperor until I was Ray—yes? So the boy will come as far as the veil," Saad said, the tone of his voice telling Sarra that she must comply, that if she did not agree he would kill the boy on the spot, kill her and be done with it all.

"So be it, Saad. The boy is my son. Let us all go to the veiled window so that Tolemy may speak and name you Ray." She turned as she spoke. Eyes stinging, she bent alongside Ott and helped him to stand. *No,* she thought, *not Ott. I can't lose him like this.* Sarra had sacrificed her marriage and her eldest children for this boy. She would not lose him now, not to Saad. The Protector knew her son's secret, but not the emperor's. *He left his troops behind. He believes in Tolemy.*

As his soldiers closed the doors, Saad tore Ott from her grip. "Follow at my heels," he barked, and she struggled to ignore him. Calmly, she offered a lamp to the Protector and lifted one for herself. "Tolemy waits," she told him, but he did not acknowledge her; he did not even bother to meet her gaze—his thumbs were tucked into his bronze breastplate, his eyes surveying the many carvings that lined the Hall of Histories. Saad was thinking about the emperor, picturing himself standing behind the veil, in the dazzling light of the god. She saw the glow on his face.

Behind him, Ott staggered and nearly fell. It was a gruesome sight, watching her son struggle while the Protector strutted. *I can't do this,* she thought, her resolve wavering momentarily. Saad stopped in front of a depiction of the Children's War, surveying the heroic image of his father, foot on the head of Koren Hark-Wadi.

"It looks glorious to me, no matter what Arko said."

"Didn't . . . he like it?" Sarra shook as she spoke, her eyes burning.

"He thought our artists had taken some liberties with the subject matter." Saad stood back a little more to admire the carving, as if his father's glory still reflected on him. "It's a shame my own father never saw it. Must be twice his height." She held her lamp high and the flickering light made the relief glow. A cool wind swept down the hall and the light vanished. Sarra struggled to control her trembling limbs, her voice.

"We shouldn't keep the emperor waiting." Sarra said, glancing at Ott, wondering what was in that head of his. He did not speak, nor did he tap his fingers. Linen wraps covered two of the digits. *Did he break Ott's fingers? What happened in the tower?*

Saad paid them no mind, speaking aloud to himself. "I'll see that the Harkan stories are changed as well, when I am Ray. There is no glory

save that of Solus, no bravery but our own." He pointed down the corridor, where carving after carving showed the hand of the Protector smit-
ing the head of one kingdom's leader or another tribe's warlord, the
position of the hand always the same, the club the identical shape, an
image reproduced over and over again without regard toward the truth.

"That would be glorious," she said, her voice flat, anger in her face and
in her words. "But the emperor must not be made to wait."

She urged him forward with a wave of her hand, but he would not
move. While her boy shivered, Saad turned once more in a circle, surveying the entirety of Soleri history illustrated in the stele.

Ott fell while Saad idled. *Mithra, let this end.*

She rushed to him, but Saad blocked her path.

"Stand," he commanded, and Ott rose to his feet, using his good arm
for balance.

Mithra help me, she thought, *or I will club Saad with my own hands. I will
strike him as he struck my son.*

In the distance, a door groaned on its hinges—Saad had reached
the end of the hall. *Thank the gods,* she thought. *I can't take any more of this.*

He pushed open the heavy door, beyond which the corridor narrowed,
the air growing cooler, mustier. She caught sight of his shadow as it passed
into a small chamber, where there was the sound of water and the flicker
of lamplight and three pale eunuchs formed a circle around the Protector. He glowered at them, at their shaved heads and white skin. They
seemed frightened, uncertain of how to proceed, waiting for Sarra's
direction. *Poor, pitiful creatures.* She caught sight of Ott, waiting in the
shadows, his head once more concealed beneath the cloak. She prayed he
was all right. She nodded for the girls to remove Saad's tunic and armor,
saw Saad wince in pain as they peeled the blood-soaked fabric from his
chest. She waited in the darkness of the corridor, hearing the splash of
water, watching Ott. He was clearly in pain, he shifted from foot to foot,
groaning a bit, mumbling, but never speaking. *Why?* She feared they
had cut out Ott's tongue when he refused to reveal some secret.

When Saad emerged, he was no cleaner than before, but the water was
now black with blood and ash. He took the Ray's ceremonial robe from
a rack. "Damned blind mice," he growled, his exposed back facing Sarra,
the skin littered with scars, long cuts arrayed in parallel lines. These were
no battle marks; these wounds were deliberate in their arrangement. She
wondered if the ragged lines were the work of Saad's father, Raden.
Was this the old Protector's method of punishment? Had he cut the boy

whenever he disobeyed a command or broke a rule? She wanted to pity Saad, but could not. All men suffered.

Saad tugged the robe over his head, the blood from his chest seeping through the fabric. Without looking at her, he stepped into the Hall of Emperors. Ott at his back, Saad perused the imperial statues, whispering the name and title of each as he passed: *Kantafre, beloved of Mithra, heir of Atum, chosen by Bes and Horu, he who united the inner and outer rings, enduring of life and strong of heart. Osokohn, beloved of Mithra, son of earth and sky, chosen by Sen and Makht, he who laid the stones of the Dromus, enduring of years and firm of mind.*

She could feel his ego growing with every word and every footstep, the power entering his every gesture. The man stank of victory. *No—this is my hall, my throne. Soon you'll be dead and forgotten. Mithra spared me from the rioters so that I could serve the line of Tolemy. That's what the people will think.* She would replace the old lies with new ones. She would tell Solus that Saad set the blaze without Tolemy's consent, that he murdered the Ray of the Sun then perished when he stood beneath Tolemy's light, that the emperor had endorsed Sarra as his First Ray. *All that stands in my way is you, Saad.*

"This is it?" he asked, and she realized he had reached the end of the corridor. Statues of the Soleri flanked the door. A circle crowned their heads, a plaque adorned the pedestal. It read MAY YOU SHARE THE SUN'S FATE. Sarra smirked at that, doubting Saad would rise again after today.

"This is it." Sarra put her hand on the amber panel. "Beyond this door is the great veil of the emperor. He will speak to you through the screen, but you will not see his face. To see the emperor is to see the sun, and no one can survive that light."

"Open it," said Saad impatiently, a drop of sweat dribbling down his cheek. He drew Ott to his side, holding the boy by the neck, keeping him close, as if the boy could somehow protect him. Saad was nervous, trembling, but she could not tell if it was the unknown he feared or the emperor himself. Either way, the boy was at the edge of his wits. He looked as if he might snap Ott's neck just to ease his nerves.

"Do it. Stop stalling, Mother. Stop playing games. This one is done."

You are more right than you guess, thought Sarra, but she held her tongue as she opened the door a crack, watching him peer inside. He wanted so much to know the secrets of the empire. *Go on,* she thought. *Have a look.* She waited until he was almost at the crack. *Now is the time.*

She faced him, unafraid at last, "Did you know that word has already spread through the capital that the Protector assassinated the Ray of the Sun, mouth of our Lord Emperor and God, and set fire to half the Waset in the process?"

"So? I've done Tolemy's bidding, nothing more," he said, his fingers probing Ott's eyes, looking as if he might pluck them out.

You do my bidding and no one else's, thought Sarra as she pushed the door open a little. Saad hurried toward the breach as if anticipating the golden glow of imperial rooms, the voice of a living god, but instead the widening gap held only darkness, a puff of ash. "Stand back," he told her. "This is my moment, god-child, not yours."

He released Ott.

She let her hand fall from the door. A shuffling sound penetrated the gap, sandals sweeping through the soot and dust.

She rushed to her son.

Saad's brow furrowed as priests flitted from the darkness, a cloud of black powder rising at their feet. She had used Mithra's Door to smuggle a cadre of priests into the throne room. They had each agreed to give their lives to end Saad's.

The Protector pushed past them, still not realizing what was happening. When both doors opened, he gaped at the burnt chamber, the crushed throne and broken beams. There was no veil, no Tolemy. "What's this?"

The first hit tore at Saad's robe, rending the fabric, destroying the costume. As members of the priesthood, Sarra had forbidden the priests to use proper weapons. She had told them to assault Saad with scraps from the burnt throne room. *Let him be bludgeoned by the thing he desired,* she told them.

Sarra took hold of Ott, her white robe fluttering in the darkness. She took him by the arms, dragging him away from the doors. Too late. Saad spun, coming at her now, dashing through the open doors, his bloody hands raised. He was disoriented, frantic. "This isn't the throne room— where have you taken me, god-lover? What lie is this?" he asked, clearly confused, angry. He reached for his sword, but the scabbard was empty. He'd been forced to surrender it.

"I don't need a weapon to wring the truth from you," he said, crushing her son's foot with his heel. "Come here, boy." Saad gripped Ott by the leg and tore him from her hands. He moved to attack, but her priests were on top of him.

"Fools, get your hands off me, I am your lord." Saad thrust one against a column, leaving a bloody spot where the priest's head hit the stone. He tore the wood from another and struck him with it. "You should have sent soldiers," Saad said. He was fighting back, and it seemed for a time that he might triumph, but between each blow he glanced at the chamber, still confused and still gasping at what he saw.

"Gods," he muttered as her priests came at him with their clubs. "You're all so bloody eager to die." He clubbed one priest, then another. Searching for better ground, he retreated to the throne, climbing the steps, tripping over helmets and broken spears, kicking dust and ash into the air. "What is all of this?" he muttered. "What happened here?" he asked as he struck one priest, sending him crashing into another. Cries echoed through the empty chamber, more dust and more ash. Saad stumbled. Blood flowed from the cut on his chest, the place where she hoped her husband had struck him. His amber skin was white, his eyes sunken. The blow dealt by her husband had sucked the life from Saad, but he was not yet ready to fall.

"Finish it," she commanded. This was taking too long. Sarra worried she had brought too few men.

Her priests came at Saad, clubs swinging. Saad took one man by the neck and tossed him from the platform. Her priest hit the floor with a thud, his neck bent in an unnatural position. "When I'm done clobbering your priests, Mother, I'm coming for you, and I won't be merciful." Saad spun, trying to deflect the next blow, but he was too late. The priest hit him once, twice—knocking him against the throne. Saad did not cry out or react, he only stared at the broken chair, his face, at last, a mask of shock.

"What's this?" he asked. "How is this—"

Sarra understood his confusion. Saad had thought this was all a ruse, a clever deception, but no more. He was gawking at the body of Suten Anu, which lay beside the empty throne. He made no effort to move or to defend himself. The shock was complete. The fight fled from his limbs, chased away by the truth of the empire. He only stared at Suten's body, pondering the empty throne room, at last realizing where he was and what had happened here.

Her priests did not hesitate.

Hit after hit bent the Protector's body into an awkward semblance of his former self, an image not unlike a child's drawing, the lines broken, the features out of order. He crumpled when the next blow bit his skin, and then Amen Saad, Father Protector of the Dromus, finally took a ragged, wet-sounding breath as his body tumbled down the steps, landing not far from where Sarra stood.

She leaned over and met Saad's eyes, the shock there slowly fading toward death. "There is no emperor," he said. At last he understood everything.

She stared at him with calm eyes. "No, there is an emperor, Saad. You are looking at her right now," she said, but Saad gave no reply. He did not breathe. He was gone. Arko was gone. The throne room was quiet.

She had won.

Alone, Sarra looked for her son. "Ott?" she called, but the boy didn't answer.

⇥ 59 ⇤

Ren stepped over bodies, tripped through fallen beams and burnt planks, stumbling down the corridor that led to the Prior Master's chambers. He had come here alone, leaving the other ransoms behind. *I can't risk their lives, but I can risk my own. I have to find Tye.*

Up three flights of steps he climbed, the smoke now thinner, and came upon a bronze door, which he forced open, slipping inside and letting it shut behind him. Inside a roof hatch was open—someone had vented the smoke, leaving the air inside clear. Bright light poured through a window, and he pressed his mouth to it and sucked in fresh air, let it fill his lungs again and again. He stood back to gauge the size of the fire, which stretched from the Shroud Wall out to the Priory, and farther still. Everywhere he looked, there was smoke and flame. The sight left an ill feeling in his stomach. There was something unnatural about the fire, something unwholesome, but he could not place it.

Three doors lined the corridor, the first two open, the rooms empty, littered with old tunics and books, the beds larger and more comfortable than the ones the boys had been used to. This had to be the prior's quarters, the place where Oren and the others had slept. It had to be.

The third door was just slightly ajar, and through the crack he spied a man rifling through an old trunk, as if looking desperately for some-thing. Ren pushed the door open with his toe, both hands gripping his blade.

The trunk was still open, but the man was gone—until the next mo-ment, when Oren put one gauntleted hand to Ren's throat and the other on his blade, his black iron-encased fingers closing around Ren's neck. Oren squeezed the dagger, twisting it from Ren's grip, the blade clatter-ing to the floor.

For years he had imagined this moment; he had dreamed of taking his revenge on the Prior Master. But now, when the moment had come, when he had approached Oren as a free man, everything had gone wrong. Ren was helpless. No friends at his back. No weapon. Fear wiped his mind clean. He was all adrenaline, kicking at Oren with one foot, driving his knee into the man's groin, punching with bare fists.

Oren squeezed his neck and knocked his skull against the stone. "Calm down, Hark-Wadi. Stop your fussing, or I'll crush your bones before your next breath."

Ren would not yield—better to die now, choked against a wall, than let Oren have time to devise something else. He knocked the Prior Mas-ter on the jaw. Another fist to his temple, a knee to his chest. Oren was strong, but still older and slower than Ren, and he had none of his fierce-ness, his desperation. Ren would claw Oren's eyes out if the man came close enough.

Oren released his grip, and Ren hit the floor. He slid toward his father's dagger, twisting his body to grasp the blade. He gripped the knife and leapt to his feet.

"Stop!" cried a new voice—not Oren's, higher and sweeter, but still familiar. It was Tye. She was bound with manacles, lips swollen, shirt torn, eyes pleading. Oren had a knife at her temple, a line of blood dribbling down her forehead. Oren held the blade by the pommel, as if he were about to drive it into Tye's skull as a logger drives a stake into a tree.

"Ren!" Tye cried.

"Your knife," Oren growled. "Put it down. Or I'll kill the bitch."

Ren let the dagger fall and Oren pushed it aside with a kick.

In one swift motion the Prior Master grasped Ren by the tunic, slammed him into the wall, and forced his hand into a manacle. Oren shackled the other hand, then raised the black-iron gauntlet and pressed it to Ren's stomach, the serrated edges piercing his skin. Pain—sharp and hot. Ren kicked, trying to curl himself up to avoid Oren's touch.

"Don't move, boy. Stay still and you'll save yourself some pain." Oren eyed the fallen dagger. He appeared to think on it for a moment. "You're not yet king. Are you? No king's escort, no Harkan soldiers. You've come alone, haven't you?" Oren kicked the door closed. "Why? Why have you returned? Not just for Tye. She's a pretty little packet, but hardly worth the effort," he said, a wicked look in his eye.

"Are you okay?" he asked Tye. "Did he hurt you?" Ren felt his blood boil at the thought.

Tye shook her head. "Is that really you, Ren?" she asked, peering through the hair that hung almost to her nose. "I thought I would never see you again."

Oren slapped Ren. "Answer the question, boy! Was it your father who called you?"

Ren gave no response; the question made no sense.

Oren asked again, "Was it your father who called you, boy? Did he call you before he met with the Protector?" Ren stared blank-faced at the man. *What does my dead father have to do with any of this?*

"You don't know, do you?" Oren asked. "You don't know your father's dead."

"You ass." Ren kicked wildly, but his old master twisted the gauntlet and Ren froze in a web of pain. He cried out, head slumping. "Of course my father's dead. He died when he met Tolemy."

Oren shook his head. "You stupid boy, he died today. Didn't you know that your father was made Ray of the Sun?"

"No," Ren said. "You lie." He spoke the words, but already he knew Oren was telling the truth. Ren remembered the talk among the refugees at the gates of Solus, something about the new Ray and the unrest he was causing. *If Oren was telling the truth . . .*

"It's no lie," said Oren, confirming what Ren knew. "I wish it was one. Arko's term was short, but real nonetheless. The fire you see"—he gestured to the windows, to the blaze that raged from the Antechamber to the Priory and beyond—"was lit by the Protector in judgment of the Ray."

If only I'd made some small inquiry, I might have learned that my father had been made Ray.

Ren understood now why the sight of the smoke had sickened him. He was looking at his father's death. Angry, he swung at the Prior Master, but the older man's reach far exceeded his own and Ren's fist met only the air. He kicked with both feet, but Oren's grip held, the black gauntlet tearing Ren's skin. Ribbons of flesh pulled from his chest, and he quit struggling. *Not now. Not like this. I won't die at Oren's hand.*

Oren grabbed him by the hair and jerked his head back. "I want to tell you something before you die."

"There's nothing you can tell me." Ren spat in his face.

"Didn't you wonder why I singled you out? Why I sent you to the sun? Why I let you take Tye's place? No boy was ever sent there for a minor infraction—except you."

"I don't care."

"Yes. you do. Again and again it was you who suffered, but it wasn't your fault. It was your mother's."

"What?"

"Sarra Amunet, your mother. She was the one who came to me."

"Fuck you," Ren spat. "I have no interest in the Mother Priestess."

"You're lying," Oren said, a smirk on his face. "I see it in your eyes. You want to know the truth and so I'll tell it to you: Your mother came to me year after year and paid me to make certain that you never slept, never found peace, that you were broken and would never take the throne of Harkana. I accepted her coin, but I would have done it without the crescents."

Even as he spoke, Ren tried to ignore Oren. *He's a liar,* thought Ren, but somewhere deep down in his gut he knew the words rang true.

The Prior Master released his grip and Ren's head fell, his eyes closing, the pain seething in his chest.

His mother had wanted him dead, had wanted him tortured, had wanted him abused, had set Thrako upon him.

My own mother. No, he corrected himself, *she's not my mother, and Merit's not my sister.* Neither had proven themselves worthy of those titles.

Darkness. Dull thumping. Was it his heartbeat, was it fading?

Then—voices, a banging sound, like a door opening, or else it was his own brain pounding inside his skull.

There were more voices, young voices, crying out. *Stop, stop!*

He opened his eyes to see Oren pinned against the big wooden desk, held down by Adin and Kollen as one after another the survivors of the Priory flooded into the little chamber, carrying burning sticks and sacks of smoking embers, practice swords, and wooden maces. One by one they took turns flailing at their old master: first Adin, then Carr, then Kollen, and the rest. They smashed Oren's head, beat his belly, broke his arm, and set his clothes on fire.

Someone lifted Ren. The manacles came undone. Hands steadied him, weak arms made strong by their desire to save a friend. Adin was standing with Tye, struggling with her chains. It was Ren who freed her, catching her right hand as it came free of the first manacle, her left as it fell from the second. Tye collapsed on him, her frail shoulders falling on his broad ones, her heart beating against his. Ren could not recall embracing her, or even feeling her touch. A warm shiver coursed through his chest. He held her for a heartbeat, maybe two, as the others fled the fire and the chamber.

It was time to go, to be free of the Priory, of everything it was or could be.

He waited while the ransoms fled, watching each one go. When the last one was gone, he paused at the doorway, Adin at his side, Tye still gripping his shoulder. He glanced at the desk, the manacles, his eyes drawn at last toward the body of Oren Thrako.

It was still moving.

They watched in disbelief as Oren lifted his trembling body from the floor, slowly righting himself, straightening his back and lifting his head, flames dancing on his chest, blood caked on his face. Stumbling toward them, his broken arm hanging limp, he grasped Ren's tunic, pulling him from Tye's arms. She fell to her knees, too weak to move. Adin was dumbfounded. Only Ren reacted, he struck Oren on the jaw, striking bones that were already broken, flesh that was already seared and blistering. The Prior Master cried out in pain, but he would not yield. He struck Ren on the mouth. The blow rattled his teeth and Ren stumbled backward.

Where is my knife? Ren cast about for his blade, saw it amid the embers. It was too far to reach, so he pointed and Adin went for the knife. In that same moment, Oren slammed into Ren with all of his weight, throwing him against the wall.

"There're three of you and you still can't kill me, Hark-Wadi. You're no king."

"What do you know?" Ren asked, ignoring Oren, searching for Adin. *Where's the knife?* He stretched out his fingers, waiting for Adin to place the dagger in his hand.

"The Harkans sing about their triumphs, but what have they done?" Oren continued. "Where is their greatness? Arko was a drunk. Koren was a drunk. What will you be? Another drunk? If the Harkans are so strong, why don't they fight?" he sputtered, the flames spreading between them, blood dribbling from Oren's lips, a broken tooth wiggling in his gums.

Ren felt the slap of the dagger hitting his palm; he gripped the haft.

"I don't care about any of those bastards," he said. "I never knew them; they never knew me." Ren drove the blade at Oren's chest, but the older man caught it. The knife twisted between them, cutting Ren, but not deeply. Adin wrapped his fingers around Oren's. The knife trembled, the three of them gripping the iron, their fingers slick with perspiration as each struggled for dominance. A push, a shove, and the blade clattered to the floor. Oren kicked the dagger into the flames.

What now? Ren thought. Then he remembered that he had another weapon, one he had never used. It wasn't a blade, but it would do the job just the same. In a flash, he reached over his shoulder and unslung the eld horn. He jabbed the pointed end at Oren. The Prior Master resisted, his fingers gripped the antler and arrested its progress. The eld horn trembled, suspended a hair's width from Oren's chest, the tip advancing by slow degrees. Adin's fingers wrapped Ren's and the two of them thrust the gnarled tip of the horn at the older man. Oren flailed, but he could not distract them or weaken their hold. Their grip was iron; neither would relent. Oren kicked, he threw his bald head at them, but the boys wouldn't budge and the horn bit into the Prior Master's skin, piercing his robe and plunging into his chest. Oren's mouth opened in shock. He convulsed, his eyes closing, a hushed cry escaping his lips as he fell to the floor, motionless. The kingsword had had its first taste of blood.

"He's gone," said Ren as he slung the horn over his shoulder and retrieved his father's knife.

"Dead at last," said Adin.

Another dead man in a city of dead men.

"Ren, help me," said a voice. It was Tye. He helped her stand.

"We're free," she said. "All of us, free at last." It was true.

Backing away from the fallen body, Adin at his side, Ren heaved a joyous breath, holding Tye for a heartbeat, meeting her eyes, a realization spreading between them: It was over. Oren was gone and the Priory was burnt, destroyed. The city itself was aflame. He was done with Solus, done at last with the Priory. It was time for Ren to return to Harkana. Time for the ransoms to come into their inheritance.

Ren gripped the door and swung it closed, hurried through the passage, out into the Hollows, through the darkness below the city, and into the light and safety above.

⇥60⇤

"I'm fine," Ott spat blood as he spoke. At his side, Saad lay facedown on the stones, his chest unmoving, his body still. The priests who had acted as assassins were all dead, having drunk the poison they vowed to consume. Ott and Sarra were alone in the throne room of the Soleri. It was the second such chamber she had seen and it was no less glorious than the first.

She sat with her back to his, supporting her son. Through her robe she felt the steady beating of his heart, the expanding and contracting of his lungs. Her son was alive. That was all she needed to know. So she sat there in the dust and ash, taking in the great throne room of the Soleri.

"It must have been glorious," Ott said, breaking the stillness.

Through centuries of dust and cobwebs she saw the empty throne, the unlit braziers, the many flower-topped columns, the empty pits where water had once splashed in pools. She saw the curious symbols of the forgotten script, the empty cups, the vacant chairs, the cracked pews. In the depths of the chamber, barely visible, she saw the vacant cages in the menagerie, the mats where men once kneeled and the drums that were once played to entertain the emperor. Burnt murals ornamented the walls, their once ornate patterns now charred and indecipherable. Above the walls sat arched ceilings, exquisitely curving vaults illuminated by jeweled mosaics, a wondrous filigree of palm and lotus motifs set in stones of agate and sapphire.

Sarra spoke, her voice hushed. "This"—she indicated the burnt throne—"has stood here for centuries, unseen and unknown. Doesn't it make you wonder?"

"About?"

"How we got here. The map, that journey through the Shambles, and the bodies we found beneath the mountain. How did we do this? How did we unearth what no one else could find?"

"You think someone helped us?" Ott asked. He too was whispering. The sight of the chamber was likely just too much to absorb. Too much splendor covered in too much dust and ash. The calamity of the thing made one want to whisper.

"Perhaps," she said.

"It makes some sense."

Sarra grunted.

"Who? The priest from the Wyrre, Noll?"

"It's just a hunch. He was the one who sent the first translations, the letters that led us to the grain silo and the chamber with the carvings. He found the map on the ceiling, and he translated it. And when we were in the Shambles, he was the one who pointed out the lights on the cliff, when I was ready to go home."

Ott was still looking at the chamber, sighing as if it at all were one big mystery, which it was. "Curious."

"It is curious—isn't it?" she echoed, her eyes settling on the Amber Throne. "When this is done—when we've hidden what happened here and I've taken my place in the Antechamber of the Ray—we will need to learn more about the dead boy, Nollin Odine. There is a mystery there. I'm certain of it."

≋61≋

The morning after the duel in the Chathair, Kepi woke with Dagrun at her side, his chest rising and falling, gray covers swaddling their naked bodies. She slipped from beneath his arm and sat at the edge of her bed, listening to the distant call of the kite. The floor was cold on her feet, the room dark, and the shutters drawn, leaving only cracks of light at the window's edges. She stepped toward the light, padded across the floor, noticed Dagrun's sword was gone, but gave no care. The servants were always coming and going, moving and removing clothes or furniture. That morning a servant had delivered a crock of amber and a platter topped with ripe blackberries. Half-asleep, she had seen Dagrun drink amber, then slip back beneath the wool covers.

Now Kepi swung open the shutters, but the light was too bright. She closed the wooden flaps, but not fully. The remaining light illuminated a gray patch of floor, her clothes and Dagrun's tangled in a pile, left where they had tossed them the day before. Spilled amber had turned his tunic a ruddy brown. She stuck her toe in the syrupy spill.

Dagrun groaned in his sleep.

Kepi closed the shutters and slipped once more beneath the covers, the lambswool scratching her limbs, making her itch, but not unpleasantly. Dagrun embraced her from behind, the heat of him warming her skin as he wrapped his arms around her slender waist. Then he rolled her to her back and kissed her neck.

He raised her hips and took her until she cried out, gasping, little sounds of mixed pain and pleasure escaping her lips. With a groan, he finished and they lay again together, shoulder to shoulder in the darkness, hearts beating in the satisfied quiet.

Afterward, alone, naked in the darkness, Dagrun drank and ate, and they talked of the war and the warlords that were gathered not far away. At times they were quiet, neither one of them speaking.

"What is it?" she asked, sensing some hesitation on his part.

"There is news from Solus." A messenger had arrived the night before. The long-delayed messages had at last come through. Her father was made Ray, but his tenure was short. Dagrun described the light on the mountain, the banquet in the Cenotaph, the trial by fire, and Arko's passing. He told her what he knew.

Kepi listened. She waited, her smile flat, eyes distant. She showed no grief, though her heart held more than she could bear. She hoped her father was at peace. More than any man, the king of Harkana had longed for, but not found, peace in his life. Perhaps, she hoped, if he could not find solace in this world he might find it in another.

"I don't know what to say . . . I thought he was dead. I . . ."

"It helps to talk," he murmured, still groggy. "Tell me something about him."

"He was a hunter," she said, thinking, welcoming the distraction. "More than anything he loved to hunt. There is a place in Harkana, the Shambles, where all things are old, where even the rocks are shattered and the trees are broken. It is a morbid place, but my father loved it and I never knew why, never understood why he went there, why he hid from his duty and now he is gone, dead, and I will never know what made him love that place, why he hunted amidst the ruins of his father's army, the crumbling towers and burrowing caves."

"We can go there together," Dagrun said, rubbing his forehead, looking pale, his eyes bloodshot.

"No." Kepi wrapped the wool around her. She had mourned her

father's passing once and did not have the heart to do it again. His arms enveloped her and she lay there, trying not to think about the past.

The room was quiet, and the hall outside was quiet too, the pacing of the guard absent. Then—footsteps rang in the corridor, a cry, a thud, and the sound of something heavy dragging across the floor. The door was flung open. Kepi startled, drawing the covers around her naked body.

More commotion, footsteps, and Dagrun was off her. The door lurched closed. *What's happening?* From her place on the bed, Kepi saw only darkness. She heard someone, a man's voice—no, a boy's—telling Dagrun to leave her alone, let her be. "You . . . you took her!" said the voice, and Kepi knew it was Seth. Seth had come in and seen them together. "Get away from her, you brute!"

"Who the hell do you think you are?" Dagrun answered. "Get out of here, boy."

Then banging sounds, bodies moving in the darkness. Kepi twisted left and right, throwing the blanket off, trying to find her clothes, her sword. "No!" she screamed, fumbling in the darkness. "Seth—no!"

Dagrun, naked, scrambled toward his discarded clothes to look for a weapon, for something, but he was moving strangely, awkwardly—something was wrong with him. Where was Seth? Where was Dagrun's sword? Then she knew that Seth had gotten hold of it somehow, that a servant had come into the room and stolen the king's blade for him.

In the darkness, Dagrun turned and caught the boy's wrist with both hands, held Seth's sword hand away from his body until the boy cried out. The blade clattered out of his hands and slid across the smooth stones of the floor, and Dagrun went scrambling after it, hoping to get there first, but the king did not move with his usual speed. He stumbled and fell to the floor, his hand resting just short of the grip. That was when Seth took out the dagger from his belt, raised it above his head, and plunged it into the smooth skin of Dagrun's back.

Kepi screamed.

Blood poured from Dagrun's wound, great buckets of blood that spread out across the floor. Dagrun crawled a few inches, his arms reaching back painfully to try to touch the wound, but his strength was failing, he was falling, gurgling sounds coming from his throat, the wet sounds of sucking breath and blood in his lungs. "Kepi," he said, "Kepi . . ."

Seth rushed toward her, dagger in hand, angry, confused, his eyes darting. "Are you okay, Kepi? He'll never hurt you again—"

But the moment he reached her, she began to beat Seth with her fists, catching him in the face, in the gut. "You stupid boy!" she cried. "I was willing. I was his wife."

Then, she saw in Dagrun's cup a wisp of red, a dark coil that wound like a serpent's tail through the pale amber. When Seth slipped into the room to take the sword he must have also poisoned the amber. That's why Dagrun was so pale, why his eyes were bloodshot and he had not moved with his usual speed. Seth had poisoned him. Surely the king would have otherwise bested the boy.

Seth was no warrior.

Even in the dark, with surprise on his side, Seth would not have defeated Dagrun. He had cheated. He had procured a poison and poured it into the king's cup. He must have made it himself, or perhaps the physician made it for him. There were many who did not accept Dagrun's reign, the king had said so himself. Seth had said so. Now those men had aided Seth, and the boy from Harkana had stolen her husband.

"The servants are revolting. They are taking over the caer. We should go!" Seth sputtered, but Kepi was no longer listening.

She fell to the floor, naked still, sobbing, her body still charged with the electricity of their sex. She crawled to her husband and covered his body with her own. "Don't leave me," she said, petting Dagrun's hair, his face. His skin was white, the poison making him look strange. His eyes were wide open, staring. He was already gone.

She collapsed next to her dead husband, Seth howling her name—and then she turned on him, the one she'd thought she'd loved, the boy who was now a murderer. "What have you done?" she wailed.

"I came to save you. I thought he—" Seth took a shuddering breath. "Kepi, I—"

"*I'm not yours to save, Seth!*" She turned on him, her eyes flashing hatred. "You couldn't have left when I gave you the chance? I told you it was all over, I set you free to go home to your family, and this is how you repay me?"

She stepped toward him, her hands clenched into fists, but he still held the bloody dagger in his hands. Instead, she went to the chest and, at last, found her sword, advancing on him with fury in her eyes. "You won't kill me," he said. "Kepi, it's me, it's Seth—don't you remember? You love me!"

"I don't love you. I told you that in the yard. I told you, but you wouldn't listen!"

Shouts rang through the door. Soldiers approached. She heard a scuffle, raised voices, and swords meeting armor. Dagrun's soldiers were here
and were fighting the men who had aided Seth. The conflict reached a
fearsome crescendo, coming closer. Seth took a step back, his eyes always on the tip of her blade. He was reaching out to push it away when he
backed up to the doorway, right into the guards who were coming into
the room, staring with horror at the dead king lying on the floor in a
pool of his own blood, the boy holding the bloody dagger, the queen defending herself with her own sword.

They took hold of the boy roughly. "I didn't kill him!" Seth lied.

"My lady?" said the captain of the guard, looking at the queen.

"It was him," she said. "He killed the king of the Ferens."

"No! It was her, it was her!" Seth cried, but the men were already dragging him away.

Even as he tried to put the blame on her, she knew why he had done
it. *You thought Dagrun Finner was no different from Roghan Frith. Two brutes,
two Ferens. You were wrong, Seth.*

The soldiers went to their fallen king, checking to see if his heart still
beat, but Kepi knew the truth already, that her husband was dead. The
floor was slick with his blood—it would never be clean again, no matter
how often it was scrubbed.

The morning light was still coming in the windows. A moon ago she
had been a girl still, a king's daughter of Harkana, thinking only of her
own wants, plotting her escape from Harkana with Seth, wishing Dagrun dead. It had all happened—Dagrun was dead, and she and Seth had
escaped Harkana. Not the way they had intended, but it had happened
nonetheless.

Kepi fetched the sparring clothes that Dagrun had made for her. She
dressed, not caring that the soldiers watched her every move, that she was
still smeared with Dagrun's blood, like a sacrifice made to the gods. She
was a widow, again. Her father was dead. She must be doomed to unhappiness. Whenever she found even a little bit of peace, a tiny sliver of
joy, it would always be taken from her. She knew that now.

There was a commotion in the corridor outside. In the muffled distance, she heard men shouting, stomping in the hall. When the next wave
of soldiers arrived, they were not Dagrun's men. They did not wear the
silvery tree of Feren upon their chests. Instead, they were dressed in
the clothes of servants, of stable boys and slaves. Thirty or more of them
crowded into the room, wielding dirks and other small arms, ones that

could be hidden beneath a cloak or a tunic. Dagrun's soldiers let go of Seth. They engaged the traitors. The king's men held the mob at bay, cutting and stabbing, piling up bodies before them, but for each servant or slave who fell, four more arrived to fill his place. The traitors were standing shoulder to shoulder, their sweaty arms and bony shoulders jostling one another, pushing and shoving, trying to get their hands on the soldiers. Most wore nothing more than loincloths or homespun tunics. They were not soldiers; they had no training and no real weapons. Some fought with bits of broken pottery, or stones, bare hands or household items, anything that was sharp: a knife, a shovel, an adze.

There are too many of them and not enough of our own men, Kepi thought as she retreated across the room. The king's soldiers would soon be overwhelmed. The turncoats were coming for Kepi. She was Dagrun's wife and queen. They wanted her dead, just as they had wanted her husband dead. "False king!" they cried. "False queen!" they shouted even louder, their voices filling up the small chamber, echoing in her ears, driving her mad.

When Seth saw that they were coming for the queen, he threw himself between Kepi and the traitors, but they pushed him aside, knocking him to the ground as if he were one of Dagrun's own men. Seth cried out. "Stop!" he said, shock on his face, terror too. He begged for mercy as they clobbered him with stones and shards of metal, trampling him as they came for the queen, their feet wet with his blood.

Kepi stood by her husband's body, but the angry mob tore her away from him, pummeling her with rock-filled sacks and wooden spoons. They threw her to the ground. The men loosened their breeches, their intentions clear, their faces screwed into menacing snarls. She would not die quickly, or mercifully. They meant to have some fun with her, but before they could get about it, more of Dagrun's soldiers charged into the king's chamber, pushing back the traitorous crowd and pulling Kepi to her feet. They made a wall with their bodies.

"We can't hold them," cried one of the soldiers.

"Go to the Chathair," said another. "The king's sworn men hold the throne room. You'll be safe—" A slender knife pierced the soldier's throat, cutting short his words, dropping him to the ground.

Kepi ran, into the corridor, stumbling over bodies, making her way toward the throne room, but the hallway was already filling up with the traitors.

Through open arches, all around the caer she saw slaves and stable boys gathering in the corridors and on the walls. The traitors had men at all of the doors, and turncoat soldiers guarding the Chime Gate. Dagrun had said there were a few traitors in his midst, but he had not grasped the true size of the rebellion. There was nothing but traitors in the caer. *Is there anyone left to help me?* The common folk and the slaves, the soldiers and the cooks, all of them had banded together. In Feren, a monarch cannot rule without the kite. She knew that, and Dagrun knew that too.

She rounded a corner, her bare feet skidding on the stones. There were more guards, more of Dagrun's loyal men lying on the floor, their skin pale, eyes red. There was no sign of conflict, no blood. "Help!" she cried, hoping desperately that someone would hear her. The caer held thousands of soldiers, but it seemed that all of them were unconscious or fighting for the turncoats. *Maybe I am alone.* In a moment she'd know the truth. The Chathair was just around the corner.

She stumbled into the great throne room, ready for the worst, prepared to find herself alone with an angry horde, but instead, men from both sides were gathering their supporters. Dagrun's soldiers formed ranks. They ushered her into their midst, surrounding her with their shields. Dagrun's loyal warlords, Ferris Mawr and Deccan Falkirk, stood at her side. Ferris shouted orders as the traitors scrambled for weapons, pilfering swords from Dagrun's fallen soldiers.

A tall, gray-haired man in blue and green clan stripes stood at the center of the unruly mob. Gallach, she guessed. *This must be the traitor.* Seth had mentioned him once or twice. He had victory written all over his face. The traitors vastly outnumbered the king's men. And everywhere there were soldiers lying on the floor, their skin looking sickly and cold—just like Dagrun's. The sight of it made her realize what had happened. The traitors had poisoned Dagrun's loyal soldiers. The scullery girls and the cooks, all of them must have been a part of this revolt. They had poisoned the amber and the bread, everything the soldiers ate. Hundreds were unconscious, drugged or dead—she didn't know.

The traitors had taken what weapons they could find and were gathering into a mob, ready to advance. *I'll make my stand here.* It was as good a place as any to die. *At least I have a blade.* Kepi would die like her father, with iron in her fist, fighting until the very end. Three years ago, in Feren, after her first marriage, she had escaped what seemed like certain death, she had evaded Roghan's cruelty and the cell his men had kept her locked in for a year, but this time there was no escape. There was no one left to come to her aid, no husband and no father. *Just as well,* thought Kepi. *I don't want to be saved by anyone—I want to fight.*

The chanting grew louder as the traitors gathered their nerve and made their final push. "Gallach!" they hollered over and over as their gray-haired leader raised a silver sword and beat his chest. *Who is he?* Kepi thought. *Some minor lord, some half-blood trying to wring power from my husband's throne?*

Seeing the traitors advance, the king's warlords chanted Dagrun's name, their soldiers leveled their blades and set their shields in a ring. The turncoats pressed in around them, slaves and servants leaping over one another, eager for blood, for revenge, for a chance to strike at the false king's soldiers. The yelling and the clinking of blades, the roar of the battle was all around her. Kepi fought from within the ring, thrusting her sword between her soldiers' shields, doing her best to hold back the rebels, but already she knew what was coming next. The circle would not hold. When the first soldier fell, the traitors would pierce the ring. They would come for her first. She was the one they wanted. So she waited for their attack, pacing in a tight circle, balancing on her toes, ready for the fight. *Get it over with,* she thought. *This waiting is worse than dying.*

The first strike came from behind Kepi. The soldier fell to his knees. The circle broke. Something ragged cut her skin, a blade cleaved her leather bracer. *This is it.* The rebels were all around her. She waited for the final blow, but it did not come.

Instead, a piercing shriek rattled the very room in which she stood. All eyes bent toward the ceiling. The cry came again and Kepi recognized it. She had heard it in the Cragwood and on her journey to Rifka, in the yard outside her chamber and on the post wall of the caer. It was the kite. Through the Wind's Eye, she watched it wheel amid the distant treetops, through the cool and the damp. It soared through the great Eye and circled the Kiteperch. Smaller birds followed behind it. One after another, the birds of the Gray Wood flooded through the Eye. They filled the air with the furious beating of wings, with terrible shrieks. Amid the ruckus, a soldier halted his blade, midstrike while another let down his shield. A slave froze in place, his dagger trembling before a soldier's brow. The servant girls put down their knives and the stable boys their pitchforks. One by one, then two at a time, both sides stopped what they were doing and watched in awe as the kite circled the room, as the birds of the Gray Wood flew through the Wind's Eye.

The sound they made was the voice of the ancient forest. It was the voice of Llyr. The kite cried out to the people of Feren, saying *halt, stay your hand, stop.*

And they did stop.

The soldiers and slaves threw down their weapons. The cooks and the physicians, the scullery girls and manservants, dropped whatever they held. All of them gawked as the Kiteperch shivered and swayed, as the birds of the forest alighted upon its limbs.

The slaves and servants reversed their attack, retreating across the chamber, leaving Kepi all alone. She stood in a clearing and held out her arm, as she had done before, in the yard—when Dagrun was still king. *You came to my aid again,* she thought, her eyes on the kite. *You've been following me since that night in the Cragwood.*

The kite cried out as it caught hold of her leather-covered wrist. It stretched its wings once, gave another cry, and settled on her arm. Kepi touched its head. *Why did you not come to me earlier?* Already, Kepi knew the answer.

It was Dagrun, the false king. The kite would not come if the false king sat on the throne. The king of the Ferens had not suffered the Waking Rite, but *she* had. She had fought for her life in the Cragwood—she'd been fighting for it for years.

Kepi stumbled to the center of the Chathair and stood in the shadow of the great Kiteperch. The tree shivered, its limbs alive with movement. Birds streamed through the Wind's Eye, one after another they landed upon the branches of the Kiteperch, the hall echoing with their grisly cries. The people of Feren had revolted because Dagrun was not a Kitelord, and he had not suffered the Waking Rite. Dagrun had given them cause to rebel, and they had done it. But the kite had returned to Rifka. It had come to the queen. The great gray-winged beast cawed, but not to Kepi: The kite sang to the crowd, its eyes black and baleful. It made a sound that shook the earth beneath her feet and made the Kiteperch tremble. It spoke with the voice of Llyr, crying in a language that spoke to the people's deepest memories, to their instincts and the minds of their ancestors. It bellowed, and its cry made those closest to her kneel.

All around Kepi the people stooped to their hands and knees. First the slaves bowed, then the servants of the house, the men and women who tended the great caer. Then the soldiers fell to one knee, one after another up the ranks, until only the warlords of Feren were left standing on one side of the Chathair, while Gallach stood alone on the other.

The gray bird cried again. It gave a loud call and then another, a string of raucous, babbling sounds that bounded through the Chathair, each cry breaking upon the walls before splitting into an even more dense chorus of echoes. The smaller birds echoed the larger, they shrieked and squawked, the cries building. They sang the Dawn Chorus, the hymn of the kite, the song that heralded the dawning of a new rule, and Kepi sang it with them. She howled till her lungs were raw.

Then she said, "Quiet." And the birds ceased their crying.

At her foot, the warlords bowed, and in a hushed silence Gallach bent the knee and acknowledged Kepi, the Kitelord and queen of the Gray Wood.

⋛ THE VOICE IN THE STONE ⋚

The boy woke and pulled himself up, unsteady on his feet. There was dust on his face, sand gathering at the corners of his eyes. His head throbbed and his fingers were stiff.

How long have I been here?

There was a thick layer of dust on his clothes. In the place where he had rested, his silhouette was outlined in the dust.

I must have been out for a long time.

The boy stumbled forward, nearly colliding with one of the twelve obsidian statues. When he saw them, kneeling before him, arrayed in a circle, his memories flooded back to him.

He recalled the black-sand beach, and the time he had spent at sea. He recalled his march to the Dromus, and the way the Gate of Coronal had rocked on its hinges. Along with a host of aged fishermen and young boys, he had traveled from Scargill, in the Stone Reefs of the Wyrre, to the mainland and the black-sand beaches of Sola. He'd eaten and drank and marched with the rest of the Scargill fishers, but he was not one of them. He was a priest, not a fisherman. He had only needed their ship, a means to reach Sola with his oilskin sack and the translated symbols it held. He had journeyed to Desouk and met the Mother Priestess. He recalled the grain silo and the curious map on the chamber ceiling. It had led them here, as he had somehow known it would, to the Shambles, to this very place. The throne room of the dead Soleri.

I am Nollin Odine.

The taste of Sarra's poison still lingered on his tongue, burning when he swallowed. *I died in this place. I drank poison and I died.*

But I am no longer dead.

How? he wondered, his gaze settling on the twelve statues. *Could it be?* Could they have saved him? Noll had dedicated his life to the study of the Soleri. From his earliest memory, the old gods had fascinated him.

Noll had felt a calling. He had given his life to the study of the Soleri and now he stood before them. The last pilgrim come to find the dead gods of Sola. It was said that Mithra's true followers would share the sun's fate, that they would rise again. *Is that what happened? Did they give me life just as they once gave life to the desert?*

"I must know," he said aloud, his voice echoing in the darkness.

"Did you wake my still heart? Did you bring me back to life? Give me a sign. Let me know that you yet live, that your power is real. That you are more than just statues."

Something unseen stirred in the distance. Noll shivered. The soldiers who drank poison were all dead, their faces white, their bodies exhibiting the first signs of decay.

Noll inched toward the ring of statues.

For all his life he'd waited for this moment, he'd dreamed of meeting the gods.

He quailed when a draft made the dust shift and the statues appear as if they were moving. He steeled himself and took a step forward. At the foot of Sekhem Den, he kneeled like a pilgrim and bowed his head.

The great chamber was quiet.

He put his ear to the stony head of Sekhem Den, but immediately recoiled.

He kneeled alongside a second statue. Then he bowed before a third, listening until there could be no mistake.

The twelve figures looked like nothing more than statues—cold, lifeless, inanimate things—but inside those black shells, the Soleri were screaming.

GLOSSARY

Adad, Enger: a Harkan general, commander of the outer legion.

Ahti and Samia: Merit's waiting women.

amaranth: the sacred crop, raised in the highland Oasis of Desouk, and tended only by the Mithra cult, a gift from the gods themselves. The leaves of the plant form a thick paste that makes the dry soil of Solus fertile.

amber: a type of ale, made from ground millet and emmer.

Amber Throne: the throne of the Soleri emperor, located behind the Shroud Wall of the Empyreal Domain.

Amunet, Pouri: former Mother Priestess of Desouk, Sarra's predecessor, now deceased.

Amunet, Sarra: the Mother Priestess of the Desouk, ceremonial wife of Mithra-Sol and high priestess of the Mithra cult.

Antechamber: the seat of office of the First Ray of the Sun.

Anu, Ined: the Protector at the time of the War of the Four, the man who drove the Harkans out of Solus, the first to call himself the Ray of the Sun.

Anu, Suten: the Ray of the Sun, the sole representative of Emperor Tolemy V, the living god.

Asar: an island in the Wyrre, birthplace of the Mother Priestess.

Asni, Garia: a lector and priest of the Mithra cult.

Ata'Sol: located beneath the Temple of Mithra at Solus, home of the Mithra cult in the capital of Sola.

Atourin: sister of Arko, married to a Rachin lord.

Atum: home of Mithra-Sol, from the time before the making of the world.

badgir: a wind catcher, used to cool Harkana homes.

Barca, Haren: a former captain of the Outer Guard of Sola, now a rebel and a traitor.

Barsip: a Harkan city, located near the Feren Rift valley.

Basin of Amen: the low desert flatland that separates Harkana from Sola.

Battered Wall: a section of Harwen's fortifications, damaged during the War of the Four and preserved as a war memorial.

Blackrock: a Harkan city, south of Harwen.

Blackthorn Chathair: an ancient ironwood stool, the throne of Feren, also refers to the room in which the stool is housed.

Book of the Last Day of the Year: one of several holy texts used by the Mithra cult, the tome that contains the prayers read during the Devouring.

Caer Rifka: the Feren citadel and high seat of power, located in the city of Rifka, home to the Blackthorn Chathair.

calash: a desert carriage favored by Harkan lords.

Catal: a desert stronghold, the ancient seat of Feren power.

Chaldaan: the Rachin code of honor.

Children's War: the second revolt, led by Arko's father, Koren, when he refused to send Arko to the Priory.

Chime Gate: the gate at Caer Rifka, made from suspended wooden logs.

Coin: a common board game.

crescent: a coin carved from the ancient currency of the Soleri Middle Kingdom, resembles a crescent moon, the common currency of the Soleri Empire.

Dalla: Kepi's servant in Caer Rifka.

Dasche, Sirin: a Harkan commander, Sarra's escort in the Shambles.

Dawn Chorus: the singing of birds before dawn; in Feren, the hymn of the kite, sung in the Blackthorn Chathair for the crowning of the Kitelord.

Dawn Crier, the: the acolyte who sings the "Song of Changes" each day, at the Temple of Mithra at Desouk.

Den: in the time of the Children's War, the surname of the emperors of the Soleri.

Den, Sekhem: last in the line of Den, former emperor of the Soleri during the War of the Four, two hundred years ago.

Denna hills: the highlands, south of Solus, home to the Desouk priesthood and the amaranth fields.

Desouk: in the Denna hills, the city of priests and scholars, home to the Mithra cult and the Repository at Desouk.

Devouring: the high festival, the solemn rite of the Soleri, the time each year when the moon eclipses the sun, when Mithra-Sol blesses the emperor and his servants.

Dromus: built during the Middle Kingdom, a circular wall running astride the border of the kingdom of Sola, separating Sola from the lower kingdoms.

Eilina: sister of Arko, married to a Rachin lord.

Elba: an amber house in Blackrock.

eld: a many-horned, four-legged species, similar in appearance to a deer, but larger, and some say a god.

Elden Hunt: Harkana's sacred rite, the right of kings; every Harkan king since Ulfer has taken the eld horns and fashioned a sword from them.

Empyreal Domain: guarded by the Shroud Wall, the precinct of the Soleri; only the First Ray of the Sun may pass in and out of this sacred ward.

Eye of the Sun: the gem worn by the First Ray of the Sun, a signifier of his power and position.

Fahran, Adin: the son and only heir of Barrin Fahran, the former king of Feren, a friend of Ren.

Fahran, Barrin: Barrin the Black, the Worm King of the Gray Wood, the former king of Feren, father of Adin, deposed by Dagrun Finner, now deceased.

Fahran, Dalach: during the Children's War, the king of the Ferens.

Femin, Khai: an acolyte of the Mithra cult, from the Wyrre.

Feren: a woodland kingdom, north of Sola, ruled by Dagrun Finner, known for its plentiful resources, its blackthorn forest, its use of slave labor, and its large army.

Feren Rift valley: a narrow defile, defines the southern border of Feren.

Finner, Dagrun: the king of the Ferens, a merchant who purchased a mercenary army and took the Feren throne by force.

First Ray of the Sun: the eyes and ears of the Soleri emperor, the only man permitted to pass through the Shroud Wall and into the Empyreal Domain.

Frith, Roghan: Kepi's first husband, a minor Feren lord, now deceased.

Garah, Seth: Kepi's lover, a servant of the Hark-Wadi family, born in the Barsip, in Harkana.

Gate of Coronel: the southern gate of the Dromus, the sea gate, located along the southern coast of Sola, on the black-sand beach, three days' ride from Solus.

Golden Hall: built during the Middle Kingdom of the Soleri, the formal and public seat of Soleri power, the place where the First Ray of the Sun observes the Devouring each year.

Gray Wood: the blackthorn forest of Feren.

Hacal, Asher: the captain of the Harkan kingsguard.

Hall of Histories: located beyond the Shadow Gate, along the path that leads to the Empyreal Domain, this corridor contains large-scale carvings depicting the history of the Soleri Empire.

Harkan Cliff, the: a massive precipice, separates the Harkan kingdom from Rachis.

Harkana: a desert kingdom, founded by Ulfer, ruled by the Hark-Wadi family.

Hark-Wadi, Arko: the Bartered King, the king of Harkana, the only Harkan king to avoid serving time in the Priory.

Hark-Wadi, Kepina: younger daughter of Arko, king of Harkana.

Hark-Wadi, Koren: father of Arko, former king of Harkana and leader of the second revolt, the Children's War, now deceased.

Hark-Wadi, Merit: elder daughter of Arko, king of Harkana.

Hark-Wadi, Ren: son of Arko, heir to the Harkan throne, a ransom in the Priory.

Harwen: capital city of Harkana, seat of Harkan power, home to the Hornring and the Horned Throne of Harkana.

hierophant: a priest of any faith who dedicates his life to the interpretation of sacred symbols.

High Desert: west of Sola, an arid region occupied by nomadic tribes.

Horned Throne: the Harkan seat of power, located in the Hornring.

Hornring: Harwen's keep, home of the Hark-Wadi family and the Horned Throne of Harkana.

Horu: brother of Mithra-Sol, god of death.

Hykso: a nomadic High Desert tribe common to the southern regions of the High Desert, as well as the borderlands between Harkana and Sola.

Jundi: the lowest soldiers of the Protector's army.

Kiltet: a service cult dedicated to the maintenance and protection of the grounds of the Empyreal Domain.

kingsguard: the black shields of Harkana, the sworn soldiers of the Harkan king.

kite: a large and gray-feathered bird, a sacred animal, worshipped in parts of Feren, the symbol of the Feren king's divine right of rule.

Kitelord: in Feren, a king or queen who has completed the Waking Rite, a divinely sanctioned ruler of the Gray Wood.

Kiteperch: in the Blackthorn Chathair, the Feren seat of power, a monumental treelike sculpture.

lector: a priest of any faith who dedicates his life to the public recitation of sacred texts.

Llyr: the *kitefaethir,* the mud god, the lord of chains, the ancient god of Feren, god of the blackthorn and graythorn trees.

lower kingdoms: the four kingdom that serve Sola: Harkan, Rachis, Feren, and the Wyrre.

Middle Kingdom of the Soleri: the Amber Age, the Age of Marvels, the time when the Soleri built the miracles of Solus—the Dromus, the Golden Hall, the Cenotaph, and the Great Circus of Re.

Mithra-Sol: the sun god, father of the Soleri.

Mithra's Door: a passage reserved for the Mother Priestess, used in the Middle and New Kingdoms, blocked after the War of the Four, this corridor connects the Ata'Sol to the Empyreal Domain.

Mithra's Fire: a literal trial by fire—if the accused live, they are innocent; if they die, they are found guilty by the sun god.

Mosi, Sevin: captain of Merit's guard, a man from the Wadi clan, one of Merit's sworn soldiers.

New Kingdom of the Soleri: the present age, also known as the Imperial Age, includes the time of the Soleri's sequester behind the Shroud Wall.

Northwoods: the lands north of the Gray Wood, an ancient part of Feren that is now semi-independent.

Odine, Nollin: a boy from the Wyrre, a scribe of the hierophantic order of the Desouk cult.

Old Kingdom of the Soleri: the first age of the Soleri, ends with the unification of Sola and the lower kingdoms.

Ott: Sarra Amunet's personal scribe.

Plague Road: the road that connects Sola to Harkana.

Priory of Tolemy: also known as the House of Tolemy, a prisonlike school where the noble-born sons of the lower kingdoms are held until their fathers are dead.

Protector's Tower: also the Citadel of Solus, the seat of power of the commander of the armies, the Father Protector.

Rachis: a mountain kingdom, north of Harkana, east of Feren, home to the mountain lords.

Re: the first of the Soleri, the first to descend from Atum, the first emperor of the Old Kingdom.

Repository at Desouk: the largest library of scrolls in the Soleri Empire.

Rifka: the High City, seat of power of the Feren king, home to the Blackthorn Chathair.

Riksard: the ancient home of the Wyrren people, from the time before the settling of the Wyrre.

Ruined Wall: a Harkan war monument, a fortification destroyed during the War of the Four and preserved by the Harkans as a memorial.

Saad, Amen: the Sword of Mithra, the Father Protector and commander of Sola's armies.

Saad, Mered: the brother of Raden Saad, Keeper of Seals, Overseer of the House of Crescents, a wealthy citizen of Solus.

Saad, Raden: the former Father Protector, father of Amen Saad, now deceased.

Salt Barrens: a flat and dry region of the High Desert, characterized by salt plains.

San: a nomadic desert tribe common to the eastern regions of the High Desert as well as the borderlands between Feren and Sola.

Scargill: an island, part of the Stone Reefs, at the southern tip of the Wyrre.

scribe: a priest of any faith who dedicates his life to scrollwork.

second death: a body must be whole to pass into the afterlife; if a corpse is dismembered it therefore dies a second death and is denied entrance in to the world of the deceased.

Shadow Gate: an archway in the Shroud Wall, the ceremonial entry to the Empyreal Domain of the Soleri.

Shambles: in Harkana, south of the Feren Rift valley, a desolate stretch of land, the home of the Harkan king's sacred rite of passage, the Elden Hunt.

Shroud Wall: the barrier that separates the Empyreal Domain of the Soleri from Solus.

Sirra, Tye: the only girl in the Priory, the daughter of a prominent lord of the Wyrre, a friend of Ren.

Sola: the kingdom ruled by the Soleri.

Soleri: a family of god-emperors, descended from Mithra-Sol, twelve in all, a father, a mother, and ten children (five boys and five girls, always interbred).

Solus: the city of light, the eternal city of the Soleri, the capital of the kingdom of Sola, seat of power of the empire of the Soleri.

Stone Forest: also the Cragwood, the site of the Waking Rite, the Feren ruler's sacred rite of passage.

Stone Reefs: also the Untamed Islands, an isolated chain of islands at the southern tip of the Wyrre.

Temple of Mithra at Desouk: the first temple of the Mithra cult, an ancient open-air structure in the city of priests.

Temple of Mithra at Solus: in Sola, the temple of the sun god, and home to the Ata'Sol.

Thieves' Moon: the new moon, the time when ransoms are traditionally released from the Priory.

tulou: a ringed desert fortress, characterized by rounded walls made of mudbrick.

turn: a half-crescent coin, part of the Soleri currency.

Ulfer: the first king of Harkana, the first to take the eld horns as his symbol.

Vimur: an island in the Wyrre.

Wadi, Dakar: in Harkana, the warden of the hunting reserve in the Shambles.

Wadi, Nirus: a Harkan king, and later the Harkan emperor, the man who held the Amber Throne during the War of the Four, two hundred years prior to the present.

Wadi, Shenn: the husband of Merit Hark-Wadi, lord of the Wadi clan.

Waking Rite: also the Night Vigil, the Feren king's sacred rite of passage.

War of the Four: during the rule of Sekhem Den, the revolt of the four lower kingdoms against Sola. Led by Nirus Wadi, the lower kingdoms joined their armies and rebelled against armies of the Soleri. The Harkan emperor held the Soleri throne in Solus for twenty years before the Protector, Ined Anu, routed the Harkans, taking back the capital city of Solus and defeating Nirus. After the war, the Soleri instituted a system of tributes to admonish the four lower kingdoms. The noble-born daughters of each kingdom were forced into politically inconvenient marriages, while the noble-born sons were kept in Tolemy's house, the Priory, until their fathers died, thus weakening the royal lines of the lower kingdoms.

Waset: in Solus, the old city, the most ancient precinct of the holy city of the Soleri, home to the Golden Hall, the Cenotaph, the Shroud Wall, and the Empyreal Domain.

Wat, Khalden: the chief adviser and main servant of the First Ray of the Sun.

Wind's Eye: in Feren, the circular opening in the ceiling of the Blackthorn Chathair, a window.

Wyrre: also known as the Southern Islands, a vast archipelago composed of more than a thousand islands.

Zagre: city of birds, capital of Rachis, seat of Rachin power.

ACKNOWLEDGMENTS

This book would not be possible without my wife. She is my coauthor, editor, and constant coconspirator. She inspired me to write and encouraged me never to quit. Praise should also go to my daughter. She's only nine, but she had the patience to listen to an abridged version of *Soleri*. Her comments were helpful. My three beta readers—John Johnston, Anji Johnston, and Jennifer Ungaro—were also tremendously helpful. My agent, Richard Abate, cannot be thanked enough. At Tor, a big thank-you goes to Bob Gleason and Elayne Becker for making this book a reality.

ABOUT THE AUTHOR

Michael Johnston was born in Cleveland, Ohio. He was trained as an architect and worked at architecture firms in both New York and Los Angeles. *Soleri* is his first solo novel. He lives with his wife and daughter in Los Angeles, where he is currently working on a follow-up novel to *Soleri*. Learn more on twitter at @mjohnstonauthor.